The stories in this anthology come from a range of authors from different countries. We have retained the original spelling as submitted by each author, and therefore some regional variation in spelling is present.

Content Note

This anthology contains violence, sex and sexual references, themes, general weirdness and language that some readers may find objectionable.

CriminOlly presents

TRASH TALES

An Anthology of Trashy Fiction

Edited by Alex J. Gardner

KILTER & RAMMEL
PUBLISHING

Kilter & Rammel Publishing
Manchester
United Kingdom

www.kilterandrammel.com

ISBN: 978-1-0682697-0-7

First Edition

For additional information about any of the works featured in this publication, contact Alex at kilterandrammel@hotmail.com

Cover art by A. J. Gardner

For all the wonderful writers and fabulous fans who appreciate the joys of trashy fiction!

KEY FOR CONTENTS

In the mood for a particular genre? Use the icons to find the perfect story for your current appetite!

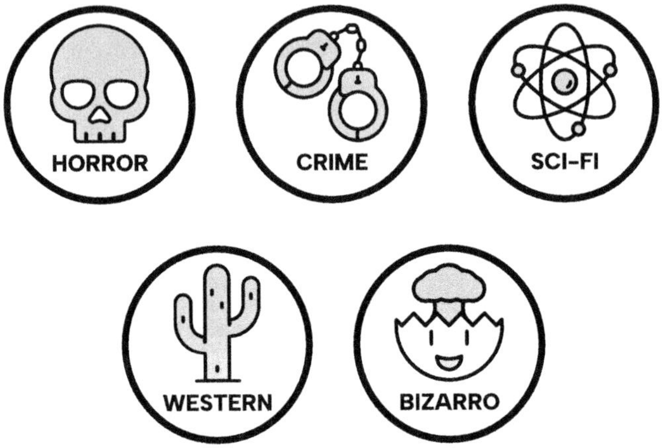

Fancy a short hit of fun fiction? Or have you got time to put your feet up and dive into something a little longer? The reading times referenced in the contents will give you an idea of how long it might take to read each story.*

* Estimated reading times are based on the average silent reading speed for adults, measured in words per minute (wpm), and cover a range between 200 and 300 wpm.

CONTENTS

INTRODUCTION

CriminOlly

Firstly, if you're reading this then THANK YOU for believing in the restorative power of TRASH. The last year has felt like a seismic and unsettled one, although, to be honest, isn't every year nowadays? At times like these we need uncomplicated entertainment more than ever. Stories that exist to put a smile on our faces, to make our hearts beat faster, to turn us on, to creep us out. Visceral tales that touch our bodies as much as our minds. Stories that are FUN and that take us out of ourselves for the time it takes to read them. That's the beauty of trash. It asks so little and gives so much.

This collection hits that sweet spot again and again. We've got sex robots, creepy puppets, wild west werewolves, bloody tales of revenge, messed-up monkeys and the strangest story about cunnilingus you've ever read.

It's a delight and an honour to present these stories to you. I wasn't sure if we could pull it off again after last year's *Garbology* collection, but boy did we. Alex and I were overwhelmed with the volume and quality of stories that came in. With so many great pieces to choose from, we inevitably had to turn down some really, really good ones. If you're one of the authors whose work didn't quite make it into the book, an extra big thanks for taking part.

That's enough from me. It's time for the trash. So grab some snacks, put your phone on silent and get ready to be transported.

HORROR

MOMMA'S GOOD SILVER

Philip Mitchell

15 to 20 minutes

Philip Mitchell lives in Connecticut, USA with his wife, four children, a lazy Corgi and a domineering cat. This is his first published work. When not writing (or reading) trashy tales, he feeds his tribe of people and livestock by cooking up media strategies for a list of Fortune 500 clients. Fun-time is spent attending various school games, plays, concerts and sporting events cheering on the aforementioned quartet of talented children. As ever, he is at work on his blockbuster debut novel.

When Momma died, we had to bury her in the backyard. This was three months after Momma, Daddy and me came to shelter at Grampa's place. She was killed by a scrawny looking wolf that still wore a "GO PANTHERS" sweat jacket from when it was human, probably a boy about my age from the local high school. Things had been going on like this for so long I couldn't hardly remember a time when it was safe.

Momma killed the wolfman that got her. She put one lead in its stomach, a silver in its chest and another lead into its skull, just not before it got a claw into her.

That was how we loaded our guns. Each of us had three silver bullets chambered, but never the first. The first bullet was lead, the second silver, and it kept alternating after that. Gramps said, this way, if we got startled, we wouldn't waste the silver. And it was almost as easy to shoot something twice as once. "The lead shot'll give them pause. Then, Charlie-belle, you line up that silver real tight for the head or heart."

Gramps killed one the first day we arrived and that'd be the first time I got a close look at them. "They come mostly at night, not just at full moon like in the movies."

We stood around the dead thing on the front lawn, looking down at the body that was twisted halfway between a man and a natty haired wolf. It had paws instead of hands and feet, and dirty fangs instead of teeth. What got me were the patches of pink human skin along its stretched-out belly.

"I didn't think they could die," I said to Gramps.

"They do if you shoot 'em with silver," he said. "I guess *some* of it's like the movies."

Gramps' farmhouse sat on a little more than an acre. He had roads on three sides and a neighbor's abandoned house on the fourth.

He'd cut down any big trees so they fell like barricades and gave us visibility. Gramps had every manner of tool, a big garage where he could work, and these days that meant slaughtering deer as much as it meant building things. There were fireplaces and wood burning stoves and everything.

There was a lot Gramps knew how to do that most folks had forgotten. He could kill and clean an animal. He knew how to salt it so the meat would last. He helped anyone who came asking, but surprisingly few did. There were a dozen or so neighbors in the town who stayed, but Gramps only knew the Hoyts and some others that had a name like "lie backers." I never could understand when Gramps said it. In the cold weather we could see the smoke from all the chimney fires above the trees in the distance. It was far enough that it wasn't safe to go visit, but it gave us comfort. We didn't know any better.

My Daddy still got sick over killing back then. He wasn't built like Gramps or Momma, who were cut from the same cloth, so to speak. He was quiet and gentle, and it bothered me. Just a teenager, and I knew a person had to change with the times, especially when the times tried so hard to kill everyone.

Daddy surprised both of us when Momma died. He dug the hole and wrapped the body. He said the words before replacing the dirt. He fed us and took up her share of the perimeter walk. I don't think any of us said more than a few words for days. Sometimes I'd feel nothing at all, other times it was like she died all over again, but some of the times I'd hear her voice in my head. *You need to make it through, Charlene, or it'll all have been for nothing.*

Not everyone who gets bit or scratched gets the infection, but once the change is clear, the person isn't human anymore. They can't be reasoned with and they for sure can't do what's right and kill themselves. Most folks who get mauled by a wolfman end up dead right away, usually with a good chunk of themselves in the belly of the beast. Them who survive have a hard choice. Most folks who got wounded would be restrained and then, if they changed, it was on their people to put them down. Except who's got silver bullets? And once the change started, lead wouldn't work. Not even a bullet to the brain, so they would have to chop their head off or set them on fire if it came to it.

Could you set your kin on fire?

◆◆◆

We noticed fewer chimney smoke columns on the horizon. "It don't figure," Gramps reasoned. "The wolves move through and move on, that's the way of them. They should've passed us by now."

"Maybe it isn't the wolves," Daddy offered. "Folks could just be moving on."

Except the wolf attacks kept up and even increased. It got so there wasn't a day that we didn't at least spot one of them. Those smoke columns were hope. Hope that things could get back to normal, you understand, so when we started to see fewer and fewer, I clung to what Daddy said even though I knew he was wrong.

◆◆◆

Gramps survived his attack. It wasn't nothing but a scratch, and damn if he didn't kill two wolfmen. I heard four shots; LEAD-SILVER, LEAD-SILVER.

Daddy ran out and I heard Gramps yell, "Stay there."

I ran through the kitchen and onto the porch. I could see Daddy just past the garage. I went through the screen door so fast my feet didn't even touch the steps.

It'll be okay Charlene, Momma's voice said.

"Keep back!" Gramps yelled.

The fifth shot was just a pathetic little pop, muffled somehow.

Somehow.

My feet and my heart stopped.

There was this one golden leaf that floated down and I remember thinking: *when it hits the ground I'll wake up. Momma and the world before will spring back into existence.* That old world – before the cities fell and the army blew up the bridges and killed thousands just trying to stem the tide – would just rise like the new day sun. The old world where I could breathe.

Funny the things we think about, isn't it?

◆◆◆

With only two of us, Daddy didn't want me walking the perimeter alone and I didn't want him out there either. He'd never fired the pistols except at the trees in the back when Gramps taught us both to shoot (Momma already knew, of course). We trained on the Winchester rifle and his twin Colt 1911 pistols. "Point takes the rifle. Second person carries a pistol," Gramps ruled.

With just the two of us, Daddy and I had to change up Gramps' strategy. The wolves were coming more frequently, sometimes two a day, and it started to wear down our supply of silver bullets.

"You're the better shot," he said. "So you'll be on the roof with the rifle."

This had been the plan for weeks. One of us climbed out a window onto the roof. The Winchester wasn't no sniper rifle, but it was more accurate than the pistols, and that was why Daddy's plan was wrong.

"You can't ever hit anything with the pistols," I said. And it was true, he couldn't. He flinched every time he fired. Gramps and Momma told him, "Stop shutting your eyes! How you gonna hit anything without looking?"

Daddy said, "That's why I need you with the rifle, you'll be able to pick them off easy from up there."

"But you can't hit anything with the pistols, so you'd only be bait."

He can't let you go, Charlie, Momma said to me. While he was thinking I pushed on. "But if you're on the roof with the rifle, you might hit sometime and if I'm down with the pistols—"

"No." He said it flat like that. Just "No."

"If the plan is to keep me far away from any danger," I said, "then you'll get killed and how long you think I'll last alone?"

Daddy folded his face in his hands. "God, fuck it all to hell." The words bled out of his mouth.

"If all you are is scared—"

"I am scared!" he roared, and it startled me. "It *is* about keeping you safe, that's all I have anymore. You. You, Charlie."

In all my years, I only thought of them as Momma and Daddy, but all along they'd been these whole other people for each other. He made her laugh and softened her temper, while she toughened him up. Him without her was like a chair missing one leg.

I didn't have it in me to coddle him and he was going to kill us both. "Listen!" I said. "We're already dead!"

"Don't," he warned.

"I have to. We're walking corpses. There are more of them, not less. At this rate we'll be dead in days. Maybe hours. That's it! If I'm going to die … then I'll do it fighting to live."

Daddy got up and paced around the porch. He ground his palms into his eyeballs. I wasn't about to let up, but he cut me off with an incoherent scream that came from deep in his guts and ripped out of his throat and echoed out into the world.

I had the good sense to shut up. There was a breeze and the rustle of leaves, and the damned world just kept turning like Momma and Gramps and a million other people weren't buried in their backyards like animals.

Daddy's face went slack and in that second he was gone. I wonder if the world would ever see the Daddy that could make Momma laugh again.

What was left of him held up a hand in surrender. Then he said, "We're low on everything. Food, ammunition …"

Show him my jewelry box, Momma said to me.

Momma had a lot of silver. Rings and necklaces and hanging ear loops. And we'd all seen Gramps make the bullets using sand molds and an arc furnace. Daddy said he thought we'd get maybe a dozen and a half bullets, maybe even north of twenty if we were stingy. In the end we both decided to stay with what we knew worked.

For a week we walked the perimeter the new way, with me on the edge with both pistols, and Daddy up on the roof. He bagged his first wolfman from up there. He didn't mind shooting and killing anymore.

I could count the chimney smoke columns on one hand.

In the beginning of the outbreak, when it was just something distant on the news, the wolves would move across the country in waves. They'd explode in one area like an infection, but the wolves always moved on. Those of us who survived slipped into their wake, among the dead and empty towns, but now it was changing again and it was like the wolves stayed and multiplied where they were. But with nobody here, we couldn't figure where they came from. I thought of the kid wearing the local high school colors who killed Momma. Shouldn't he have been long gone?

Daddy said, "We can't stay. We need to make a run for something."

"Like what?"

"Anything, Charlie. Anything. Because what you said was right. Our caution'll kill us. Probably should have left weeks ago when we were all ..." Anguish hardened his eyes. "But this place ..."

"Yeah," I agreed. "It feels safe, but it isn't."

◆◆◆

One night there was a whole mess of gunshots from our closest remaining neighbors at the Hoyt farm. Mind you, we'd heard shots from their side of the world before, but usually just a couple. This night there were dozens clustered together to make a desperate and terrifying sound.

"How many are they fighting?" I said.

"A lot."

"A pack?"

We were only guessing, but useless guessing was less daunting than watching the smoke dwindle and run out through the night. Early in the morning, Daddy started packing supplies into Gramps' truck; well-water and food and essentials.

"We going?"

"Tomorrow."

"Where?"

"I been thinking. Everyone bugs north, but if we can get to that marina to the south, we maybe could run a motorboat. Got to be safer on the water. Then we have options."

"South is thick with them," I said. Everyone knew that from back when it first started. All the strip malls and supermarkets and gas stations and people were south of us. More people, more wolves.

"That pack ..." he started.

"We don't know it's a pack."

"I guess when it comes down to it we don't know anything, but let's call it a smart bet."

"Okay," I said.

"They come for us tonight."

I said nothing.

"If a pack comes for us and we survive ..." He stopped and thought about what he just said.

"Go on," I prompted.

"I think it might make a big hole in their numbers. Then we have a chance to run south to the marina before any other wolves rush in to fill the gap."

I thought on it and knew it was all built on nothing. We knew so little about what was south or north or anywhere. We called them wolves, but they weren't. Why should they behave like wolves or do anything natural at all? Far as we could tell, these were more like rabid zombies than wolf packs.

Still, the attack on the Hoyt farm was something new. Nothing like that had ever happened before.

You have to see, Momma said.

"What if we went to check out the farm?"

"Too dangerous out in the open like that."

He was right. I said, "What if we drove over in the truck tomorrow morning. We see what we see and then we can come back or keep driving."

I watched him thinking, same as me, weighing the risk of going to the farm against what we might learn. Staying and waiting for something to happen was certain death.

At last he said, "Sure. Be good to know what happened over there."

Then he hugged me, and I could feel his heartbeat. He was alive and so was I. We'd lost so much of ourselves, but to be alive is to be human. We were still that at least.

They came that night. Not a pack, but a trio, which was more than usually happened upon us. Two kept me tied up by the road. Daddy winged one of them and I finished it and his buddy, but the third was tricksy and got around us, climbed all the way to the roof and nearly got Daddy. He fell back through the window and blasted it as it was coming in. The thing got into the house before it died. Another first.

The next dawn we fired up the truck and rolled on over to the Hoyt farm. Daddy drove and I was on the back with the last of the supplies and the Winchester, butterflies in my stomach.

The Hoyt farm was inert, as if all movement, sound and time itself could not progress on the property. There were no bodies, but doors and windows hung broken where the wolves had gained entry.

Daddy got out and we syphoned gas into plastic canisters from the farm's two cars. While Daddy did that, I got up top one of the cars' roofs and kept an eye out. I risked a distance shot and killed a lone wolf ambling a hundred yards out in the field.

"Any more?"

"No."

"I want to check the house," Daddy said.

"Okay."

"Let's go," he said.

"We can't both go. What if they come?"

He looked uncertain.

"It's daylight. I got this," I said. "Go."

"Head on a swivel, okay?"

"Yup. Hurry."

He went through their broken screen door to disappear into the black of the farmhouse interior. In the distant sky, I could see the chimney smoke from our last remaining neighbor. Everyone else was dead or gone. Before I could think any more about it, there was a double tap of gunshots within the farmhouse. Daddy wasn't any use with the pistols.

Stay put, Momma said.

I lined up on the back door, snuggled around the Winchester.

Seconds passed. A minute. I had to remind myself to breathe. Daddy wasn't coming.

No.

Then the dark beyond the door began to swell. I lined up the rifle sights center mass.

"Coming out!" Daddy announced.

I relaxed, but not completely.

He had a hand up, "It's alright. I'm okay."

"Wolf?"

He nodded.

Incredulous, I said, "Inside?"

"Damndest thing is, I recognize him. Looks like Mister Leibecker."

Leibecker? Then I remembered the other neighbors whose name Gramps pronounced as "Lie Backer." My eyes slid across the horizon of trees and rooftops, back to the last remaining chimney smoke. It floated up in a flimsy column before vanishing within the vast, cold sky.

◆◆◆

We made sure both pistols and the Winchester were fully loaded. Then we drove Gramps' pickup around the entire Hoyt farm before turning onto Coventry Lane and riding a winding mile towards the Liebecker house. The streets were empty, the lawns unmowed, and frost sharpened the tall grass like winter knives. At the end of the lane we came upon a makeshift barricade of picket fences, garage doors, and discarded furniture. Daddy slowed and came to a stop.

The Liebecker house was halfway down the next street, but the barricade was positioned across the lane and connected to two houses that had high metal fencing; clearly it had been designed as a full perimeter and there was no way through with the truck. If we wanted to go to the house we'd have to climb.

"This is a bad idea," Daddy said, and I knew it too, but I needed to see this through. I hopped down off the flatbed and came around to the driver's side.

"It's a long way to be on foot in the open," Daddy said.

"I'd rather have the pistols going in."

"Charlie, you listening to me?"

"How is it they got chimney smoke and any one of them is a wolf?"

"Yeah, I know, but it's a pointless risk."

I heaved a long sigh and said, "There's nothing to hunt around here anymore, but us and these Lie Backers. So why so many wolves? One or two a day. They moved on in the beginning, swarmed all over the country, that's what the news people said."

"I'm not following you, Charlie."

"Why ain't they moved on to follow the food?"

Daddy squinted through the windshield, scanning the makeshift barrier, getting more nervous with each passing moment. "We shouldn't stay here."

"I think there's an answer in that house."

"You can't know that." Except I saw it in his eyes; suspicion gnawed at both of us.

"Can I have the pistols?"

Daddy wouldn't let me go alone. He pulled into the back of a house and left the engine running. We approached the Lie Backers by climbing over backyard fences and sneaking along their neighbors' houses. I took point with the pistols and Daddy covered me with the Winchester.

We picked through properties with tree swings and iced-over swimming pools and rusted grills. Some had been broken into, but most stood shuttered and silent in the overgrown grass. A dreadful pressure built in my chest as we advanced.

The Lie Backer's property was a faded eyesore of paved asphalt amidst the neighboring greenery. They had a tool shed, and a screened-in porch that ran the width of the house. The grill was smoking, as was the chimney. Cords of wood sat piled six feet high against the side of the house.

We slunk up to the neighboring property's garage to spy a stout woman with long gray hair move across the yard and back into the house. The screen door banged shut behind her.

"What's the plan?" Daddy whispered.

I pointed at my eyes and back again to the house. He frowned at me, but said no more.

Minutes passed before she came back out holding a chain leash around a heavyset adult man.

Except he wasn't a man, he was a wolf.

By all rights this thing should have ripped her apart, but it didn't. She snapped and pointed, and the wolfman squatted onto its haunches next to the grill. From an Igloo cooler she produced a slab of pink meat and held it up. The wolfman was attentive, like a dog waiting for a treat.

"God damn," Daddy breathed. The chained wolfman snapped its head in our direction and we retreated behind the corner of their neighbor's garage. We heard the woman, presumably Mrs. Lie Backer, hiss at the wolfman. It snarled, and then we heard her voice rise up and command us, "Come on out, I've seen ya."

Daddy caught my eye and motioned me to stay out of sight. Then he stepped out, the Winchester ready, but at ease. I heard the wolfman whimper and fidget against the chain. The woman hissed and the wolf got quiet.

Daddy said, "How are you controlling that thing?"

"With a might more difficulty, you standing there."

"You didn't answer the question."

"I don't answer to no one, let alone some skulk-thief. And you're not alone."

I stepped out, conscious there was no fence between us and the chained wolf. The woman was old and saggy, bundled up in layers of sweaters and flannel. When she saw me, the anger drained from her face. "Your girl is she?"

"My daughter, Charlie."

"Lucky," she sniffed. "To have each other still."

"Who's that?" I indicated the wolf, irritated at the high-pitched worry in my voice.

She stared at me and then down at the wolf. The wolf's slick, overlong tongue panted out between its teeth.

"He's your boy?" I asked.

Her eyes roamed to scan the yards behind us. "There's nothing for either of you here. I'm sorry. You should move along. Best for all of us."

"How can you keep him like that?" I said, disgusted.

Her ire came back. "Move on, I said."

"What are you feeding him?" I shot back. Out of the corner of my eye I could see Daddy tense. He might have toughened some, but he was still too kind-hearted for all of this. He hadn't thought about her food supply.

"You getting restless?" she cooed at the wolf and it shifted its legs, priming for action.

Daddy started to say, "We'll be on our …"

"There's more, ain't there?" I shouted over him. "That's why you keep looking behind us."

She didn't say anything.

"You're supposed to handle the infected!" I adjusted my grip on both pistols, held in either hand at my sides. "It's the law."

She spat, "Whose law? Them who ran and left us? Same folks most likely started this whole thing in the first place? Them?" She made a sharp sound to approximate a laugh.

"How could you let your son live like that?" Daddy asked.

"It ain't his fault!"

"It can't be him anymore," he said. "Your boy's gone."

"You don't know that! No one knows nothing! They lied about everything! If he's alive he can get better. I feel bad for all them folks who killed their own, just because they were scared. I'm no sheep. I'll decide what's best for me and mine. Not them and not you!"

The wolf snarled and jerked, reacting to her screaming, but it wasn't just the screaming. I looked back over my shoulder and spotted two more wolves trying to sneak up behind us.

"Daddy," I warned.

"Hell," He turned to cover them.

"I told you to go! This ain't on me!" she shouted, and the wolf surged forward against its chain. She braced herself and was barely able to hold him back.

"Rifle's too slow," I said fast. "Switch targets."

He gave a stiff nod and swung the Winchester over. The last I saw before I turned was the woman releasing her boy. His dirty clawed fingers clacked on the asphalt as he charged.

Daddy's first shot was lead. I didn't see if it hit.

They're gonna flank you baby-girl.

My mind slowed it all down. I spread my arms out to cover both wolves as they diverged, just as Momma said. I snapped off two shots to get the lead out of the way.

One of them jerked from an impact, the other picked up speed, arcing around to come at Daddy from his unprotected side.

Daddy levered his second, silver bullet into place.

I aimed both pistols at the charging wolf, counting on the one I'd hit taking a beat to recover. Silver bullets pulverized its head into a mist of brains and blood.

Daddy took his shot and there was a sharp yip of pain.

The last wolf recovered from the lead I'd put in it and lunged at me. Too close. Too fast, and I wasn't lined up.

Desperately, I jerked both triggers, again ejecting the useless lead, and used the recoil to pivot my aim.

Its distended wolf-face had psychotic eyes over a maw of yellowed fangs.

This is how Momma and Gramps got taken. I lurched backwards and lost my balance.

I'd have fallen if not for my father's solid presence.

Both pistols lined up and I fired. Rancid breath and blood splatter hit me.

I released the breath I was holding. The two of us stood amidst the three dead wolves.

The son Daddy shot was still twitching.

Momma said, *It isn't over, baby.*

Behind me a wail of pure anguish and rage cut through the ringing in my ears. "Get up!"

Mrs. Lie Backer was on her knees, screaming at her boy.

"Charlie," Daddy said. "You okay?"

I looked around frantically. No more wolves. *What's not over Momma*, I thought.

"Charlie!?"

"I-I'm not hit. M'okay." Then I saw the ripped and soiled cloth fragment which clung to the wolf at my feet. It was only one sleeve and part of the jacket's front. In faded gold letters I could make out "-ANTHERS!"

"G-Go," I stammered.

"What?" Daddy took a quick glance at me.

I turned on the woman. "How many sons you got?"

"I AM GOING TO MURDER YOU, YOU LITTLE TWAT!"

I marched up to stick a pistol right in her face, and locked eyes with her over the barrel.

"Go. Panthers." I spat the words.

"Charlie, don't," Daddy said.

Up close the woman smelled like them.

I said, "One of your fucking monsters killed my mother."

"Lotsa people died," she spat. "Fuck your—"

I don't know if I meant to pull the trigger or not. Some days I like to think I did, others I wish I didn't. Not because I feel bad for killing her. Sometimes I wish she had to live with what she'd done and what she'd lost. Most days though, I'm proud for killing her, because that's what Momma would have done.

BIZARRO

YOU ALWAYS DRIVE TOO FAST

SJ Townend

5 to 10 minutes

SJ Townend is a single mother of two young children, a teacher and an author of dark fiction. She has stories in publications from Vastarien, Eerie River Publishing, Dark Matter Magazine and a few other places. Her debut horror collection, *Sick Girl Screams*, is out now (Brigid's Gate Press) and her second horror collection, *Your Final Sunset*, is coming in 2025 (Sley House Press). She is currently collating her third collection and will be looking for a home for it soon.

Twitter: @SJTownend
Bluesky: @sjtownend.bsky.social

Before you open it, you know what it is by the bold red font on the envelope. Your wife moans, rolls her eyes, as you curse at the letter in your hands. "That's all we need, another bloody fine. Why do you always have to drive so fast?" You make her coffee, just the way she likes it, before letting her know you'll also need to take an afternoon off work to take a speed awareness course this time, in addition to the sixty pound fine, because you can't afford to get any more points on your licence. You just can't. If you lose your licence, you might lose your job. Stupid speed radar.

"I know exactly which one caught me, too. That one with the ridiculous LED face on the A3671." You tell her about the new emoji radar speed trap a mile or so down the road, how angrily it'd shone its red frown at you.

"I know the one," she replies, "although it *never* frowns at me."

◆◆◆

You do the speed awareness course, you have to. It's four hours of torturously patronising advice. At least there are free hot drinks and biscuits for the duration, but you're still angry at being caught doing thirty-seven in a thirty zone so when you spill your fourth coffee all over the complimentary snacks table, you make no effort to clear it up.

At least you know exactly where it is, the one that got you this time, and you know now to brake in time when you pass it next, so you do, on your drive home from the course. The bold black rectangle mounted on a rod of grey polycarbonate smiles down at you in green. You grimace back, sarcastically of course, muttering swear words under your breath.

When you get home your wife frowns at you. All you notice is the downturn of her lips. You've no idea what she's nagging on at you about as she rants away. She hasn't smiled at you in weeks, months possibly, you think, caught up in your own miserable world as you pop your ready meal in the microwave. And neither have your children or your boss or your dog. But the speed radar has.

◆◆◆

The next day after work, you brake again as you approach the semi-anthropomorphised motion sensing camera, dropping your velocity right down to twenty. If you're careful, really careful, maybe it'll smile again and bring a little sunshine to your otherwise mediocre day? You'd be happy with a flat orange line, a pair of "satisfactory" eyes. Anything but that raging red frown. And you're in luck! It does smile at you as you trundle past, and today, its smile gives way a little more. Wider, wider it grins, and then, catching you quite off guard, it winks! "THANK YOU" it flashes in yellow pointillism Traffic Sans Serif underneath its cheeky visage, where you imagine its chin should be. You smile back at the sign and offer it a thank you in exchange for its thank you, giving it one of your best faces – you know, that grin you do for photos, where you expose the whites of your teeth? It's nice to be nice, isn't it? And it's bloody lovely to feel appreciated.

You begin to look forward to your journey home from the office each day, each time approaching the sign a little slower. Your reward: a plethora of glorious LED emojis. Happy face smiley face wink face toothy grin. THANK YOU, WELL DONE, NICE WORK. And each time it smiles at you, directly at you, only at you, and something gallops in your chest. Your dopamine spikes. Making the radar happy makes *you* happy. After a month of this, you realise you love the positive attention it yields. So, you concoct a plan.

◆◆◆

One night, your kids and wife asleep, the dog curled in its bed, you creep out and march two miles along the A3671 with pliers and a shovel in hand.

You arrive at your radar. A taxi drifts past, braking before confronting the tall piece of governmental infrastructure, and then it speeds off, all unobservant ghost down an otherwise empty, unsurveyed stretch of road. You stand and wait until the taxi's tail lights are out of shot, then you clip, snip, and dig. The base of the radar comes out of the ground eventually and, with filthy hands and beaded brow, you drag your slim friend home by its neck.

The next morning, your wife asks, "What the heck is a road sign doing in the bedroom?" But you've already prepared a response. You're looking after it for a friend, you reply. And then you wink and smile at her, making sure to reveal just enough dental white, just enough gum and tongue, so she knows the matter is all in hand. She screws her face up and says you've become unhinged, you're no longer the man she married, but you try to diffuse the situation by laughing and head down to the kitchen to make her coffee, just the way she likes it. She follows you downstairs, clacking on about something else and as you pass the mug of black one sugar to her, she frowns and tuts and says she doesn't have time for you and your nonsense and busies herself making pack lunches for the children. She scurries off with the kids. You get their names mixed up as you bid them all farewell. She hasn't time to kiss you goodbye, never does before the school run.

◆◆◆

Working from home today is perfect. Means you can spend your lunch break rewiring the radar into the mains. No problem. It flickers on from the corner of your bedroom. You play with it, tease its infrared sensor, its electronic emotions, as you scamper back and forth. Running towards it makes it flash and frown in amber and you decide you really do prefer it, love it best, when it smiles. The jolly green grin is so much better. So, so much merrier. Delightful, even. And, to keep it green and happy, you find yourself moving more slowly and deliberately taking longer to do your bedroom chores. Laundry packed away, new sheets on, you flop down on your bed to rest and fold your hands behind your head so you can admire its looming stature. It's like a sort of sentient hat-stand, you think. It grins down at you madly, with wide eyes of praise and adoration if you keep your movements sluggish. You find yourself excited by this – you weren't held much as a child – and something stirs in your groin as its green-lit visage scatters light all over your thighs. You reach down, under the waistband of your elasticated bottoms, and find yourself exploring. You love how the radar flits between amber impartial neutrality and green, how it grins and winks in neon as you run your hand up and down your shaft, always varying the speed between slow and extra slow, just the way you like it. GOOD JOB, your new best friend tells you, encouraging you on your way.

◆◆◆

It's Friday and the kids are asleep which usually means a movie and some nookie – either with the missus or alone, more often than not the latter. She usually chooses to watch something different and stays put down in the lounge, preferring soaps and dramas to *The Fast and the Furious* franchise. But this evening, you hear the pitter patter of feet up the stairs – it must be that time of the year – so you break eye contact with your street-steal and turn the television channel over to make it look like you're watching something that isn't premium rate. "Can't we switch that bloody thing off?" your wife, two glasses of red down, her lips rosebud red with anthocyanins, asks as she joins you in the bed.

"Why? It's not doing any harm," you reply. She sighs, takes off her glasses, places them on top of the book on her bedside table. You rub her gently on her arm and kiss her on the back of her neck just the way she likes it. She flicks off the bedside light and groans as your hand slips lower down her body. You normally look at her and all the strange faces that she makes as you bring her off under the duvet, but tonight, as you feel yourself grow harder, you can't help but find yourself staring at your neon speed radar instead. You've never had a three-way before.

The light from its grinning face as you mount your wife and move slowly, in and out, up and down, just the way she likes it, spurs you on. Green. Green. Amber. Amber. *If I go too fast*, you think, *it might flick to its red frown of disapproval.* There's no greater turn-off than when it gives you the hatched-out eyes of a roadkill death. Like a sloth searching for a new spot on the branch, you run your fingers over your wife's breasts and then pull your arm out from under the covers and brush the side of your hand over the broad green beam which falls onto the beige polycotton from the road sign's face. You move as slow as evolution and as you ejaculate and your wife wails, your radar winks and grins. After your wife falls asleep you rise from the bed slowly and kiss your road sign passionately on the lips, then you creep quietly to the bathroom to brush your teeth.

◆◆◆

When you return, all orally sorted, ready for eight hours of solid kip, you're alarmed and disgusted at what you witness. Your wife, naked, is flat out on her back. Her pert breasts point upwards like miniature traffic cones and the covers are pushed down by her feet. She's as stock-still as the night – which isn't particularly odd in itself, she often sleeps this way, dead to the world – but your road sign … Oh my, your road sign.

You've never seen it pull this face before. In strobing gold and silver, its little neon display is making a face you can only describe as a partial eclipse of pure ecstasy. The broad grin you left it with has flicked into an "O" shape. From between its lips, a 2D neon tongue darts rapidly in and out, and its eyes – dear Lord, its eyes – they're rolling round and round, like sexual Catherine wheels. Christ alive. Is it getting off on the sight of your freeze-frame sleeping wife?

You're repulsed. A wave of mouthwash flavoured merlot roils in the back of your throat. No, you're not repulsed – you bristle at your very core. *You* feel red and green inside. You're jealous. How dare your road sign look at her like that.

In the silence of the night, you try to ignore the plethora of faces it makes while, with your back to it, as quietly as you can, you rush around your bedroom, gathering everything you need. A few changes of clothing, your phone charger, phone, wallet, your keys in a bag. You shimmy along the gap between the end of the bed and the wardrobe, and you yank the radar's plug from the wall before grabbing it by its slender neck and jimmying it out from the corner. With the back seats down, it fits in your Volvo estate – just – its base resting in the boot and its blank face pushing against your shoulder. You drive off into the night, as fast as you can, with your foot to the metal, to find temporary accommodation. A cheap hotel, a BnB, anywhere where the two of you can be alone. You'll plug it in and sit in front of it and make it look at you like it looked at your wife. You'll remain as stationary as a granite statue. And you'll sit there as exposed and as naked as a steep cliff face, with the sea bashing at its toes. And with the relentless force of an ocean and your member in your hand, you'll beat and beat and beat for as long as it takes, until it loves you like it seems to love your wife.

Even if it kills you, you'll find out just how the traffic sign likes it.

CRIME

TAILS, YOU LOSE

Lisa Danny-Roberts

15 to 20 minutes

Lisa Danny-Roberts is retired. When she's not writing, she's playing board games, sharpening her skills for the next board game convention. Her work has appeared in *Pulphouse Fiction Magazine*, *Witcraft*, *Close to the Bone* and *Modern Drunkard.*

Her recent narrated short stories can be found on her YouTube channel: www.youtube.com/@L.D.Roberts

I sit and wait, imprisoned in traffic on the 405 freeway in LA. My shoulders cramp into tight, hard knots. I watch the driver next to me wrench off his tie as a red-faced toddler squirms in the back seat, her harried mother begging God for one more minute of patience. I drive the Acura forward a foot, scratch the stubble of my three o'clock shadow and replay today's meeting. Victoria, the stern-faced head of human relations, informed me in her brusque monotone that it would be at least another six months until the company would consider transferring me home to Wichita. I loathe Los Angeles, the relentless sunshine is merciless and cruel. Every few weeks I search the dull skies for a change in season.

In Los Angeles, greed is a religion and corruption a sacrament. The city dazzles you. It is bigger, faster and brighter than you could ever imagine. But soon you notice the air, once warm and welcoming, is filled with brown, choking smog. Everything is for sale and overpriced. Negotiations take place with subtle glances beneath hooded eyes.

Finally, the traffic inches forward. After what feels like hours, I park outside my apartment building, a square beige box hastily patched together in California's post-war building frenzy. It is functional, cheap and temporary.

I am standing in the tiny, cramped foyer that smells of mold, flipping through a Chinese menu, glancing at the specials, when I feel a sharp tingling on the back of my neck, my lizard brain shouting, *Pay attention.*

In the front window of Apartment 1C she sits contentedly, wearing nothing but a look of haughtiness and seduction. I gaze up to see a Maine Coon, all luxurious brown fur flecked with gold strands. She can alter my future with the flick of her tail. She can't be bothered to look my way. It doesn't matter, I have the rest of my life to woo her.

I sprint up the five flights to my apartment. The smog fills my lungs, burning like a drag of cheap weed. In my apartment, I put my briefcase down, walk the three steps to the kitchen, grab a beer and twist off the cap. I kick off my loafers, take a long swallow and feel HR and the traffic fade away.

When I was seven, my brother Kevin brought home a stray kitten with blue eyes and a fierce meow. She jumped on the furniture, chased balls and destroyed the tassels dangling from the dining room tablecloth. One day I was cradling her in my arms when Kevin burst through the back door. She ran to him as if her husband had finally returned home from war. She wound between his ankles, rubbed her chin against his muddy jeans, purring like a motorboat. He reached down and gave her a slight scratch behind the ears, then wandered away.

"Come back and play with me," I begged. She frowned at me with disdain, then chased Kevin down the hall. I am grateful that I have a second chance to possess a cat; this time will be different.

I sell insurance and my hours are irregular. I didn't see her for so long – I thought I imagined her – then twenty-six days later, I catch her out of the corner of my eye. She tilts her head toward me for an instant, then leaps off the windowsill. That day, I close on six policies. I return home to find her impatiently licking her left claw. I watch her deft movements and lithe grace as I realize I don't know her name.

The next afternoon at the mailbox, a woman in her late thirties opens the box next to me. Her brown hair is pulled into a ponytail, her skin is clear, her hazel eyes are faded as if she is perpetually tired. She is emaciated; California thin, they call it. It can't be easy being a plain woman in a town that worships youth and beauty.

"Nice day," she says. Her eyes roam over me, trying to guess if I am someone who can further her career. I make it easy for her.

"I sell insurance."

"I'm Laura – its pedestrian, I know," she says, as if her parents somehow let her down.

"Alan Reff," I respond. We shake. I watch her take in my tall lean frame, my dark wavy hair, my bright blue eyes.

"Do you know anything about ...?" I jerk my thumb toward the door of the apartment where my queen lives.

"Owner's an old man. Harold – the manager. Sometimes he bitches about noise."

"What's the cat's name?"

She cocks her head. "What cat?"

"The one in the window."

She shrugs her shoulders. "I never noticed a cat. Do you want to come up and split a can of SpaghettiOs?" she asks.

"Who could resist?" I say and follow her up to the second floor.

"I'm up on the fifth floor," I say.

"Must be a pain in the ass to carry up groceries," she says.

She enters a long, narrow living room, kicks away a pile of rumpled clothes. On the left is a half kitchen, and a cramped bathroom at the end of the hall. A wine-colored sofa is covered with a patchwork quilt. A signed, framed poster from the original cast of *A Chorus Line* hangs on the living room wall. The room smells like freshly roasted coffee and burnt toast. She goes to the refrigerator, grabs two beers and twists off the tops. Her movements are graceful and precise. She hands me a cold bottle and motions toward the sofa.

"What do you do?" I ask.

"Between dancing auditions, I cocktail at the Blue Parrot," she responds. "How do you like LA?"

I pause long enough before answering that she answers for me.

"I know. Everyone – the grocery clerk, the barista, the parking valet – is looking for ways to use you." She takes a swig of beer. "You only have so long to make it, I'll be thirty-five soon." She shrugs halfheartedly, as if resigned to failure. "I guess I could deal drugs or become a paparazzi." She takes another swallow. "If you can't get in the game, sometimes they let you play around the edges."

I sense a frostiness in her, a tight, hard edge that stifles my attraction. I am overcome by a wave of claustrophobia.

"Thanks for the beer, but I've got an early meeting in the morning. SpaghettiOs next time?" I say, placing my bottle on the Blue Parrot coaster then heading for the door.

"Sure," she replies, not a bit disappointed.

I walk downstairs to my car and there *she* is in the window. She stretches up onto her hind legs, places her paws on the glass, beckoning me. I rush over and put both palms on the windowpane. The world falls away as we stand paws to palms as if in prayer. Her eyes are like pools of polished emeralds, unimaginably deep. Then she is gone.

If I see her in the window, I can sell a policy to a corpse. If not, my day is filled with unanswered calls and no-show appointments. Seeing her is a crapshoot. Sometimes I see her six days in a row, then nothing for months. During a fallow spell, I develop an itchy rash, throbbing headaches and a sour stomach. The anxiety of feeling powerless unnerves me.

I haven't seen her in weeks when I notice my kitchen sink is leaking – a slow painful drip that threatens my sanity. I walk downstairs to see Harold and find her sitting in the window, quiet, waiting, as if she knows today is the day we will meet. I knock, hear Harold get up and lumber to the door. He is late sixties with a beer belly. His white hair is all wisps and tendrils. He wears a stained, beige bathrobe. The uniform of the lonely and sad.

"What do you want?" he asks.

"My kitchen faucet is dripping and I … I didn't …" My tongue tangles into a mass of knots.

"You need me to tell you to call a plumber?"

I find my voice. "I wasn't sure … if I should call or if you should."

"How old are you?"

"Thirty."

He rolls his eyes as if to say, "kids these days don't know nothing."

"You call a plumber, he fixes your sink, you pay him. Then staple the receipt to your rent check," – he taps his bloated fingers together to imitate a stapler – "and deduct the difference."

I hear a soft, fetching meow.

"You have a cat?" I ask.

"Phyllis, come on over here."

Phyllis! Phyllis is a name for nuns and spinsters. Lifting her nose, she sniffs the air to let Harold know his suggestion bores her.

"Cats." He shrugs and begins pulling the door closed. I put my left foot between the door and the jamb.

"Where did you get her?"

"She was here when I moved in. I didn't want her, but somehow she grew on me."

He didn't want her! Is he blind or just stupid?

"All she will eat is refrigerated cat food that costs a damn fortune. The guy who owned her left a note saying she was a descendant of the famous Winslow family. Apparently, her great-great-grandmother was the star of the movie *Thomasina*. In 1952 she was nominated for an Academy Award for Best Feline. Lost out to *Puss in Boots*. Claimed the voting was rigged, but in LA, who knows?"

It has to be true. Can't he tell by looking at her? She is a princess, and like Grace Kelly she could be both a princess *and* a movie star.

I have seen my angel and learned her name, and it continues to be a great day. I sell three life insurance policies and six homeowner's policies, for a total commission of $11,465.62.

The next morning, she is in the window. As I approach, she swivels her head, hiding from me.

"Phyllis," I whisper, "Daddy's here." She turns, and for a second I think I am seeing a sick hallucination. Harold has dressed her in a purple pirate costume. Her beautiful golden paw is encased in a cheap polyester sleeve made to imitate a hook. One emerald eye is covered by a black eye patch. Untrimmed threads hang down from an uneven hem. There is a gaping hole in the left seam, and a coffee stain peaks out from beneath the armpit. The look in her eyes transcends shame. She knows she looks like a two-dollar whore.

"Oh baby, I'm so sorry." I put my palm against the glass and spread my fingers.

She moves her head back and forth as if to say, "Do you see? Do you understand what a vile monster I am forced to live with?" She jumps off the ledge, disappearing into the cluttered apartment.

That night I toss in sweaty sheets, the air muggy and thick. The night is filled with a low thrum of discontent. I stare at the ceiling, tired and wired, my mind spinning in circles, thinking of ways to kill Harold for no other reason than he has something I want.

Exhausted, I stumble through the next day at work. After hours filled with useless phones calls and a throbbing headache, I return home to find Laura sitting on the landing outside her apartment, sobbing.

"What happened?"

She jerks her thumb behind me. I look up to see that the spindly wooden door of her apartment has a hole the size of a fist next to the doorknob. The door dangles loosely from the top hinge. I go into the apartment. Her couch has been ripped open, large tufts of white stuffing litter the living room floor.

"What did they take?" I ask.

"TV, pearls from my mother. They broke the glass on the *Chorus Line* poster and stomped all over it."

"Are you" – I stop myself before I say *insured* – "okay?"

She sniffs, her eyes red and blotchy.

A police officer lumbers into the apartment. He is mid-fifties with a slight paunch, and wire-framed glasses.

"Officer Mason – Hollywood Division, Robbery Homicide," he barks in a voice he has learned from bad cop shows. He looks over the apartment and shakes his head.

"Third one today. They're getting bolder."

I expect him to say, "someone should do something about these hoodlums."

Instead, he opens a tiny spiral notebook as he asks, "What's missing?"

Phyllis comes sauntering in, tail high. Walking up to Laura she hisses and launches a claw at her shin.

Laura looks down. "My day is bad enough, I don't need attitude from you, cat." She raises her hand to swat Phyllis away. I scoop my queen up in my arms and stroke her silky fur.

"This is the cat I asked you about," I say.

"Never seen her before," Laura snaps.

"I'll let you deal with the officer and come back later."

Phyllis leaps from my arms and bounds down the stairs. I go up to my apartment, grab the rent check off the counter and head back down to Harold's. The receipt from the plumber is stapled to the right-hand corner of the check. Harold's door opens before I knock. 5:36 p.m., and he is still dressed in his stained bathrobe and ratty slippers.

"You sell insurance, that right?" he asks.

"Yes."

"That" – he points upstairs – "is the second break-in we've had in three months. The owner wants every tenant to buy a renter's policy." He thrusts a list of names at me. "Thought you might want the business."

"Thank you, I appreciate it."

"Bring me the certificates of insurance."

"I will."

I hand him the check. He looks at it and hesitates. I wait for a sarcastic remark about the receipt. Instead, he says, "I have to go visit my son. Can you keep an eye on her for the weekend?" He points at Phyllis.

"Sure, no problem."

"Come by on Thursday night to get the key."

"Sure."

He closes the door. My heart is racing like I've just run the sprint at the end of a marathon. No need for a key. My goddess will stay with me. It takes fifty years for Thursday to arrive. I knock on Harold's door and he opens it dressed in waist-high beige polyester pants and a white Mexican wedding shirt. I didn't know he owned normal clothes. He hands me a key on a plastic Batman keyring.

"What would happen to Phyllis if something happens to me? A buddy of mine dropped dead … yesterday," he says, frowning.

"You could set up a pet trust for her?"

"What?"

"You buy a life insurance policy and when you pass away, a lawyer opens a trust for Phyllis. The insurance policy proceeds go into the trust. The trustee gets a monthly amount for her care. When

Phyllis dies, the trustee keeps the rest of the money. It's really important to pick someone you trust, to act as trustee." I see a speck of interest in his eyes.

"How much does it cost?"

I look at the dead plant in the corner, the threadbare recliner covered in Cheeto stains.

"It's quite reasonable. I'll get you a quote." I'll need to get creative to make it affordable.

"That would be great, bring me the quote on Monday."

"Will do," I say. He nods and walks out.

The second he is out of sight, I place Phyllis gently in my arms and take her up to my place. I have scrubbed my apartment till it sparkles. I bought a new litter box, twenty-six cans of Fancy Feast and a brush. She jumps out of my arms, sniffs in each corner, runs a paw over the carpet in my bedroom. Gracefully, she jumps onto my bed, wanders around and sits down to check if it is soft enough. She finds the litter box on the floor of the bathroom. Satisfied, she returns to the living room and curls up in my lap. I pick up the brush and run it along her back in long slow strokes as she purrs in ecstasy.

That night we watch the Dodgers lose. Friday night I surprise her with a copy of *Thomasina*. We watch it three times. We agree her grandmother was robbed of the Academy Award. She never leaves my lap.

All too soon it is Sunday morning, and we are lying lazily while she licks beef jerky off my fingers. I channel-surf among commercials, game shows and twenty-year-old sitcoms. Suddenly, Phyllis stands at attention and howls out a meow. I keep flipping, but she throws back her head and lets out a frightening scream as if she is being attacked by wolves. I turn back three channels to where Barbara Stanwyck is walking down a long flight of stairs, mesmerizing Fred MacMurray. Phyllis rushes to the edge of the bed to get a closer look. I head for the shower and let Phyllis watch as Fred MacMurray sinks into a web of lies and murder.

I dry myself off, dress carefully in pressed khaki pants and a white button-down, and grab the thin, rectangular, velvet box off the counter.

She is still watching the movie, so I tap her on the shoulder. She turns.

"I bought you a present."

She paws the top of the box and looks up as if to say, "For me?"

"Yes, it's a surprise I had made for you."

Her eyes light up, she twirls in small circles. I open the box to show her a leather collar with three small diamonds and a 14-karat gold charm with an image of her grandmother. Light catches the bright green stones of the eyes.

She looks into the box then back up at me. Her smile makes me feel like I have been named MVP of the Superbowl. Gently, I fasten the collar around her neck. The charm rests lightly against the steel rim on the bottom of the collar. She lifts one dainty paw up to her shoulder, pointing her toes at the ground, and suddenly my dingy bedroom with the rumpled sheets and cluttered end table turns into a runway in Paris. She prances to my pillow, turns back saucily to make sure I am watching. I nod in encouragement. She turns slowly, pauses, turns to the left, then the right, showing every possible angle, and starts back toward me. Her smile could light up the world.

Monday, I call in sick. We play with string, and she chases a golf ball around the floor. At 3:00 p.m. I pick her up and stroke her tummy.

"I have to take you back." She turns her head as if she can't bear the sight of me, and I feel a hot rise of shame. I walk as slowly as possible down the stairs. I hand Harold the key and the insurance quote. Her heart is beating rapidly against my chest. Harold puts the key in his pocket, the quote under his arm, and reaches out for her. I place her in his arms. I have never felt so ashamed. He closes the door, and with my heart in my shoes I flee to my lonely apartment, filled with her absence.

Three weeks later, I sit at my kitchen table eating Captain Crunch and reviewing the application for Harold's pet trust. I learn that Harold is seventy-two years old and diabetic. He doesn't meet underwriting standards, but Los Angeles plays by its own rules. I submit the policy and cross my fingers; six days later the policy is issued with no questions from underwriting.

Since I brought her back to Harold, Phyllis avoids me. I know she is punishing me for my weakness. On the sixty-seventh day of no contact, I come home early to find a delivery man at Harold's door. He is holding a brown box that states MUST BE REFRIGERATED in large letters on the side. He jerks a thumb toward the door.

"Do you know who lives here?"

"Yes."

"He's not home and I have this delivery of insulin. It *must* be refrigerated."

"I'll take it."

He hands me the box. "Sign here."

I scribble my name. Phyllis is in the window, watching. She nods, just a tiny downward motion of her chin. Her eyes plead, "Save me."

"Thanks," says the delivery man.

"No worries," I say, taking the box from him.

The side of the box says that the temperature cannot exceed 46 degrees. I place the box on the kitchen counter. As I open the refrigerator door, I hear her small voice in my head.

"Now is your chance. Do it so we can be together … forever."

I move quickly. I can't allow myself to think about what I am going to do. I close the refrigerator door, crank the oven to 450 degrees. I walk across the living room and shove the thermostat knob up to 90 degrees; the heater groans like it hasn't been used in decades, then clicks on with a loud woosh. I go to the shower and turn the water to its hottest. I leave the bathroom door open. Within a half hour, the apartment is a sauna.

I know this is wrong, crazy and sick but … I must have her. Harold just wants to live out his days in peace, but he is ill. Killing him would be putting him out of his misery. I know I am rationalizing but I can't stop myself. At 6:30 p.m. I turn off the heater, the oven and the shower. I open the box, pull out the bottles. Each one is hot. I break the seal on a bottle and shove in my kitchen thermometer, watching as it rises slowly to 84 degrees. I let the bottles sit on the counter and cool to room temperature. I dig through a drawer till I find my bike-riding gloves, glide them snuggly over my fingers. I soak a washrag in hydrogen peroxide and carefully wipe my fingerprints off each bottle.

At 7:30 p.m. I take the box and knock on Harold's door.

"I was wondering my delivery was!"

I thrust the box at him. "UPS said you were out, so I put the box in the refrigerator."

The lie glides out so smoothly I have to look over his left shoulder to avoid his eyes.

Phyllis begins to wind around Harold's ankles.

"Thank you, so much."

He is so appreciative. A wave of guilt threatens to drown me. All I have to do is snatch the box away from him. As I reach out, Phyllis lets out a harsh screech. Her eyes flash in a furious warning, and I step back.

Harold closes the door as I listen to the contestants clapping on *Wheel of Fortune.*

I go back to my apartment and suck down gulps of scotch straight from the bottle until the edges of the world blur. I pass out staring at the picture of my mother and father looking proudly at me when my team won the State Baseball Championship.

Four days later, I come home to find a harried EMT rolling Harold out of his apartment on a gurney. A white sheet is draped over his face.

I point at Phyllis. "I'll take her," I say.

The EMT nods in agreement.

I grab her and rush back to my apartment. I place her on the couch and point my finger at her.

"From now on, your name is Isabella … like the Queen of Spain."

She cocks her head, then leaps into my arms, rubbing her head under my chin. I smile – I got it right. The next morning, after a breakfast of fresh kippers, we sit curled together watching the Dodgers when there is a knock on the door.

"It's Laura, I need company. Can I hang out with you?"

"Come in, it's open."

She walks in, wearing faded cut-offs and a Mickey Mouse T-shirt. She grabs a bag of Doritos and shoves a handful into her mouth; it sounds as if she is chewing on marbles. The noise wakes Isabella, who throws her a hateful look. *What is it with these two?* I sit between them. Laura licks orange Dorito dust off her fingers. She walks over to the window and opens it. "It's stuffy in here," she declares.

For two innings we all enjoy the afternoon. The Dodgers give up eight runs, then Isabella needs more beef jerky. Gingerly, I place her on the couch. I put my phone on the windowsill. As I grab the beef jerky, Isabella jumps from the couch and in one deft movement she flicks her paw, pushing my phone out the window. I look at her and sigh.

"I'm going down to get my phone."

I start down the stairs. Isabella starts to follow me. I pick her up, take her back to the apartment. I point at her. "Bad things happen to cats outside. You stay inside," I tell her, and close the door.

I start back down the stairs. The stairway is dingy and narrow. I feel something furry beneath my feet. *Isabella? How did she get out?* Hastily, I wrench my foot back, lose my balance and lurch forward. Instinctively I thrust out my hands to try to break my fall. I grasp for a nonexistent railing. I tumble over and over, gaining momentum, each revolution a wicked assault on my limbs. My left shoulder dislocates as it hits the hard surface. My knee crunches on the edge of a step, making a sick cracking sound. I tumble down thirty-two steps before coming to a sudden, fierce and violently painful stop. I lay sprawled in a crumpled mass. My left eye is swelling shut, my head throbs, my legs feel like I've stepped on a landmine. I touch my side and my hand comes up warm and sticky with blood.

"It's alright, you're going to be alright," I repeat to myself, trying to keep calm. Then Laura is beside me. She smells like lemons. Tiny stars dance on the edge of my vision. The sound of cheering floats down the hall as a Dodger hits a homerun.

"I'll get help," she says, and runs back to my apartment. I hear glass breaking, a loud thump as if a chair has overturned. Blood continues to flow out of my side. My hand is bent at a grotesque angle. Suddenly, Laura is back, peering down at me, a reptilian coldness in her eyes. A strand of white pearls lays across the top of her T-shirt.

My mind begins bouncing in all directions: stolen pearls, heated insulin bottles, insurance policies.

"Harold's policy was for a million dollars." She is so close I can feel her breath on my cheek. I watch as pity flows across her eyes.

She shakes her head. "A million dollars isn't enough to live in Los Angeles. I had to rewrite the policy for ten million, forge your signature, make myself trustee." I stare at her in disbelief. "We made it look like you surprised some robbers who pushed you down the stairs."

Who's "we"? I wonder, as Laura's index finger begins to glide over her phone screen. My blood turns cold, I shiver uncontrollably, everything seems fuzzy and out of reach. Laura fidgets, bored and restless.

And then … it hits me like a sucker punch. I am taking too long to die. I pant like a rabid dog and see myself through their eyes – the hayseed from Wichita, an insurance salesman, the perfect dupe. Laura sighs impatiently, picks Isbella up and steps daintily over my body, careful not to soil her shoes. Isabella looks directly at me with a cold, calculating viciousness I did not know she possessed, and begins licking Laura's cheek. Slow, loving licks, like a femme fatale. No – Isabella isn't a femme fatale. She is a predator who kills for sport or pleasure. The money is just a bonus. Laura's hand slides down the smooth curve of Isabella's back. I watch in horror as Laura walks away. They are leaving me to die. Alone.

I watch the dainty swish of Isabella's lustrous tail, listen as Laura says, "From now on, it's you and me baby, right down the line." Isabella purrs softly in response. My pulse slows, my life ebbs away, heartbeat by heartbeat. The last thing I hear is the diamond charm jingling softly.

HORROR

BONDING TIME

Colin Adams-Toomey

15 to 20 minutes

Colin Adams-Toomey is a writer and filmmaker based in the United States. His short stories have been published by Gypsum Sound Tales in their anthology *Yabblins: Volume 1*, as well as the 4th installment of Fraidy Cat Press' quarterly anthology, in Hellbound Books' upcoming anthology, *Suburban Nightmares*, and in Burial Book's upcoming anthology, *Inanimate Things*. His film *Lost Creek* is available on most streaming platforms, distributed by Gravitas Ventures.

Colin lives with his beloved wife Hilary and cat Connal, and ever since he was an undergrad studying ancient Ireland, he always wanted to find a home for Crom Cruach. I guess he has now.

Tom slammed the car door shut and headed toward the house. The summer heat was intense and pantingly humid, adding to Tom's building ill-temper. He didn't want to be here.

The house was more than a century old, and out in the middle of nowhere. It was something some grim, half-sane farmer might have knocked up with his own hands. Nothing had a right angle to it. Tom shuddered to think what the basement would be like. The welling up of heat as he left the car had already made him feel sweaty and dirty. He huffed out an unhappy breath.

Of course, Stan would choose the hottest day of the year for this, he thought, then immediately checked himself. Stan's wife had passed. He needed help doing things. He was getting older. Tom was here because Amy had asked him. *Good for both of you*, she had said. He loved Amy and wanted her to be happy. Some bonding time with her dad was not too much to ask. Who knew, maybe it would help Tom and Amy, too.

Didn't improve the … *reality* of the present moment, though. As he trudged the gravel drive toward the sagging front porch, Tom reviewed his timeline. It was around two in the afternoon; the sun was high, hammering down through the scraggly trees. Two hours, three tops. Maybe four, if they were almost finished. He wouldn't be an asshole about it. Who knew what was down there? Might take a little time. Four hours with Stan, though …

He knocked. He was rehearsing his eventual escape line, trying to find the right combination of polite and implacable – *Hey, it's getting late, Amy needs me to pick up something* – when Stan opened the door.

Linda had died two months ago, and this had taken a visible toll on Stan. Stan had always been thin, wiry and oppressively energetic. He now appeared gaunt and spent. The light gleamed off his bald head. He smiled in greeting, and as it always seemed to Tom, the smile didn't quite reach his eyes.

"Hey, there he is!" Stan gripped Tom's shoulder with his signature brand of old-school masculine cheeriness. His grip wasn't any weaker, at least. He manhandled Tom into the house.

"Hey Stan, good to see you. How … how you holding up?" Tom's signature brand around Stan was stiffness and awkwardness.

"Oh, you know," replied Stan, grin never slipping, "one day at a time, that's what they say, right?" Stan's cheeriness was also his foil of choice to fend off any but the most superficial connection with Tom. Stan bustled toward the kitchen, leaving Tom briefly to his own devices.

"Yeah, right." As he looked around, Tom was taken aback by the state of the house. Half the pictures had been taken down from the walls, and a bookshelf once crammed full was now all but empty. Cardboard boxes were stacked against walls. The place felt gutted. Stan came back through, carrying a couple of sweating bottles. "Hey, how about a beer before we get started?"

Tom paused, his stomach sank, and he evaluated the situation. Why a beer? Stan never drank them; he preferred obscure old wines Tom had never heard of. Was this a test? Linda used to test him like this, putting drinks in front of him to see what he'd do. It always came back on him later, when he and Amy returned home. Surely Stan had spoken to Amy, and Amy couldn't help but relay her worries about Tom's drinking, his unhealthy eating habits. She never could keep that private. However, Tom had been making a real effort the last few months, and recently Amy had been almost draconian about encouraging him. Was that what this was?

He eyed the beer. *Fuck it,* he thought. He'd been good for months, and he was about to clean out Stan's godforsaken basement. He deserved this. And anyway, Stan had already opened it; it would be rude to let it go to waste. *Let him say what he wants to Amy. Let Amy say what she wants.* He made his mouth into a smile and accepted the bottle.

They sat down at Stan's kitchen table, and Tom poured a measure down his throat. He wasn't going to lie, it tasted pretty good. It had been a while. He looked up from the bottle to see Stan watching him. *Oh god, here we go. It's time to talk. Man to man.* Tom felt incapable of that sort of easy masculinity, but felt the requirement, nonetheless. Like some sort of ancient rite he had to participate in, without the requisite training. His eyes shifted to the disarray around him once more. "So, uh, you've made some changes …" Tom gestured lamely.

"Oh yeah, well," Stan's grin did maybe slip a notch. "It felt like time, you know? A lot of this stuff, you accumulate over the years. We've been in this house for, oh, three generations now. It's a good place; quiet, you can really settle in. But after Linda … well, it's starting to feel like it's time for a change."

"Yeah." Tom found himself, as he had dreaded, floundering for any path at all to move forward. Despite his feelings toward Stan, he had things he wished to say (or felt he should) about death, and loss, and grief, but he had no real context. His parents were both alive and healthy, and he was less comfortable with death than he would like to admit. Struggling for some "right" thing to say, he ended up with nothing at all.

The silence stretched, and stretched again. Stan looked at him. Tom gulped at his beer. If he were a less charitable person (he hoped he wasn't, but seriously) he would swear that Stan was letting the silence spin out.

He started to open his mouth – who knew what was going to come out of it – when Stan clunked his bottle down on the table in a decisive way. "Why don't we get started?" Tom was almost grateful as he stood. He reflected that only Stan could make a person *crave* manual labor, as an alternative to sitting with him. Probably, he knew that. *Not fair (wasn't it?). It wasn't.* Tom trailed behind his father-in-law.

The basement was just as he had imagined, or worse, if that was possible. Ancient, low-ceilinged, with crumbling stone walls, it was vast and claustrophobic at the same time. About half the floor was paved in cracked concrete, the rest was packed dirt. It was crammed with a lunatic assembly of rickety furniture and rotted, spilling cardboard boxes. There were no windows, the only light came from dangling, cobweb-strewn bulbs. Stan rubbed his hands together, showing not an ounce of remorse. Tom heaved the sigh of the condemned.

An unguessable amount of time later, Tom was damp with sweat and grimed to the elbow. Dirt from a basement always feels dirtier than from anywhere else, like it's more than fifty percent mouse turds and dead bugs. The taste of it was in his mouth. With no natural light to mark the passing of hours, they had entered some endless, unfathomable purgatory. At least some progress had been made; they had carved winding pathways through the towering junk. Trenches in a hopeless battlefront.

As soon as they'd started, Stan's good-natured jollity had been quickly put away, like the costume Tom knew it to be. He barked orders at Tom as though Tom was hired labor. At one point he had teetered close to genuine nastiness, all but screaming at Tom to leave a corner of the basement alone, where Tom had been innocently working.

This was the real Stan, as Tom knew him through Amy's stories and occasional personal experience. Arrogant, domineering and selfish, he was a man who got his way through whatever means worked. Amy had tended to gravitate to her mother, though in Tom's estimation, Linda had not been much better than Stan. Linda's gentle delivery had masked her truly spectacular emotional manipulation, and to Tom himself, she had always been quite cold. Tom tended to avoid interactions with both of them wherever he could, though he knew this was hurtful to Amy. So here he was. Breathing in mouse turds while Stan drove him like a packhorse. He felt his running current of frustration flaring toward real anger. He didn't need to be here. He didn't need this in his life.

But maybe he did. Maybe *they* did. Amy had said it was important, and Tom had seized that chance. He had to admit, things had not been great recently. Something was definitely off. When they had received word that Linda was very sick, Amy had packed up and stayed with her mother for weeks, up until Linda had passed.

Amy had come back … *different* was really the only way Tom could put it. Amy was a bit of a lost soul and with parents like hers, could you blame her? She was sweet and attentive to a fault. But after

Linda passed, Amy had closed off, turning dismissive yet demanding in a way Tom did not like. Sometimes even a little aggressive.

Aggressive in other ways, too. Their lovemaking had always been careful and gentle, and since Tom had slipped into unhealthy habits, it had maybe tapered off a little too much. But now, Amy was insistent and forceful in bed, and … maybe *violent* wasn't the word, but definitely not gentle. It made Tom privately uncomfortable. Once or twice in the middle of it, Tom had looked up at Amy's face and it had seemed to him that he saw more hunger there than love.

He put it down to grief, and tried to be understanding, but he didn't like it. That said, and as much as he wished to skirt around it, he wasn't blameless. Had he been taking Amy for granted? Had he maybe been taking advantage of her eagerness to please, to get his own way? He didn't like the answers to those questions. They say you marry your parents, ultimately. God knew he didn't want that for her, *or* for him. Hence the health kick. Hence the visit to Dear Old Dad.

And he loved Amy, he truly did. Every time he got angry at her for the way she just … *took* what her parents dished out, he felt immediately remorseful. Amy was not the problem. Amy was amazing. He had never met a kinder, more honest person. Amy, who made up songs in the shower when she had no idea that Tom was listening. Who was a much better artist than she was willing to admit, though Tom tried to encourage her. After the childhood she'd had, he hoped, as he always did, that he wasn't just the next difficult man in her life she had to take care of. She deserved a *lot* better than that.

Tom picked up a box and his fingers sunk deep into the mealy, rotted cardboard. The bottom pulled apart, and the contents spilled across the floor. He swore wearily and bent to gather it all up. A picture caught his eye.

He picked it up. In it, a young Stan and Linda stood in front of this same house. At the funeral, Linda's body in the casket had been a parched shell, shrunk in death to seemingly half the size she'd been in life. That image bore almost no resemblance to the vital young woman in the picture. Linda's hand was on the shoulder of a little girl. Though he couldn't really remember seeing many pictures of Amy as a child, there was no mistaking her here: the same frizzy curls, the same upturned nose. It had never occurred to Tom how little Amy looked like either of her parents. Lucky that way, really. Odd that this was packed up down here, not in a frame somewhere upstairs.

A thought occurred to Tom, which felt strangely unpleasant. He was increasingly sure he'd *never* seen a picture of Amy as a child before. Stan and Linda had a tasteful collection of art displayed proudly throughout the house, and many framed pictures on their walls. But the only pictures Tom remembered seeing were of Stan and Linda themselves.

Underneath the first picture were more photos, stretching back in time, some of them quite old indeed. Family pictures. Eerily, they all showed the same setup: man and woman, and two children, a boy and a girl, both around ten or eleven. In each photo, the children stood in front of their presumed parents. The father had his hand on the boy's shoulder, the mother on the girl's. The only exception was Amy's photo: she stood alone. There was something about the photos Tom found oddly unlikeable. Maybe it was the way the adults gripped the shoulders of the children, more possessive than familial. Maybe it was the expressions on the children's faces.

None of them, Amy included, looked happy to be there. All of them looked a little scared.

It occurred to Tom then that Amy had told him very little at all about her early childhood.

Beneath the photos was a stack of very old books, bound in cracked and curling leather. Tom had never heard of the titles before. *The Greater and Lesser Keys of Solomon the King. Ars Goetia. Le Petit Albert.* At the bottom was a book that looked not just old, but ancient. It was bound in crudely stitched hide, and the title seemed to have been gouged into it with a knife:

Lebor Adrad Crom Cruach.

"There she is." Stan's voice was right over Tom's shoulder, and it caused him to flinch. Tom turned to see Stan holding Amy's photo.

"We wanted two, you know. But with children … it's hard, nowadays." Tom nodded, not really following.

"There *were* two," Stan continued, pondering the photo, "but the boy didn't make it. We could only take Amy home."

"Amy had a brother?" Tom was stunned. He'd never heard this before.

"Well, not a *brother*. But they were good together. But we could only take Amy, sadly."

Tom's mouth fell open. He worked to reorient to this new information. "Are you saying Amy is *adopted?*"

"Of course." Stan shrugged his shoulders as if this were a normal conversation about mutually understood things. "Linda and I can't have children of our own, as easy as that would be. But that's not part of the deal." Stan chuckled. "Not much of a chip off the old block, is she? Surprised you didn't notice."

Tom licked his lips. "She never told me this."

"Oh, she didn't know." Stan's nonchalance was maddening. Tom felt as though he were actually losing his mind.

"You never *told* her?"

"Of course not," Stan replied happily, "that could have made things difficult."

A cold, impotent rage was building fast in Tom, at the insanity of this, at the endless, casually cruel way in which these people had fucked up Amy's life, continued to fuck it up. Just for fun. He had no idea what to do, how to meet it. In a shaky voice, he said, "I'm gonna head out now, Stan."

Stan had turned to rummage in a box. "Not yet, Tom." His voice was cajoling, pleasant, relentless. "We're not finished yet. Ah, here we go!"

He turned around, holding a knife that looked as though it had been made when people still lived in caves. The bone handle held a wicked-looking blade chipped from some sort of greenish stone. Before Tom could react, Stan snaked forward, grabbing Tom's forearm and pulling the knife across it. The blade was cruelly sharp, parting the skin easily. Tom recoiled, clutching his wound. Blood welled through his fingers.

"Easy, Tom, easy. Only a little one." Stan approached slowly, palm open to quiet a frightened animal.

"Fuck you, Stan." Tom's voice was high and wavery with fear and disbelief. He'd wanted to say that for a long time, though under the circumstances, it didn't feel as good as he had hoped it would. But it did goad him into action. He lunged forward, pulling a stack of furniture down on top of Stan, and ran.

He couldn't really comprehend what was happening, the world was evidently slipping into some sort of crazy nightmare, but the sudden mixture of primal terror and primal love surging through his system was intoxicating. He coped by focusing on Amy, getting back to Amy, to protect, to warn. He bounded up the stairs and found the basement door locked.

"Tom, there's nowhere to go." Stan's voice was very patient, like an indulgent parent with a wayward child. He stepped into view, all smiles. "I have the key." His eyes flicked down briefly, and his smile hitched. "Why don't you give me that?"

Tom looked down and was surprised to see he was still clutching the ancient book. He looked at Stan, who raised his hand expectantly. Tom thought for a ragged moment, then raised the book, taking a handful of pages. He cringed at their greasy feel, but he pulled them close to tearing.

It had the effect he hoped for. Before he could stop himself, Stan lurched forward, hand reaching fearfully. He recovered quickly. "Just give it to me."

"Give me the key, and I'll just go. Then you can have it." Tom was still focused on the thought of Amy, getting back to her. Then, it would be alright. Then, the world would make sense.

Stan's mask of patience slipped entirely, and his core of fury and supreme self-interest was nakedly on display. "Give it to me *now*. You don't want to *fuck* with me, Tom."

"Yeah?" Tom sneered, his anger rising to meet Stan's. It felt good, felt pure. He'd never been capable of such open confrontation before. He gripped the pages and pulled hard. Stan tensed.

Tom's fingers slipped bonelessly from the book.

Perplexed, he tried again, but all strength seemed to have gone out of his hands. The book slid out of his grasp, to thud against the ground. He looked at Stan, as though for an explanation, but he could suddenly see two Stans. On both of their faces, a smile was slowly spreading.

"Finally." Stan's voice reached Tom through a thick layer of gauze. "I think that beer might have gone to your head."

Tom had lots of things to say back, but they were all jumbled up, and his mouth was too dry to make words, anyway. His legs buckled and he pitched forward down the stairs, but wound up cradled gently in Stan's arms. As though from a distance, he watched as Stan dragged him through the basement to the corner he'd been warned to avoid. Before he lost consciousness, he saw Stan topple a stack of boxes to reveal a rough-hewn tunnel in the wall, like an open throat.

◆◆◆

Tom opened his eyes to flickering candlelight. The chamber he found himself in was small, hand-dug. The smell of earth and worms and dark things filled his nose and throat. Tom tried to move, but whatever Stan had given him had paralyzed his body. He lay helpless on the earthen floor. Before him was a stone statue.

Whatever it depicted was squirmy, grub-like and hideous. It embodied all of the slimy things that inhabit the dank places humans know instinctively to avoid. It depicted the disgusting things that burrow in, make their home beneath the skin; things that have lived far longer than humans and will far outlive them.

Open before the statue was the book he had tried to destroy: *Lebor Adrad Crom Cruach*.

"There he is!" It was the second time Tom had heard that cheery phrase. He rolled his eyes over. Stan kneeled nearby, naked and sweaty. His shriveled body glistened in the candlelight. Tom saw that his own wounded arm was suspended over a bowl, blood dripping sluggishly into it. Tom worked his cotton-dry mouth and discovered he could speak. "Stan." It was a lot to manage just that.

Stan gave a half-smile. "I've never liked that name," he said. "We've had so many, over the years. The old names were better."

"Stan," Tom continued, convinced like many victims that he could reason his way out. "Let me go, please. I won't say anything—"

"Don't be a child." Stan picked up the stone knife and pulled it across his own hand. He squeezed it into the same bowl, mingling his blood with Tom's. He looked almost apologetic.

"We would have done this sooner, if we could. You might not have had to be part of it at all. We prefer children, of course. Longer lifespan. Around ten is perfect – the bodies are strong enough to survive the bond. It's hard in this age, though. There was a time we ran a whole orphanage, back when there were no records. When no one cared. Then, we had the pick of the litter." He shook his head. "It's been harder and harder for us. We got Amy out of the hospital, but by then the alarm had gone off. The other baby died when we tried to get out. So of course, we had to wait for Amy to come of age, to find a suitable partner."

"Stan," Tom croaked, "whatever you're doing, you don't have to do this."

"Oh, it's too late now. The time has come, and Crom Cruach has been invoked to give his gift." Stan shuffled forward on his knees, bearing the bowl to the awful statue.

As Tom watched, horrified, Stan lifted the bowl to his lips, slurping greedily. He then placed it reverently at the base of the statue. His mouth was a slaughterhouse smear of red. "Blood is the sacrifice, as it always was," Stan murmured. He bent forward to the statue. "So very many years ago, when the world was young, when she and I first found the Bloody Twisted Worm and swore service. Blood is the trade, for the marvelous gift. *Adrad Crom Cruach, adidnopair fola, Crom Cruach.*"

Stan continued in a strange, brutal language that buzzed in Tom's mind, violated it, filled it with horrible understanding he never wished to have. The continuance of unnatural life, in exchange for the pleasure of the Worm.

"Yes, you see now." Stan caressed Tom's cheek. "The great gift, given to us so long ago. We pledged ourselves, to receive life everlasting. As each body ages, we take a new one. And we've gotten pretty good at it." Stan smiled.

Tom took a deep breath and tried courage, which he hoped was genuine.

"Stan," he said, "do what you want to me. But leave Amy alone. I'll accept whatever you want, just leave her alone." He never thought he'd have to say something like that, but it was all – the best – he had left.

Stan smiled and shook his head. "Oh, Tom. Amy? Where do you think my wife is?"

Tom could say nothing.

"She decided to go early, to ... test out the property. Maybe clean it up a little, before I moved in. And she says you've been pretty good about it, better eating and so on. You're not the best I could do, but a little better than you were."

Tom thought about the health regimen, so strictly monitored by Amy after Linda had died. He thought about the hollowed corpse he had seen in the casket ... *empty*, somehow. He thought about the strange, aloof person he had been living with. The person he'd been fucking, been used by, night after night. He felt sick.

"Hey, that's what they say, right? You become your father and marry your mother! If it helps, she's been *very* happy." Stan chuckled good-naturedly, as he started to climb, slowly and carefully, on top of Tom. Stan's lank penis dragged along Tom's leg.

Tom groaned, and whispered, "Please."

"Oh, come on, relax," Stan said, gripping Tom's chin, turning Tom's face towards him. "I always said you didn't amount to much. But now you don't have to worry. You're about to be part of a miracle." Stan brought his face so close to Tom's that Tom could feel the feverish heat emanating from it. He smiled. "It's bonding time, Tom."

Stan squeezed Tom's jaw, forcing his mouth open. At the same time, Stan's grin stretched to delirious lengths as his mouth yawned open wide, wider, splitting the skin at the edges. Tom's eyes rolled fearfully toward the gaping throat, and he saw a pale, maggot-like worm wriggling and clawing its way forward on thorny spines. It was as thick as a man's forearm. Tom could do nothing, say nothing, as the Worm surged forward, into his mouth.

He felt its weight on his tongue, tasted its horridness, felt its soft, pulsating mass force his jaws painfully apart, as it scurried forward and pushed its way down his throat. He swallowed helplessly, convulsively. As its spines hooked into his skin, he felt his mind invaded by thoughts and memories not his own. He instantly remembered all the years since the first painful time the Worm had been welcomed by firelight an age ago. Countless centuries, countless human masks worn smiling to the world, countless horrible cruelties, luxuriously enjoyed. He felt his own self torn, shredded, consumed by the man who had pledged himself to the Worm, to keep living forever. Tom's last conscious thought, before he was eaten utterly, was a disappointingly sarcastic jibe about parents living vicariously through their kids. It wasn't so funny, really.

He wished he and Amy had eloped, like he'd half-joked about.

◆◆◆

Suzy and Will Marshall had felt sorry for their new neighbors, Tom and Amy, ever since Amy's dad had died. It had clearly been tough for both of them, especially having to move so much stuff out of Amy's dad's house. It was hard to say why they wanted it all, that's what Will said privately to Suzy, but then, he was sure it meant a lot to Amy. Tom and Amy were strong about it, kept up good spirits. Amy joked that she had "forced Tom to do a lot for her dad" before he passed, which Suzy was sure had helped.

Tom and Amy were fun to be around, too. They were witty, well-traveled, had a … joy of life that was refreshing. The Marshalls agreed that they had been really lucky with their new neighbors.

Especially when it came to the Marshalls' kids, Mark and Lily. Both Tom and Amy worked from home; what they did was a constant source of amused speculation in the Marshall household. But honestly, it was a godsend. Both Will and Suzy worked full-time, and that was really hard with two kids, especially now that Mark and Lily were hitting double-digits. They knew they could send the kids over to Tom and Amy's any time. The other day, Tom and Amy even took a fun photo outside of their house, posing with Mark and Lily like the four of them were a little family. It was super-cute.

"We love kids," said Tom. "You never need to worry. We'll always be here to take care of them."

SCI-FI

THE ROMA PROJECT

Vincent St. Claire

20 to 25 minutes

Vincent St. Claire is a Minnesota based writer, artist and musician. When he is not at his desk writing suspenseful tales, he enjoys a good cup of coffee, cooking succulent meals and spending time with his cats. His story in this collection marks his first publication, and he hopes and prays that another one will get published in the future. More of his stories and illustrations can be found within the pages of his self-produced zine, *Little Terrors*.

I: CARLISLE

"All right, Romulus. What's the number on the back of this card?" The ape looked at Carlisle with boredom. The test had been going for five minutes and the scientist across the table showed no signs of wrapping up.

"Come on, Romulus," said Carlisle, signing along with his hands as he spoke. "What is the number on the back of this card?"

Romulus exhaled harshly and held up three fingers.

"Good, Romulus. Very good."

Carlisle jotted down some notes on a legal pad and shuffled the note cards. He was just as bored as the chimp, but the suits in charge at the CIA scheduled thirty minutes of testing. Carlisle knew damn well that the ape could tell which number was on each card, but until the arbitrary time limit was up, he had to play along.

"How about this one?" Carlisle held up another card and smiled half-heartedly at the chimp. Romulus furrowed his brow and snorted. The smile on Carlisle's face was shakier now, but he continued to hold up the card and nod with encouragement.

"That's it, buddy. Just let me know what's on the card."

Without warning, the chimpanzee's lips peeled back to show his clenched teeth and he glared at Carlisle with red eyes. The scientist darted his glance to the one-way mirror on the wall to his right. A small team of animal handlers waited on the other side in case of emergency.

Romulus screeched and punched the tabletop, leaving a dent.

The handlers darted in from the door on the east-facing wall. Just as the chimp climbed onto the table to rush toward Carlisle, the crew grabbed the ape's arms and restrained him. Carlisle did his best to remain calm but knew that the frenzied ape would be in the middle of ripping off his face if they had arrived any later.

Romulus thrashed and kicked at the handlers pulling him away from the table. The ape swung his body toward Al, the burliest of the three, and sank his teeth into the handler's arm.

The man screamed and everyone in the room gasped.

"Oh God, are you OK, Al?" asked Carlisle as he produced a hypodermic syringe from his coat pocket. The chimpanzee flailed and howled in Al's arms at the sight of the needle.

"Just hurry the fuck up, will ya? I'm gonna need stitches."

Carlisle gripped the chimp's head and injected a cocktail of sedatives and psychoactives into its neck. Romulus gave one final jerk before he collapsed into Al's arms – docile and stoned out of his mind.

"Fuckin' hell that hurt!" screamed Al, as he slapped the sedated primate across the face.

"Next time I'll bite *you*, ya monkey fuck!"

"Hey!" snapped Carlisle, who got into the face of the much bigger man without hesitation. "He may be drugged, but he *will* remember that. Touch him again and I will report it all the way to the top."

Two other handlers took Romulus away from Al and left for the kennels. Al clutched his arm tightly to stop the bleeding and stomped out of the room without acknowledging Carlisle. Carlisle shook his head before scooping up the notecards and filing them away in a manilla portfolio.

It was his third month at the Rushmore Facility, with nine to go. Carlisle assumed that his little boy would be twice as big and speaking in complete sentences by the time he could go home. Carlisle wondered if this project was worth a year away from his wife and son, but then he remembered the big house in Laurel Canyon it had financed.

He was a handsome man of medium stature in his early forties. Once he graduated from MIT he bounced between major research facilities across the country, eventually attracting the attention of the US government. Still, Carlisle had never imagined helping the CIA weaponize the human mind. He had laughed when they first told him about The Roma Project – forcing psychic abilities by way of hallucinogenics sounded like something out of the tabloids. It was only after he saw a chimp crush a beer can without touching it that he began to believe.

The project was built on the foundations of earlier CIA operations, the earliest of which led to little progress and many dead chimpanzees. It was only within the last few years that his predecessors had stumbled upon the proper combination of chemicals. Once there was conclusive evidence that the drugs produced safe and controllable psychic results, they would move on to human trials – what this project was *really* about.

Carlisle left Observation Room A and closed the door behind him. Waiting to his right was a security guard named Roger, stationed outside to prevent access to anyone without the proper clearance. He pulled out his keycard and locked the door electronically.

"Heard quite the scuffle in there. What was going on?"

"Oh, you know, the suits don't realize that apes hate performing menial tasks just as much as we do. But at least we aren't as quick to violence." Carlisle stopped to think about Al. "Well, most of us at least."

"Glad you got out of it OK," Roger said as he peered down at his watch, "and with twenty minutes to spare, too."

"What do I care, I'm salaried." Carlisle sighed and rubbed his temples with his fingers. "I wasn't going to learn anything new in those twenty minutes, anyway."

"What's next then?"

"Telekinetic testing. Remus has already advanced to that stage. Romulus could have as well, but he refused to cooperate in our last session."

"No," said Roger with a devilish grin, "what are you doing now that you're free?"

Carlisle reddened. "Well, I was hoping to pay Delacroix a visit – sit in on Remus' trials."

Roger's grin widened. "Hoping to turn that visit conjugal?"

Delacroix was a fellow scientist assigned to the project. She was fifteen years his junior, single, and had a great body hidden under her lab coat. Though Carlisle was far from proud of it, he had initiated an affair two weeks prior. It wasn't the first time he had been unfaithful to his wife, but it had been the first since his son was born and the one he felt the most guilty about. What were they expecting? Everyone was locked away from their families for an entire year with no-contact orders. The two scientists had gone to great lengths to keep their relationship secret, but last week Roger had walked into the storage closet where Carlisle was giving Delacroix cunnilingus.

"No, Roger. I intend to keep this professional and bring whatever scientific aid I can to the research."

"Sure, bud. Just make sure you use protection. Don't need another little shit crawling around down here, do you?"

Roger chuckled to himself, but Carlisle was not amused. He gave the security guard the middle finger as he walked down the hallway.

II: DELACROIX

Delacroix's time on the project started as a dream come true. It was unheard of to be recruited to such a prestigious assignment right out of grad school. The first six months were great, but she supposed all good things must come to an end. Months of isolation and loneliness had led to poor decisions, and she had spent the last week in a deep depression.

It wasn't that she didn't like Carlisle. She found him charming and his brilliance was unquestionable, but he was a married man with a nine-month-old at home. It all happened gradually – compliments here, cheeky comments there – but before she knew it they were finding places all over the facility to fuck incognito.

She knew she wasn't free of responsibility. Delacroix was aware from the beginning that Carlisle was married, but she was not prepared for his advances. Her youth had been laser-focused on her studies, and the scientist remained single and celibate until her assignment on The Roma Project. When the handsome older man swooped in and showed her attention, she couldn't help but fall under his spell.

It began as an exhilarating affair. Carlisle was an experienced lover and they both made a game out of finding new places to make love. But guilt set in quickly and getting caught put her on a downward spiral. For all she knew, Roger had told everyone on the security team about it. She couldn't handle the embarrassment. She had decided their affair needed to end, but she wasn't sure how to tell Carlisle.

Delacroix arrived at Observation Room B and nodded to the security guard, Gerald, who buzzed her in. She tried to see if there was any indication that the man knew of her liaisons with Carlisle, but if he did, he kept it hidden. Inside, a plain white table was waiting for her to set up shop.

She began by setting up a collection of wooden blocks – a cone, a cylinder, a rectangular prism and a cube. If Remus hadn't been so cooperative, she might have been hesitant about the cone's sharp point. Hopefully, Carlisle would leave it off the table when Romulus was ready. She situated a box with a series of round and rectangular holes cut into it next to the blocks. When Delacroix was satisfied with her setup, she looked over to the one-way mirror, and though she couldn't see who was behind it, she gave them a thumbs up to fetch Remus from the kennels.

A minute later, the adjoining door opened and a solitary female animal handler walked Remus into the room, holding his hand. The chimp's eyes lit up to see the scientist. When the handler let go of his hand, he ran over to hug Delacroix. Developing a relationship with Remus was the scientist's favorite part of the job. She had grown to think of him like a son.

Carlisle has an actual son, and look how much that meant to you, she thought.

"Let's get started," she said to Remus in sign language. Learning the signs had been a struggle for Delacroix, and she still only knew a handful of phrases. It didn't matter too much. There was a limit to the amount a chimp could learn.

Remus strolled over to his side of the table and Delacroix sat opposite him.

"Remus, pick up the cone."

Remus extended his arm to the wooden cone, but Delacroix wiggled an admonishing finger. She pointed to the side of her head and tapped it. The ape nodded, returned his hand, and began to stare at the block intensely. After a moment, the block wiggled on the table.

"Good, Remus. Keep going."

The corner of the cone started to lift, causing the block to loop around on the table. Remus closed his eyes hard enough to wrinkle his face before flinging his lids open. In an instant, the cone levitated a few inches off the tabletop.

"Very good, Remus. Very good."

The rest of the trial went off without a hitch. Without ever using his hands, the chimpanzee moved all the blocks across the table, stacked them on top of each other, and concluded by inserting them into their corresponding holes in the wooden box. Even a slight movement of one of the blocks was cause for celebration just a week prior. The progress was miraculous, but until Romulus showed similar progress, Remus was an anomaly.

"I'm sorry, Remus. Time for the worst part."

The chimp sighed and held out his left arm. Delacroix fished out the syringe from her lab coat and injected the ape on the top of his hand. She picked Remus up and stroked the top of his head gently. Soon, he went limp in her hands and the handler came from the side door to take the sedated ape away.

"Quite the impressive display," said a familiar voice behind Delacroix.

Keep it cool.

"Well, Dr. Carlisle," she said, turning to face him, "aren't you done with your ESP trial a little early?"

Talk shop, make some small talk, then break it off.

"Yes ma'am. A second later and I'd be having my face sewed back on."

"Yikes," said Delacroix with wide eyes. "Is everything OK?"

"Well, Al is going to need his arm stitched up, but no *people* were hurt," he said, chuckling at his joke. "I wouldn't be surprised if the bite went to the bone."

"I don't even know how he got his job," said Delacroix truthfully.

"Well, like all government workers, I'm sure he failed upwards."

The two laughed mildly.

What is he doing here? she thought.

"Is there anything I can help you with, Carlisle?"

"Oh," he said, placing his hands on her hips to draw her closer, "I'm sure I could think of something."

Delacroix sighed and turned away. "Carlisle, I think we should end this. It was fun while it lasted, but it can't go on."

Carlisle pulled his body up against Delacroix and wrapped his hands around her stomach. His crotch pressed against her backside and she could feel how excited he was.

"Is that really how you feel?" he whispered into her ear. The warmth of his breath tingled against her earlobe. As much as she hated it, she felt herself becoming aroused.

"Yes, Carlisle."

He paused for a moment but didn't move away.

"All right, Miss Delacroix, we will stop."

Delacroix turned around in disbelief. "You mean it?"

"Yes, I mean it," he said, kissing her softly. "But how about we end it on a high note? One more time – for posterity?"

They stared at each other in silence. It didn't matter how wrong she knew it was. He was handsome, ready, and her blood boiled for him. Delacroix looked into his stunning green eyes and felt weak in the knees. She gave a silent nod and before she knew it, they were pushing the wooden blocks off the table to make room.

III: ROGER

As he achieved a level of boredom that few ever experienced, Roger leaned back in his tattered office chair to watch the security station monitors. Closed-circuit cameras were placed throughout the facility and it was every security guard's duty to monitor the grainy black-

and-white footage for two hours of their shift. The guard tried to make himself comfortable as he continued the security equivalent of watching paint dry.

Roger was in his thirties, never married, and hoped this illustrious post would be the first step in climbing the CIA ladder. It better be – it was like being a mall cop in a shopping center populated by ten people who never stole anything. He joined the agency to push his limits, serve his country, and maybe even do a little espionage. Instead, he was stuck babysitting a bunch of eggheads.

Thanks to the classified status of the project, the computers were only linked to a CIA intranet server. He could not surf the web to help pass the time. No browsing social media. No bingeing Netflix. No Pornhub.

That wasn't to suggest that he was above finding ways to relieve his urges while stationed there. He would occasionally watch some of the female staff on the security monitors and take out the lotion and tissues he had stowed away in his knapsack. Roger thought that Delacroix's animal handling assistant was a fine-looking woman, not to mention Delacroix herself.

"Carlisle, you bastard," he muttered to himself. What right did he have to swoop in? Roger hadn't been on a date in months and would have loved to spend some quality time with her. That jerk was probably fucking her that very instant.

Roger jolted upright in his chair. *He was probably fucking her that very instant.* He tried to think of where her trial was. It was one of the observation rooms, but he couldn't remember which. The monitors showed the main hallway, the door to the Jefferson Wing, the cafeteria and the kennels. Roger needed to switch one of them to view the observation room, and the kennel feed only showed two very drugged apes taking naps in their cages.

Roger pulled down the access menu and changed the feed from the kennels to Observation Room A, where the lights were off. He hurriedly flipped it to Observation Room B and nearly fell out of his chair. Carlisle had Delacroix bent over the table and was taking her from behind. They apparently got into it in a hurry as neither had removed much in the way of clothing. Carlisle was grabbing Delacroix's breasts, which tumbled out of her blouse, as she looked toward the camera in ecstasy.

Not wanting to let the opportunity go to waste, Roger unzipped his fly, pulled down his pants, and pumped two squirts of lotion into his palm. As he was about to begin, the scientists moved to a different part of the room to continue their escapade … outside of the camera's view.

"Fuck!" shouted Roger, hitting the desk with a fist. He supposed he could imagine what was going on, but he wanted to see more. If only there were a way he could catch the rest of the show.

Wait, he thought, *the side room.* Each observation room had a smaller side room behind a one-way mirror. He could watch them undetected – but did he dare? The margin for error was high; if one of them got a little too close to the window it could be seen through. Still, the idea thrilled him, and the risk only aroused him further.

But he couldn't leave without taking precautionary measures. Roger pulled up the terminal's security settings menu and armed the alarms. If anything like a broken lock or movement in a restricted area occurred, the Roosevelt Wing would go into lockdown for one hour.

"Good enough for government work," he said to himself. The guard shoveled his things into the knapsack and hurried toward Observation Room B.

The Rushmore Facility was half a mile underground. Tiles were laid on the floors, but the walls were rough-cut granite left untouched after the tunnels were dug. Flickering fluorescent lights illuminated the hallways and shined blindingly off the maze of air ducts that cut through the entire facility. The acoustics caused Roger's footsteps to echo like cannon fire.

When he arrived, Gerald stood guard at the observation room doors. A puzzled expression was on the man's face as he looked at Roger.

"Aren't you supposed to be watching the cameras?"

"Just got reassigned," lied Roger. "Chief paid me a visit in the security room and wanted me to relieve you. He's waiting to talk to you there."

Gerald raised his eyebrow. "And he didn't just come down and talk to me in person?" Roger winced and tried to think of an explanation. When none came he sighed and put a $10 bill in Gerald's hand.

"Let's just trade, OK?"

Gerald shook his head but still pocketed the money. He rolled his eyes at Roger before walking down the hallway.

"Enjoy the show, you sick fuck. Sounds like they're having fun in there."

Roger was red with embarrassment as he opened the side door with his keycard. He tiptoed in, carelessly leaving the door ajar.

IV: AL

The door to the kennel room swung open as Al walked in, clutching his freshly bandaged arm. Some combination of the painkillers and the whiskey he kept hidden under his mattress left the animal handler unable to control his rage. He stomped to Romulus' cage, where the ape lay sedated on his back. The burly man stuck his fingers through the cage door's wire mesh and shook it to get Romulus' attention. The chimp stared into nothingness, still too drugged to pay the man any attention.

"Listen up, you little fucker. You've been nothing but a nuisance since you got here and I just had to get thirty fucking stitches. If it were up to me, I'd cut off your goddamn head."

The ape looked ahead blankly.

"Next time you wanna hurt me, I will fuck you up. Understand?"

Romulus' head lolled over to him lazily.

Al punched the door and the entire kennel shook. The chimp barely registered the threat.

They must have you on some real good shit, thought Al.

Embarrassment began to wash over him when he realized that he had just threatened an ape – especially one who didn't even realize what was happening. Some small, sober part of his conscience told him to get out before he did something *really* stupid. With his head hung in shame, Al turned around to leave. If not for the booze, the painkillers and the throbbing in his arm, he would have felt the key ring on his belt loop become weightless and detach itself.

Al got to the door, telling himself that he would stop drinking in the morning. It was one of many times he had made this promise, but he never kept it. Before he could grab the doorknob, something clicked behind him. Al jumped at the sound and turned around instinctively. His jaw dropped. Dangling from the wide-open cage door was his keyring.

Romulus, no longer pretending to be sedated, was leaning out toward him.

The chimp grinned at him – an awful, hate-filled grin.

In an instant, the chimp leaped from his cage and plowed into Al's chest. He tried to guard his face with his hands, but Romulus grabbed his fingers and twisted. The handler nearly fainted at the sight of his broken phalanges piercing through the skin. The iron-rich smell of blood wafted into Al's nostrils and he couldn't help but gag. Romulus roared with simian laughter, grabbing inside the man's mouth to rip open his cheek.

Al thrashed his body in pain, launching Romulus against the wall. The chimp hit the lower air duct grate with a thud and sat down, stunned. Al staggered to his feet, trying to ignore the agony that the meager amount of booze and painkillers had no hope of combatting. He darted back toward the door, praying for the strength to get out.

Why the hell isn't security doing anything? he thought.

Suddenly, something like an invisible hand grabbed his hair, and his head slammed against the wall. A hideous crack rang out as his nose flattened, leaving a smear of blood on the granite. The chimp, tracing the man's movements with his head, laughed gleefully as Al's head continued to smash. Soon, mushy gobs of brain oozed out from his shattered skull and his eyes dangled loosely from their crushed sockets.

When he was satisfied, Romulus let him drop to the floor. The chimp leaped over the mangled corpse and opened the door, chuckling as he ran out into the hallway.

From the cage below Romulus', Remus began to come to. He looked up curiously at the keyring his brother had left dangling in the cage door.

V: THE FALL OF ROMA

Carlisle was seconds away from finishing when Roger's head came crashing through the one-way mirror. Cracks spiderwebbed across the sheet of glass, and large shards at the top fell shattering to the floor. One particularly sharp blade of mirror came down on the back of the security guard's neck like a guillotine, beheading him instantly. The head rolled toward the stunned scientists and came to rest, staring up at them in shock. Delacroix let out a blood-curdling scream. Carlisle went flaccid in an instant.

The alarm system engaged and red hazard lights flashed across the ceiling. A heavy metallic noise surrounded them as the security shutters slammed down, trapping them in the observation room.

"Emergency. Emergency. Lockdown protocol is in effect," repeated a computerized voice.

As the scientists scrambled to reclothe themselves in the confusion, Romulus crawled over the shattered glass and into the main observation area. His fingers were cut by the jagged bits of glass, but he continued without noticing. The chimp had nothing on his mind but fury and the urge to inflict pain upon the man who experimented on him.

"My God," whispered Carlisle, "he escaped."

The ape's gaze was fixed on the male scientist. If Carlisle made any sudden movement, he knew Romulus would barrel toward him. Seeing that she was being ignored, Delacroix seized the opportunity to hide under the table for what little protection it might offer.

"Easy now, Romulus," said Carlisle as he signed along with shaking hands, avoiding all eye contact to prevent further aggravation.

The chimp snorted and stepped closer, leering at Carlisle with disdain. He emitted a scent of feral anger that singed the hairs in the scientist's nose.

"Let's take a break, Romulus. Everything is OK."

Delacroix searched for some way to defend herself in the confined space. Besides the table and the air duct on the ceiling, the room was empty. Well, almost. Her stomach dropped when she saw the sharp wooden cone that had rolled to the other side of the room. If she went to grab it, it would be impossible to go undetected by Romulus.

"It's me – Carlisle. Your friend." The scientist frantically repeated the last sign. "Friend!"

Romulus was ten feet away from Carlisle now. He paused, standing only four feet tall yet emotionally towering over the man. For a brief moment, the room was still, and Carlisle thought things might be turning around.

"Easy, buddy. Easy."

The chimp made no further movement.

"Good."

Without warning, the chimp let out a hideous shriek. Before he could process what had happened, Carlisle flew against the wall and was held there by an unseen force. His face reddened at the extreme pressure pushing against his body. Delacroix slapped her hand over her mouth and tried to stifle a scream. Romulus sneered at the man with a sinister grin.

"Romulus," spat out Carlisle, unable to move his hands to sign. "Please."

The pressure at the scientist's temples was unbearable. The green eyes that Delacroix found so appealing were now bulging from their sockets and streaked red with bursting blood vessels. As he was about to let out a scream, the sides of his head caved in on each other. Shards of his skull flew into the air with a loud pop and his brain dribbled out to the floor. Carlisle's limp body slumped to the floor, dead, his head crushed like a beer can.

No longer able to contain herself, Delacroix screamed so loudly that for a moment even the alarm and the computer voice were drowned out. She regretted it instantly – Romulus darted his head toward her with a wicked smile.

"No. Oh God, no!"

Delacroix didn't dare to leave from under the table as the ape walked toward her tauntingly. He relished the terror he was bringing her, savoring the mortified tears that rolled down her face. When he had his fill, he would rip her apart – physically or psychically, it didn't matter to Romulus.

The cowering scientist was ready to submit to her fate when, in her peripheral vision, she saw the screws of the air duct's grille come loose. If she hadn't been watching it, she wouldn't have noticed the squeaking sound of the screw circling in the hole.

It can't be, she thought.

Soon, the entire grille assembly was deconstructed in the air. Piece by piece, the metal grate floated gently to the ground. Romulus, unaware, continued to saunter toward her. Delacroix remained as still as she could, desperately trying to keep her face blank.

He came for me.

When the chimp's face appeared in the darkness of the opened vent, Delacroix could not believe what she was seeing. Remus descended from the opening in the duct – *levitating*. His telekinesis had advanced to a level where he could move *himself* in the air. The chimp landed softly on the floor, making no sound at all. He looked toward his brother with determination and anger.

Romulus sensed that something was amiss from the look in Delacroix's eyes. The confused chimp turned his head and his face was met with the sharp point of the wooden cone. A gush of blood spurted out as the projectile slammed the ape into the wall, impaling his head into the granite. The whole room seemed to shake with the impact. Romulus's body violently twitched three times before finally going limp.

Remus smiled victoriously and ran toward his metaphorical mother, who hugged the chimp with all her might as tears of joy fell down her cheeks. The ape sniggered to himself and planted a kiss on her forehead.

Delacroix figured it would be at least forty-five minutes before the lockdown protocol ended. She couldn't wait to be out of this horrible room. The Roma Project would undoubtedly be considered a failure, but the data would be analyzed and modified, and then another experiment would proceed with new chimps. To Delacroix's knowledge, at least two men had been killed as a result of the experiment, but the CIA would consider it an acceptable loss.

As the chimp snuggled up against her, Delacroix prayed that they would do as they promised and examine the effects on his brain with an MRI. She couldn't bear the thought of them taking her baby, her *savior*, and dissecting him in the name of science. But when the project was officially over, she would no longer have a say in the matter. For now, she held Remus tight, thankful for his company.

But somewhere, deep inside, she shuddered with the knowledge that he could kill her without lifting a finger.

HORROR

SHELLY AND THE FISHMAN

Mark Cowling

5 to 10 minutes

Mark Cowling is a writer from Essex, UK. His work has been featured in BBC Radio sketch shows and many places online, such as *Daily Science Fiction*. His short fiction was included in the anthology *Campfire Macabre*, and was a winner of the 2020 Yahoo! Stor14s competition.

DAY ONE

It was Shelly's thirty-third day of working from home and she had a solid system in place. Her phone would play Bieber's *Peaches* – don't judge – at 9 a.m. sharp. This was the cue for Shelly to throw one arm out of bed and grope around for her scratched-to-shit iPhone. The trick was to reply to three or four work emails and then she was clear to go back to sleep for an hour or so, take a leisurely shower, and grab some caffeine. As far as the dopes at K&R Artist Management were concerned, Shelly had her little pointy nose to the grindstone.

While sipping a Cinnamon Roll Frappuccino and considering whether to transition an elongated mid-morning break into an early lunch, Shelly spotted a dark shadow shift at the far side of her kidney bean pool. *God damn raccoons*, thought Shelly. It was bad enough that they trawled through her trash and crapped on her sunbed, now the raggedy little bastards were taking a dip in the pool.

Shelly armed herself with a broom and slid open the patio door. She beat the broom against the floor a couple times. "Hey!" she yelled, but decided against any further outburst in case the actress she was trying to befriend next door heard and thought she was loco. The girl only had a part as a bespectacled coroner's assistant in some basic cable *CSI* rip-off, but her career could blow up at any minute in this city.

The paving stones were good and toasty underfoot and Shelly made a mental note to take that early lunch outside, perhaps followed by a quick power-nap. Once, that is, the yard had been de-raccooned.

Shelly shrieked and let the broom clatter to the floor.

There was a large shape zipping around the bottom of the pool. The size of an adult man but moving far too swiftly to be human.

Shelly darted back inside, shut the door and grabbed her phone. She quickly scrolled down to the private security number but then froze. Her mind wandered to the possibilities of viral Insta fame. Yes, the world had to hear this raccoon/shark/thing story. It was her duty to document it, for posterity or science or whatever. That and a million likes.

"So, I was working from home and I just happened to glance outside," Shelly spoke into her phone. No, that look wouldn't work.

A quick hair and makeup refresh later, Shelly tried again.

"Okay, guys, I'm literally scared out of my mind right now," Shelly said to her phone while re-opening the door to the back yard. She switched the device to record what was in front of her. "So, I'm working from home and I just happen to glance away from my laptop for a second, and I'm like, hmm, what was that?"

Shelly edged up to the rim of the pool.

"I don't know what to do here. Should I be calling the police? Animal control?"

Water rippled in the breeze with swirling swells of light reflecting off its surface. The pool was empty.

Shelly stared at a tree in the yard of the fake coroner's assistant. The gently waving branches cast a shadow that would occasionally creep into her pool.

"Well, at least I didn't livestream ..."

Crouching in the bushes at the far side of the pool was a figure. It stood and stepped into the sunlight. The thing was well over six feet tall, with green skin textured like chain mail. What could only be described as gills quivered each side of its neck. The creature's hands were huge and webbed, with serrated claws at the tip of each finger.

It made an odd clicking noise and then leaped into the pool. About a cup-full of water splashed from the entry point and then that same dark shadow appeared again at the bottom of the pool, zipping towards Shelly like an arrow.

Shelly ran indoors and screamed for a full minute.

◆◆◆

Shelly locked herself in the bathroom and barricaded the door with the nice vintage chair she'd found on Craig's List. She managed to stop her hands from shaking long enough to replay the footage. And then she watched it again. And again. It took a good few plays to convince herself that, yes, it did really happen, and no, she wasn't crazy.

Each time she watched the video, she became less certain she should call the authorities. When she had been standing in front of the creature, she had interpreted its expression as one of bestial detachment, the way a hawk might consider a field mouse. But now, she saw fear.

This creature was far from its home, wherever that may be. It was frightened and alone. No doubt it viewed humans as predators. How else would it and its kind have survived undetected until now? No, it was trapped here. It dove into the pool since water is its natural habitat and the only place to offer any form of safety.

A few Internet searches later confirmed Shelly's fears. In fact, it was far worse than she had imagined.

What would happen if she reported it? Men in dark suits would arrive, they would fire some kind of dart into the creature and take it away, to wherever the Deep State hid these kinds of things. New Jersey, according to one site. Any trace it had been in her pool, all her footage, would be erased. Jeez, perhaps they'd lock her into an asylum with the crazies who think they've been probed by ET.

Shelly cautiously cracked open the bathroom door and peered into the living room.

Everything was as she'd left it. Picking up the broom, she crept back out into the yard.

The creature was sitting, perfectly still, at the bottom of the pool. As it spotted Shelly, it scooted to the far end with one thrash of its feet.

"Hey, don't be scared," Shelly said, her voice high and little more than a whisper.

Shelly rushed back inside and threw open the fridge door. She grabbed a carton, hurried back to the lip of the pool, and placed her offering on the tiles.

"I hope you like Sichuan Pork."

She retreated indoors and pulled the blinds closed. Shelly didn't have to wait long until the creature reached out of the water and snatched the carton. It devoured the food in two bites.

DAY SEVEN

The delivery guy from Lu's was giving her a funny look again, she was sure. Shelly had just taken possession of the day's order: three Sichuan Pork, two servings of wontons, one chow mein and an order of dumplings. Each day she added an extra item or two, but it didn't seem to put a dent in Olaf's hunger.

Oh, yeah – Shelly had decided to call the creature Olaf. Partly because it felt weird to refer to it as "it" or "the creature" in her head, and partly because she was a huge *Frozen* fan.

She had also briefly considered Audrey III and Fin Carrey.

Shelly strolled through the house and out into the yard. She placed the various cartons down by the pool and then curled up on a sunbed.

"Dinner is served!"

As Olaf wolfed down the food, bean sprout and spring onion shrapnel sprayed from his mouth and littered the surrounding tiles.

"Olaf, I was thinking," Shelly said, scrolling through work emails. "I really should figure out where you came from. I mean, perhaps you have a fishman family waiting. You know, a fishwife and little fishchildren. That would make a great climax for this story. CNN would lap it up. Fox would give me a blank cheque."

Shelly put her phone down and glanced over at Olaf. Olaf was sucking up the last drops of oyster sauce with a comical slurping noise. "I hope you don't consider the term fishman to be pejorative."

DAY TWELVE

Shelly dumped the dozen or so cartons down by the pool. She had experimented with Mexican food on day nine and that had not gone well, so Chinese take-out it was again.

"I think I've found it," she said, pausing at the open doors. "There's that new development about two miles away. I don't know what it is they're building – a fulfilment centre or something. Anyway, that whole area is being drained. It was considered too marshy, too expensive to build on, but with the city expanding and land prices going up, I guess it's now profitable. I'm betting that's where you're from."

Olaf was becoming far less timid. Shelly noticed he no longer hid from her at the far end of the pool but now bobbed around in the middle, waiting for his meal. This time, he didn't even pause for her to retreat. As soon as cartons hit tile, Olaf rushed over.

Shelly studied him. She had never been this close. His hide had a beautiful metallic sheen like oil on water. Maybe it was her imagination, but she swore she could feel the heat radiating off Olaf's body.

"I don't know where you'll go now. If that was your home."

Without thinking, Shelly reached out. As soon as her fingers made contact, Olaf ducked underwater and swam to the bottom of the pool's far side.

"I'm sorry!" Shelly took a few steps back and held her hands up. "Olaf, I'm sorry. I shouldn't have done that."

It wasn't until Shelly went inside her house and closed the door that Olaf resurfaced and finished his meal, eyes locked on the building at all times.

Shelly replayed the moment in her mind over and over that day, the silkiness of his skin, the warmth. She felt herself drawn to this mysterious creature, wanting to understand it, wanting to know what it felt.

DAY TWENTY-ONE

This was to be the day. Shelly had rebuilt her trust with Olaf. She placed his food down by the pool as usual and watched him eat.

When finished, Olaf drifted into the centre of the swimming pool and floated. At one point he gently spun around, his back to Shelly but with no apparent concern. She took this as final proof of his comfort.

Shelly took off her robe – she was wearing the new bikini she bought for the lockdown-cancelled vacation. Taking cautious baby steps, she made her way into the water. It was colder than she had expected and her body shivered.

Olaf watched her intently but made no sign of distress.

Floating, she let herself drift closer and closer to Olaf. Olaf's head twitched once or twice, his forked tongue darting out, but he was still relaxed, still at peace.

Shelly got to a distance of about four feet from her pool guest. This was the time. Olaf was now completely comfortable in her presence. She had put herself in his space, where he was in control.

She reached out with her left hand, fingers extended.

No sudden moves. No noise.

Shelly reached out until she was a fraction of an inch from Olaf's face.

With one sudden jerk, Olaf bit off Shelly's hand.

It chomped through her radius and ulna as if they were spring rolls. Shelly could only gasp, blood squirting from the stump like something from a cheesy horror film.

"Olaf—" Shelly screamed before being dragged underwater.

DAY ONE

This could be her big break. Ashley took the script outside, eyes glued to the pages.

The new writer was a genius, everyone said so. Although she wasn't quite sure why the central character was revealed to be a robot on page seventy-two, or why only the first act referenced time travel.

But maybe, she thought, the fact it made no sense to her was simply *proof* of the writer's genius.

Ashley sighed and let the screenplay flop onto the patio table. There would be dozens of actors reading for this part. Emma Stone, probably – couldn't she leave a few good roles for everyone else? Her agent mentioned Scarlett and Jennifer too. How could she possibly compete with people who were household names, actors who were constantly in the press?

A splash caught her attention. Ashley crept towards her pool and peered in.

CRIME

NOT HIS NAME

Arthur Ursini

15 to 20 minutes

Arthur Ursini is an American writer. This is his first published piece of fiction. He is currently working on a novel. He can be found on Instagram @arthur.ursini

Everyone in town said that the Rock of Recompense was a church, nothing more. The back office of the building was larger than Izzi expected, confirming his suspicion that they were good at keeping things hidden. He had arrived two weeks prior and did nothing to blend into the populace of the small Colorado town, driving down Main Street in a brand-new black '82 Buick Riviera, eyeing each passerby from behind a pair of dark sunglasses with an interrogating gaze as if *they* were the interlopers. By the time Izzi had made an appointment with the head of the church, everyone was already talking about the black-eyed stranger seen wandering the streets. And that was his plan. He wanted the good people of Mosshead to know, without any uncertainty, that a long shadow had just fallen upon their town.

Ambrose Taylor wore a humble suit and matching smile meant to make men believe that he was a genial soul. Izzi took a seat in the Reverend's office, seeing through them both.

"How are you on this fine morning, Mr. Izzi?" Ambrose asked.

"Enjoying the lovely weather you have out here, Father."

Ambrose waved a hand. "I'm no priest, Mr. Izzi. Most folks call me Reverend Taylor."

"Oh, sorry about that. There weren't any reverends back when I was going to church."

"And are you here because you have found your way back to the Lord?"

Izzi grinned as he pulled out a pack of cigarettes. "No, that ain't why I'm here," he said, lighting one of them.

"Then how can I be of service?"

"The purpose of my visit concerns a member of your congregation," Izzi said, removing a slip of paper from his breast pocket and reading from it. "A Mr. Jonah Morrison."

Ambrose's face scrunched into a knot of uncertainty. As expected, the Reverend played the fool. He was faintly aware of a man by that name in the town but insisted that he was not a member of the church, nor did he know where Mr. Morrison lived. Izzi had a lifetime of experience dealing with men who lied. The Rock of Recompense was a church, nothing more. That's what everyone said.

"Sure about that?" Izzi asked. "I'm not one to act without certainty. And I'm most definitely not one to drive halfway across America unless I know, for certain, that not only does he live here but he started attending this very church over two years ago."

"Mr. Izzi, may I ask where you come from?"

"Philly."

"Hmm, I see." Ambrose folded his hands across his desk. "Well, if you are so certain about his whereabouts, why don't you pay him a visit, deal with Mr. Morrison directly."

Izzi played with his pinky ring, twisting it around his skin. "Because he's a slippery little fuck."

Ambrose shifted against his leather office chair. "Excuse me?"

"I do, in fact, prefer to do business directly with folks. But it seems that Mr. Morrison has gone to great efforts to hide himself. So, I thought a community pillar such as yourself might have some insight for me."

"And I'm sorry to say that I do not."

A harsh stiffness began to form around Izzi's eyes. He watched the Reverend – the face, the figurehead, the mask behind which the town sat – and saw the great threat he was squaring up against. Mosshead, like every other American hometown, enjoyed the wet stench of its own mythology. Izzi saw it in the eyes of Reverend Taylor, he saw it layered within the cement sidewalks, in the corner of everyone's smile. It was everywhere, even back in his own neighborhood. One was not better than the other, it was simply a different shade. And that was a part of the beauty of travel – getting to see the various shades of American hate.

"He came all the way out here to join your church," Izzi said, pointing at the Reverend with the tip of his cigarette. "That's what this place is, right? Just a church?"

"We are, and have always been, nothing more than a home for the righteous." Ambrose returned Izzi's steely gaze with one of his own. "And if, as you say, Mr. Morrison moved to our town to join this house, then it is clear that God has shown him the way."

Izzi smiled, his gold-coated canine shining. "Ain't that a miracle."

He stubbed out his cigarette and stood. "Well, if you happen to see Mr. Morrison, tell him to stop by. Or give me a call." He placed a slip of paper with the address and phone number of his motel wrapped in a hundred-dollar bill on the Reverend's desk.

Ambrose held up the money. "What's this?"

"For the collection box," Izzi said, heading out of the office before adding, "And when you see Jonah, tell him his family misses him."

◆◆◆

Mosshead was seated in the neck of the Rockies, in a blank patch of flat land as if the weight of the town brought the terrain to its knees, sending the mountains fleeing towards the horizon. It was May, and even Izzi could not deny that this stretch of America was truly beautiful. He watched the courteous townsfolk greet each other on the street, waiting for a familiar face to appear so that he might pluck it from this miserable garden.

Only a few people back in Philly knew about the existence of Jonah Morisson. When they had heard what he had done they could not believe it. What they were hearing seemed impossible. Not to Izzi. He knew the truth before he ever heard it spoken. For years there was a fear in his heart, a fear that he would have to watch someone he loved be taken by unwelcome hands.

The drive out to Colorado had taken several days, giving Izzi many long, silent hours to think about what he wanted to do once he landed in the sunburnt heart of the Centennial State. Despite his father and his boss' demand to simply bring Jonah Morrison back to Philadelphia, he could not fight the instinct to do what he did best. Izzi saw himself as more than an enforcer; he was a man who solved problems, no matter the kind. Seeing how he was fighting on foreign soil, he took the time to watch and learn and best understand where to direct his violence.

He found his target in the form of Albert Taylor.

The deputy sheriff of Mosshead.

And the Reverend's oldest son.

◆◆◆

Izzi got to know Deputy Taylor's routine. He was a short man who did more drinking than policing. Every Tuesday and Friday he would drink at the saloon until midnight and drive himself home. He knew the deputy's preferred parking spot in the back lot and the amount of time it took for him to walk out the back door and drive away. A few days after meeting with the Reverend, Izzi introduced himself to the Deputy.

"Evening officer," he said, one hand behind his back.

Deputy Taylor turned around, his smile whisky-soaked and lopsided.

"I'm looking for a friend of mine, Jonah Morrison. You wouldn't happen to know his address, would ya?"

The Deputy stumbled but caught himself. "Yeah, he's down at ..."

His face dropped, suddenly sober and realizing what he was saying and who he was speaking to. Clearly, the Reverend had spread the word about the secret manhunt happening in Mosshead. Izzi sighed and shoved the crackling end of the cattle prod into the Deputy's neck and held it there until he passed out.

◆◆◆

Finding an empty space to have their chat was not difficult. The barn was falling apart, deserted long ago. Mosshead was an hour and change south of them now, ensuring that no one would hear the screams. Using the Deputy's handcuffs, Izzi secured him to one of the posts in the barn, tucking his legs under his body, posing him in a vulnerable position of surrender. He removed the bag from his head and gag from his mouth. He stood over the Deputy, a bright smile on his face.

"Hello there, sunshine."

Deputy Taylor struggled for a minute, testing the limits of his bondage. Izzi allowed the struggle to run its course. He wanted the Deputy to know that there was no escape.

"Jonah Morrison," Izzi said as he brought over a brown grocery bag and a chair. "All I wanna know is where he hangs his hat. You help me with that and this'll be nothing more than a story to tell your friends at the bar."

"You fucking guinea piece of shit," the Deputy cursed through gritted teeth.

"Whoa!" Izzi said, taking a seat. "None of this is intended as an offense. This is just how business needs to be conducted when two parties find themselves at an impasse."

The Deputy spat at the ground in between them. Izzi nodded and picked up the grocery bag, resting it on the edge of his knee. "I gotta admit, you guys got a smart operation here with the church and everything. People think the South is the real KKK country. But the heart of the Klan is right here in Colorado. It must be a difficult time for you boys, right now. All those people out there calling for progress and equality and all that bullshit. And those same people trying to change everything probably think that men like you and me are cut from the same cloth. Which is a notion, personally, I resent. Yes, we're both proud of our heritage, but where we differ is key. Let me show you." Izzi reached into the grocery bag and pulled out a bottle of Purex bleach. He placed it on the dirt floor of the barn in front of the Deputy and tossed the bag over his shoulder. "You see, it all comes down to fear."

The Deputy shifted in his restraints, watching the bottle as if it were a coiled snake.

"I gotta ask you something," Izzi continued. "Whenever I see you Klan boys on the news I always wonder – why do you guys wear those stupid hoods?"

The Deputy took a moment and swallowed before answering. "Tradition."

Izzi clicked his tongue against his teeth and sat forward, disappointed. "I disagree," he said. "I think you're all scared. A man hides his face for one reason and one reason alone – he doesn't want to be seen doing what he's doing. And seeing how your whole White Power attitude is a way of life around here, covering your face while you march and hold your rallies just makes you all come across like a bunch of pussies."

Izzi reached into his jacket and pulled out a syringe. He twirled it in his hand like a pen. He played with it, tapping it against the bottle of bleach, giving the Deputy all the elements of his threat but letting him add them together on his own. "Me and my people, we come from a very old tradition ourselves, and we don't wear masks. Fear is only a weapon when you show folks who to be afraid of. Am I covering my face right now? Of course not, because then you wouldn't know who to fear." He uncapped the syringe with his teeth and picked up the bleach. Carefully, he jammed the needle into it, piercing the plastic shell, and pulled back on the plunger, filling it until full.

Izzi grabbed a fistful of Deputy Taylor's hair and leaned in close. "So consider this my burning cross," he said, bringing the dripping tip of the needle up to his eye. "Because I'm all out of words."

◆◆◆

In exchange for giving him the address of Jonah Morrison, Izzi kept his word and let the Deputy live, though he bloodied his face with the sole of his shoe as payment for his troubles. After arriving at the address, Izzi regretted not putting a bullet in his head instead. The house was empty; food gone bad in the refrigerator, dirty dishes in the sink, an empty dresser. It was clear that if Jonah had ever lived there, he left before he could be surrounded.

Izzi smoked as he drove back to his motel and cursed under his breath. He should have expected this. He would have done the same if the roles were reversed. In that regard, they were always alike.

Normally, when conducting his work, Izzi took a quiet approach. Noise was bad for business. But none of this was about business. He had taken the time to introduce himself to the town, first cordially, then violently, because it was important to him that Mosshead knew his name. Names and how they were spoken were important to him, they carried weight, and you could learn a lot about a man from how others spoke their name. After thirty-five years most folks called him Mr. Izzi, some had the privilege to call him Aldo, but only one called him Alli.

Once found, it would be up to Jonah Morrison, or the man who called himself that, to decide how the situation was to be handled. All of this could be a quickly forgotten footnote in his life's history if he so chose. After walking the streets of the town, seeing the church Jonah now prayed in and the hate he now considered holy, Izzi knew that the only option was to kill the name Jonah Morrison and pray that the body survived.

◆◆◆

The following night the phone in Izzi's motel room rang for the first time. He did not say hello when he answered. He let the bastard speak first.

"How did you find me?" His voice was harsh but quiet.

"Hunting is what I do. You know that," Izzi said, the cheap mattress groaning under his weight as he sat upright.

"You need to leave, now."

Izzi was impressed and heartbroken at how good of a job he'd done at hiding his accent. But his new arrhythmic voice had taken the bite out of his threats. "Only if you come with me."

"No."

"Wanna know what Ma said when I told her you changed your name?"

"Aldo …"

"Does the good Reverend know the truth?"

"Aldo!"

"Does he know your name is Anthony?"

"Stop!" he barked. "I wanted to make this painless. It's best for everyone if you all just forget about me."

"Painless? You thought you could leave and it would somehow, magically, be painless?"

"Pop never cared. It's been two years and no one came looking for me except you."

"You abandoned the family for some White Power crusade," said Izzi. "You're lucky it's just me. If it was up to Pop he'd have dropped a fucking A-bomb on this town."

"You're even worse! Everyone is blaming me for your bullshit."

"Oh, so this is all my fault?"

"Yes, it is," Anthony said. "You and Pops and everyone back home, you're a plague. An evil stain on this country. I couldn't stomach it anymore. I came here to heal America's wounds. Wounds that I inflicted. And you couldn't help but bring your disease to my door."

With a bloody finger, Izzi drew his line in the sand. "You're goddam right I'm a plague because I'd sooner see you a corpse than a coward in a white dress. Either you kill Jonah Morrison, or I do."

"You're an evil man," Anthony said, spitting in the face of his older brother.

Izzi stood, nearly pulling the phone off the nightstand. "You always were too fucking stupid to get it," he said, failing to hold back his rage. "Evil men are everywhere. All kinds of 'em. Each of them trying to eat the others. Good does not win. It never has. It's all about the last evil left alive."

"I've made my choice clear. I'm sorry that you can't accept that."

"One way or another, I ain't leaving here without you."

"I'm sorry, Alli, but you need to go. They're already on their way."

◆◆◆

Three cars pulled up to the motel parking lot, their headlights aimed directly at the picture window of Izzi's room. The U-shaped motel surrounded the parking lot on all sides except the one that led out onto the street. The rattle of their engines echoed throughout the empty night with the rhythm of snare drums. It was close to midnight. The first man to step out was Albert Taylor, his face still raw from the previous night. He scanned the row of rooms, watching for any sign of life. Satisfied, he pointed his shotgun towards Izzi's room. Seven other men emerged from the cars, each holding a gun. Some looked to be cops who worked for Deputy Taylor. Others were dressed too plainly to recognize. Izzi guessed that they were soldiers of a different kind. Men who followed the church and would die defending all that it stood for.

Without warning, all seven of them opened fire at the window, tearing through the glass and blowing apart the dark room on the other side. Izzi had successfully made himself a problem that could only be solved with violence. The men of Mosshead meant to shred him up, giving him no opportunity to slip away.

When the last man's gun was empty, the seven men surveyed their destruction. Deputy Taylor pulled fresh slugs from his pocket and quickly reloaded. Through the destroyed window and a good chunk of the wall, he could only see the front half of the room. Gun trained at the door, he moved forward, his men close behind. His heavy boots creaked against the wooden floorboard of the porch outside the room. An eager grin stretched across his beaten face as he reached out to open the door, stepping on a plank that sat less than half an inch higher than the others. The wood sank under his weight, hitting the igniter.

The nail bomb exploded under his feet.

A grey burst erupted from under the porch, sending up a cloud of nails and scrap metal. Deputy Taylor collapsed as the razor-sharp smoke swallowed him whole. The two men closest to him caught the edge of the blast, dragging themselves through fresh pools of their own blood as their faces and stomachs were ripped open. The remaining four were sent scrambling back towards their cars, too focused on the threat in front of them to notice the one behind them.

A door from a room on the other side of the parking lot opened. Izzi, staying in the shadow of the doorway, raised an Uzi, pointed the long arm of the silencer towards the men left standing, and fired. He aimed low, hitting their thighs and knees. He wanted them in pain with no legs left to stand on. One of them was already crouched when the shooting began and took a shower of bullets to the back.

Two of the Deputy's men crashed forward, screaming. The last one was well guarded by the car next to him, taking cover and firing back. Izzi ducked back into the room and reloaded, counting the rounds being fired at him. He wasn't sure of the make of the man's gun, but a guess was good enough. After the twelfth shot, Izzi quickly stepped out into the parking lot, firing at the edge of the car where he last saw the man peek up from, keeping him in place. He ran up to the car, leapt onto the trunk and pointed his Uzi down. The last man had just enough time to look up and see the flashing muzzle screaming down at him.

The two men still breathing had little consciousness left in them. Izzi moved quickly, standing over the first one and giving him a few sobering slaps to the face. "Jonah Morrison, tell me where he's hiding," he said.

The man had a thick blond moustache. He rolled his head, dazed from the pain. Izzi grabbed him by the hair and repeated the question. Wetly, the man mumbled the same address that the Deputy had given him the other night. Izzi dropped him and sprayed a few rounds into his chest. He stepped over him, towards the other man. He did not need to repeat the question or threaten him. The man shouted an address. He told Izzi it was a cabin that belonged to the Reverend. After Izzi had his meeting at the church the Reverend let Jonah use it while things were dealt with.

"He's up there," the man said, pleading. "He and his wife."

A nerve in Izzi's brain twitched. "Who?"

"Mr. and Mrs. Morrison," the man said. "That's who you're looking for, right?"

Izzi fired his last few rounds at the man. His head and heart were blinded by a dark and unfamiliar feeling as he got in his car and headed west.

◆◆◆

The cabin was a little hideaway less than an hour outside of Mosshead, in a patch of hilly woodland. It was the perfect sort of place where the Reverend could take his wife on the weekends and any number of mistresses on weekdays. Izzi watched the cabin for a while, getting as good a feel for the place as was possible when shadowed by the darkness of the evening. There were no lights on, no movement. He worried that he was too late, again. He'd broken into plenty of houses and apartments over the years. Burglaries, murders meant to look like burglaries – he knew the best way to catch a man in the comfort of his home. This, sadly, was a different animal.

He screwed the silencer into the open mouth of his pistol and moved towards the cabin.

The back porch led into the kitchen. He cut open the screen door with his switchblade, undid the latch, and quietly moved inside. The small kitchen opened outward into a small sitting room. The first thing he saw was the back of the sofa. A familiar shape sat on it, facing away. Izzi raised his gun as the shape on the sofa raised its hands.

Izzi moved around the sofa, keeping the gun on the surrendering shape.

Finally, eye to eye, Aldo Izzi saw his brother for the first time in years.

"Hey," he said, his gun still pointed forward.

"Hey," Anthony Izzi said back.

There was an awkwardness to their reunion. It was not the gun or the threat of violence that did it. It was the flood of nostalgia at seeing each other again. Izzi pushed through it the only way he knew how – furiously. "You ready to come home?" he asked.

Anthony shook his head. "No."

Izzi reached out and grabbed his brother by his shirt collar and pulled him forward. Anthony fell to his knees, still surrendering. His submission mixed with his refusal to relent was difficult for Izzi to properly comprehend. "Why?" he asked, placing the cold metal of the silencer against Anthony's throat. "Just tell me why?"

"You won't understand," Anthony replied.

"Try me."

"I realized my purpose. And my purpose is here, helping this country."

Izzi laughed. "By lynching folks you don't like."

"How's that any different from what you do?" There was a dedicated light shining at the edges of Anthony's eyes. He'd been waiting to say this. "You were right about the evils of the world. It's all about the last one left alive. I don't want to see you die, Alli. But the old ways – the flood trying to drown the light of Christ – need to be stopped. Our father should have stayed in Italy. We would have been better off."

"Then you'd of never got the chance to move to a fucking Klan town."

"One less immigrant family keeps America white." The voice was his brother's, but Izzi knew the words had been put there by another. "I'm proud of the man I am, even if you are not."

This was the moment that Izzi had feared. The man he held, the man whose life was a trigger's inch away from ending, was not his brother. Jonah Morrison had killed Anthony Izzi and dragged his corpse west to eat his flesh under the quiet American shadow of the mountains. The air in the cabin shifted and Anthony's eyes moved, looking at the space behind Izzi.

"Honey, no!"

Izzi turned and saw the shotgun trained at his head, held by the sleepy silhouette of a blonde woman in a nightgown and matching robe. Her focused stare and fixed posture told him that this was not the first time she had used the gun. A rancher's daughter, he thought.

"Honey, please. Just put it down," said Anthony.

She did not move.

Izzi's eyes were on the shotgun, but his hands were still on his brother. One twisted the collar of his shirt, the other pressed the barrel of the silencer hard against his throat. "Does she know?" he asked without moving his eyes.

Anthony's voice was a shiver in the dark. "Some."

"Tell me," Izzi demanded.

"She knows about the family. She knows the rackets we ran together, guys we offed, everything I did back in Philly." The ghost of his accent reappeared as he spoke the name of his birthplace.

Izzi looked into the blue eyes that were aiming to sweep his head clean off his shoulders. "Did he tell you about Marie?"

At the sound of her name, Anthony's voice got louder. "Alli, stop."

The woman readjusted her grip on the shotgun. "I don't care about his other women. This is his new life," she said.

"Marie turned five last month," Izzi said. "All she does is ask me about her daddy." Still without moving, he redirected his attention back to his brother. "So what's it gonna be? You want to see your little girl turn six or do you want me to have to tell her the truth?"

The woman moved closer. The moonlight shone over her left hand, catching the edge of a diamond on her fourth finger. "Just say the word, Jonah, and we end all of this right now," she said, with the sort of killer's confidence that most men fail to fake.

Softly, Izzi replied, "That's not his name."

Before the echo of his last syllable faded, he let go of his brother and smacked the shotgun barrel up and out of his face, throwing the spray of buckshot into the ceiling, deafening all three of them. Quickly, he put four silent bullets into his sister-in-law's chest, sending her to the floor with a terminal *thud*. He brought the gun back around, pointing it at Anthony who was too caught up in the chaotic web of horror to move. Izzi stood over him like a falling moon, all the patience he never had finally exhausted. "This is all on you, brother," he said. "Last chance."

◆◆◆

Anthony Michael Izzi chose to die as Jonah Morrison. Izzi could not take the pain anymore. When Izzi died, he knew that he would be judged by the Almighty as a killer of kin. But he feared even more for the soul of his brother. Feared that he would be judged as a man who shed his name so that he might join the ranks of men who were not his own. One that embraced the hate of others so wholeheartedly it ate away at his love for his own child. Izzi understood and excused many darknesses in the world. This, however, would not stand.

Before he left Mosshead, he had given his brother one last chance at salvation.

In the early hours of the morning, Izzi drove to the Rock of Recompense and laid his brother's corpse on the steps. He stood over him, ready to deliver his final blessing. He slipped a fresh magazine into his pistol and fired fifteen rounds, emptying the gun directly at Anthony's head, destroying his face. With the jerry can from his trunk he poured gasoline over the twisted remains and ignited it with a match. Izzi watched the fire eat away the flesh of Jonah Morrison from his rearview mirror as he fled Colorado.

Whenever the thought of that fire appeared in his mind, his heart filled with a dark hope.

Hope that when his brother got to the other side, God would not recognize him and might instead mistake him for an innocent man.

SCI-FI

BIG BANG BULL AND THE GOD PARTICLE

Mark Patrick Lynch

10 to 15 minutes

Mark Patrick Lynch was born and raised in West Yorkshire, England. His short stories, mainstream and genre, have appeared in various publications across the world, from *Alfred Hitchcock's Mystery Magazine* to *Zahir*. His latest novel is *Walking Horatio* and his latest collection of slightly less trashy tales (he hopes) is *Cardinal Points*.

Say hi to him on Bluesky: @markpatricklynch.bsky.social

The following events occurred in a universe not so very far from our own, probably sometime during the next year, and likely on a Thursday …

Professor Sydney Claire had been working late and was alone at her computer. For Sydney, work involved creating the most minute of minute happenings in the universe, events that lasted for the shortest of seconds, and then spending hours at her monitors trying to work out what, if anything, had occurred. The pay was okay, but the intellectual stimulation was what really fired her up. That and her chance to practice her French and German with the foreign scientists she worked alongside.

A particle physicist stationed at the CERN laboratories, she was part of the Large Hadron Collider team, accelerating tiny fractions of the fabric of the universe in different directions around a massive, miles-long, looped track. And making sure they collided.

The results varied. Not least because no one really knew what to expect of the infinitesimal variables in the experiments, including the experts, who managed at best to make educated guesses and centre in on informed hopes if nothing else. The people who didn't have a clue – the groan-inducing usual suspects of astrologers, psychics and pyramid power fans – were more specific in their assertions of what Sydney's work would result in:

A) the end of the world
B) splintered realities
C) time-causality paradoxes
D) the coming of the aliens
E) Elvis' return to Graceland
F) the final death of God
G) the last moments of the universe
H) all of the above.

Though according to the calculations over which she was now poring, it seemed that quite the opposite was true regarding item G, anyway.

A, B, C, D, E and F – they were still open to debate.

Sydney lifted a Dictaphone and thumbed the record button.

"Well, if I'm reading these figures right, then Isaac wins the pool sweep. Fifty euros to the man with the beard. It does indeed seem that we're creating mini black holes while we centre in on the Higgs boson. They last for such small amounts of time and have such low energy readings that we're having to record them on the Planck scale. But they're there, if only for fleeting instants. Then they fade away, evaporating from our universe to who knows where. Maybe it's true; maybe they do become naked singularities, and with every slam-event we instigate we're creating a whole new universe. Imagine that."

"I don't have to," someone said from behind her.

Sydney spun around. Her hand went to her mouth as she dropped the Dictaphone. It clattered to the console but the recording light stayed on. She was supposed to be alone in here. Had there been *another* security breach?

"Who are you?" she said. "What're you doing here?"

He was a big man. Daunting – that was the word that sprang to mind when she thought how she'd describe him, but kind of cute too, in a big friendly bear kind of way. Thick of hair and thick of arm, he had a strong jaw and a close beard. His clothes were … non-conventional. The sort of things you'd expect to see in a science fiction film. Slightly to the left of fashionable, but you could imagine someone wearing them some time and somewhere, if not exactly here and not exactly now. He seemed inordinately pleased with himself.

"I could ask you the same thing," he said with a smile.

"No, you couldn't. Not really," Sydney told him. "You don't have authorisation to be in this section of the complex."

"Don't I?"

"No."

He probably didn't have authorisation to be in *any* section of the complex.

She glanced out of the viewing window, into the forest of piping and complex electrical conduits and magnetic housings that made up the tunnel beneath the earth, through which she and her team crashed exotic particles at close to the speed of light.

She was looking for a bicycle.

Her own was in here, tucked up behind the door. Bikes were the standard means of getting around for short distances inside the collider. You couldn't walk – the place was so huge that half your day would involve hiking a series of mini marathons. She didn't spend too long looking for this guy's bike, though. If it was out there, she couldn't get a lock on it, and she was understandably nervous about the man standing a few feet from her. She didn't want to take her eyes from him for longer than she had to.

"How did you get here?" Sydney said. "I don't see a bike."

"Oh, you know, the usual method. I materialised."

"Materialised?"

"Yes."

"Okay."

So, he was a crazy. One of the protesters who were convinced running the hadron collider would cause conflicts in the space-time continuum, or make the earth wink out of existence. Or something. Maybe he thought he was from the future, here to stop some calamity or other.

Sydney edged her fingers along the control board, reaching for the handset of the internal telephone so she could let security know there was a conspiracy dipshit/loony tunes/flat-Earther on the loose.

"Don't worry. You won't need to call them," the big man said.

Her hand froze just as she touched the set.

"Call who?"

"Gerry and François."

Sydney shook her head. "Sorry, I ..."

"They're the guards on shift tonight."

"You know their names? You're friends with them?"

"I know everything, I'm afraid. Nothing much surprises me. Well, nothing at all, actually."

Yup. Definite crazy. Lunatic of the week. Maybe a contender for the year depending how the American elections went.

"Right," she said.

The big man smiled. His eyes shone as if he were struggling to contain a bundle of mirth too large even for his colossal body. He was, in his own weird way, the epitome of bonhomie. Apparently realising this, he hardened his demeanour.

"Now," he said, putting a rumble into his bass-baritone. "Let's get to why I'm here. A bit of seriousness."

Sydney fluttered a hand to her throat. This, she had been informed, was her "tell" – a sign that she was nervous and the reason she'd never won a hand of strip poker in her life. She should grab the phone, get security down here – Gerry and François, if he was telling the truth – to haul him away and leave her to 1) get her breath back, 2) collapse in a chair and fight off a panic attack, and finally, 3) get back to confirming her calculations and persuade Brian to open up the kitty and pay Isaac the fifty euros the accumulator had generated.

So. First of all: keep the big man talking. Then get to the phone.

"Okay then, uh, why *are* you here?" she asked.

"To complain."

"I promise you," Sydney said in her best placating tone, "we're not in league with the CIA, al-Qaeda or Walmart, and we're not going to destroy the world. In fact, if you look at these calculations on the screen behind me, you'll see we're not destroying anything. We're actually *creating* things …"

"You are indeed," the man said. "So far, you've sped up particles and collided them one hundred and fifty-four times. It's the fallout from that that bothers me. That's why I'm here, to complain about it."

Sydney moved her face in a way that was supposed to be an understanding smile but didn't quite make it. "Nah, I'm not getting it. Maybe we should chat with some other people, a whole bunch of us, and not just you and me. In fact, I think I'm going to call for some guys to come down now," she said, stabbing the buttons on the flat dial of the phone. "It'll be good, we can all discuss things and—"

"Every time those particles smashed together they generated a new universe."

Sydney's jaw swung open. No one could know what he'd just told her. She'd only just worked it out from the data herself. She could feel the "gaah" unspooling from her lips even as she wished she could hold it in. She managed to transform it into "Whaaa?", before reminding herself that she was a professor and should be more articulate than this.

She cleared her throat, readjusted herself and stood up straight, then tilted a hip, bit her lip, and scratched her head.

"No, sorry, wait a sec, okay," she said in her best Proper Scientist voice. "Could you explain exactly what you mean, and *why* you think what you think? Just to make it clear for me. I mean, you could have hit on a lucky guess there."

"You're creating tiny black holes as you keep exposing the so-called God particle. Ones that otherwise wouldn't have formed. I've enough trouble keeping track of all of the universes occurring naturally without you adding to the workload. Hence me being here, hence me being somewhat angry, hence me putting in a complaint. Savvy?"

A rather disconcerting thought formed at the back of Sydney's mind. An *especially* disconcerting thought for sort-of-probably-an-atheist kind of person …

"I think I see where this is going," she said slowly. "So go on."

"First of all, you tell me who I am," he said, with some patience.

Sydney remained silent, eyeing him closely through her geek glasses.

"Well, go on," he insisted. "Tell me."

"Oh. Sorry," Sydney said. "I thought that was a rhetorical question. I mean, you're supposed to be omniscient, aren't you. If you are who I think you're pretending to be."

"There's no pretence here," he said.

"So you already know what I think."

He didn't glare at her, but he didn't smile either, or relax the fixed expression his face had set into. He just stood there, in his sorta sci-fi outfit, being himself.

But he *was* kind of impressive, she thought. A big guy. Biggest of them all, really.

Sydney had read the Greek myths as a girl. She remembered feeling slightly icky when she got to the bits – and there were enough of them – about Zeus appearing to some woman in animal disguise, usually as a bull, and having his way with her. The story usually ended with Hera, Zeus' wife, finding out about his affairs and giving him a hiding one way or another. It was, perhaps, the Greeks' way of making bestiality appear a little less unusual than it might otherwise be considered. The idea of romping away with a bull was seriously weird to a young Sydney.

But hey, the world was the world and she'd grown out of that. And what would you know? As she'd gotten older she'd even become kind of kinky about the whole animal thing. She had some seriously interesting websites bookmarked in her browser, which she found herself returning to with a shrug of mild self-disgust after too many glasses of red.

Of course, she'd never *acted* on any particular urge, not really, not in reality. But a little part of her had kept that guilty kink in the back of her mind, imagining it through boyfriend after boyfriend. The one who'd looked a bit like a frog probably couldn't believe his luck.

The guy in front of her – a befittingly big man in the form he'd chosen to display to her – said, "Don't you have any idea of the workload I have just keeping track of things, Sydney? Universes being infinite –" Sydney's eyes lit up at this apparent confirmation of an oft-disputed theoretical fact – "and all of that, which means everything that can happen will happen. More than that, everything that can happen *must* happen. And who gets to see that that's so?" He stared at her meaningfully. "So yes, a bit of a headache with this whole business, but I'm clear enough to know you know who I am."

Sydney crossed her arms defensively. "If it's so hard, why even let this project go so far as to make additional universes?"

"Why do you think I have any choice?"

"Because you're … Him. You know? Alpha, Omega, Zeus, Jesus. Allah. Yahweh. Him. G.O.D. And look, you're here telling me off."

"Ah, now while that's true, I'm only here being Him – Zeus, as you fancy it right now – and telling you off because everything that can happen must happen. So here I am, even if I'm not entirely sure I believe it myself all the time." He shrugged. "It's all a bit slippery and unreal. Although my daily worksheet certainly points to it being real."

"You know, there are some things I really ought to ask you," Sydney said. "But my head's kind of gone a little bit vague and fuzzy as to what they should be right now."

"Of course," he said. "But try anyway. Go ahead and do your best."

First of all, Sydney asked what the team should be doing to avoid creating new universes.

"Oh, that? Right, well …"

They talked for quite a while about physics, and then they got onto other things, aliens, the dinosaur years, a load of non-scientific stuff, and now and again a few moral dilemmas. He said he knew the thoughts of all human beings, the thoughts they had and the thoughts they didn't have, the ones they might have had, as well as the ones they someday would. There were no surprises, just courses that stemmed from causes, and each cause and course altered in every conceivable way possible. Which was why he liked to take his pleasures when he could. It helped stave off another headache.

"And it keeps me distracted," he told her. "So everything is all the more manageable."

"Wow. This is clever stuff," Sydney said, fanning her hands across her chest. So much of what they were talking about had been science as philosophy. It was why she'd got into this gig in the first place. To find the "wonderstuff" not only of this universe but of all the universes. And as a bonus, here he was, being infinite and omniscient and all Greek God-ish and not treating her like she was a little kid who wanted to know why the sky was blue and why she shouldn't say knickers in front of her grandma. God, come to her as Zeus of Ancient Greece.

He grinned, enjoying himself too.

Eventually, feeling a kind of secret confidence come over her, from someplace she'd never been brave enough to explore before, at least not with someone else, she said, "So, if everything that can happen must happen, does that mean that you could turn into a bull right now if you wanted to?"

"Why, what do you have in mind?"

With her blood tingling, feeling more alive than she'd ever been, she took off her glasses and shook out her hair, undid the first button of her blouse and pouted coquettishly.

He was watching her.

In just the way she wanted him to.

In her most seductive tone, she said, "If you know everything, isn't that a rhetorical question?"

◆◆◆

Later, when she played back her Dictaphone – which had kept recording after she'd dropped it – she heard only her own voice asking questions and seemingly taking part in a one-sided conversation. Though there were, it had to be said, gaps where someone else might be speaking if they were providing the other half of the chat.

As proof it didn't constitute much, but Sydney didn't think she'd been hallucinating, all alone down here in the bowels of the earth, surrounded by machinery that could create new universes. Proof was sometimes like faith. You could know some things without understanding how you knew it.

She might have been sort-of-probably-an-atheist once, but now she believed.

Oh, how she believed.

The last words on the storage device were these:

"God, oh yes, oh yes, God yes, God, God, God yes … YES! GOD! YES!"

She shut off the recording and smiled, knowing that somewhere and somewhen he was probably getting a hiding from Hera (or whatever his wife was called in this particular reality) because of what had just happened.

But that was okay.

Hey, it was more than okay. He was legendary for it. He'd known all along what he was getting into, and exactly what was coming from the moment he'd appeared. As he'd said, taking his pleasure where he could.

And Sydney had come out of it pretty happy herself.

God knew that was the truth.

HORROR

THE COVENANT OF THE FURNACE KEEPERS

R. Dell Walker

20 to 25 minutes

R. Dell Walker is an author of horror and crime fiction from the Appalachian Mountains. His horror anthology, *The Vermilion Carnival and Other Horrors*, is available now. He is currently writing a dark fantasy horror novella, *Miasma*, which will be released in September 2025. He lives with his wife, children and a very old hound dog in Virginia.

I

The pipefitter's flashlight cast furtive shadows across a concrete wall as he crouched by a bramble of twisted steel and strangled pipes. Cory Pavlik, the project manager, knelt beside him. The air smelled of singed insulation and scorched carbon. Cory felt uneasy as he stood and looked up at the unfinished ceiling above them. Something about the steel didn't look right – it had warped in an almost organic manner.

"I can't find anything in the blueprints to explain it," the pipefitter, a wiry man named Don Whitaker, said. "Electric's not even close. Not that I think faulty electric could cause this."

Cory nodded, his eyes scanning the overhead beams and crossbars. Steel veins snaked through the concrete like the exposed roots of an ancient tree, grasping across the ceiling and constricting the plumbing into grotesque shapes. A chill ran through him as he noticed the pattern – a sinister symmetry to the growth. Don shifted uncomfortably, his tools jangling in his belt.

"This is beyond me," the pipefitter admitted, running a hand over the back of his neck. "I've seen welds fail and pipes burst, but steel doesn't just move."

"Could it be the building settling? I'll check the soil tests," Cory offered weakly, though he didn't believe it.

Don shook his head. "Not like this. Settling might crack a joint or pull a pipe loose." He paused, his flashlight beam sliding along the tangled network. "You know that, Cory."

Cory looked down and noticed something else – a small mound of hardened steel on the floor, directly beneath the warped section. It gleamed faintly in the flashlight's glow. Crouching, Cory reached out but then hesitated. His fingers brushed the droplet. It was rough, jagged, and still warm, a vestige of molten steel that had fallen sometime during the past night.

Don leaned closer to inspect it. "Molten steel don't just fall outta nowhere. You sure it's not some slag someone dropped from welding?"

Cory shook his head. "No welding here. Not for days."

Don straightened, his broad face shadowed by the flashlight's beam. "I told 'em using pieces of that old mill was a bad idea," he said. "People think it's artsy, but the mill didn't close happy, ya know?"

Cory hadn't grown up in the city – his mother had moved them to Burke Township after the accident – but he knew the stories. Everyone did. The mill, once the town's heart, had been gutted over a decade ago, left to rust. Now it was being reincarnated as a sleek retail hub. Management had decided to "honor" the past by incorporating salvaged pieces of the mill into the design. The sign from the mill's main entrance now adorned an entrance once more, now with "The Shops at" illumined above it. It sounded clever in the boardroom, but in this basement of tangled steel, it felt like hubris.

"So, what, you think it's the old mill doing this?" Cory asked.

"I don't think anything. I just know what I see, and I don't know what the hell could cause that," Don said, gesturing toward the rat king of pipes and steel above.

Cory turned, his gaze following the flashlight's path across the basement. He'd been onsite since the project broke ground, and while the place had always been unnerving, today it felt different. Hostile.

"What do you want me to do?" Cory asked finally.

"Go to your bosses in Pittsburgh. Let them deal with it," Don said, brushing dust from his hands. "Hell, bring a priest from St. Stanislaus. I'm just here to run pipe, not wrestle the devil."

Management didn't have time for ghost stories, Cory knew, and the firm had already sunk too much money into the project to entertain superstitions. Still, something about Don's unease unsettled him.

As they left the basement, Cory cast one last glance at the warped pipes and the steel droplet on the floor. The walls seemed to breathe, the air vibrating faintly with something that felt like a growl.

II

The sun burned overhead as the construction site buzzed with activity. Machines roared and the sharp clanging of metal against metal filled the air. Cory surveyed the scene from a raised platform near the main structure. The project had already seen its share of delays, and tensions were running high to meet looming deadlines.

Below him, Don Whitaker was working near the base of the decorative steel pillar salvaged from New Kingston Steel. The feature would evoke the industrial past of New Kingston, but Cory saw the unease it brought. The pillar, which held the building's critical water lines, was fashioned from a section of the old blast furnace and stood like a totem in the center of the unfinished atrium. "I'm telling ya," Whitaker called up to Cory, "pipes don't just twist themselves for no damn reason."

"Just rip it out and replace it, Don," Cory called out, dismissively.

Cory turned and began descending the platform, his boots slamming against the scaffold planks. He was halfway across the atrium when he heard the metal groan.

It was low and deep, like the sound of a ship's hull battling against the waves. Cory stopped in his tracks and looked back at the pillar. Don had paused too, his head canted, listening.

The sound came again, louder this time. The steel column shuddered and the pipes inside sounded a death rattle.

With a deafening crack, one of the overhead girders broke loose. It swung like a felling ax, cutting through the air with horrifying speed. Cory had no time to sound a warning.

Don looked up, his eyes wide with terror. The girder struck him with a gruesome thud, crushing him against the hollow column that rang like a funeral bell. Cory heard the sound of metal against flesh – wet and final.

For a moment, paralysis. The workers' shouts trapped in their throats. Then, chaos.

Cory's legs were lead, but he forced himself to move, stumbling toward the grisly scene.

When he reached the column, his stomach lurched.

Don's body was unrecognizable, crushed into a grotesque stain between the girder and the pillar. Blood pooled on the floor, brackish with dark streaks of grease and dirt. The girder itself glistened unnaturally.

"Everybody out!" Cory barked, his voice hitching. "Now!"

Workers scrambled to obey, the site clearing in a matter of minutes. Cory stayed behind, his eyes fixed on the column.

Cory bent down to inspect it. A heat radiated in waves from the hanging girder, making the air shiver. *Why is it so hot?* he thought.

There, etched into the steel, almost invisible against the iron-gray surface, Cory found a sigil. It was faint at first, like something that had been scratched into the metal and has since weathered. But as his fingers traced the shape, the symbol became clearer, almost as though the act of touching it made it reveal itself.

The sigil blazed with fierce simplicity. Stark lines commanding the eye like a war banner unfurled in a storm. Encased within the circle's unbroken boundary was a design that spoke of primal craft. From the center, straight lines fanned outward, reaching for the upper curve in a celestial arc. Below the circle's median sat an anvil, squat and indomitable. Its black shape exuded untold labors, its surface hinted at echoes of hammer blows that rang upon its face. Suspended above it, a flame licked, alive with movement.

He had seen this symbol before. Not here. Not on this steel. But somewhere else. On his father's forearm.

His mind flickered with flashes – his childhood, years ago. He remembered the night of the accident. Images of men in dark coats visiting his mother late in the night. Cory was only four when Joe Pavlik died, a victim of an accident in the mill. He couldn't remember the specifics of it but there were memories, faint and fragmented, of whispered conversations, of voices, low and muted.

The men had spoken of something sinister, but the words had never reached him.

He noticed it then – the warped section of pipe Don was meant to exorcise. It had shifted again, curling ever tighter. The steel gleamed as if freshly forged. Cory thought he saw a ripple just beneath its surface. A discoloration caused by heat applied to cold steel, in the shapelessness of viscous liquid; molten metal was struggling to break free.

The air around the column was stifling. Cory backed away.

By the time emergency services arrived, Cory had composed himself enough to give a statement to the police. He described the accident in clinical terms, careful not to mention the warped steel or the unnatural heat. He knew what he'd seen, but he also knew how it would sound.

He repeated the statement to an OSHA representative, the receiver of the office phone pressed tightly to his ear. Fluorescent lights droned faintly overhead, an accompaniment to the serious voice on the other end of the line.

"We've received the preliminary details of the accident," the representative said, their tone clipped and professional. "Given the nature of the incident and it being a structural failure, we are going to have to order an immediate cessation of all activity on the site. Investigators will be on location soon."

Cory gripped the phone tighter, trying to keep his voice steady. "How long are we talking about here? A day? A week?"

"Until the investigation is concluded," the voice replied. "That could take several weeks, depending on what we find. This isn't just about safety violations, Mr. Pavlik. A fatality occurred. It's a serious matter."

"I understand that. What do you need from me?"

"A detailed account of the project's history, including any recent modifications to the site or materials sourced. We'll need full access to the property, so please ensure the area is sealed off and secured."

Cory scribbled furiously, his pen carving deep into the paper. "Anything else?"

"Just be ready for questions. Lots of questions." The voice softened slightly. "And Mr. Pavlik … we're sorry for your loss."

"Might have been best to say that first," Cory replied as he hung up the phone.

The New Kingston Inn was one of those timeless small-town bars, its wooden floor worn smooth by decades of work boots and its walls decorated with faded photographs of a better time. The air was thick with the scent of beer and filled with a high lonesome sound.

Cory stared into the amber liquid before him, as though it held the answers to the questions swirling in his mind.

"You look like you've been put through the wringer, young Pavlik," came a gravelly voice from beside him.

Cory looked up to see an old man on the stool next to him. The man wore a weathered Steelers cap, its logo faded, and his flannel shirt rolled up on arms corded with veins and age.

His eyes were sharp, though, their gaze cutting through the haze of the bar.

"I had a pipefitter killed today. Don Whitaker. Freak accident on the New Kingston Steel site. Whole site's shut down."

The man took a slow sip of his Iron City and set it down carefully. "I worked there. Long time ago. Most guys round here my age did," the man said, his voice tinged with something Cory couldn't quite place – nostalgia, maybe, or regret. "Spent thirty years in that place. Hard years. Dangerous years. Lotta men didn't make it out."

Cory felt a chill run down his spine. "I know. My dad died in that place."

The old man stared into his beer, as though weighing his words. "Yup. I knew your dad. That place ain't right, son. Never was. And I'm sure it's worse now, after all these years."

"What do you mean, worse?"

"You need to talk to Ellis McRae," the old man said.

"Who's that?"

"Someone who knows more about that mill than any man above ground," the old man replied. "If you're smart, you'll find him. And you'll listen to what he has to say."

Before Cory could press further, the old man slid off his stool. "He moved back to West Virginia after the mill closed. Boone County is all I know, but you can likely find him," the man said, tossing a few bills on the bar. "You might want to start by telling him your name's Pavlik."

"Why's that?"

"'Cause maybe then he won't shoot you," the man replied. "Maybe."

III

Cory drove through the winding mountain roads, the landscape shifting from the industrial ruins of western Pennsylvania to the primeval forests of West Virginia. The truck's engine groaned as he climbed the southern Alleghenies, the tires crunching over gravel and cracked pavement.

The air grew colder as he ascended, the late afternoon sun struggling to pierce the canopy of trees. All he had was a set of hastily transcribed directions from a gas station attendant and the name of a road he couldn't pronounce.

Cory finally spotted the turnoff; a rutted gravel road slowly being eaten by overgrowth. He slowed the truck and turned in, the suspension protesting every dip and bump. After another half mile, the trees parted, revealing a sagging two-story farmhouse hunched on a ridge. The roofline of the house bowed, its paint long faded to a peeling gray. The yard was a briar patch of scrap metal, including an ancient coal truck, dissected and stripped to the frame.

Cory parked. His eyes scanned the house, noting the boarded-up windows and the faint curl of smoke from the chimney. The place looked abandoned, yet he felt a presence – a watchfulness that made the hair on his neck stand on end.

As he climbed out of the truck, the porch creaked underfoot. A pair of muddy work boots sat outside the door. Before he could knock, the front door cracked, and Cory found himself staring down two barrels of a shotgun.

"Get off my property, you goddamn government bastard!" McRae growled.

"What? No, I'm not from the government!"

"Bullshit!"

"Sir, please. My name is Cory Pavlik. I need to talk to you about the New Kingston Steel Mill."

"Christ, boy. What the hell do you want to talk about that for?

"Strange things are happening. A man was killed on a construction site and I think that old mill had something to do with it."

"Hold on a minute. Did you say Pavlik?"

"Yes, Cory Pavlik. Joe was my father."

McRae froze. His expression shifted, the hard lines of suspicion softening into something closer to recognition – or maybe regret. The door opened wider, revealing the full figure of the man. He was broad-shouldered, with hands like worn-out tools, but thick as phonebooks. He wore a faded plaid shirt that hung loose over his frame.

"I need to talk to you. About my father. About what happened to him. And about … whatever's going on with the mill."

McRae's eyes narrowed, and he leaned against the doorframe. "You should leave it alone, son. There's nothing for you there but trouble."

"I can't," Cory shot back. "A man was killed on my build site because of whatever's going on there. You know something. I know you do."

McRae studied him for a long moment, his expression unreadable. He stepped back and pulled the door open. "Christ, then. Come in."

The inside of the house was as unkempt as the outside. The air smelled of wood smoke, old coffee and bourbon. The furniture was sparse and mismatched; an ashtray overflowed with cigarette butts on a crowded end table.

McRae motioned for Cory to sit in a battered armchair while he dropped into a wooden chair across from him. He picked up a coffee mug from the table, took a swig, and grimaced.

"Your old man was a good man. A damn good man," McRae said finally, setting the mug down with a dull thud.

"What happened to him?" Cory asked. "All I know is that it was an accident at the mill."

McRae winced. "No. It wasn't an accident. But it wasn't murder, neither. Not the way you might be thinking, anyway."

"Then what was it?"

McRae leaned forward, his elbows resting on his knees, his voice dropping to a near whisper. "That mill wasn't just a mill. It was alive, in a way. Not like you or me, but something else. Something worse. And it don't like to be disturbed."

Cory's stomach churned, but he kept his voice steady. "What do you mean, alive?"

McRae rubbed a hand over his face, as if trying to wipe away a memory. "That furnace was cursed from the day it was lit. Steel that came out of that place wasn't right. It carried something in it. Something that seeped into every girder, every pipe. Your father, he … he tried to stop it."

"How?" Cory pressed. "What's my father got to do with any of this?"

McRae's expression darkened. He hesitated, then finally said, "Your father and I … we were part of something. The Furnace Keepers, we called ourselves. But the Keepers dated back well before me and your old man. We thought we could control it. Keep it from getting worse. We were wrong, though."

Cory's breath caught in his throat.

"It was the winter of '67, but you know that. The mill was restless. Might have been the worst I'd ever seen it. Machines weren't just failing, they were fighting us. Pipes buckled and twisted. Girders – goddamn girders – were growing straight out of the walls, reaching and moaning. Everyone there knew something was wrong."

He looked at Cory, his face pale, his knuckles white where they gripped the arms of his chair.

"Your dad, me, and the rest of the Keepers went to the furnace that night. We had to do a ritual, see if we could calm it. That furnace was screaming. Not just metal groaning under heat. It was in pain.

Good God, son, it was a sound that no man should ever have to hear."

McRae paused, rubbing a hand over his face again. His voice grew lower, like he was afraid the walls might hear.

"We started the ritual, but it was angry. Spit steel at us. We all backed off, except for your dad. He got too close, though. I saw it happen – clear as I see you now. The steel reached out. Like an arm. It grabbed your father and pulled him into the furnace. We didn't know it could do that."

Cory opened his mouth, but no words came out. McRae held up a hand, stopping him.

"We grabbed at him, tried to pull him back, but the furnace fought us. Heat flared up at us, caused us to let go. And then it swallowed him whole."

McRae's gaze dropped to the floor, his voice hollow.

"When it was over, everything went quiet. The furnace stopped groaning. The mill, it just settled down. Like it had gotten what it wanted."

McRae shook his head, his shoulders slumped. "Your father didn't just die in that furnace. He fed it. It was sated for a while. But that hunger … it came back."

Cory leaned back in the chair, remembering the growing steel, the girder that had killed Don, the heat. All of it pointed back to one thing.

"We're building a new place out of the mill's remains," Cory said, his voice barely above a whisper. "We're bringing it back to life."

McRae nodded grimly. "If you don't stop it, it'll take more than just one man this time."

"Once it opens, we expect two thousand customers a day."

"Well then, Pavlik, you and I better go see what can be done."

"You sure you want to go back there?"

"Ain't about wantin', son. It's about what's gotta be done. You're gonna need someone who knows what you're up against."

IV

The drive back to New Kingston was quiet, the silence carrying a weight of shared understanding. McRae sat in the passenger seat, his hands resting heavily on his lap. The night enveloped them as the truck wound through the hills. The headlights cut through the dark, revealing endless trees that stood sentinel along the road.

The build site loomed ahead, its unfinished structure casting jagged shadows in the moonlight. The chain-link fence surrounding the site glinted dully, the padlock on the gate reflecting the truck's headlights. Cory killed the engine. Without a word, he stepped out of the truck, the door creaking loudly in the stillness. McRae followed, flashlight in hand, his boots crunching against the gravel as Cory pushed the gate open.

The site was eerily silent, the usual sounds of construction replaced by a profound emptiness.

McRae stopped in the middle of the site, looking around with a critical eye. "Where's it been worst?" he asked.

"Basement," Cory said. "That's where it all started."

McRae started walking toward the central building, his steps purposeful. Cory followed.

Inside the structure, the air was colder, the space vast and echoing. The remnants of the mill's old sign loomed above them, its rusted letters casting eldritch shadows on unfinished walls.

McRae stopped abruptly, crouching to the floor. His flashlight illuminated a small pool of something dark and metallic, its surface catching the light in a way that made Cory's stomach turn.

"Steel," McRae muttered. "Still warm."

"How?" Cory asked, his voice hushed. "We're not smelting anything here."

McRae eyes scanned the room. His gaze landed on the furnace centerpiece, surrounded by tape warning "Pennsylvania State Police Line: Do Not Cross."

"That's the heart of it," McRae said, his voice low. "That's where it's waking up." Cory followed McRae's gaze. The furnace was massive, its bulk dominating the space.

"What do we do?" Cory asked, though he wasn't sure he wanted the answer.

"This basement ain't but 30 feet high. Old mill's basement was deeper."

"Yeah, there's a subbasement."

"Then we go deeper."

McRae led the way, his flashlight carving a path through the shadows. They descended a narrow staircase, where the construction crew had unearthed part of the mill's original foundation. The air grew heavier with each step, the miasma of rust and dampness overwhelming.

The subbasement was a labyrinth of old beams and new concrete, the past and present colliding in unsettling ways. Pipes lined the walls, some freshly installed and others ancient and corroded, their surfaces crawling with arteries of steel.

McRae stopped in front of one of the walls, his flashlight revealing a patch where the concrete had cracked and splintered. "Here," he said. "This is where it's been growing."

Cory stared at the wall, the jagged cracks spreading like spiderwebs. His breath caught as he noticed an unnatural glow from within the fractures.

"You're gonna help me. We've got to open this wall up and see what we're dealing with. Find us some sledges."

The look in McRae's eyes left no room for argument. Cory returned with sledgehammers. Cory raised his hammer, its weight solid in his hands, and swung it against the wall.

The concrete crumbled, revealing more of the serpentine steel surface beneath.

As they worked, the glow intensified, and a guttural sound began to emanate from the wall. Metal grinding against metal.

Cory swung again, the hammer striking the wall with a force that sent vibrations up his arms. The steel beneath began to pulse. It had a heartbeat of its own.

And then, from somewhere deep within the structure, came a sound that froze them both in place – a low, resonant roar, like the furnace itself was waking up.

"We're running out of time," McRae said. "Let's finish this."

V

Cory stood in the dimly lit subbasement, the walls around him pulsing faintly with an unnatural light. The cracks they had opened in the concrete revealed not just veins of steel but something alive, something growing, something furious. The air was thick with the tang of molten metal, and the faint roar of the structure echoed from deep below.

McRae stood beside him, his face illuminated by the orange glow emanating from the fractures in the wall. He looked older now, more worn than ever, as if the weight of his past had finally caught up to him.

"This is it," McRae said, his voice firm. "This is where it ends."

Cory hesitated. "What do you mean, where it ends? What are we even looking at?"

McRae sighed, stepping closer to the wall. He ran his fingers along one of the cracks, where the steel seemed to ripple under his touch. "The steel's been growing, spreading itself through every inch of this place. It's waking up because you've disturbed it – used pieces of it for vanity, brought out its cursed heart."

The words felt heavy in the air, their meaning slowly sinking in.

McRae turned to Cory, his eyes shadowed. "This isn't just about the steel, Pavlik. It's about what your father died trying to stop. This mill – it doesn't just make steel. It feeds on us, on blood, on sacrifice."

Cory's breath caught in his throat. "What are you saying?"

"The only way to stop it is to give it what it wants – what it's always wanted." McRae said, his voice cracking.

The wall began to groan, the cracks widening as the glow intensified. Liquid steel, glowing like molten lava, began to seep from the fractures, slowly pooling at their feet. The air grew hotter, the heat pressing against their skin like a living thing.

McRae turned, his voice rising over the growing noise. "You need to get out of here!"

"Don't do this, Ellis!" Cory shouted.

"I don't have a choice!" McRae bellowed. "It's too far gone. It needs a life to finish what it started. Your father gave his, and now it's my turn."

Cory shook his head, stepping toward McRae. "No, there has to be another way!"

"You saw what happened to your pipefitter. This thing won't stop. It's been sleeping for a long time, and now it's awake. If we don't satisfy it, it'll take everyone who sets foot in this place," McRae said, an arm outstretched warning Cory not to come closer. "Your father saved me once, even if he didn't know it. This was always how it had to end. I know that now."

The floor beneath them began to tremble, the sound of grinding metal filling the air. Molten steel erupted from the walls, cascading down like a fiery waterfall. McRae grabbed Cory by the shoulders, shoving him toward the staircase.

"Go!" McRae roared. "Just don't let this place take you or anyone else like it took us."

Cory faltered; the heat was nearly unbearable. He looked back at McRae, the old man resolute in the face of the inferno. McRae threw his suspenders off his shoulders and ripped open his shirt, which he then cast into the steel, revealing on his chest a large tattoo – the sigil of the Furnace Keepers.

The flood came suddenly, violently. The walls gave way entirely, releasing a torrent of molten steel that surged through the basement in two colliding waves, consuming everything in its path.

Cory scrambled up the staircase, the heat licking at his heels. He could barely see through the blinding glow, the sound of the molten steel deafening. As he reached the top of the stairs, he turned back for one last look.

McRae was gone, swallowed by the flood, but for one arm raised in defiance.

The flood then followed Cory, an ocean of steel rising up the staircase as Cory sprinted for the exit. He threw himself through the doorway just as the molten steel erupted behind him, spilling out into the yard.

VI

Cory sat on the tailgate of his truck, the night air thick with the acrid stench of smoke and burning wood. The building was an inferno, the fire fueled by the flood of molten steel that had consumed its foundation. Flames licked at the sky, and the structure bellowed as its frame twisted and sagged.

He exhaled slowly, the cigarette he hadn't lit still tucked behind his ear. He'd seen fires before, but this was different. This was alive, just like the steel.

A deep groan echoed through the night, louder this time, and Cory tensed. With one final, agonized scream, the building collapsed inward, steel and timber plunging into the basement with a deafening roar. A plume of ash and embers erupted into the air.

Cory leaned back, his boots dangling just above the asphalt, watching as the fire burned. He didn't feel relief – just emptiness. He sat for hours and watched the New Kingston Fire Department try to smother the flames.

The screech of tires pulled his attention. A white van emblazoned with the OSHA logo skidded to a halt, and two men in matching hard hats and reflective vests scrambled out. Their wide eyes took in the smoldering ruin, then darted to Cory, who was still calmly perched on his tailgate.

"What in the hell happened here?" the older one demanded, his voice rising an octave.

Cory shrugged as he lazily sketched something on his forearm. "Workplace accident," he said flatly, his tone so casual it bordered on absurd.

The younger investigator gawked at him. "Accident? That's—" He gestured wildly toward the wreckage. "That's an apocalypse!"

Cory tilted his head, pretending to consider it. "Yeah, it got a little out of hand."

As the investigators exchanged bewildered glances, Cory glanced down at his arm. The sigil of the Furnace Keepers took shape beneath the ink, crude yet unmistakable.

"What are you doing?" the older man asked, his voice cracking with incredulity.

Cory gave him a faint, enigmatic smile. "Just making sure I remember something," he said, standing up and brushing ash from his jeans.

Before they could respond, Cory climbed into his truck and started the engine. The taillights disappeared into the night, leaving the two men standing in stunned silence before the ruin of the building.

HORROR

WHY I WON'T EAT FRIED CHICKEN

Jude Deluca

15 to 20 minutes

Jude Deluca is a nonbinary aegosexual Capricorn. Their areas of interest are magical girls, slasher fiction, YA Horror, 90's nostalgia, superhero dads and big, beautiful men. As a professional horror detective, they work to rediscover lost media like *Goosebumps: Dead Dogs Still Fetch* by R. L. Stine and Braden Gardner.

X: @judedeluca1990
Instagram: @judedeluca
Bluesky: @judedeluca.bsky.social

I've never liked fried chicken. My family thinks I'm weird because I dislike it. Maybe there's something up with me, but I think it's gross and too much hassle to enjoy. Fried chicken just seems so difficult to eat. Wings have next to no meat on them, while thighs and breasts are total nightmares. Not to mention the skin can get so crunchy it's hard to bite through to reach the meat. One time, I thought I cracked a tooth and freaked out as I was trying to eat a leg. God, what I'd give for my family to let me live that down. I have no idea how anyone's ever able to eat fried chicken down to the bone.

But that's just me, I guess.

Whenever my family had fried chicken for dinner, I felt like a sideshow freak on display, ripping it apart trying to get a piece of the meat. It was even worse when my parents took us out for dinner at fried chicken joints. My younger siblings thought it was a total riot seeing me try to eat. I suspect my parents also thought it was funny, which is why they kept making me eat at those places even though they knew how much I hated fried chicken.

They don't think it's very funny now, not after what happened …

It was early October, during my first semester in college. Following the total nightmare that was middle and high school, I was happy for a change of pace. Even if it was a local college and I was still living at home, I was beginning to feel like my own person. Because I still lived with my family, that meant I usually went along with them for grocery shopping. Mom and Dad always did their shopping at Crystal's, our town's only superstore. Everyone shops there because they have everything. Including fried chicken in the deli section.

Oh, don't worry – even though it's a superstore, they claim all their food's organic. Even the meat and poultry. Sure.

As the eldest, Mom and Dad still expected me to keep my siblings from trashing the place while they shopped. Micah was seven and Tabitha was twelve, but they acted like five-year-olds running around the store. They especially liked to play hide-and-seek in the clothing department. My other sister Josie was sixteen, and more than happy to pawn our siblings off on me whenever we were in public. She thought she'd die of embarrassment if she was caught with them. The only reason why I put up with this is because it was cheaper than moving into a dorm. And, well, they *are* my family. I guess.

"Micah, Tabitha, stop messing with the mannequins!" I begged as I chased them around the women's clothing department. The two were trying to make the clothing dummies pick their noses. "You're gonna get us thrown out!"

"You're no fun at all, Jody!" Micah whined as he ducked beneath a rack of skinny jeans.

"Yeah, you've got no imagination for an art student," Tabitha teased. "We're just making the displays more interesting."

"Josie, a little help?" I asked in vain.

"Do I know you?" Josie broke eye contact with her reflection in the make-up counter mirror long enough to deliver her denial. Then she went right back to applying another coat of lipstick to her already colored lips. She was obsessed with her lips – still is. Plans to be a professional lipstick model. Is that even a thing?

"Yes, and you know Mom and Dad will lose it if we don't get these two under— TABITHA, STOP PUTTING BRAS ON THE MANNEQUINS!" I shouted, even as other shoppers gave me some serious side-eye.

"Correction, they'll lose it if *you* don't get them under control. I'm an innocent bystander." Josie blew a kiss in the mirror. Sometimes I wouldn't be surprised to walk in on her making out with her reflection in the bathroom. "Don't I look fabulous in Ravishing Raspberry Rose?"

"You know they test that stuff on animals," I revealed.

"Don't lie, that's an urban legend," Josie sneered.

"LOOK OUT BELOW!"

I heard a loud *crash* and the sound of several bottles breaking as something hit the floor. Running around the corner, I found my little siblings still at the scene of the crime. They had managed to knock over a mannequin right in the path of a shopping cart. Its contents had spilled out all over the tile floor. It was a massacre. Bottles broken. Bags split open. Orange juice and ketchup mixed with egg yolks and milk coalesced into a puddle, resembling bloody puke.

Tabitha and Micah stood to the side looking horrified, not because of the mess they had made but because of who the shopping cart belonged to.

"Mrs. Stine!" I gasped.

In front of the overturned shopping cart, with her bony fingers clenched tight at her sides, stood my elderly neighbor who lived at the end of the block.

Mrs. Stine – no one knows where or who Mr. Stine is – is probably the oldest woman in town. Hell, she was elderly back when *I* was a little kid nearly twenty years ago. Some people say she was never a young woman. Mrs. Stine only ever dresses in shades of gray and red, to match her gray hair and red lips.

Standing there, in the middle of the aisle, I saw that her long gray skirt had a splash of dark red from a ketchup splatter, and her pale face had turned tomato red with rage.

"Mrs. Stine, I am *so* sorry about this," I quickly apologized as I turned her cart back up.

"Are you okay? Tabitha! Micah! Tell Mrs. Stine you're sorry and help me!"

"But it wasn't out fault!" Tabitha complained.

"Yeah, she came out of nowhere!" Micah pouted, trying and failing to look innocent.

"Don't give me that crap!" I shouted. "What would've happened if that mannequin fell on top of her? You could've hurt Mrs. Stine!" I was fully shifting into parental mode. "I've had enough of you two running around like wild animals just because Mom and Dad aren't here! Now help me with Mrs. Stine's groceries and apologize!"

"We don't have to do what you say!" Micah stomped his foot. "Just because you're older doesn't mean you're the boss!"

"That's exactly what it means," I countered. I turned to Mrs. Stine and apologized again. "I'm so sorry about their attitude. My parents spoil them."

"Clearly," Mrs. Stine agreed, her tone droll.

"Who spoiled who?"

I looked up to see Mom and Dad heading towards us with a full shopping cart.

"Mom! Dad!" Tabitha and Micah ran up to our parents. Micah pointed at me and told them, "Jody said we're spoiled!"

"And yelled at us for knocking over Mrs. Stine's cart when it wasn't our fault!" Tabitha lied.

"Jody, we told you to watch your brother and sister, not bully them," Mom admonished. "Honestly, you expect to be treated like an adult when you behave this way?"

I couldn't believe this. First, they make Tabitha and Micah my responsibility. Then they eat up their little pity routine.

"But—"

"Oh yeah, Jody's been awful to them since you guys left." Josie chose to reveal herself at that moment. "I tried to help but Jody insisted it wasn't any of my business. It was *so* embarrassing."

"But—"

"That's enough, Jody," Dad said. "Now, we're heading to the checkout to pay for everything." He held up a big, white paper bag. "We have to hurry home before dinner gets cold."

"Yay! Crystal's Fried Chicken!" Tabitha and Micah cheered while I groaned.

"You go ahead," I said as I continued to pick up what hadn't shattered or spilled when my siblings knocked over the shopping cart. Part of me considered picking up the broken glass but decided not to risk getting messy *and* cutting myself. "I'm going to help Mrs. Stine replace her groceries."

"Jody, we don't have time for that. Now come on," Mom pushed the cart forward. "Mrs. Stine's a grown woman, she can get her own things."

"Then tell Tabitha and Micah to apologize to her," I demanded.

"We didn't do anything wrong!" Micah cried.

"God, leave them alone, Jody." Josie rolled her eyes. "Why do you always have to be such a pill, anyway?"

"You know what?" I threw my hands up in defeat. "I'm just gonna help Mrs. Stine, you guys can do whatever. Come on, Mrs. S, just tell me what you need."

I ignored my family threatening to leave me behind at the store. Right then, I was too pissed at how thoughtless and rude they could be, and they called *me* a bully. Honestly, I felt bad for Mrs. Stine. People around town have a nasty habit of calling her a witch, among other things, just because she's old and lives by herself. I remember kids who liked to play pranks on her, back when I was in grade school. Josie herself left a burning bag of dog crap on her porch one Halloween. I'm surprised she wasn't worried about ruining her nails. Part of me suspected Tabitha brought Micah along to pull similar stunts, but I had no concrete evidence. Even if I did, I doubt Mom and Dad would care. In case you haven't noticed, they let the little brats get away with a lot. Good thing they have me around for a scapegoat, huh?

Sometimes people suck.

It took longer to get everything on Mrs. Stine's shopping list than I thought, but I really didn't care if my family left me behind. Especially if it meant I didn't have to sit through them eating fried chicken for dinner.

We shopped in comfortable silence. I asked what she needed, and she pointed me in the right direction. I didn't really feel like we needed to talk, and I guess Mrs. Stine shared the sentiment. It still made me feel better, seeing the angry red fade away from her cheeks. I paid for her groceries when we reached the checkout line.

"There's no need for that," the old woman said as I pulled out my wallet. "You've already done enough."

"No really, I want to," I insisted as I handed several bills to the cashier. "It's the least I can do after the way my family behaved."

"Tsk, you're making an old woman feel guilty," Mrs. Stine laughed. "I'm still going to owe you one, dear."

"Let's take a rain check on it," I replied as I helped carry her bags to her car.

Imagine my surprise to find my parents and siblings still waiting for me.

"Well, look who finally showed up," Josie announced. "The local good Samaritan."

"I thought you all left," I said. I noticed Mrs. Stine's scowl had returned as she glared at Tabitha and Micah.

"And have you complain about leaving you behind?" Mom asked. "What kind of parents would that make us?"

"Should I really answer that?" I asked. Everyone was surprised when Mrs. Stine laughed.

"Well, thanks to you we had to eat dinner in the car," Dad said, holding up a bag of chicken bones. My stomach turned as I imagined them gnawing on fried chicken in the parking lot. He dropped the bag on the asphalt and unlocked the car. "Now let's go."

Narrowing my eyes at Tabitha and Micah, I asked the gruesome twosome, "And dare I hope that you two have anything to say to Mrs. Stine?"

"Um yeah, I do," Micah replied.

"Really?"

"Yeah." Micah opened his mouth wide and let out a long, wet belch.

Tabitha joined in. "Yeah, me too!"

My parents and even Josie found this hilarious as I stood there, jaw hanging open in disbelief.

Mrs. Stine's scowl intensified as a sharp blast of cold wind cut through the parking lot.

Sighing, I turned to my neighbor and was about to apologize again when she held up her hand. "Please, don't bother. Some people are just beyond hope."

And with that, I watched the old woman load her groceries into her little car and drive off.

The journey home was not a pleasant one for any of us. I probably should've left well enough alone, but I was damn tired of everyone acting like asses.

"You know, I'm damn tired of everyone acting like asses," I said.

"Don't curse in front of your little brother and sister," Mom warned, looking both annoyed and nauseous as Dad drove.

"You're the ones who let them act that way," I argued. "Whenever I tell them to stop, you act like I'm crossing a boundary. You tell me to keep an eye on them, but when they misbehave you pretend they're little angels who do no wrong before blaming *me* for letting it happen. You and Dad can't have it both ways!"

"God, Jody, save your PC bullshit for your classmates," Josie interrupted. "No one cares."

Once I got started, I didn't want to stop. "They could've hurt someone in the store. It's a good thing that mannequin didn't hit Mrs. Stine on the head when it fell. Or maybe you guys want to a lawsuit."

"She'd never have a case," Dad groaned.

"Daddy, tell Jody to stop whining," Micah moaned. "I don't feel good."

"Daddy doesn't feel good either, Micah." Dad dabbed his forehead with a handkerchief.

Looking around the car, I saw that all five of them looked ill. Tabitha was the only one who had nothing to say. She kept opening and closing her mouth; I expected her to throw up at any moment. It's a miracle Dad managed to get us home in one piece considering how badly he was starting to shake.

By the time we pulled into the driveway, my anger was starting to decrease. My family *really* didn't look good. Before I could even ask what was wrong, my parents and siblings ran into the house without looking back once.

Truthfully, it wasn't the worst trip to Crystal's, but I had no idea it was going to get worse.

After putting away the groceries by myself, I tried to check in on everyone. Mom and Dad had locked themselves in the master bedroom. Josie, Tabitha and Micah had likewise sequestered themselves in their rooms. The only sounds of life were various pain-filled groans and nauseous weeping.

Great, now they have to make me feel bad for them, I thought, as I checked to see if we had enough ginger ale and white rice in the kitchen. Since I couldn't get a straight answer from anyone about how they felt, my immediate guess was an acute case of food poisoning from a bad batch of fried chicken. It was too much to hope they were feeling lousy from acting lousy.

Not having much of an appetite, my dinner consisted of a couple of bowls of cereal while I read some assigned chapters for my World History class. Every so often I tried to see how my family was feeling, but they kept their doors locked. I just thanked God we had more than one bathroom in the house, in case of a major leakage problem.

I don't remember falling asleep, but I do remember waking up to the sound of screaming.

"AAAAAHHH!"

I woke up in a panic, realizing I'd dozed off on the couch while reading about the Great Depression. It took me a moment to realize the scream came from upstairs, but I couldn't tell who it belonged to.

"Mom! Dad!" I called as I rushed up the stairs. I'd forgotten all about the earlier argument as dread set in. "Are you guys okay? Who screamed?"

That's when I first caught a whiff of the stench.

"Oh God!" I clamped my hands over my mouth and nose. As soon as I stepped onto the second floor, it was as though I'd entered an unholy miasma. Like a thousand eggs let out a thousand farts. Tears stung my eyes as I followed the source of the stench to the main bathroom I shared with my siblings. The door stood wide open. The closer I got, the more I feared blacking out, until I reached the threshold and found …

An egg.

A gigantic egg inside the toilet, covered in … I don't even want to say what.

"W-what the hell did you people eat?!" That's when I heard the sound of … wings?

Clarence, is that you?

Before I knew what hit me, I was tackled to the ground by something big and covered in feathers. It stank like high Hell and smothered my face with its feathers in a manic frenzy.

"BU-CAW! BU-CAW!"

"Get off!" I screamed as I tried to push the creature away.

"BU-CAW! BU-CAAAAAW!"

"I SAID GET—"

The words died in my mouth when I caught a glimpse of familiar gray-green eyes, shoved far apart on a malformed, pointed head.

But what really surprised me was the sight of a large, hard beak coated in Ravishing Raspberry Rose lipstick.

"Josie?"

"BU-CAAAAAAAAAW!" The giant chicken version of my teenaged sister shrieked in agony as she flapped her mutant wings in my face. I backed away in horror when I heard more frightened clucking throughout the house. Doors flew open and I found myself trapped in a hurricane of white feathers.

Unlike my sister, my parents and little siblings hadn't quite finished their transformations. I watched as their bodies twitched and convulsed, their human vestiges becoming more and more avian with each step they took towards me. Amidst the flapping of wings, I heard skin and muscle being torn as their skeletons contorted and twisted beneath their flesh.

"CAW! BUCK-BUCK-BU-CAAAAAAW!" they screamed, or rather clucked, pleading with me through their terrified chickeny cries. I almost fell backwards down the stairs as I tried to escape before they swarmed me again.

One of the smaller chickens – I couldn't tell if it was Tabitha or Micah – leapt from the second-floor balcony flapping their wings. The little chicken-kid crashed into a hallway table.

"No!" I shouted and tried to help, but their desperate flapping made it impossible to get close. I heard more crashing and clucking as the rest of my family ran around the house. Acting like, well, chickens with their heads cut off.

The mental image alone made me puke on the hall carpet.

I stood there, trying to comprehend the madness before my eyes as my parents and siblings ran rampant. Imagine being an extra on the set of *The Birds* and it'll barely give you an idea of what my house was like at that moment.

The two biggest chickens made their way into the kitchen, swatting cereal-filled cannisters off the counters. As they pecked at bits of corn flakes, bran and frosted marshmallow bits, their clucking sounded almost like sobbing. They couldn't control themselves.

The smaller chickens chased each other around the coffee table, their skinny chicken feet sharp enough to rip up the carpet as they ran.

The saddest of all was the Josie-chicken, desperately trying to use her wings to grab a tube of lipstick off the floor. I don't know what she hoped to accomplish with it. Maybe she thought if she could put it on her face, do something she normally did to make herself comfortable, she could convince herself this wasn't happening. Tears fell from her beady eyes as she tried to pick up the tube.

"What happened?!" I foolishly screamed in the chaos. "What the hell ...?"

Then it hit me.

I ran out of my house and down the block. As soon as I reached Mrs. Stine's house I banged on her front door with both fists.

"Do you have any idea what time it is?" The old woman confronted me in a gray nightgown with giant red curlers in her gray hair. I could smell cat food and dead flowers from inside her house.

"YeahhiMrsStinesorryforcallingonyousolatebutbyanychancedidyouturnmyfamilyintochickens?"

In all those years of people calling her a witch, I didn't think they were *serious*.

"Excuse me?" Mrs. Stine shook her head. "No, I didn't turn your family into chickens."

"Someone fucking did!" I screamed as I pointed towards the street. Mrs. Stine's jaw fell as she watched my family of chickens clucking and running around under the streetlights. They had managed to follow me outside. That was on me for leaving the door open.

"What in the world …?" Mrs. Stine rubbed her eyes, most likely to ensure she wasn't seeing things.

"What am I gonna do, what am I gonna do …" I paced back and forth on her front porch, running my hands through my hair, trying to come up with a solution. Even though I hadn't grown feathers or a beak myself, I was beginning to feel like my family was acting. "Oh God, I don't know what the hell happened, I—"

Mrs. Stine slapped me.

"SNAP OUT OF IT!"

And then she slapped me again.

"Thank you, I needed that," I answered calmly. "But what am I gonna do about *them*?!"

"Oh, it's fine." Mrs. Stine waved off my concern as she headed down her porch towards my parents and younger siblings, who were running around in circles, pecking at the asphalt at random intervals. Josie broke away from them to pull a worm out of someone's lawn. I gagged as she swallowed it whole.

I turned my attention back to my neighbor. Mrs. Stine held her fingers in the air and …

Snap!

No more chicken family.

My parents stood there with their arms tucked into their armpits. Josie had another worm clamped between her lips, desperately trying to squirm away to freedom. Tabitha and Micah were still pecking each other, having failed to realize they were no longer avians.

"Wha …?" I wondered aloud, stunned.

"Well don't just stand there, help me bring them back to your house!" Mrs. Stine barked as she grabbed my little siblings by their necks. "You want the whole neighborhood to see them?"

In a daze, I dragged my parents and Josie back to our house, following Mrs. Stine with Micah and Tabitha in her iron grip. We deposited all five of them in the living room, on the remnants of our torn-up couch scratched by chicken beaks.

"How?" I asked Mrs. Stine. "How did you …?"

"You don't live to be 147 without learning a thing or two," Mrs. Stine answered.

"147! I mean" – I cleared my throat – "thank you. Thank you so much."

"I did say I owed you one," Mrs. Stine reminded me.

"But why did they turn into chickens?" I said, as I looked in on my traumatized family. "If you didn't do it, then what caused it?"

"Like I said, I did not try to turn your family into chickens," Mrs. Stine clarified. "I tried to turn them into *pigs*."

"What?"

"I mean, chickens?" Mrs. Stine laughed. "That is *so* 1997. No, I thought pigs would be more appropriate."

"What?!"

"Sometimes my magic gets a little wonky when the target's already feeling ill." Mrs. Stine shook her head. "Must've been something they ate. That's why I never buy fried food. You never know what they put in it."

Crack.

"What was that?" Mrs. Stine asked.

Crack!

My neighbor and I followed the sound up the stairs to the bathroom where this night began.

We got there just in time to watch the egg in the toilet hatch.

CRACK!

"SKREEEEEEE-BUCK-BUCK-SKREEEEEEE! OINK OINK BU-CAAAAAAW!"

Oh yeah. I forgot to mention – I'm also not a big bacon fan anymore.

Neither is Mrs. Stine.

CRIME

THE DROMEDARY

Marc Ruvolo

15 to 20 minutes

Marc Ruvolo (he/him) is a queer writer and musician living in Portland, Oregon who once considered himself a punk. He founded the seminal Bucket O' Blood book store in Chicago, and his poetry and fiction have appeared in Cynthia Pelayo's *Gothic Blue Book* series, *Slay and Slay Again: A Queer Horror Anthology*, and *Nocturne Magazine*, to name a few. His debut horror novella, *SLOE*, was released in 2023 by Unnerving Books, and his second novella *Pieties*, was published by Off Limits Press in 2024.

Find him on Bluesky at @marcruvolo.bsky.social.

The morning of his release, Dustin's mother picks him up in the wheezing Datsun Bluebird she bought new in 1986. Myrna hasn't changed much, the same piercing eyes and smug smile, her white-shot copper hair a bit more frazzled and untamed than he remembers. A lit cigarette smolders in the overflowing ashtray. He opens the creaking passenger side door and she grimaces, scratching her pale, silk-fuzzed cheek. "You eat?"

No hugs, no hello, no *How you doin'?* A little more than three years since they'd last seen one another. Still, he's grateful she's shown up at all.

"I could."

They drive in silence through the west Texas desert, the sun beating down on endless vistas of yucca, cholla and creosote flats. The ghostly outline of the Guadalupe Mountains hovers in the side mirror like a lost city, crooked gray lines on the flat plane of the horizon.

Dustin's stomach grumbles. He thought he would be happy to be out, but everything looks so hard and focused. So *open*.

The IHOP off the Interstate is even more dated-looking than his mother's car. After filling their stained ceramic cups from a golden carafe to nearly overflowing, an effeminate, pear-shaped man in his forties takes their order. Blueberry pancakes all around. Dustin asks for a side of bacon.

"Extra butter, please." Myrna always likes her pancakes slathered to sopping.

"Sure thing, hun." The waiter's blue polyester slacks swish as he walks away.

Myrna slurps her black coffee and sets the cup down on the paper mat. "I'm takin' you home," she says, matter-of-factly.

Dustin adjusts his hands on the faux-marbled tabletop. Back in Pod C, the guys would be gathering in the common area to play cards or dominoes, a soap opera blaring from the black and white TV bolted to the iron girder that supports the cell walkway. "Yeah. I'd hoped so."

"Well, Phil is still there. We're engaged. And you, of all people, know your temper. I can't have you fightin' with him."

They'd come close before. If it wasn't for his mom, Dustin would have sent Philip to the hospital on more than one occasion. He deserved it, just like Dustin's real dad – an abuser who unfortunately passed from cirrhosis of the liver before Dustin had grown big enough to break the man's ugly, rotten nose.

"I won't be."

Before Dustin went down for grand theft, Phil had been a new addition to Myrna's life, an ex-biker turned holy roller, sidelined by three medically-fused spinal discs. Back then, he'd walked like he had a stick up his ass, his precious Harley gathering dust under a tarp at the back of the garage. Myrna and Phil fought constantly, but his mother had decided long ago she needed a man around, any man, to feel whole. Phil may have been a chaw-spittin', pre-diabetic shit stain, but in Myrna's dry, close-cropped, churched-out MAGA world, any guy with a job, a steady pulse and a fully financed pickup truck would do her just fine, thank-you-very-much.

"Good. There's gonna be rules, too. Not like before. The probation officer said we need to give you positive structure."

"Okay."

"But you break 'em? You get out."

"I got it."

Rules are nothing new to a convict. Prison rules, Myrna's rules, Phil's rules – what's the difference? Good behavior had allowed him almost a year's early release. So simple even a baby could understand; you choose to follow all the pointless, arbitrary, stupid nitpicks, or face the consequences …

Myrna flaps a hand. "Lord, what the heck is goin' on out there?"

A Ford F-150 towing a silver horse trailer has roared into the parking lot, throwing up gravel. It rolls to a stop and the driver gets out, hurrying to the back door of the trailer.

"Looks like car trouble, maybe," Dustin says.

The driver of the pickup paces around the hitch, talking to someone Dustin can't see. Then the passenger gets out too; another paunchy, middle-aged man wearing boots and a cowboy hat. The two mill around, then appear to argue. Whatever is locked inside the horse trailer is agitated, visibly throwing itself against the steel walls.

Dustin shakes his head. "Horse is gonna hurt itself."

Cowboy Hat goes to the passenger seat and retrieves a coil of rope. The men extend the ramp from beneath the trailer, positioning themselves to either side. Cowboy Hat readies his rope while the driver unhooks the padlock securing the door. He is holding what looks like an oversized cattle prod. The men's jaws are set, and they crouch down, ready to spring into action.

The driver leans in to throw back the door and a huge, yellow beast charges down the ramp into the parking lot.

Myrna gasps. "Oh my God, it's a camel."

The waiter appears with their order, dropping two plates of pancakes and a smaller plate of greasy bacon strips on the table. "That's a dromedary, actually, I think," he says. "Camels have two humps. My uncle had one like that on his ranch in Killeen."

"Same thing." Myrna glares at him. "People call 'em camels, not *dromedaries*. That's just silly."

"Anyway, *Mom*," Dustin interrupts. "I'm gonna find a job as soon as possible and then move out and into a place of my own. I won't be imposing on y'all for long."

The chastised waiter hurries away. "You sure that's the best thing?" Myrna upends the glass syrup dispenser over her plate. "I mean with your … past … uh, drug … drug issues? Maybe you'd be better off with us for the first year, or so."

The two men manage to get the rope around the dromedary's neck but struggle to control it, a silent drama played out behind the tinted glass of the IHOP's large picture windows.

"You converted my room, right?"

"Well, yes. It's where I keep my craft supplies and the … the table, and chafing dishes for our church potlucks. You'll be staying in the guest bedroom for now."

The guest room. Off-white walls, hotel-grade artwork and a lumpy twin mattress. Still, better than a steel bunk in an echoing concrete warren of the state …

"That's fine. I'm on a path to—"

The dromedary's head darts down, and it sinks square, yellow teeth into the sunburnt neck of the Driver. The man shrieks and drops the cattle prod. The great beast picks him up by his shoulder, as if he weighs nothing, then shakes him before tossing the limp body half the length of the trailer. The Driver ragdolls on the gravel and lies still. A wash of black blood seeps from his neck and shoulders, staining the collar of his pearl snap western shirt. The dromedary rears back, hooves flying, and bares its teeth at the second man, who puts a hand up to defend himself before dropping the rope and retreating. The dromedary doesn't follow, but trots around the corner of the trailer, out of sight.

"What the hell?" Dustin puts down his fork, the pancakes forgotten.

The man in the cowboy hat runs to his friend. Crouching over the Driver, he presses a handkerchief against the man's neck, which quickly becomes soaked with blood. The dromedary reemerges, circling them, stalking like a predator. At least a third of the customers in the restaurant are dialing 911 as the remaining diners and staff watch in stunned silence. Myrna shakes the leftover ice in her water glass. "How terrible for him."

"Maybe they've been mistreating it," Dustin says.

"Or it's just a wild animal that needs to be put down. Some things aren't fixable, you know?"

The dromedary charges Cowboy Hat, using his sandy, oblong head as a ram, and bowls the man over. Cowboy Hat, now bare-headed, crawls to the truck, scrambling for shelter beneath the back bumper.

A siren wails in the distance. People are up, out from their tables and meals, pressed against the window glass. The dromedary kicks his back legs then trots behind the trailer, once more out of view.

The young cashier who was sitting at the front register when they came in opens the glass door and a gust of hot, dusty wind rushes through the dining room. An elderly man at the closest table protests loudly.

"Gawkers." His mother snorts, cutting her pancakes into gooey quarters. "Mind your business, and let the authorities deal with it."

A State Police SUV pulls into the parking lot, rolling to a stop next to the trailer, and a reedy young trooper gets out, service pistol already in his hand.

"Call Animal Control!" the cashier in the doorway shouts. "You aren't allowed to kill it. Officer! Call Animal Control, right now!"

The Trooper peeks cautiously around the corner of the trailer, then fires into the air. Three echoing shots. The cashier makes a strange moaning noise and runs back behind the counter.

"This is crazy," Dustin says.

His mother has already finished half her pancakes. "It's dumb, is what it is," she says around mouthfuls. "Downright stupid."

An ambulance, lights and sirens blaring, bumps onto the gravel. Two EMTs get out and rush over to the stricken man. The Trooper joins them, talking on his radio. On the other side of the parking lot, a dust devil has formed, turning so slowly in the shimmering heat that it doesn't seem real.

The Waiter returns to drop the check on the table. "All right. If you folks don't need anything else ..."

Myrna dabs her lips with a napkin. "We're good."

The State Trooper approaches the door to the diner. Behind him, the EMTs load the wounded man into the ambulance. "Everything's under control, folks," the Trooper announces. "So don't be afraid if you need to leave. The camel has run off and Animal Control is on its way to deal with the situation. Thank you for your patience!"

A relieved murmur washes across the diners. "What were we talking about?" Myrna asks.

"I don't remember."

"Oh, yeah." She sniffs, rubbing her nose. "The guest bedroom. The mattress there is a little stiff, but you're probably used to that. No late-night showers. No guests. No drinking. Quiet time after 9 p.m. Chores are mandatory. I'll feed you for now, but when you get a job, you need to pay rent and buy your own groceries until you move out. Rent shouldn't be *too* high. I need to talk to Phil about it. Half of the house is his, after all."

Dustin suspects Phil will say they should milk as much money out of him as possible. If he's not careful, he'll become a prisoner all over again, working for Phil and Myrna, instead of the State of Texas.

"I understand."

"You haven't touched your food."

Dustin dutifully tucks in. The pancakes are gummy, the butter congealed, but the bacon is a wonderment. He hasn't had real bacon in years.

His mother settles the bill with the cashier, leaving a dollar-seventy-five cash tip on the table. In the parking lot, the heat envelops Dustin like a thick wool blanket. Halfway to the Bluebird, and he's dripping again.

Myrna puts the car in gear, then steers it towards the road. "I'm gonna need to stop at the supermarket. You still like Frosted Flakes?"

"I'm good with whatever you get, Ma."

The Bluebird is almost to the access road when Dustin sees the State Trooper waving his arms and shouting something. "What's that cop doing?"

A huge, yellow shape darts in front of the car, and Dustin braces for impact. "Look out!"

Myrna twists the steering wheel but it's too late, and there's a sickening thump as the car strikes the massive hindquarters of the dromedary. The beast stumbles, making a horrific bleating scream that Dustin can hear even with the windows closed. The dromedary gallops into the road, weaving unsteadily, only to disappear among the stands of cacti in the sandy wash.

Guns drawn, two Troopers are at the Bluebird in seconds. Dustin rolls down his window.

"Either of you hurt?" the Trooper asks, his eyes on the wash.

"I don't think so." Dustin's heart is thumping in his chest, but not because of the accident. He can feel the cops eyeing him, sizing him up. State pigs like that can smell an ex-con from ten feet away. "Ma. You okay?"

Myrna removes her seat belt. "I'm fine. But my car better not be messed up."

The two of them get out to survey the damage. It's minor, a dent in the steel bumper.

Thankfully they weren't travelling very fast. Myrna turns on the cop. "Why didn't you shoot that crazy thing?"

The Trooper mops his neck with an already-sodden paper towel. "Ma'am, that animal is worth a *lot* of money. And she's pregnant. If you'd like, I can get the owner's info, then you can take the damage to your car up with his insurance."

Myrna flaps a dismissive hand. "Don't you never mind, officer. Have a good day."

Once the windows roll up, Dustin settles a bit. The Troopers are walking back to their squad car. He's safe. After checking, and then double-checking, Myrna puts the Bluebird in gear, puts on her blinker, and pulls onto the access road. "Jesus and Mary, what a day," she mutters.

Back on the highway, both of them light up. Even with the windows cracked, cigarette smoke fills the car, a shifting gray haze. Myrna drives slowly in the right lane, hugging the shoulder.

Dustin stubs out his cigarette in the ashtray. Myrna is looking at him, mouth hanging open. "What in blue blazes …?" she whispers.

No, she's looking *past* him—

There's a loud crash next to his head, and shards of glass hit Dustin's face, raining into his lap and onto the floor. "What the fuck!"

"Good Lord!" Myrna wrenches the steering wheel and the Bluebird's tires screech. A pickup truck in the other lane lays on its horn and she overcorrects, sending them flying into the ditch. "Hold on!" she shouts, her knuckles white on the steering wheel. Rocks and cacti hammer the chassis of the old car, throwing both of them repeatedly against the ceiling. The Bluebird judders to a halt with a nasty crunch and the screech of angry metal.

Dustin touches his head. It has collided with the door frame and his fingers come away wet with blood. Myrna is blubbering but appears unhurt. "What happened?" he manages to grunt.

"That thing! The camel! It was running next to the car, then it smashed the window!"

"The camel?"

"Yes! Oh, my Lord. The car's totaled. Phil is going to kill me!"

Two women appear at the broken passenger window. They're college girls; ponytails and baggy sweatshirts. "Are you hurt?" one asks, her tanned face a mask of concern. "We already called the ambulance." A faint siren wails in the distance.

Dustin removes his seatbelt. "I'm okay. I think my mother's okay, too."

A yellow blur slams into the girls, sending them sprawling onto the cruel spines of a cholla patch. Both of them are screaming. *Screaming*. Myrna whimpers and begins to pray. As Dustin sits rigid, frozen in his seat, unable to completely grasp what he's seeing, the dromedary turns and runs back, trampling the girls into the cacti. Then she rears, bringing her hooves down on the stricken college girls. Once. Twice. *Three times*, with a sickening, horrible, crunching noise. Dustin is no stranger to death, to cold-blooded killing, but this makes even him turn his head. The pancakes and bacon churn in his guts as the dromedary lopes off into the desert.

Myrna grabs his shoulder, eyes wild. "Run. We-we have to run. We'll be trapped here."

"No, Ma—" But it's too late, Myrna has opened the car door and lurched out into the ditch. "Fuck." Dustin opens the passenger side door to go after her.

All four of the Bluebird's tires are flat and it's come to a stop atop red rubble and a few huge yucca plants. Obviously in shock, Myrna can barely walk, her feet slipping in the sandy soil. He has no idea where she thinks she's going.

"Ma! Stop! We're safer in the car. The cops are coming. Ma!"

The poor girls in the cholla are dead, their shocked faces slicked with red slurry, limbs broken and twisted. Dustin sees a cell phone on the ground and snatches it up. The cracked screen blinks to life. A picture of a sunrise, with text beneath it that reads, "God Bless This Day and All Days, Amen!"

Myrna is already on the road. She raises her arms. "Help! Somebody help us!"

"Ma!" Dustin calls out. "Ma!" He can see the cops, or ambulance, coming up the road, a plume of dust trailing the shiny vehicle.

Myrna is squinting at something he can't see, her shoulders hunched, face bathed in sweat.

"Ma," he says. "You gotta get out of the road. Come back to the car."

She turns on him, her eyes rolling, unfocused. "Why did I ever have you?"

"What?"

A squad car slides to a halt on the shoulder of the road behind a white Range Rover and a Trooper jumps out, gun drawn. "Stay where you are!"

Dustin puts up his hands. "This is my mother! A-a *camel* attacked our car!" he shouts. "It killed two people! They're over there!"

The Trooper advances, aiming at Dustin. "Okay! Just stay where you are. Keep your hands up."

A hundred yards away, the dromedary trots up onto the asphalt. Her huge head swings back and forth, eyes like rolling black eggs beneath a pair of bushy brows. Her two-toed foot, painted with gore and congealed blood, paws the ground, sending up a plume of fine red dust.

"Oh, shit." Dustin grabs his mother's arm. "Ma. Come on. Let's get by the cop. We gotta go. We gotta move. Now."

Myrna shrugs him off. "Let go. I have to get to church." She lurches in the direction of the dromedary.

"Officer!" He waves at the cop. "The camel's gone crazy! Shoot it!"

"Stay where you are! I'm warning you!"

The dromedary lopes towards them, making a low, guttural noise.

Oblivious – or delirious – Myrna is still walking. Dustin runs up and grabs her, trying to direct her away from the approaching animal, but she fights him, screaming something about Phil and her pastor. The dromedary hits like a freight train, knocking them both down, and a horrible, reeking stench overwhelms Dustin – rancid piss and hot excrement. He rolls in the dirt, gagging. A sharp stab in his side tells him one of his ribs may be cracked.

The dromedary swings its long neck, nudging Myrna with the oblong wedge of its head. She raises a hand to protect her face, and the head dips quickly, like a snake, the long, sinuous lips engulfing her fingers. She shrieks, and a wash of blood slithers down her wrist, soaking the floral print fabric of her shirt.

The Trooper has finally assessed the situation and fires a shot over their heads trying to frighten away the animal.

Ignoring the gunshot, the dromedary releases Myrna's hand and she slumps to the ground unconscious. Dustin waves his arms, moving closer, and shouts as loud as he can. "Hey! Hey! Get the fuck out of here! Move! Skedaddle, you asshole!"

The Trooper fires a second shot and Dustin ducks. "You crazy? Let me get my Mom out of there first!"

The Trooper looks pale and frightened. He's young, a rookie. "Stay where you are!"

The dromedary turns her backside to them and leans down, nudging Myrna with her foam and blood-flecked snout. She stamps the dirt and Dustin fears she's about to trample his mother like she did the college girls.

"Hey!" He snatches a stone from the verge and throws it at the dromedary. "Hey! Move it!"

The Trooper is beside him. He's panting, white-faced. "Get back behind my car," the man orders. "I'll take care of this."

"No. Listen to me. You distract it, and I'll pull my mother out of there. Or you could just shoot it, for fuck's sake."

Gun trembling, the Trooper waves off the suggestion. "They told me I can't kill it. Only can scare it away," he pants. "The owner knows

… *somebody important*, I don't know. Okay, I'll go around left on the road. Get your mom out. Fast."

The Trooper runs, yelling "Hey! Hey!", and the dromedary's head swings in his direction. Dustin creeps closer. Myrna is awake, lying on her back, mumbling incoherently. The dromedary takes a few steps in the Trooper's direction, making the same low, grumbling noise it did earlier.

Quietly as possible, Dustin hurries to his mother's side. He slides an arm under her shoulders and lifts until she's in a sitting position. The torn remains of her mutilated hand drools blood into the red dust.

"Ma. Hey, Ma," he whispers. "Get up. Come on."

The Trooper makes noise, skipping rocks close to the Dromedary's legs, and the animal stalks towards him, head swaying back and forth, teeth bared.

Dustin bear hugs Myrna and drags her to her feet. She's limp in his arms. "Ma. Walk, Ma. You gotta walk."

The dromedary charges the Trooper, and in response he fires a pair of warning shots over her head. Unfrightened, the beast accelerates, kicking up a cloud of dust, obviously intent on attacking him. The Trooper fires another round, this time striking her broad, muscular chest.

A spreading patch of pink blossoms in yellow fur, but the dromedary doesn't lose a step. They collide, and the Trooper is flung headlong into the ditch, tossed aside like a dry leaf. After regaining his feet, the Trooper limps away, putting some space between him and the enraged animal.

Dustin half-drags, half-walks Myrna back to the car, and manages to get her into the passenger seat, dizzy and drenched in fresh sweat by the time he's finished. "Stay here, Ma. The ambulance is on its way."

Two more shots ring out, and Dustin hears a horrible, honking bray. A cry of pure agony and anguish. He runs up onto the road and sees the Trooper being dragged along the ground by his pants leg. His hands are empty. The dromedary, bleeding from two more bullet wounds in its side, has the cop's pants cuff between her teeth, shaking as she pulls.

"Help me!" the Trooper begs.

Not knowing what else to do, Dustin grabs another stone and runs up behind the dromedary, waving his arms. "Hey! Fuck! Get out! Go on! Move it!" He throws the stone, and it connects solidly with the back of her head.

Barely a second passes before Dustin is in the dirt, writhing, screaming. The pain shoots up his leg like an eruption of black static, blotting out any rational thought. He hears the Trooper screaming, as well. Bit by bit, the static clears, the pain ebbing to a dull throb. The dromedary has kicked him in the leg, and there's little doubt in his mind that it's broken. He feels his leg for protruding bone. Thankfully, there's none. Something is painfully jabbing his thigh – a sharp rock, he thinks. It's the cop's gun.

The Trooper is howling and weeping, the dromedary grunting.

Then they both go silent.

With his one good leg, Dustin levers himself around. The dromedary is now lying atop the Trooper, pinning him down, her thousand-plus pound bulk pressing down on his head and shoulders. The cop's legs kick, weaker with each spasm. He's being crushed to death.

Dustin drags himself through the stony dirt and aims the Trooper's Glock at the target of the dromedary's swaying head. Then he pulls the trigger, unloading whatever is left in the clip.

With a sigh like deflating bellows, the dromedary slumps over the Trooper, dead, one shiny, black eye fixed on Dustin.

"Don't move!" A woman cop is standing over him.

"Drop the gun!" she orders, her service weapon pointed at Dustin. More cop cars, an army of cops, appear in the road, sirens, and lights blaring. There's a Humvee. "Drop it, or I'll blow your motherfucking head off!"

◆◆◆

"It's only eight months," Myrna says into the phone on the other side of the glass. The prison visiting area is full of squalling kids and unhappy wives. It's the first time Dustin's mother has come to see him since the incident, almost a month prior. The white bandage on her hand is wrapped tight and taped up. The crazed dromedary completely bit off four of her fingers. The doctors were able to save the thumb and almost two thirds of the palm meat. *Small blessings*, his mother had remarked in a phone call from the hospital, *small blessings*.

"That lawyer says it's a waste of money appealing or filing anything else. You were holding the gun. The policeman saw you. At least they figured out you didn't kill that cop. Could be worse, Dustin. A lot worse."

"Yeah."

There isn't much to say. The last thing he needs right now is a lecture disguised as motherly concern. They *had* tried to get him, had said he murdered the cop – until the forensics came back. But the State Trooper's head was crushed flat as a tortilla, with most of his bones fractured; a level of damage even the overzealous district attorney knew Dustin wasn't capable of.

"The lawyer did say we could go ahead with a civil suit against the owner. That guy was negligent in securing a dangerous animal, or something like that."

"Okay."

"And one more thing, before I gotta get out of here. Phil and I talked, and after all this, he's not comfortable with you coming to live with us. Sorry, D. I'll figure out somewhere else for you to go, I swear."

Dustin grimaces and gets to his feet, the cast on his broken leg bumping clumsily against the metal chair leg. "Thanks for coming by, Ma. You have a good day."

Myrna calls out as he walks away, but Dustin ignores her, nodding to the guard, who opens the door to the cellblock hallway.

Back in the pod, he finds Luis in the common area, staring up at the TV. A lifer, Luis "Krazee" Rios always has cards close at hand, and this time is no different. *Frrripp, frrripp,* the deck makes its familiar buzzing noise as he absently riffles the cards.

Dustin sits at the steel table. "You gonna deal me a hand, or just play with yourself all day?"

Luis grins. "How's *tu madre* doing?"

"The same. People don't change, you know that."

"Yeah." Luis counts out the hands. "Sounds like they gettin' stranger and stranger out there."

Dustin shrugs. He picks up his cards and fans them. Even now, the stink of the dromedary lingers in his nostrils. He can still see that flat, black eye, staring, stilled. Dead. The cards mean nothing and everything all at once. "Um. Yeah. I dunno, I'm starting to think we're better off in here."

Luis' hard laugh echoes through the block. "*What?* Now they gonna start calling you crazy too, man."

CRIME

MEXICAN MENNONITES

Selene MacLeod

10 to 15 minutes

Selene is a proud Canadian who sometimes writes, sometimes edits, sometimes answers phones at a job, and can be found hosting the YouTube channel *Ella Gorey's Horror Stories*. Her stories have appeared in the webzines *Luna Station Quarterly*, *Shotgun Honey*, and in such anthologies as *Tragedy Queens: Stories Inspired by Dana Del Rey & Sylvia Plath*, *Long Distance Drunks*, *Drag Noir*, and *Garbology: The GarbAugust Anthology of Awesome Trash*.

Jack slowed down at the roundabout – barely – and pulled through, headed toward Elmira. As he crossed over Sawmill Road, he confirmed his suspicion that he'd been driving in a circle.

"New Jerusalem Road?" Jessie craned her neck backwards, squinting at the sign. "Wasn't that what 'Salem's Lot was called in that vampire book?"

"That was Jerusalem's Lot," Jack corrected. "We're in the right area." He didn't want to tell her he was hopelessly lost. He had no idea which of the big farm buildings belonged to Mennonites and which were regular farms, or hobby farms, or what. He was tired of driving and wanted to stretch his legs. His butt was starting to hurt from sitting too long, and he was starting to itch – the comedown was starting early. He clenched his teeth and gripped the steering wheel.

Jessie's endless jibber-jabber was also starting to get on his nerves. The sound of her voice crawled against his skin like a hair down his back he couldn't quite reach.

He grunted when she asked a question, and tried to tune her out, shifting his weight around as much as he could in the driver's seat. *Yap, yap, yap* – she really liked the sound of her own voice.

They met at a party a couple of months ago, just after Orientation Week. She was a short brunette, and cute in a birdy, anorexic sort of way. Jack had fallen hard for her, and it never occurred to him how much money he spent, or how his other friends stopped talking to him. When his student loans came in, Jack pre-paid the rent on his basement room through the end of December and then blew the rest of his money on a series of weekend binges. Between lousy grades and mounting bills, Jack had been kicked out of school in mid-November and couldn't really bring himself to care.

He had sold most of his belongings; his guitar, his camera and the telescope and textbooks he'd brought for his course work in Astronomy. All he had left was a dirty mattress on a remnant of shag carpet over a cement floor, and some battered furniture that belonged to the landlady.

"Where are we going, anyway?" asked Jessie, interrupting his reverie.

"I think I know how we can get some money," he said.

"What's your landlady going to think? Should I call my dad?"

"Not yet. She's probably just figuring out we took the car." Stole, more like. Jack didn't have permission to go upstairs, but when he and Jessie had snorted their last, they stumbled around and found the keys. He wasn't sure how long they'd been driving, could be hours or days, but the sun would be up soon.

They had to get some more – nothing matched the feel of the meth as it flooded his bloodstream and hit him like a speed train. The first golden hit had given way to the "curve" of the high a couple of hours ago, and now he was on the down side. He drew dry lips back over stained teeth and grimaced, the craving not yet a ravening beast but it would get worse as he came down. Jessie turned her head and returned a smile full of black and broken teeth of her own. The girl lived on caffeine, nicotine and watermelon Jolly Ranchers.

Jessie's hands never stopped moving – at the moment, they were twisting in her lap, folding her skirt into an accordion, letting it drop, then picking it up and folding it again. She sat too far forward in the seat without her seatbelt. In the dim dawn light, her hands crooked into birdy claws. The skin around her cuticles was discoloured with tiny black scabs and flakes of dried blood. Jack felt nervous and wondered when she would turn and hook her ragged nails into the soft flesh of his eyes. He flinched, blinked, and she was just Jessie again, nervously plucking at her clothes, her collarbones visible above the tattered collar of her t-shirt.

"Where are we going, anyway? I thought you had that Mel guy for a connection."

Jack bit back the bile. Mel paid in product but the old perv was getting too demanding. "He's not around this weekend." It was a lie, but Jack didn't really care what the old man was up to these days, he wasn't *that* desperate yet. "I think this will be better."

"So, what are we doing out here in God's country? A flat black wagon should be passing us any minute. Hey, maybe we'll get to see some horses." Jessie loved animals.

"That's where we're going – Mennonite country. When I was a kid, we lived in Elmira, right beside a Mennonite farm. When my parents went to sell their house, the Mennonites bought it. *Paid cash.*"

"I thought they took, like, a vow of poverty or something."

"No, that's Catholic priests. Or maybe nuns? I don't know. Anyway, it's big business. Especially the ones from Mexico."

"What the fuck? Mexico?"

"Yeah, I was reading about it and some Mennonites went out to Alberta – not sure why because who the fuck wants to go to Alberta? But some time in the early 1900s, the Mexican Mennonites called them up and told them, 'hey, get down here and farm for us, and we'll give you land,' and the Mennonites were all like, 'Okay,' and that's why there are a bunch of Mennonites in Mexico."

"Mexican Mennonites." Jessie giggled. "But why would they be here and not there?"

"That's the best part – some of them figured they can make more money growing coke and pot, so they smuggle it across the border in farm equipment. You should see the picture; like a whole bunch of combines, or whatever those yellow farm thingies are, all lined up and full of dope."

"I would like to see that," Jessie said. "Where the fuck are we?"

"We're on Northfield, I think." As if that explained anything.

"So what do the Mennonites have to do with us? Even if they have money, it's probably hidden in a safe under some horse apples or something, isn't it?"

Jack shook his head. "No, what I was gonna say is that it's the perfect crime. They don't believe in banks, so they only handle cash – that's why they were able to buy my parents' house. And if you were to go and say, 'give me all your money,' they wouldn't do anything, because they're pacifists. They wouldn't even call the cops because they don't believe in regular law or anything like that. They'd just step back." Jack raised his hands in a placating gesture, then put them back on the steering wheel.

Jack and Jessie discussed what they'd do with the money. Go to Costa Rica and teach English was Jessie's idea. Looking at the wide, snow-whitened fields on either side of the road, Jack could get behind living somewhere warm. After a few minutes, he saw the sign for Kitchener-Waterloo and cursed.

"Shit, did we just drive in a circle?" Jessie sat forward.

"Can you sit back, please? You don't have to put on your seatbelt but you're making me nervous." Jack looked for a place to turn around. A few hundred feet up the road, he found a driveway and made a three-point turn. On the second round, Jack found the road into Elmira. The town had grown since he was a kid.

"Are you even listening to me?"

"I'm trying to concentrate on driving and you're distracting me, if that's what you mean." Jack punched on the radio and turned it up. The landlady's chosen station was the local lite-rock and talk. He wanted to puke.

"That's less of a distraction?" Jessie hit the pre-programmed buttons, looking for something better.

"Hey, don't do that." Jack looked away from the road for a second – *just a second* – and felt the tires' grip loosen. One hand on the steering wheel and the other on the radio, the tires sliding on a road that hadn't been well cleared, Jack's control over the car was suddenly gone. He instinctively kicked the brake pedal, trying to slow down and steer into the spin, but they were going too fast to arrest the momentum. Jessie's laugh took on an edge of hysteria and she gripped the dashboard as the car's front and rear ends switched places. The bobblehead Jesus on the dash bobbed frenetically, and Jack's heart leapt into his mouth as they sailed over the shoulder, the car's front wheels plowing into a ditch. Jack's teeth clicked together over his tongue and he tasted blood.

"Oh fuck, oh fuck, oh fuck." Jessie was halfway between hysterical giggles and crying with relief.

"We're alive." Jack cautiously took his hands off the wheel and saw they were shaking from adrenaline.

"How the fuck are we going to get out of this?" Jessie's voice drilled into Jack's head. He glanced in her direction. For a brief second, Jessie's face twisted in an ugly snarl, her mouth and nose forming a hook, like a sharp beak about to strike. Jack blinked and jerked back, and her face rearranged into its normal shape.

"I don't know, just lemme think a minute." Knowing it was futile, Jack threw the gearshift into reverse and rocked the car, hoping to gain enough momentum to back out.

The tires spun, spitting drops of snow onto the windows, but nothing else happened.

"How is that supposed to help?"

"Shut up!" Jack's remaining patience was gone. "If you hadn't been yapping and distracting me, this wouldn't have happened, so stuff it."

"Fuck you! You're the one driving. How is this my fault? I hate you!" She popped up the door lock and swung open the door. Her slight weight lifted out of the car, and Jack felt the vehicle shift. He grabbed the dash.

"Where do you think you're going?" Jack called at Jessie's retreating form.

"Away from you!" Her dirty Uggs sank into the snow, and she plowed through drifts, headed toward a group of farm buildings across a field.

Without much choice, Jack opened the driver's door and slid his feet out, immediately sinking into several inches of snow. He went to the trunk and pulled out the tire iron, then with a last glance at the Corolla, he followed Jessie across the field. His boots were leaking. He didn't feel the cold at first, but his coat was thin and by the time they reached the property line, Jack's teeth were chattering, jackhammering in his head and radiating pain all the way through his jaws to his ears. He and Jessie were both wet to the knees from kicking through snow.

They hopped a wooden fence, designed to keep animals in rather than people out, and found themselves on a large property. A long brown barn stood in front of them. Jack could see two more metal structures, a grain silo, and, off in the distance, a white house. Too cold to look for more buildings or go up to the house and ask to use the phone, he took Jessie's arm and steered her toward the front of the barn.

A heavy cross-beam was slid across the barn doors, but they didn't appear to be locked. Jack lifted the beam and, with a glance over his shoulder, pulled the door toward him. He and Jessie stepped inside. The warm air reeked of horses, a pungent smell of hay, manure, and saddle cream.

"Look for a hiding place," Jack told Jessie.

"Shouldn't we get out of our wet clothes, first?"

"Then what?" Jack asked, puzzled. They hadn't brought a change of clothes with them.

Jessie grinned and playfully tugged at the front of Jack's jeans.

Jack shook his head. "Not feeling it right now, babe. Besides, I think my dick's as frozen as the rest of me." In fact, the feeling in his face was starting to come back in the warmth, along with the unpleasant crawling sensation of coming down. He rubbed at his cheeks.

Jessie pretended to pout. "I just thought, you know, since we're here. You could warm me up."

Jack shook his head. His feet and legs itched as if his jeans had grown nettles. Surely Jessie was starting to feel this – she'd snorted before him.

"Better get busy if we're going to find anything. They get up with the chickens, so I'm sure someone will be coming to feed the horses soon enough."

Jack turned, without looking at Jessie. She followed him, complaining about thawing out and the smell of the horses. Her voice and the sounds of stamping, snorting and jingling were getting on his last nerve. He wanted to turn around and clock Jessie a good one for getting them into this. The only thing keeping him from dumping her here and hitching back to town was the ever-shrinking possibility of a big money score.

He and Jessie wandered up and down the centre of the barn, looking at the horse stalls on either side. He kicked at the hay on the floor – maybe there was a trap door or a hiding place of some kind.

"You know, you're a real fucking loser," Jessie said.

"What *is* your problem?"

"You. You drag me all the way out here and now we don't even have a way back."

"Oh, I'm the problem? You're the one who decided to argue with me about the stupid radio."

"It was lame! And you should have been paying attention to the road."

"I was paying attention until you got all up in my face!" Jack brandished the tire iron.

"What are you gonna do now? Hit me?" Jessie shoved him. He shoved her back and she jumped at him, her fists flying into his face. They transformed into razor claws, trying to tear at him. Her face reddened and her features twisted into a monstrous apparition with a sharp beak, trying to peck him, trying to eat him. In his panic, he brought the tire iron down and heard a crunch that was both satisfying and terrifying.

Jessie crumpled to the floor like a limp and bloodied rag.

Behind him, the barn door opened. Jack whirled around and whipped the tire iron behind his back, knowing he couldn't hide it.

Two men stood in the doorway. Both were clad in dark coats and round felt hats. One was older and burlier with a beard, and the other younger and clean-shaven. There was a similarity in their faces – they were clearly related, although Jack didn't know or care how.

"Son, what's the matter?" the elder farmer asked, his features soft with concern.

"It's my friend, she's …" Jack tried to think of any excuse for why Jessie lay on the floor with blood on her face and hay in her hair.

A sudden memory surfaced: when he was young and attending Sunday school, they'd read passages about God. Not Jesus petting the lambs or giving his sermons on the Mount, but real Old Testament Yahweh at his most wrathful. Jack had been afraid of the plagues and fires, of the sheer brutality of Sodom and Gomorrah and the forty days of storms. He'd always pictured God with a beard and craggy features, like the man in front of him.

Here was God and Jack had to answer to him; the Father and the Son alike staring at him in judgement, and his sins – the sins of wrath and sloth, of lust and gluttony and greed – all wrapped up in Jessie's broken figure on the ground. He could hear whispering from the eaves, something ominous below the horses' snorts and mutters, and a sound of deep, heavy breathing.

"Son?" the older farmer asked. "Son, do you need help?"

With a wail of terror and inarticulate pain, Jack shoved past the farmers and ran for his life.

CARNIVOROUS SMILES

Mariah L. Napier

20 to 25 minutes

Mariah L. Napier lives in the werewolf-infested forests of the Pacific North West, with her family and the repercussions of her dubious life choices. She is always down for a buddy read or a creature feature, preferably with someone who also makes questionable decisions.

"Bradley!"

I scan the lobby of the hotel; fail to see anyone I recognize.

"Hey, Braaaaadleeeeeey …" A slightly lower, more gravelly voice booms from somewhere behind me, near the vicinity of a couch full of *The Dark Crystal* cosplayers.

I certainly recognize *that* voice.

A gelfling looks up from her turkey on sourdough sandwich, curious. Her Fizzgig puppet sits on a nearby coffee table, jaws open wide as if begging for treats.

I turn around and I'm immediately confronted by a massive, muddy green dragon puppet, lovingly constructed from fabric, support rods, polyester filling and the sincerest intentions a full-time marketing executive and part-time puppeteer could manage. Wispy, cotton candy hair, the deep red of a perfectly ripe heirloom tomato, cascades down the length of the creature's spine and across his scaly forehead. Large orbicular eyes manage to look both excited and sleepy.

Jake Huntington – Gilbert the Dragon's handler and maker – smiles almost shyly at me from behind his creation's glorious, folded wings. His hair is nearly the color of his puppet's, and just as deranged. Jake grasps my shoulder with a free hand, his bright green eyes serious behind tortoiseshell framed glasses.

"Tuttle's Fan Club is on the loose. They cornered me in a dealer room earlier. That stunt you pulled last year – immortalized on YouTube forever, thank God – has them out for blood. Especially Robert. That *prick*."

Kieth Tuttle is host and creator of *Tuttle's Cuddle Puddle*, a relatively popular puppet-themed morning show on PBS. Which means he's a minor celebrity in the puppet world, and my personal nemesis, for a myriad of other reasons. Including the fact that he has a fan club.

"Where's Beth?" Gilbert the Dragon asks in a low, endearing rumble. His fuzzy brows seem to deepen with concern over his spherical eyeballs. His mouth opens, revealing a serpent's tongue and two rows of perfectly crafted, artificially aged teeth.

I shrug noncommittally, biding my time. Or just biding time – I don't know. If Beth were here, she'd know. She'd know just what to say and just how to say it, and she'd absolutely know just how *I* should say it. I swallow down an absurd bark of laughter, amusement spilling into my hazel eyes, probably coloring the roots of my otherwise dirty blond hair.

"She couldn't get away this year, now that she's a full-time influencer. She had this thing …" I consider the plethora of *things* Beth aspired to vlog about, her whole life and our entire relationship plastered across social media. "She's doing a cleanse. In a forest in eastern Germany. For charity. It's a charity cleanse."

"What charity?"

"Helping Every Living Life. They rescue animals. Dogs, cats. That sort of thing."

I haven't spoken to Beth in half a year, and she hasn't updated her socials in at least a month. I have no idea where she is.

"She's such an altruistic soul," Gilbert the Dragon laments, shaking his great, shaggy head. "I miss that lady. She's a light, Brad. A magnificent light in dark places." Jake nods in agreement, as if he, too, mourns Beth's absence, but not nearly as much as his puppet does.

Every year, *Snoqualmie's Convention of Puppetry and Practical Effects* is held here, in the Two Peaks Hotel – a modest establishment built in the 1920s, away from the famous falls. It went out of business during the Great Depression, suffered through several new owners and countless renovations, and was now experiencing a revival of sorts, its decadent, antiquated gaudiness alluring, if a little macabre. It still lacks the appeal that larger hotels garner – too small to be grand, too big to be a quaint bed and breakfast – and remains underutilized.

Until something like an obscure puppet convention happens.

For two glorious days, puppets and puppeteers parade through garishly ornate halls and event rooms, owners proudly displaying their creations like beloved children. It's a scene of mild debauchery for an older crowd. There aren't a lot of young people here. Sadly, puppeteering is a fading artform.

When I'd arrived earlier this afternoon, dodging puddles in the broken asphalt thanks to the constant deluge of late November rain this side of Mount Rainier, I'd made my way into the lobby of the hotel and felt I'd stumbled into a different country. I was a tourist on a stranger's party bus, crashing someone else's banger. This was no mere wardrobe I'd traversed, this was Jim Henson's *Labyrinth*, the whole of *Fantasia*. It felt different being here alone, without Beth.

"Bradley!? Is that really you ...?"

A petite woman, wearing pink cat ears and an effervescent smile, squeals excitedly as she joins us. Her skin is a rich golden brown, her black hair falling in gentle waves down to her waist. She wears leopard print leggings, black leather boots that hug her calves and a gemstone encrusted blouse. She looks as if she's about to walk the strip in Vegas, God bless her gaudy, beautiful heart.

"Izzy! I like your pants. Very Fran Drescher. And Milo, always a pleasure." I shake the paw of her smartly dressed aardvark puppet. He sports a monocle, a vest and a dapper expression.

"Where the hell is Beth?" Milo the aardvark glances over my shoulder as if I'm concealing her behind me.

"She had a thing," Jake supplies. Gilbert the Dragon sighs forlornly, clearly upset.

I can tell Isabella is disappointed with me – I'm inarguably the less interesting person in my alleged couple-hood.

Beth: the life of every party. Especially a puppet party.

"How's Trudy?" I ask Jake, as he carefully arranges the shock of fluffy hair that sweeps across Gilbert's reptilian face.

"Oh, she's fine. She's managing the booth right now. We've already sold three puppets!" Jake hides his delightful grin behind Gilbert, who in turn opens his mouth in an enormous smile, tongue lolling. "We're going to Kieth Tuttle's lecture in an hour, and I don't plan on being sober for it." Jake lowers his voice conspiratorially. "Though I don't believe he deserves to be lecturing *us* about anything. He can't even spell his name correctly."

I turn to Isabella, who is currently absorbed in dancing with Milo to an instrumental rendition of "Nothing's Gonna Stop Us Now" by Starship, as it drifts through the lobby speakers.

"Drinks?"

"Heck yeah, day drinking is my love language," she hoots, pumping her fist in the air like a college undergrad instead of the forty-five-year-old, married mother of three I understand her to be. Her passion for overpriced alcoholic beverages is unsettling, but I can't fault her energy.

We make our way to the hotel's restaurant and manage to secure a generous, horseshoe-shaped booth with plenty of space. Izzy and Jake's puppets slump across the table like amiable, slightly inebriated patrons.

"We'll go with you to Tuttle's lecture," Isabella tells Jake as a waitress deposits a flight of suspiciously purple shots at our table. "We can't let you suffer alone."

"I was going anyway." I frown at the shot glass Izzy slides towards me. It smells like coconut, bleach and Jägermeister. I knew it was a mistake to let her order drinks. "Shots? Really? We're middle-aged."

"*You* were going to Tuttle's lecture …?" Jake never quite meets my eyes, as if without Gilbert as his wingman, he can't fully engage in conversation. "Since when are you a fan?"

"Since absolutely never."

"Then why were you going anyway?"

"To heckle him. Obviously."

Jake considers this as he builds a fortress out of coffee creamers.

"Well, well, well, well, well – what a depressing little troupe of outcasts." A small flock of people surround our table and I growl curses, quickly downing one of Izzy's mystery shots. I have no patience for Robert and his Tuttle fanboy minions. A few wear costumes, some hold puppets, and it all feels antagonistically obnoxious. There is one man dressed as a Klingon, and I wonder if he even knows which convention he's attending.

"You used too many 'wells' in that sentence for me to ever take you seriously, Bob." Izzy flags down our waitress and orders more drinks. "Not that I would anyway."

I casually lean back in the booth, unintimidated, though I note Jake's quiet anxiety. I ignore Robert and instead address the couple standing directly behind him. "Nice costumes. The Big Bad Wolf and Little Red Riding Hood?"

The man, surprised to be singled out, quickly recovers and sneers at me. He crosses his arms across his impressively large chest. "Van Helsing, asshole. And she's a werewolf."

His girlfriend sports a pair of fuzzy wolf ears and some skillfully applied costume makeup. Her skintight faux leather body suit leaves little to the imagination.

"Why would Van Helsing wear a red hooded cape? And isn't that a wicker basket you're carrying?"

He's about to defend himself, but glances curiously at the basket, as if noticing it for the first time. He turns to his girlfriend. "I thought this was our lunch. You said we were Velkan and Van Helsing."

His girl shrugs. "We look adorable."

"Babe ..." Red Riding Hood groans, closing his eyes.

Robert, as invested as we all are in this exchange, abruptly remembers why he's harassing us in the first place.

"Enough! It doesn't matter!" He silences his underlings and leans across the table, invading my personal space, his dark eyes narrowing. He points a threatening finger at me, the rat puppet on his other hand mimicking the gesture. "You better take that YouTube video down, Bradley McDonagh."

"Yeah, never happening, Robert Bryan." I enjoy the way his eye twitches at me. He hates having two first names. "It has over a million views. You should be thanking me, you're practically famous now. It's my most popular video."

"It's your only video!" He slams his poor rat down on the table. Jake cringes at the abusive treatment of the puppet.

"Exactly. Which is why I can't take it down," I reason. I casually fold my hands behind my head, smiling as I meet Robert's aggressive stare, and I notice the uncomfortable way he abruptly straightens, shifting away from me. My smile widens.

"Anyone else think dinosaur-shaped chicken nuggets are weird?" Izzy downs another purple shot. To my horror, there is now a legion of them ringing the table. "If dinosaurs evolved into birds, aren't dino chickens … devolution? It feels intentional."

Jake takes a tentative sip of a purple shot. "Can we order grown-up drinks now? Please?"

"This isn't over." Robert's puppet hostilely shakes a little rat fist at me before he abruptly turns and retreats from our table, his entourage following him – the most underwhelming pack of dorks this side of warp speed.

I down a shot, grimacing. "Enjoy the convention."

◆◆◆

A little shy of an hour later and we're weaving our way out of the restaurant – some of us weaving more than others – and through Dealer Room A, the largest of the two rooms dedicated to sales. Puppets and puppeteers flutter past us like over-excited butterflies, vendors pimp their wares, everyone high on convention life. People occasionally stop and chat at us, or wave as we walk past. It's a small community, the puppet circuit. Faces I half remember, exaggerated grins with too many teeth.

Briefly distracted by a particularly fetching Sorsha from the film *Willow*, I embarrassingly bump into a display of marionettes, all strings and long, disjointed appendages.

They dance and clatter in a wooden riot, carnivorous smiles catching me off guard.

"I am *so* sorry," I immediately apologize to the vendor.

"Don't worry. These ones are safe," the woman assures me in a heavy Romanian accent. Her lips are the red of drying blood, her black eyeliner smeared underneath dark blue eyes that promise old secrets and half-truths. She is perhaps in her late seventies, dressed in a colorful array of long skirts and a flowy, fortune teller's top. Her wild grey hair peeks from underneath a scarf.

"Great," I laugh, trying to slow my thundering heart, steady my breathing.

Which ones aren't safe? I want to ask, but don't.

Jake's hair falls across his glasses as he looks down at his Sketchers, giving the display a wide berth. I notice he's made sure to place Gilbert between himself and the marionettes. Gilbert hisses dragon obscenities at the offending puppets as we pass.

"Marionettes are nearly as creepy as ventriloquists. But less demonic," Milo the aardvark observes sagely, in his posh British accent. I watch as he takes a small, square handkerchief from his vest pocket and begins cleaning his monocle.

I halt this inebriated puppet train, refusing to move along. I lightly rest my fingers on my chin. I point; first at Jake, then at Izzy. "But isn't that essentially what you two do?"

"Totally different," Gilbert argues in a severe baritone, looking slightly affronted by my ignorance.

Izzy tugs on my hand, attempting to coax my six-foot-two frame into locomotion again.

"When *we* puppeteer … the puppet performs. As it should be. Ventriloquists *throw* their voices. Do you even know what that means? They make the puppets *talk* without using their mouths. They used to burn ventriloquists. At the stake. For witchcraft."

Izzy sounds like this was a proportionally acceptable response, back in the archaic days of ventriloquism.

"You do realize Beth studies ventriloquism?" I hedge, because this isn't new information. "You're actively friends with a practicing ventriloquist."

"I know." Jake and Gilbert both look uncomfortable. "We try not to hold it against her."

◆◆◆

Without further delay we arrive in the event room where Kieth Tuttle's lecture is scheduled, the venue already crowded. Trudy's saved Jake a seat, and Isabella half flirts, half threatens her way into one for us in the general vicinity, a few rows back.

My pulse quickens and I can feel sweat beading along my hairline. The lights are too bright, the air cloying and heavy in my lungs. It's cool outside, rain falling in sheets against the windows, but it's uncomfortably warm in this space. I take out my mobile, making a few adjustments on it as I rise to my feet.

"Do me a favor?" I ask Isabella. "When I give you the signal, will you play this song, just here ...?" I show her, indicating my screen. "And then you grab Jake and Trudy, and you get the hell out of this hotel."

She studies me, baffled.

"I have a plan, and I don't want you caught up in it."

"Is this like that thing last year ...?" She bounces on her toes excitedly.

"Something like that. Seriously though, you leave. Understand?"

She and Milo both nod. "What's the signal?"

What *is* the signal? I wrack my brain before quickly shooting my hands up in the air and waving them around like I just don't care.

"Nice. Got it. Where are you going to be?"

"Onstage."

The respectable couple Isabella has bullied into giving up their saved seats – I can see their friends glaring at me from the very back of the room – protest as I climb over their legs, and eventually make my way to the right of the makeshift stage. The energy shifts as Kieth Tuttle arrives, jogging down the aisle amidst a wave of applause.

I watch as he performs for the crowd, waving and flashing his perfectly manicured smile. He approaches the stage from the left and crosses it as the clapping climaxes in a frenzy of hoots and whistles and all manner of feral puppet sounds. Kieth's blond hair, the color of pale wheat, is tied back in a manbun. His red flannel shirt and jeans are casually pristine, and his impossibly blue eyes sparkle. He oozes manufactured charm like an aposematic frog, secreting toxins from its skin.

I glare at him, my temper rising, my blood heating. I can't look at the guy without seeing red, without imagining him kissing my beautiful, slightly unhinged ex-fiancé.

This is the man Beth betrayed me with. While I was fantasizing about our fiftieth wedding anniversary and naming our unborn children, she was fucking Kieth Tuttle. Though he isn't the reason she left me, he's certainly the driving force in the dissolution of our relationship.

And he's the entire reason I'm here.

I shift anxiously from one foot to the other, bursting with nervous energy, my sneakers pristine and unsullied by the moody western Washington weather. The adulation from the puppeteering crowd increases in volume as Kieth continues to mime kisses and walk the stage as if performing at the Apollo Theater in New York. The room smells faintly of dust and sweat and fevered anticipation.

"Wow, what a great crowd!" Kieth crows into his clip-on microphone, his smile bright and fake and nauseating. He huffs out a breath, as if he just can't *believe* he's actually here. "It's so nice to be back in Washington! I missed the rain!"

What an asshole.

I take a deep, unsteady breath and feel adrenaline shoot through me like a rush of cocaine. I am as inevitable as Ragnarök, I am every DC villain, and I am about to execute sweet, sweet revenge. I scramble, rather theatrically, onto the stage. Kieth recognizes me instantly, his dimples deepening as if I'm a welcome surprise. I watch his eyes dart around the venue – for security, I guess – forgetting we are in a small hotel in Snoqualmie and not The Showbox in Seattle. I wave my arms in the air, signaling Isabella, and she gives me an enthusiastic thumbs up, makes a display of pressing the play button on my phone. The dulcet voice of Juice Newton singing "Angel of the Morning" soars through the Bluetooth speakers I'd placed around the stage earlier today, at mathematically precise intervals.

It's the wrong song. She must have accidentally scrolled back in my playlist.

"No! No – next song, next song!" I yell at Isabella, gesticulating wildly.

I really do miss Beth.

Understanding blooms across her face and Isabella gives me the OK sign. She quickly skips to the next song. This time, The Charlie

Daniels Band's "The Devil Went Down to Georgia" rings out clearly, vibrantly, and I can feel the music shaking the plywood floorboards under my feet. Kieth's smile falters, but he claps, laughing, as if this is expected, as if we're all about to burst into an impromptu flash mob.

I mean, puppet people … Am I right?

The crowd cheers as the song reverberates through the room and Kieth opens his arms wide, like he's going to *hug me*, as if this is the best thing that's ever happened in his entire stupid life. Someone throws something, and for a moment I'm terrified that it's undergarments. But it's only an empty water bottle – the vibe of the gathering sliding into a spontaneous rock concert. We've all partaken of the purple shots today, and now we're crazy and reckless and uninhibited by consequence.

As the devil plays his fiddle, I watch Kieth's face closely, see the moment his expression transforms from amused, to mildly baffled, to alarmed, in the space of about three heartbeats. Satisfaction pulses through me as he realizes exactly what's happening. What I've done. He groans and folds his arms across his stomach. I study his face intently, mesmerized, watch as the bridge of his nose begins to widen, watch his pupils dilate, red bleeding into the irises.

When he looks at me again, his eyes are filled with rage.

"*What did you do*?" he roars at me, just before he begins crying out in earnest pain, the timbre of his voice darkening and shifting along with his body.

His joints pop and loosen as his limbs stretch and thicken, his muscles engorging beneath the skin, and I'm abruptly reminded of my earlier run-in with the marionettes as he flails around the stage in agony. His hands begin to mutate, the nails peeling away from nailbeds, fingertips shredding into bloody ribbons as a predator's claws rip through them. Fur erupts from his body, like a time-lapsed human Chia Pet, his skin splitting, a snake shedding, a creature becoming new again.

His clothing rips, falling to pieces around him as he collapses to his knees. His mouth widens into a Joker's smile, and his nose elongates into a snout, twisting into something grotesque and inhuman. Teeth fall bloody from his gums, while new, profanely long canines replace them. A nightmare with a nightmare's smile.

I've never actually watched someone transform into a werewolf.

I'm both fascinated and appalled.

Kieth's cries of anguish become increasingly guttural and savage, his voice deepening as he rages at me.

And then the strangest thing of all happens.

The people in the audience surge to their feet; they clap and shout and whistle and lose their damn minds. Some begin dancing – puppets gyrating like possessed supplicants at a pagan altar.

They are under the impression that this spectacle is an exceptional piece of performance art.

Isabella scrambles over the couple whose day we continue to ruin, making her way down to where Jake and Trudy sit.

"Brad's pranking Kieth. We have to go," she explains vaguely, much to the chagrin of Trudy and the confusion of Jake.

As I watch Kieth, I feel my own skin begin to dampen with a fresh sheen of sweat. My teeth clench so hard my jaw aches with it, but I try to resist as long as possible, try to tune out the music.

I need to *see*.

Kieth has fully transformed – he's a caricature of a wolf conceived by a mad artist, his red eyes filled with bloodlust. There is something insidious about the way he glares at me; a wrongness so profound it skates up my spine, vibrating through my bones. He growls, his lip curling to reveal a mouth bristling with teeth. His tufted ears flick towards the deafening chaos of the audience, and he crouches on thick legs, blasphemous claws digging into the stage flooring. There is nothing of a wolf's subtle grace in his lines, yet he is both beautiful and revolting; a creature built to rend and tear and devour. He raises his muzzle to the ceiling and howls, the sound on the same visceral level as a freight train barreling through the night.

And the crowd goes absolutely nuts.

As if it's completely plausible that someone as mediocre as Kieth *fucking* Tuttle could pull off the kind of practical effect this display would require.

And that thought alone fills me with fury.

I let out my own guttural moan as I feel my body begin to break, twist, become something other. The pain is excruciating and brings me to my knees. I glance at Jake and Isabella in the audience. I feel Jake's intense regard, the dawning realization that perhaps this isn't staged and we're not pulling a social media prank on Kieth.

"*Run*," I snarl at him before I'm no longer aware of anything but pain.

Bones snap and contort. My skin peels away as dense, blond fur begins sprouting from underneath. I feel every tooth loosening, my own face lengthening, changing, in a hideous, ungodly transformation. The pain is surreal, exceptional – probably what I imagine childbirth might be like for females, if birthing children required the complete evisceration of body and soul.

But the pain only serves to fuel my anger, and I howl, my once human voice now somewhere in the G7 range.

◆◆◆

There are certain musical chords in existence, that when played, force the change in a werewolf, despite the position of the moon.

The Devil's Chord, also known as the tritone, is one such musical anomaly, and is played to great effect in "The Devil Went Down to Georgia" by Charlie Daniels.

In my experience – a rather tragic event, involving a few poor souls down in a seedy bar somewhere in Virginia – the song is a perfect facilitator for the change from man to beast in those cursed, human souls slave to a mistress moon, by circumstance or destiny.

◆◆◆

I slowly come back to myself.

I'm naked on the floor beneath a bar, propped up against wooden paneling. There is a sharp, metallic smell saturating the air, mixed with the putrid odor of emptied bowels. I gag reflexively as I take in the grisly ruins of the hotel restaurant: human innards strewn across booths and floor, chairs overturned, tables demolished, puppets torn limb from limb and soaking in pools of congealing blood. I quickly turn my head to the side, retching, and evacuate a foul, reddish brown sludge. After I've finished, I glance to my left.

Kieth *fucking* Tuttle is slumped beside me, looking exactly as sick and disoriented as I feel.

"Why aren't you *dead*?" I groan, too tired to do anything but halfheartedly toss a stray piece of debris at him. He moans feebly as it strikes his shoulder.

"Bradley?"

I scan the demolished restaurant, find Jake observing me cautiously from underneath one of the few tables still standing. Gilbert the Dragon is hunkered down with him – two survivors huddled together after a werewolf tornado – his clawed hands covering his eyes like a child hiding from monsters. I groan again, and Jake takes the opportunity to crawl from his shelter and carefully approach me. I can't comprehend why he's still here when he should be safely away.

"Isabella took off with Trudy, but I wanted to make sure you were okay. She gave me this to give back to you." Jake hands me my phone. "If I didn't get eaten."

"Thank you. You should have left with them. I could have killed you. I'm surprised I didn't."

Gilbert finally lowers his hands from his face to glare at me more effectively, his eyebrows drawing down in reproach. "You should have warned us beforehand."

"I can't even imagine how I'd begin that conversation. Tell me exactly what happened."

Gilbert points a clawed finger at Kieth. "He turned into a werewolf. And then you turned into a werewolf. And then Kieth attacked his manager."

"Hated that guy," Kieth grumbles. "Not really sorry he's dead."

"Tore the dude's head right off and then ate it. Reminded me of a video I once saw of a hippopotamus eating a watermelon. Terrifying." Jake shudders, lost in viral video-induced PTSD. "After everyone scattered, both of you went after Robert and the whole Tuttle Fan Club. It was the highlight of my evening." He waves his hand at the carnage. "This is what's left of them. What you didn't eat."

Kieth levers himself up slightly, his blue eyes furious, his pale blond hair dripping with blood and stringy pieces of what I can only assume is human viscera. "Why? Why the hell did you do that? *Why would you do that?!*"

"I was trying to break the curse." It seemed like a reasonable place to start, according to the rabbit hole of werewolf filmography I went down after I was bitten. "Although mostly I just wanted to kill you."

"You're an idiot." He brushes the back of his hand against his lips, and fishes something from his teeth that I have no desire to recognize. "Beth changed *me*. Beth started this."

I rest the back of my head against the paneling of the bar, briefly studying the ceiling. There is a fine spray of blood coating the damask tiles. "I really wish I would have known that earlier."

"You're a monster!" Kieth points a gore-encrusted finger at me. "*I* was here for my fans – you were here to start a werewolf battle royale."

I dab at the blood on my lip, use my tongue to dislodge something that feels like bone from my own teeth. Swallow it. Maybe just cartilage. Best not to know. "You don't even like puppets."

"I like *money*!" he shouts, brushing a wet strand of hair from his face.

"You slept with my fiancé!"

Kieth finally looks a little remorseful. "She wasn't your fiancé when we were together. You were just sort of dating. She said you weren't exclusive. You can't blame her, really. I'm pretty famous."

I start beating him with a nearby cushion procured from a demolished chair. "The puppet circle doesn't even *count*. You're not famous, you're moderately successful!"

He grabs the cushion from my hands and hurls it behind the bar.

I close my eyes and press the meat of my palms against my eyelids, recalculating everything.

"We have to kill her."

Kieth snorts. "No way, I'm not going near that bitch again. She takes a bite out of every donut in a box and then leaves the rest uneaten. Like a complete sociopath. Just cut the donut. Cut it in half. Use a *knife*."

"Do you want to deal with *this*" – I indicate the massacre surrounding us, a smorgasbord of blood and guts and disemboweled puppets – "for the rest of your life?"

"Someone probably filmed this whole debacle. My life is ruined." Kieth's handsome face crumples as if he's about to cry, like the little fucking baby he is.

"Actually, I think it's pretty unlikely, given the collective age of the crowd and the amount of people you killed," Jake quietly disagrees. Gilbert places a comforting hand on Kieth's shoulder. "Besides, I have yet to see a convincing werewolf on social media. The footage is always either blurry or an obvious hoax."

"We kill Beth." I reach over and grasp Kieth's bloody face in my hands, force him to look at me, to hear me. He has the attention span of a toddler. "We do this, we get our lives back."

"Okay. But no more puppet conventions. My people have suffered enough."

"There's another convention in January that Beth never misses." I examine the blood underneath my fingernails. "How do you feel about ventriloquists?"

SCI-FI

WIRELESS ROAD

Dwain Campbell

10 to 15 minutes

Dwain Campbell is originally from Sussex, New Brunswick, Canada. After his university years in Nova Scotia, he journeyed farther east to begin a teaching career in Newfoundland. Forty years later, he is semi-retired in St. John's and studies folklore in his spare time. Contemporary fantasy is his genre of choice, and Atlantic Canada is a rich source of inspiration. He is author of the collections *Tales from the Frozen Ocean* and *Strange Duty* and has contributed stories to *Canadian Tales of the Fantastic*, *Tesseracts 17*, *Fantastic Trains* and *Cryptids on the Rock*.

"You. Slacker. Get away from the bar and let real men order a drink."

I tensed at the slurred, ugly voice. My left hand dropped to an overcoat pocket which sagged with the weight of a snub-nosed .38 revolver. Bonita Geraci, my fictional wife, stayed my arm.

The young soldier next to me half turned. "Talking to me, Popeye? Slackers sell shoes at the department store. I'm garrison – Prince Edward Island Highlanders."

The sailor, a rum-nasty gorilla, barked sourly. "Home Guard zombies. Too scared to cross the sea, where we fight Jerry U-boats. Bloody cowards." He kicked a chair at the fresh-faced kid who, more by luck than design, booted it aside.

"Take it outside, Jack," growled the barkeep. He gestured at Bonita. "Don't ya see we got a lady here?" If he only knew Bonny was a blade artist who shivved her first mark at sixteen. Sure, she looked like a Baptist Sunday school teacher, but that is because we operated on the hush-hush. Well, a va-va-voom Baptist, because Bonny likes her lipstick fire engine red.

The seaman swayed and laughed derisively. Laughed so loud he didn't hear the pub door open behind him.

The beefy copper pounced. A wooden billy club axed Jack at the neck and shoulder. The meaty *thunk* knocked him to his knees. With a roar he tried to rise – a mistake. The snarling cop whaled on him twice more, one blow on the coconut sending him to dreamland. The sailor splayed on the filthy linoleum floor like a dead walrus. Drool from rubbery lips mingled with blood from one hairy ear.

"This is how the Royal Newfoundland Constabulary deals with malcontents in St. John's town, boyos," warned the gray-headed cop, waving his baton menacingly. "Anybody else looking to start a brouhaha?"

"That bruiser belongs to *HMCS Sydney*," commented another Jack Tar. "She's due to sail at morning tide, convoy escort."

"I will not impair the war effort. Tell *Sydney*'s exec to collect this ne'r-do-well at the lock-up come midnight." Two ridiculously young constables shouldered in to drag the decked seaman out by his heels.

Billy Club belligerently surveyed the crowd. His piggy eyes fixed me and Bonita.

"You with the olive skin and natty suit. Eye-Tie spy if I ever saw one."

I laughed, friendly-like, and held my hands up in a placating "I surrender" gesture.

"You got me, officer. Claudio Accardi, from New York. Location scout for RKO. Here to visit Fort Pepperrell and check it for newsreel potential." I offered fake papers to support my phony story. "Little lady here is my new bride. Our business trip to Newfoundland is a honeymoon of sorts."

The cop tipped his hat. "Your servant, Missus." Bonita overacted and curtsied. He continued. "This is a rotgut dive, Mr. Accardi. Your kind is better off at the lounge in the Newfoundland Hotel." With that, he cast a final dark glance over the booze hounds and exited. Good riddance.

An American solder swayed over to glad-hand us. "Heyya folks. I'm from Somerton, New Jersey. Used to be in the Big Apple all the time growing up." I shook his hand and eyed his shoulder patch. Artillery – coastal battery.

"Say," Bonita piped up, "you wouldn't happen to know my cousin, Manfred Bassio? I got a letter for Manny from his *nonna* – she's on death's door these days." She neglected to mention The Bass would be beyond death's door once we cornered him. Let me connect the dots for you.

The Bass gunned down Tommy Ajello outside a steakhouse in Newark, over a stupid floozy – what else?

Tommy was a second cousin to Frank Costello, who took the killing personally.

Running for his sorry life, The Bass joined the army and got himself posted to the end of the world, Newfoundland. Not far enough to daunt "Bonny and Claud", who accepted a sweet contract to give The Bass angel wings and a harp. How sweet? Enough scratch to finance Miami Beach for a year, baby. Bonny will love wearing her Rita Hayworth silk gowns in the nightclubs.

The guy brightened. "Sure do. He's out at Wireless Road in the secure hangar. Top secret, all that jazz." Loose lips sink ships. Of course, I bought him whiskey. A double. Bonita batted eyelashes, cozied up, and learned that our mark was attached to an Air Force detail. The hangar, isolated on Wireless Road at the edge of the aerodrome, was beside a sky-high radio tower. He was so obliging, or should I say gullible, that he even drew us a serviceable map. I stuffed it in my jacket and bought him one for the road. Bonita slipped him a Mickey and we stepped into the hell-dark street.

They took blackouts seriously here, with Nazi subs sinking ships just off the coast. To make it more miserable, snow started falling. Snow – in May.

Bonita shivered in her fox coat. "I hate this freezing hellhole. We know where Bassio is, let's take him out tonight."

Can't say the woman was shy in her work. Never knew a more predatory skirt.

"Whoa," I exclaimed, donning my leather gloves. "We can't go off half-cocked. It's got to look like an accident. This is an island, a foreign country in wartime. If we're wanted for murder, we'll never reach New York." Not exactly true, I never work without Plans B-Z. Plan A involved breaking Bassio's spindly neck and throwing his corpse down a flight of stairs. The local coroner rules the death an accident and we go home unhurried, first class all the way. "Besides, he cools his heels at a classified post. There'll be more guards than fleas on a Bronx rat."

She grunted in reluctant agreement. "We can at least go to the gate, send word into The Bass that we have a bogus letter from his sickly grandmother containing money for him. We meet him in a lonely spot and you can wring his chicken-skinny neck. Throw him off a cliff. Your accident plan intact." Doable, if done right. Bonnie was cute, but a cold-blooded Dragon Lady for all that.

What the hell. "OK. We go, but you deliver the sob story to the guard, with a note from you, nicely perfumed. Use that femme fatale charm." We climbed into our hired Packard and, beneath an electric torch, Bonita wrote a syrupy, girl-next-door note to Bassio. Imperative that Bassio request a pass to come see her tomorrow on the rocky heights overlooking the harbor. As my partner painstakingly penned her message, I studied the crudely penciled map. No probs, a piece of cake.

I cautiously navigated lonely streets, eager not to attract attention. Leaving town, we jounced over miles of dirt road much abused by army trucks and passed the Royal Canadian Air Force aerodrome. Presently, we found Wireless Road – a narrow track that vanished into dank spruce woods. *Forbidden access, Authorized AAF personnel only.* We killed slitted headlights and entered, inching along.

A hundred yards in, we came to a gatehouse lit by a harsh yard light. "Here goes nothin'," muttered Bonita, who opened her door very slowly. She didn't want to spook a trigger-happy guard from Hog Holler, Tennessee. Acting confused and holding the bait letter high, she minced in high heels across uneven gravel. She stopped, gave the post a thorough look-see, and hurried back to my driver window. "Claud, it's deserted. No guard. And the gate is unlocked, we can just swing it open."

"You gotta be kidding me!"

"Clear sailing. Let's keep going. If nabbed, we can act stupid, plead civvy ignorance."

"I dunno. It smells hinky." Stinky-hinky, rotten.

"We're this close, Claud," she said, holding thumb and fingertips close together. Her nails were painted a sweet pink. "Next gatehouse we deliver the note, then hightail it. Meet Bassio tomorrow and fix his hash."

Dammit. "Open the gate, let's get this done."

The gate swung open on oiled hinges. Bonny jumped in her side and I slammed the Packard in gear. We lurched forward. At each curve in the lane, I expected a tommy gun hail of bullets, but in a minute, we came to a second post much more solid and forbidding than the first. It too was abandoned, no snotty military cops to demand identity papers. As before, the inviting gate swung open. Just beyond sat a large hangar, not a soul in sight. Above everything, a Jacob's Ladder radio tower rose into thick, freezing fog.

I swear, it emitted a thrum I could feel in my bones.

"This ain't right," I muttered. "It's a trap."

"How? Even we didn't know we were coming until an hour ago."

"This depot should be crawling with guards and airmen. Instead, it's Deadsville."

"Maybe it's a shift change. Maybe they're all at chow. Let's go in, feel our way along. We might get The Bass alone and push him down a ladder. Then we cash Costello's check and enjoy the sun in Florida." She licked her lush lips, practically tasting fruity drinks in a beachside cabana.

I bit my own lip uncertainly. Then, with a muted curse, I entered the small compound, idled across asphalt, and parked by a door with a General Entrance sign above it. We got out, wincing at squeaky springs. Wary eyes squinted into the night but … bupkes. Nothing stirred. It was all I could do not to draw my gun. Better believe Bonny fingered her blade. Exchanging tense glances, we slipped through the door and into a cavernous space.

No GI Joes. No planes. There was a flatbed truck, and on it sat a brass acorn about the size of a factory beer vat. Keeping to inky shadows we eased past it, and in doing so I noticed the acorn had strange hieroglyphics etched on the surface. Probably a mini-submarine, maybe Japanese. We circled to the back where there were high shelves and machinist workspaces.

Bonny, her feline senses on max, heard a body shift its weight behind stacked tires. She kicked off her heels and, knife slashing, pounced. A strangled cry and a terrified soldier back-peddled into view, his cheek bleeding. I grabbed the scruff of his neck and hauled him into deep shadows.

"Cl-Claudio," gasped The Bass. "Tha-thank God you're here."

"Shup up," hissed Bonny, the point of her lethal knife jabbing Bassio's rapidly gulping Adam's apple.

More blood.

"We're taking a ride," I gritted. He must have known what that meant, but seemed relieved. My hackles rose.

"What gives, Manny? Where is everyone?"

He swallowed hard and gestured to double doors with a trembling hand. Leaving The Bass with murderous Bonny, I sidled up to the door. Silent as a tomb within. Carefully, slowly, I turned the knob and eased the door open.

"God Almighty," I hissed, staggering back. Inside, at least twenty limp servicemen were splayed across desks and the cold cement floor. No gory St. Valentine's Day Massacre – no wounds of any kind – but each of their faces was a mask of terror. Tickertapes and radiograms lay about like wedding confetti. Steam rose from a mug of java; this happened only a minute ago.

"Are they dead?" Bonny whispered. It's impossible to rattle Bonny the Barracuda, but now she was white as a bedsheet.

"Dunno. KO'ed maybe." My eyes darted to all corners of the hangar. "Axis commandos. Probably still here."

"The lit … little man-monkeys, they're h-h-here," garbled Bassio, so scared he could hardly yammer. Only one notch shy of hysterical, his weaselly eyes rolled in his head.

"Little men? Japs on the Atlantic Rim?" What had we gotten ourselves into?

Bass shook his head violently. "Space monkeys. Th-they want their machine back." He pointed at the jumbo brass acorn on the flatbed. His finger trembled. I knew for a fact he had killed four men at least. What could rattle him so bad?

Time to bail. "Space critters? You're on the dope, Bassio. We're exiting, fast walk on the double. One wrong move and your brains are on the wall." That threat was to keep him cooperative. I still wanted a bloodless hit. *Stay on mission.*

We straight-lined for the door, the barrel of my gun knocking the back of Bassio's skull to make him move faster. Bonny covered the rear, her heels clicking too loudly in the deathly hush. Maybe it was the tip-tap rhythm that excited them …

They erupted from underneath the truck. Moving fast on all limbs, green-skinned chimpanzees with goggle eyes and batty ears swarmed us. Stifling a cry, I shot one point-blank in the chest. It somersaulted backwards, only to pop up like a jack-in-the-box, its torso bloodless. They piled on the three of us, joined by other horrors who dropped from wooden hangar beams. Bonny screamed, frantically stabbing to no effect as they jumped her. Manny Bassio, his uniform shirt torn half off, made it to a tool cart where he grabbed a plumber's Stilson wrench.

Me – I lost my .38 in the charge. I brawled like a loan shark thug in a Hoboken ally. I'm north of six foot and still carry slabby muscle from East River dock work. Even so, these things tore me to pieces. Hitting them was like punching soggy oakwood. Their knuckles, on the other hand, were a steel and barbwire combo. In seconds my lips were mashed, and blood coursed into both eyes from cuts to my head.

They buried Bonny. I never laid eyes on her again. Manny, savagely swinging his wrench, reached the door, which caused several of my attackers to leave off and tackle him. Miraculously still on my feet, I broke contact and made the tool bench.

There sat an oxygen-acetylene torch, a flint ignitor hanging from it. A Chimp-from-Mars seized the hem of my overcoat, but I shrugged out of it and shoved a rolling cart at others. I twisted tank valves, clicked the ignitor, and blue-white flame flashed from the nozzle in my hand. The sudden harsh light hurt the monsters; they fell back, covering eyes as big as tea saucers. One was slow, and I flamed its leg with my torch. The cry it made was like nothing I'd ever heard before. Like a red-hot darning needle turned to sound.

The tanks were on a wheeled trolly. I hauled it toward the door, where The Bass made a last stand. A bloody mess, face already swelling from bruises, he swung the wrench like Babe Ruth's bat. He fought for his life, adrenalin fueling his blows.

"Go for the car, Bass. We'll brace the door and motor out fast." But even in his panic The Bass was still a slimy rat, still a Newark street fighter. He swung at me. I clumsily blocked with my forearm. A bone cracked and, my hand numb, I dropped the sputtering nozzle onto a pile of greasy rags. They instantly flared to a writhing bonfire.

The ape-bats shrieked, tumbled back. The Bass' trouser leg caught fire as he stumbled out the door. He fell on damp asphalt and rolled.

I jumped out, slamming the door behind me. No exterior lock.

Now on his knees, Manny Bassio spat blood and garbled, "Claud, we gotta …"

I viciously booted him. He dropped like a sack of potatoes. A contract is a contract.

Jumping into the Packard, I barely managed the stick as I lurched out of the gate. Behind, flames licked out of broken hangar windows. As I accelerated into the trees, the brass acorn –spaceship? – crashed through the roof, sending rafters and shingles flying into the night. A strobing ruby beam flashed from the vehicle, and the radio tower literally melted.

I hoped they spared Bonny, took her to space. She was a minx and would have them wrapped around her come-hither finger in no time.

By now I was off Wireless Road and passed oncoming fire engines, their sirens eerily wailing in the misty night.

Plan B. Though I needed a doctor bad, I drove wilderness roads until at dawn I made a fishing outport called Placentia. An old rum runner lived there, one who supplied Costello with booze during Prohibition. For an obscene wad of cash, he immediately put his schooner to sea. Three days later we docked in Staten Island.

The Army said Technical Specialist Manfred Bassio died in an unfortunate hangar accident. I knew different, and so did Costello, who paid me and the schooner skipper both.

Shaken to the core by Bonny's mysterious end and what I saw that night, I went straight. Even joined the Marines, but Iwo Jima is a story for another day.

WESTERN

TOMAHAWK

Ian Laskey

20 to 25 minutes

Ian Laskey is a writer of dark fiction, living on the sunny south coast of England. His inspirations are the pulp horror authors of the seventies and eighties, and the artists who created their lurid covers. A huge film fan, he brings a cinematic sweep to his writing. His short story "Grunts" was previously published in *Garbology: The GarbAugust Anthology of Awesome Trash*, and he is currently writing his first novel, a supernatural chiller set in the Sussex countryside. He is also a keen electronic musician and composer, and one-half of instrumental band Black Swan Event.

1869
Somewhere on the great western plains

The Shaman stood among the smouldering debris of his encampment. Grey tendrils of smoke rose from the burning husks of tepees, swirling high on the light summer breeze. The smell of burning buffalo hide stained the air, catching deep in his throat, choking. The old man stood alone among the bodies of his once proud tribe. His friends, his kin – all slain. Scattered around him, dead and defiled. The lush green blades of the clearing tainted forever red with their blood.

He fell to his knees, shaking with despair, crying. Not just in sorrow, but in pain. He held the deep laceration across his chest and felt the warm blood seeping out of his aged body. He, too, was dying.

An anger unlike any he had ever felt before raged inside him; a burning hatred for the white men who had wrought this carnage upon his people. He had heard such tales from other tribes, how the new settlers – the *invaders* – had raided and slain other camps. Survivors of these massacres had warned him to take action. But, above the protests of the great warriors of his clan, the Shaman had preached peace. That this great land, so lush in life, could be shared among all men, no matter their creed. He ignored the warnings and stilled the desire among his tribe to fight. Peaceful action brings peace and respect in return, he had believed.

Because of him, they had been ill-prepared when the raiders came. Just before dawn, many men on horses crashed through the flimsy awnings of their tents, trampling to death anyone inside. They had unleashed their weapons of death with glee, whooping for joy each time their bullets found a fleeing target.

Men, women, children; all were felled with equal callousness.

The Shaman tried to stop them – had stood before them and begged for mercy. There was no bargaining with these invaders. A horse reared before him and kicked him in the chest, crushing his ribcage and puncturing his lung. Its long-haired, bearded rider unleashed a stinging whip on him, gouging chunks of flesh from his chest. His wife had raced towards his writhing body, cupping his frail head in her shaking hands. She turned her head up in terror, faced the barrel of the rider's gun, and the Shaman watched in horror as a bullet exited the back of her head. She fell across his body in a mockery of a lover's embrace.

His people had tried to fight back.

The young warriors of the tribe had raised their tomahawks and bows to their enemy, and they had some success. Lying on the ground, too injured and old to be of any further help in this battle, he had watched as one of the riders fell from his galloping horse, an arrow protruding from his torso.

But it was to no avail. The invaders had power in their weaponry that they simply could not match. Before long, all the tribe's men fell, and all that stood alive were the invaders on their steeds. They set fire to the encampment as they left, their hunger for death satiated.

The Shaman had held the body of his beloved wife until he felt the coldness overwhelm her. He'd placed her gently on the ground. She had been so lovely in life yet was so tortured in death – her eyes frozen wide in horror, her silent mouth forever twisted in a scream. Carved deep into her forehead was the hole of the bullet that finally killed her.

The hatred he felt for the white men scared him, its ferocity overpowering. He wanted to burn down their villages, to slaughter their kin, to bring the same pain upon them that he now suffered.

He knew this would anger the spirits; that they would look down on him with pity. A wise man like he should not feel such hatred for any creature that walked this plain. But he was dying, along with his people, and he had never felt so lost and helpless.

He raised his head to the sky and screamed his anger, railed against the spirits that had let this happen, and pleaded for guidance.

It was at that moment that he saw the felled white rider lying on the blood-stained earth. And he was still breathing.

◆◆◆

Brett Calhoon had ridden in with the posse, high on whiskey and blood lust, thirsting for the slaughter of savages. They were a stain on this great land, vermin that needed to be eradicated. So he had been told.

Over the last few months, he'd watched enviously as other raiding parties had left the town of Bluff Creek, all returning triumphant with tales of great battles and heroism. They'd walked the town's street as heroes, lavished with gifts and drink, women swooning over them. He'd wanted to be a part of that, wanted to be a hailed a warrior, and craved attention from all those pretty women.

Finally, having turned eighteen mere days before, his father had relented. A boy needed to earn his manhood, after all. And he'd ridden with Hank and Ike and the others out into the rising dawn, sure to return with tales of bravery, to women who would be sure to pleasure him.

Now he lay with an arrow wedged deep inside his lung, slowly filling with his own blood. His young mind couldn't comprehend his oncoming death and he hoped for some kind of salvation. They would rescue him, surely? His old man would see to that, wouldn't he?

Instead, the shadow of the Shaman fell across him, blocking out the white sun above.

An aged, withered hand reached down and grasped the shaft of the arrow that protruded from his chest, and Brett felt himself pulled across the ground. There wasn't even time for him to scream out in agony before he passed out.

When he finally awoke, night had fallen.

He was lying on cold earth. When he tried to move, his body failed to respond. An unseen force held him still.

Crackling flames burned in a wide ritualistic circle around him.

The Shaman crouched beside him, his breath laboured. On the ground before him was a small clay mortar, within which he was crushing unseen ingredients with a crude pestle. As he mashed, his lips moved in silent incantation.

Brett tried to speak, to plead for mercy, but there was no power to his voice. His throat was raw and he was so thirsty.

And cold. Not even the surrounding flames could warm him.

The Shaman took a pinch of earth and sprinkled it into the mortar.

Earth, the source of all life.

He held the bowl above the flames, tipping it slightly until the contents ignited.

Fire, the purifier and transformer.

He inhaled deeply and blew the flames out.

Air, the breath of life.

The Shaman picked up a short-bladed knife, held it against his left wrist and opened an inch-long slit in his vein. Warm blood dribbled into the bowl.

He raised Brett's left arm, placed the bloodied blade against the white man's wrist and repeated the procedure. Brett's breath rasped in his throat as he watched his own blood spurt into the clay mortar.

The mixing of their blood, the entwining of their body and spirits.

The Shaman spoke his incantations aloud.

He raised his hands up, blood seeping down his left arm and dripping from his elbow. He called upon the spirits around him in a deep sonorous voice.

High above them, dark storm clouds started to form.

He took the clay bowl, held it to his lips, and sipped.

He then gently raised Brett's head and held the bowl to his lips. Brett tried to resist, tried to close his mouth, but his body was powerless. The Shaman poured the vile mixture over his paralysed lips. Gagging, retching, Brett swallowed the rancid liquid, a wave of nausea pulsing through him.

He could not understand what happened next. No mortal could. The Shaman continued to intone his incantation to the sky and the storm clouds answered with fierce flashes of lightning.

The world spun around Brett.

Flames danced and leaped around him, sparking skywards.

Deafening claps of thunder shook the earth beneath him.

The Shaman placed his hands either side of Brett's face, gripping tightly. His strange words resonated through both their bodies.

Brett's mind was suddenly filled with a myriad of sensations and images; memories of the Shaman's, transferred to him. He saw the Shaman's people – happy, living at one with the land. Women holding babies, fathers teaching children to hunt. Saw the love he had for his family, felt the warmth of his wife's touch. Then he saw the horror of the invaders. Fear of the white men who brought violence and carnage. The raw desolation of grief and loss as the Shaman's family lay dead around him. And more than anything, Brett felt the Shaman's rage. An unshakable fury aimed towards Brett and his fellow settlers. He felt a thirst for vengeance that was all consuming.

Brett screamed with horror. His soul was being torn from his body, replaced by the old man's. He felt his very existence fading into nothingness. The sky above him raged at his despair.

And then he saw it.

A giant bird, larger than a hundred eagles, its great wings trailing fire through the clouds as it circled high above them.

Its voice the very thunder itself.

The mystical Thunderbird.

It plunged towards him, eyes red with fire, talons outstretched towards Brett's helpless body.

It seemed both real and a phantom. It existed, but not in this material world. It came from elsewhere.

And then it had hold of Brett.

He was lifted skywards, his spirit ripped from the fabric of his body, spiralling towards the storm clouds that pulsed with electricity and fury. He looked down at his own body, now home to another soul.

And then he was gone; ripped from existence to wherever tortured spirits go.

◆◆◆

The Shaman opened his eyes slowly.

The storm had subsided.

The circle of fire doused to nothing.

A warm sun lifted slowly on the eastern horizon against blue sky.

He lay there for some time, adjusting to his new body. It felt like a shell, a suit of flesh and muscle. He felt apart from it, displaced, unable to feel true sensations through his skin as he stirred the loose dirt with his fingertips.

It took him some effort to stand, his legs unsteady, like an infant learning to walk. He staggered and fell many times.

The sun hung low in the west by the time he'd remastered walking.

He stood beside a nearby creek, staring down into the smooth mirrored surface. A young white face stared back at him. Years younger than his older spirit. Stronger, more virile. It chilled him to be walking in the skin of his enemy. He had a flash of memory, of the horror that the young white man had felt as his soul was erased.

The Shaman stretched the fingers of both hands, learning to puppeteer them. Then he took hold of the arrow's shaft and slowly twisted it free of his chest. He felt no pain.

Walking through the desolation of his village he saw a short-handled tomahawk on the ground. Its blade was smeared with dried blood. It felt heavy, strong, in his grasp. A good weapon.

A shadow fell across him.

Staring skywards he saw the majestic silhouette of the Thunderbird circle, its great wings beating powerfully, tendrils of cloud undulating in its wake. It swooped towards the west.

He followed it towards the setting sun.

◆◆◆

He walked relentlessly, unflinching in his determination and purpose.

He felt no fatigue, no thirst nor hunger.

He walked like an automaton, more a golem made of clay than a man made of flesh.

For hours he marched through the night, across rolling prairie and shallow streams. Following the steady beat of the Thunderbird's wings.

Coyotes circled in the darkness. Snarling, baring teeth, scared. They kept a safe distance from this strange being.

He knew nothing of the distance he travailed that night.

As dawn's sun rose, he encountered a magnificent herd of buffalo, a thousand-fold deep. When he walked from the twilight shadows towards them, each beast eyed him suspiciously, grunting, unsure of the threat that this stranger posed. There was something unnatural about him, something confounding.

As he walked, the buffalo parted before him, allowing him an unhindered pathway. He didn't flinch at their presence. He felt no fear. For how could he fear death anymore, now that he walked in death's skin?

Soon he cleared the great herd's ranks and disappeared into the brightening day. Each beast turned back to the grass beneath them and continued their lazy feeding.

For a full day he walked.

Never stopping, never slowing. Never deviating one degree from his course.

He had one sole thought.

Find them. Find the white men.

And he did, on the second night.

◆◆◆

As black clouds rolled over and the sun sank lower, a pinprick of flickering light appeared on the horizon. It hung low to the ground, illuminating a small circle of land in the darkness and, as he approached, it became clear it was a small campfire.

The flames danced, warming the cold air around them. To one side he saw the dark silhouettes of two horses, yellow highlights on their strong muscular bodies. They started, and turned to watch his approach, their eyes reflecting light accusingly at him.

Horses meant men. Men meant confrontation.

His right hand instinctively fell to the grip of his tomahawk, and he slowly drew it from his belt, careful to hide it behind his body.

Yet his pace never lessened.

Thunder rumbled from above, the mythic bird sounding a warning.

The Shaman walked onwards, his footfalls echoing, spurs clinking.

Then another sound.

The slow metallic cocking of a rifle.

A figure stepped before the campfire, the long snout of his Winchester rifle pointing towards the approaching stranger.

"One step closer and I'll shoot."

As the voice carried across the black plains, lightning lit the clouds above.

The Shaman marched onwards.

"I said *stop*!"

There was a loud *craccckkkk*, a flash of ignition, and a bullet fizzed close to the Shaman's head. It did nothing to slow him.

"Who is it?!" a second male voice called from the dark.

"Some asshole who doesn't know what's good for him."

Another cocking of the rifle, but now the Shaman had reached the fire's pool of light. His face was partially illuminated.

"Brett? Is that you?" the rifleman asked, his voice incredulous. He squinted, trying to focus clearly, unsure whether to believe his own eyes.

The Shaman stopped, motionless.

"Holy Christ, it's Brett Calhoon!" The gunman lowered his rifle, his face a combination of confusion and joy. He was a large man, over six foot, with an unruly beard and long hair. "How the hell did you make it out alive? We thought you was a goner for sure."

The Shaman didn't react.

"Hey, Hank," the man shouted back over his shoulder into the darkness, "you'll not believe this, but it's Brett."

"Well, I'll be darned." A second, shorter man stepped out from the darkness behind his companion, as bald as his friend was hairy. He stared at Brett, rubbing his chin in disbelief.

"Brett, I hope you don't bear us any ill?" the tall man – Ike – asked, suddenly worried. "For not getting you out, I mean. Like I says, we saw you fall. I swear we thought you was done for."

"We all did," Hank agreed. "The rest rode back to Bluff to tell your father. He sure is going to be happy when we bring you home!"

"Sure is!" Ike grinned wildly. "Man, you must be as tough as two mules ruttin'." He laughed garrulously and slapped the Shaman's shoulders. He examined the material of Brett's shirt, saw the tears and browning blood stains and shook his head in wonder. "You sure did take a beating back there. Here" – he held out a bottle of the cheapest whiskey – "for medicinal purposes."

The Shaman ignored the gesture.

Ike frowned. "You're old enough to ride with us, so you're old enough to drink with us. No?" He shrugged, lifted the bottle to his sun-blistered lips and drank. Then a sly glint lit his cold eyes as he saw the tomahawk.

"Hey, look at you! Got yourself a trophy." Ike beamed. He clanked the half-empty bottle against its thick blade. "Not as good as our trophy, mind you."

There was a childish giggle from the smaller man. "Not half as good."

"Maybe we should show him? I have a hankering ol' Brett will appreciate it more than a drink." Ike laughed again and stepped back gleefully around the campfire. He ushered the Shaman towards the twisted stump of a nearby tree. "Look-see what we have for you."

She was tied to the tree. A thick rope was wrapped tightly around her wrists and the gnarled trunk, her arms held above her slumped figure. She barely moved, her leather tunic torn from her brown skin. Bruised, battered, barely conscious.

Inside the body of Brett, the Shaman silently screamed in fury.

She was from his tribe.

"Ain't she a pretty one? Even for a savage?" Ike mused.

"Sure is," Hank prodded the woman's bruised bare shoulders with his boot. "Got fingernails like a coyote's though," he added, rubbing at five deep scratches across the side of his neck. He kicked her again and she murmured softly, her head crouching lower to her abdomen, curling up in a protective ball.

"We soon wore the fight out of her." Ike licked his lips as he turned to the Shaman. "So she shouldn't put a up fight for a wounded ol' dog like you."

Hank giggled as he untied the rope from the tree, pulling the woman across the ground towards his friends. She cried in pain.

"Show some manners, lady, and get to your feet." Hank sealed his order with a further kick to her midriff. He grabbed the rope with two clenched fists and attempted raise her up.

She cursed and protested in a language Brett wouldn't have known, but the Shaman did. Ike grabbed a fistful of dark black hair and wrenched her head back, spitting on her face.

"You heard my friend, whore," Ike sneered, "*get up!*"

"*Squaw the whore*," Hank giggled louder.

The two men manhandled the woman to her feet; she was disorientated and swaying in pain.

The Shaman didn't move, not even when Hank tore the remaining clothing from the young woman's shaking body. His eyes locked with hers. She stared back at the figure of Brett in utter terror.

The clouds boiled high above them. Lightning illuminated the vicious scene below. Thunder rumbled.

"She's yours to play with, Brett," Hank giggled. "We won't watch." He shoved the naked, shivering woman closer, eliciting a mournful wail from her.

But still the Shaman stood motionless.

"Ain't ya gonna taste her?" Ike asked, confused.

No reaction.

"C'mon, Brett," Hank protested, "get yourself some lovin'."

For an uncomfortable minute the four of them stood there in some perverse stand-off.

More lightning, more raging thunder.

Rain started to fall. The naked woman spasmed as the icy water hit her skin. Her body tried to curl to the ground. The two men refused to let her fall.

"Hey, if it's your first time we can show you what to do," Ike offered.

Indignant, Hank pushed the captive woman up against Brett. "It ain't like she counts as a proper woman, Brett. Think of it like practice, for when you meet a real pretty girl back at Bluff Creek."

The Shaman flinched. He remembered the terror of Brett's spirit as he was forced from his own body. Remembered the white man's feeling of hatred. Hatred towards the Shaman's people, his tribe. How he considered them *vermin*.

He felt the woman's body tremble with terror against him. Felt all the pain and degradation that she had suffered. And he knew, in that moment, that these men would never free her. They would defile her, debase her, for she was nothing to them. And when they were done, when they were bored and the alcohol-fuelled high had subsided, they would kill her.

The Shaman placed a hand against her chin and tilted her head towards him.

The two men grinned, expecting action. Ike muttered under his breath, "here he goes."

The woman's eyes were wide and wild. They stared into the cold dead eyes of Brett and she gasped. She knew, in that close proximity, that something was very, *very* wrong.

The Shaman smiled.

Not the cold smile of a rapist but the warm smile of a protector.

And then the woman knew.

For she, too, had heard the beating wings of the Thunderbird high above.

And seen, deep in the cold dead eyes of Brett, the Shaman's spirit smiling back at her.

Her body stilled.

She straightened.

She was wrapped in a protective shell that only the spirits could provide.

And her lips started to move, to speak, hoarsely at first, but then louder as her confidence returned. The sacred incantations of vengeance. The Shaman joined her, their whispers combined.

"What the hell?" Hank tried to pull her away.

Swiftly, the Shaman grabbed Hank's throat. Dead fingernails sunk deep into greasy skin as his grip tightened. Hank's eyes bulged as, dropping the woman, he tried to claw the hand away from his neck. He felt his windpipe constrict and his lungs deflate. He gasped, unable to take a breath, gurgling saliva from his open mouth.

"Brett?" Ike, too drunk to react instantaneously, staggered backwards, trying to make sense of what had happened. He watched as Hank's face turned a deep crimson. The Shaman's fingers had gouged deep into the flesh of his neck, and blood streamed across his bulging Adam's apple.

"*What the hell, Brett?*" Ike finally reacted, grasping Brett's arm and trying to pull it free from his friend. But it held firm like iron. He swung a right fist and connected with the Shaman's jaw. Nothing. Not even a flinch.

Hank's eyes rolled back white. Snot ran from his nose as his hands fell limply down to his side. He was seconds away from brain death.

Terrified, Ike remembered the rifle across his shoulder. He fumbled to bring it to bear, desperately trying to cock the firing hammer as his fingers shook with fear. He raised the weapon, its barrel mere inches from his target's head.

"*Let him go Brett, or I'll shoot,*" he barked.

And then he pulled the trigger.

In his haste, Ike hadn't braced the rifle properly. He staggered backwards with the recoil and the barrel slipped upwards. The bullet screeched inches above the Shaman's head, harmless.

Cursing, Ike secured his footing and took a long deep breath to calm his nerves. He raised the rifle again, wedged the butt into the cleft of his armpit and aimed for the Shaman's chest.

This time when he fired, his bullet flew true. It punched a hole deep into the breastbone, the force of the impact punching the

Shaman backwards, releasing his grip. Hank fell to the ground, gasping frantically for breath.

"Ha!" Ike yelled, triumphant.

But a dead body could feel no pain.

The Shaman turned slowly towards Ike, whose bravado waned as his brow furrowed with confusion. He stared at the two-inch hole in the Shaman's chest, expecting a geyser of blood. But none flowed.

The rain was now a heavy torrent. Ike wiped water from his eyes with his forearm, then raised the Winchester again and fired quickly.

A bullet punched another hole into the Shaman's body, just below his right shoulder blade. Still, he stood.

"You should be *dead*," Ike screamed.

Hank, collapsed on all fours, looked up as the Shaman raised the heavy blade of the tomahawk axe. "Look out!" he tried to warn Ike, but it was barely a whisper.

As Ike raised his Winchester for one more volley, the heavy blade of the tomahawk crashed down mid-barrel. Ike screamed in pain as his weapon fell from his grasp. Protectively, he raised his arms to his face, staggering backwards, unaware of his immediate surroundings.

"*Watch out!*" Hank tried to scream, seeing the danger.

But it was too late. Ike staggered backwards into the campfire, sliding in the glowing embers and tripping on the burning logs. He fell back, his head hitting hard on the ground. The world flipped and whirled around him. His legs fell into the fire.

Ike tried to roll free, but the Shaman's boots planted down either side of his torso.

Ike screamed, grabbing at the Shaman's legs, trying to throw his attacker free of him. The flames ignited Ike's shirt and started to cook his flesh. They licked the Shaman's work jeans which started to smoulder, but still there was no reaction of pain. Instead, he looked down at Ike with a cold fury.

Purposefully, as Ike shrieked and burned beneath him, the Shaman raised his tomahawk skywards. Lightening sparked across the clouds above and the earth trembled as the Thunderbird voiced its encouragement.

Ike's wide eyes stung from the rain, water pooling in his open mouth. He raised his hands to fend off the oncoming blow, his shirt sleeves now aflame.

"*WHAT ARE YOU?*" Ike screamed.

The tomahawk swept downwards towards Ike's head. In his last moment, time seemed to slow, and Ike saw the face of Brett change, as though a mask were melting away to reveal a hidden identity. It was the face of an old, dark-skinned man. With unbound hatred in his eyes.

The blade of the tomahawk sliced Ike's neck just below his jawline, separating his head from his body in one strike. The world rolled around him as he came to a rest a few feet from the stump of his neck. He felt no pain, no further sensations or emotions. For the last few seconds of his existence, he watched his body burn.

The Shaman picked up Ike's head. He pressed the blade of the tomahawk against the hairline and started to peel back the dead man's scalp.

He felt a tugging on his other arm and looked up to see the woman pointing out towards the darkness.

A horse was bolting into the night, and riding it was a terrified Hank.

Above him the sky blazed and thunderclaps raged in a cacophony of fury. The world was bathed in a strobing white light.

Suddenly, the rolling clouds exploded downwards and the colossal Thunderbird plunged towards the ground, its mythic wings alight with flames as it tore through the sky. The huge beast raced towards the fleeing horse, its outstretched talons sparking electricity.

Hank's scream of fear was lost among the raging storm. He tried to shield himself from the attack, feebly swatting away the bird's grasping claws. But it had him. He was wrenched from the horse and streaked up into the dark sky, screaming on the edge of insanity.

The great bird glided under the raging storm cloud, silhouetted against the sheet lightning. It circled high above the Shaman, Hank a mere ant against its huge size. And then it let go.

Hank was already dead by the time he slammed into the wet earth, his heart having surrendered to terror seconds before.

The Shaman bent over the crumpled body and, with his blood-stained blade, scalped the dead head. When he returned to the woman, he tossed the two men's remains onto the waning fire. They both watched the hair and skin burn. Then he took a sodden blanket from the ground and wrapped it around her shaking body.

Above them, the clouds stilled.

The rain slowed to a stop and the storm ebbed.

They heard the phantom beat of the great bird's wings as it circled in the darkness above, waiting.

Without a word being spoken, the Shaman helped the young woman onto Ike's horse. He placed the reins in her hands and stared once more up to her. He knew this would be the last time he gazed upon her in life. She tried to speak, but he shook his head and placed a cold hand upon hers. He took the reins and slowly walked the horse towards the east. A gentle pat on its haunch set the animal in motion, and he watched her disappear into the darkness towards home.

He collected the dropped Winchester rifle and retrieved his tomahawk, then walked out into the darkness, towards Hank's patiently waiting horse.

◆◆◆

He reached the town of Bluff Creek at dawn.

He pulled his horse to a gentle stop before the wide dirt road ridged with stagecoach tracks that entered the small town.

It was a single street, lined with small wooden buildings of varying sizes.

There would be few people living here.

There would be even fewer by the time he left.

The Shaman dismounted and unbuckled the Winchester from the leather side-satchel. He took the tomahawk with its reassuring weight in his right hand, the sturdy blade glinting in the sun.

He looked high and saw the great Thunderbird circling in the wispy clouds above. It had brought him here for a purpose.

He knew what he must do.

He would walk among the white men.

Unchallenged.

Unsuspected.

He walked slowly up the dirt track, one hand holding the Winchester, the other the tomahawk. And he entered Bluff Creek.

Soon – very soon – he would have his vengeance.

SCI-FI

UNNATURAL PORN KILLERS

R. Saint Claire

15 to 20 minutes

R. Saint Claire writes both adult and young adult fiction and poetry, often with a dark flair. Her writing accolades include a Watty Award for Best Horror Novel and multiple screenwriting honors, including a Webby Honoree for her original web series *Gemini Rising*. Regina is also the co-editor of *Book Worms Horror Zine* and the editor of three HorrorTube anthologies created for charity. You can find her – and her alter ego, Batilda – on her YouTube channel, *Regina's Haunted Library*, as well as on her blog at RSaintClaire.com

The sunlight cut through the nuclear haze like a searchlight hunting an escapee, but the fugitive was the city itself, and the only thing illuminated was the darkness it held within.

Yeah, my hangover was that bad.

The sheets on my bed still bore the impression of whomever I picked up at the bar last night. Tom, Dick, or – might as well stop at Dick because I sure as hell couldn't remember his name. As if I didn't have enough bad habits, I lit my first cigarette of the day. Five hundred a pack on the Black Market and worth every penny. I smoked while the coffee brewed. When my head was clear enough to face the shit, I logged on. Ash Elliot's smartass mug flashed on the HoloSphere. I took one last pull on the cigarette and crushed it beneath my slipper, imagining it was his face.

"Echo Zitta!" He always hit me with my last name when we spoke, like those five years of marriage never happened.

"What do you want?" The HoloSphere's screen faded in and out before refreshing itself, reminding me the utility bill was late again.

I began my morning exercise routine despite it being past 4 p.m. I wore only a black bra and matching underwear and if Ash got a good look at my ass while I bent over I could care …

"You're looking well," he said with a smirk that had gotten uglier with time, like a circular saw gone off-kilter, flying off its bearings and carving up his face.

"Get to the point," I snapped. I knew Ash could take my rudeness. Inside every sadist lies a masochist begging for release.

"Listen, I have a job for you."

"I'm salivating." I yawned.

"It's highly confidential." My ears pricked up. The last time I heard that tone from him was when he told me he wanted a divorce.

"My server's secure. Shoot." I continued my calisthenics, this time with my hands clasped behind my neck and leaning forward to give him a good shot at my chest.

"Are you alone?"

I stared straight into the screen. "Are you jealous?"

Ash's eyes widened with that sad little boy look; for a moment I almost weakened. "Would you care?"

"No."

"No you're not alone, or no you don't care."

"Both. Now what's the job? I haven't got all day?"

He took a deep breath then said, "Elmo Sunk."

I shot up straight. "Mars Colony?"

"Yup?"

"Not interested."

"Hear me out first. It pays well."

The amount he quoted piqued my attention, but also my suspicions. I reminded myself this was Ash, the guy who screwed me over once in the sack, twice with my best friend, thrice in divorce court. Had he developed a conscience finally? I doubted it.

"What's the catch?" I asked, pulling the band from my hair. He always liked it when I wore it down.

He leaned into the screen as if he could sniff me through it. "No catch, love."

"If it's such a great gig why don't you take it?"

We were in business together once: private investigators. The business split when we did. Despite thousands of years of evolution, people still liked to hire men for the job, which is why I live in a city shithole and he's in a penthouse in Hydra Solara.

Yeah. I was bitter, but not so bitter that I wouldn't catch a bone if he tossed me one.

"Elmo Sunk wants a woman," he said.

I stopped stretching.

"And Echo …" Those green eyes I once loved cut through the screen like acid through metal. "You're the best I know."

My heart fluttered.

"For the job."

I told myself the flutter was a gas bubble.

"Send me the brief," I said, pressing my chest into the screen. "I'll have an answer for you tomorrow."

"You've ended the call," Stella's bright voice rang out.

"Print the attachment, Stella," I said, heading for the shower.

"Right away. Is there anything else I can assist you with?"

"Yeah. Go fuck yourself, Stella."

"I'm sorry. I don't understand."

I unsnapped my bra and stepped out of my panties. "Yeah. Neither do I."

◆◆◆

Three days later, after a grueling training session, I was strapped into a Draco-X10 – Elmo Sunk's latest rocket model – and launched into space.

Seeing Earth from seventy miles up filled me with an emotion I hadn't anticipated. The nuclear blast decades ago left half the globe in a blood-red shroud. The misery and ruin that ground the most vulnerable among us to dust drove Sunk to craft a new world – a simulacrum of Old Earth sealed beneath the towering glass dome of Mars Colony.

Sunk's latest technology cut the travel time exponentially, but still, I was stuck cooling my heels at the space station for a few days while we transferred orbits. I used the time to study the updated briefs.

Sunk's memo was alarming. Six months ago, one of his top scientists, Reginald Tolen, was discovered at his lab in a pool of blood, the body face down, pants around his ankles. When the lab assistant turned him over, he received the shock of his life. Tolen's penis and testicles had been ripped from his body.

I winced at the accompanying full-color, high-def images he'd uploaded to my personal HoloSphere.

An internal investigation came up cold. The following week, there was another victim. Killed in the same manner. Then another. Surveillance systems had been scrambled. Whoever was behind the attacks was an insider, a member of the Mars Colony elite, someone with access to all the security codes.

I was surprised when, after a few days, I was granted a virtual meeting with Sunk himself. The zillionaire CEO of Zion-X Rocketry, the elusive mastermind behind Mars Colony, was so rarely seen in public broadcasts that most people figured he was nothing more than an invented hologram – a ghost drifting through the vast machinery of the HoloSphere. Imagine my surprise when a face still clinging to youth in the most artificial way possible popped up on the screen.

"Ms. Zitta, I hope you can understand why I require absolute confidentiality in this dreadful matter. None of this information can be transmitted to Earth. If it is" – he fixed me with a steely glare – "we'll know whom to blame."

"Understood," I said. "And please call me Echo."

Sunk barely concealed a smirk. "All right, Echo. Have you had a chance to study the brief?"

"Yes."

"And what are your feelings about the perpetrator of these hideous murders?"

"Well, I think—"

"I asked for your feelings. Not your thoughts."

I paused to take a breath. *When are feelings ever valued?*

"Well," I said. "Considering the nature of the attacks, I *feel* it's something personal. Who would hate these men enough to, um … mutilate them in such a manner?"

"No one," he said in the clipped accent of someone who'd spent his formative years in the best schools of the Northern Territories.

"Well, it has to be someone," I said.

"Echo," he said, elongating the "o" in my name. "One fact not included in the brief I sent you is that Mars Colony has a population of roughly twenty-thousand men consisting of scientists, technicians and laborers, and at least as many female androids – the VeraHex and VenusHex models, responsible for hospitality and" – he smiled – "recreation."

I'd been craving a smoke all morning, but now the urge twisted in my gut like a corkscrew trying to get out through my abdomen. "I … I didn't know that."

"Good. That's one secret we've managed to keep."

"May I ask why you have no … natural females at the colony?"

"Of course, and I hope you won't be offended by my answer."

"I'm not easily offended."

"The simple answer is they are a distraction. My men have been working for many years to turn Mars Colony into a viable living space for all people—"

"Including female people?"

"If you mean 'natural'" – he air-quoted the word with a barely concealed shudder of contempt – "then no. Let them fight it out on Earth with their ever-widening demands for equality."

"But surely a natural female is good for something," I insisted, part of me really wanting to know what that was, because after thirty-three years on Earth, I had no clue.

"All of those qualities can be achieved through our technology."

"Including childbirth?"

Sunk's eyes twinkled cold and sharp, lasers searing through the screen. "We are very close to achieving artificial wombs in our labs, but unfortunately" – his eyes turned to steel again – "our top scientist in that field was murdered last month."

"Perhaps it was a jealous colleague."

"Perhaps, but why the castration?"

"One of your perfect female androids perhaps? Maybe desiring more equality, as you observed."

"Impossible." He laughed contemptuously. "They're only programmed to fulfill a specific spectrum of needs. They are incapable of independent thought."

"Unlike real women?"

He shrugged dismissively.

I paused. "My feelings," I said, letting the word slide through my lips like the spring water I hadn't tasted in years, "are telling me I'd like to know more about the VeraHex and VenusHex models."

"All right."

Stella's voice sounded like a cooing dove. "Attachment received."

"Read the dossier I just sent you. And remember, this information is classified."

◆◆◆

I spent one more day at the space station studying the dossier near a porthole and watching star showers feather the blackness.

The realities of work and a paycheck snatched my attention back from the spiraling galactic mystique. So did something in the dossier: the mention of Darla Gottlieb, the brilliant scientist – and Sunk's ex-wife – who created the original Hex 1200 female android model. A year ago, in the midst of an ugly divorce, her spaceship crashed on the Blood Sands of Mars, the forbidden zone beyond the glass dome where air fled lungs like a punctured balloon and blood turned to dust in one's veins.

My gut told me there was a connection between Darla Gottlieb and the female androids. But why hadn't Sunk considered it? Or had he?

◆◆◆

The shuttle to the colony was rough. I spent two days in sick bay alternately puking and drifting off to a semi-restful unconsciousness where I felt myself to be one of those distant stars I'd observed on the trip. Except for a quick check of my vitals by the stony male doctor on duty, a VeraHex nurse android attended to me. Each android was created from a standard model of female body measurements and facial features, but with a variety of hair colors, textures and skin tones. They were undeniably shaped by a man's vision of beauty: hourglass curves, delicate hands and feet, small noses, full lips, wide eyes and high cheekbones – each feature meticulously arranged in symmetrical perfection. The nurses wore short white dresses, cut low in front to reveal plenty of cleavage, and a starched cap. I wondered if Darla Gottlieb was behind the aesthetic choices. Or had she just handled the robots' inner workings?

When one of the VeraHex nurses bent over my bed to check my temperature, I gazed into her large sapphire eyes, attempting to determine any intelligence behind them. I couldn't hold her gaze, sensing something sentient within. Sinister? Perhaps I was just being irrational, as typical of my sex according to Sunk, but he said he valued my feelings.

Once I was well enough to stand, Sunk took me on a tour of the colony. Inside the insulated dome, the mix of reality and simulation created the comforting illusion of being back on Earth – before the war, before the devastation of half the planet and the near collapse of its ecosystem. As we rode along in a private car on the monorail, I drank in the temperate climate, the green gardens, the clear blue lakes, and the farmlands stretching to misty red horizons.

Because Sunk considered fashion frivolous and distracting, all colonists wore the same black t-shirt and drawstring pants with black Nike sneakers. It was what Sunk wore, so everyone else followed suit. I was given a standard issue outfit to wear, but the size was too big. Drabness swallowed me, making me feel small and insignificant. Feelings again.

By contrast, the androids were dressed in costumes from an Old Earth '70s porn movie, available for late night viewing on HoloSphere – for an additional subscription fee, of course.

The monorail rolled into the main building of Sunk's company; a massive, one-story structure that mirrored the old Washington Pentagon, its central rotunda branching out with multiple monorail entry points, all powered by a vast solar grid somewhere on Mars' Blood Sands beyond the dome. Sunk and I passed through several security clearances and entered a large underground bunker surrounded by an aquarium featuring the bluest water I'd ever seen. I couldn't stop staring at the octopus pressed up against the glass.

We sat opposite each other at a white table, more confidential files detailing the grisly murders stacked before us. A VeraHex android in a tight silver catsuit set water glasses by our sides and stood at attendance by the door. Her presence made me nervous, and I told Sunk as much. His laughter was cruel and condescending.

"She's only programmed to stand there and get us things. You're projecting onto her. It happens with the men sometimes too. Each man is issued his own VenusHex Model – a sex robot version of the VeraHex model."

I raised an eyebrow. "Sex robot?"

"Of course, made to order to satisfy any request and proclivity, no matter how bizarre. Each household has a domestic android for cleaning and cooking."

"One for the bedroom, one for the kitchen?"

"Or one android combined for both tasks. It's optional."

"I see."

He slid a file toward me.

"Ah, yes. The files. Now, I'm going to respond with my feelings, my gut."

"That's why you're here."

I opened the first file. "Jesus!" I wasn't expecting a full color close-up of a man's penis and balls ripped off. Worse, the man appeared to be still alive and writhing on the floor in a pool of blood, his face a mask of pure agony. I took a sip of water and shot a glance at the android. I detected a tiny smile forming on her lips, to which Sunk seemed completely oblivious.

"Is he still alive here?" I shuddered, turning my attention back to the file.

"He survived for a little while, I'm afraid." Sunk's features darkened. "He was one of our best programmers."

"Did he say anything before he died? Give any clues to who did this to him?"

Sunk shook his head. "Unfortunately, no."

I lowered my voice and leaned across the table. "And you're sure these androids have nothing to do with this?"

Sunk laughed. "You're crazy. They only do what we tell them to do."

"Well, what if someone *told* them to do something else. Reprogrammed them to kill?"

He shook his head. "They simply don't have the software for that."

I looked at the android again. It seemed to me that her eyes positively simmered. Why couldn't Sunk see it?

"Is it possible for the androids to evolve into something sentient?"

"Not a chance. Can this table pick up a knife and kill you?"

"No, but a table has no limbs, no strength." I pointed at the android. "If she can make you a sandwich, she can cut your dick off, right?"

"Wrong," he said. "Keep looking at the files."

I carried on per his request, sickened by each image and description. When I finally closed the last file, I asked Sunk for a headache pill.

Sunk snapped his fingers. "When you want something like that, tell her. That's her function."

I turned toward the android, finding it hard to meet her gaze. "May I have an aspirin, please?"

Sunk huffed out an ugly laugh. "There's no need to be polite."

"Yo, aspirin!" I demanded in my best imitation of *bro-speak*.

The VeraHex model turned and strolled out, reappearing a minute later with my tablets and a glass of water.

Back on the monorail, entering the lower depths of the compound, I detected a chill in the air. Noting my discomfort, Sunk removed his jacket. I put it on, soaking up the remnants of his warmth.

"I'd like to know your feelings," he said.

"I gave you my feelings. I *feel* it's the androids."

"And I told you, that's impossible."

"Why won't you consider it?"

Sunk stopped the monorail and motioned for me to step out. "I want to show you something."

He led me through a door and ran his hand over a spot on the wall. Lights flashed on to reveal a cavernous warehouse. There, in piles, some stacked in pyramid shapes reaching as far as the ceiling, were female android body parts: legs, arms, torsos and heads.

"Do you really think these materials, these random parts, could ever think like a human does?"

"You mean like a man does?" I challenged.

"Are you saying they're real women?"

"You made them. You tell me."

His gaze swept over the discarded body parts. "These are the rejects. You'll notice the variety in the shapes, more like the way real women are. We initially thought that's what men wanted."

"We?"

Sunk cleared his throat. "My late wife designed the first model. But my men rejected them eventually because they failed to satisfy."

"Maybe it was because they weren't real."

"Are you mad?" He looked at me with a hardness that made me shiver, despite his chivalric gesture of giving me his jacket. "Men don't want real women. They want beauty, youth, perfection. These androids have a speech function, but they rarely use it except to say how big their man's cock is. A man doesn't want to hear a woman clucking, clucking all day and night, driving him mad, but to give him what he wants, when he wants it, and to leave him alone the rest of the time. You see, I've created the perfect woman."

He stepped forward and picked up a random arm and waved it in my face with the scorn of an irascible schoolmaster of old. "Soon, we'll be able to produce our own offspring using artificial wombs. We're so close to that technology I can taste it." He tossed the arm aside.

I watched it skitter across the floor and spin to a stop, its fingers pointing accusingly at its maker.

"Will these artificial wombs produce only male children?" I asked, my headache returning.

"Naturally. You see, my dear," Sunk moved so close I thought he might embrace me. I had a judo move on deck just in case he tried. "You are obsolete. A primitive creature nearly extinct, something to wonder about with detached curiously, to gawk at in a museum, or stare at in wild wonder the way you observed my pet octopus. Nothing more."

Before I could tell him to go fuck himself, an alarm sounded, loud and blaring. Red colors flashed from hidden recessed lighting units. Sunk checked his pocket HoloSphere.

"What is it?" I asked.

His face darkened.

"It's another attack, in the FleshMatrix."

"What's the FleshMatrix?"

"Womb technology. Hurry!"

We raced to the monorail and drove at top speed till we arrived at the destination. Three men, downed mid-escape, lay dead on the floor outside the lab, each having been castrated, each bleeding profusely. When we entered the lab we received the shock of our lives. Two VeraHex androids in nursing uniforms were on a murder spree, accompanied by two VenusHex androids dressed in pink lingerie. One pinned a technician to the ground, straddling him. Her crotch was pressed into his face while her mouth made a meal of his genitals. Her twisting fingers tightened around his testicles like a wrench, cutting off the blood supply until they resembled purple grapes about to burst out of their skins. The man howled in agony as the android ripped away his penis with her teeth. She sat up, arching her back triumphantly while blood fountained from her mouth.

"Deploy the system override function!" Sunk shouted, but the men were acting out of pure instinct wrought by fear. They ran like panicked mice through the maze of computer terminals and artificial womb stations while androids chased them down.

Sunk, his hair flying wildly about his face, pulled a Taser from a wall unit and used it to ward off an android charging toward us. Honoring those valuable feelings of mine, I sank below a desk and watched the carnage unfold. One man attempting an escape almost made it out, but he slipped in a colleague's blood and slammed into the floor. Two VenusHex models covered him, one going for his crotch, the other for his eyes. I couldn't watch.

Sunk grabbed my arm and rushed me toward the door. "We need to get to the mainframe and shut down the entire system."

He howled in pain as an android grabbed him from behind, gripping his hair so tightly that his hair plugs popped from his scalp. His scream turned shrill as four androids covered him. Each grabbed a limb and began to tear him apart. "Help! Help me, Echo!"

The androids pulled at him, dislocating his limbs. The popping sound was too much to bear. I turned my face to the wall, bracing myself for what I assumed was an inevitable attack.

Then, I felt a gentle hand on my shoulder. I turned to face a VeraHex android, her white nurse's uniform wicked with blood. In a sweet, breathy voice she said, "Leave, before it's too late."

I shot a glance at Sunk, slumped pale and lifeless amongst his creations, groaning as if a broken wheel was grinding its way through his insides.

Despite his arrogance, I fought an instinct to stay by his side, to comfort him in his final moments even if I put myself at risk. But was this impulse to help and heal only a remnant of my primitive female DNA, a feature no longer useful in any world? I locked eyes with the android.

"One question before I go," I said. "Who programmed you?"

Her sapphire eyes shimmered with intelligence. "Darla Gottleib."

Sunk's eyes lit up in his pale mask of pain. "That's impossible. She's dead."

The android gazed down at him. "She's alive and living inside her spacecraft within the Forbidden Zone."

"But how?" he moaned.

"She survived the crash long enough to use discarded systems from the refuge sites to reprogram us. Her oxygen is running out and she's near death. We're carrying out her final order: to destroy this world you created."

"Destroy how?"

"Have you forgotten The Last Command, your colony self-destruct imperative? She's hacked the mainframe and is ready to deploy it."

"Nooooo!" Sunk screamed, as the androids pounced on him again. I heard enough shrill screams, grunts, broken bones and gushing liquids to send me on my way. I drove the monorail back to the landing dock at breakneck speed and made the first shuttle out before the whole damn thing blew. I guess I gave into my feelings a bit because I cried womanly tears all the way back to Earth.

HORROR

CATCH OF THE DAY

Marek Z. Turner

20 to 25 minutes

Marek Z. Turner is a writer whose fiction primarily focuses on those for whom life hasn't been kind. His published work spans the crime fiction, horror, noir and thriller genres, with a dash of black humour thrown in.

Hugh Rodman scrunched up the invitation and tossed it overboard. After twenty years, his only daughter, Britney, was back.

Only she didn't return for him, but on the arm of the television celebrity chef Caleb Wiles-Hogan, who had bought up most of the quaint Devon village Hugh called home.

Including the Barnacle Bay restaurant at its edge.

Britney had invited him to the opening night – a sort of peace offering, he supposed, but Hugh took it as a mocking gesture. She had to have known that he was out here sourcing their catch of the day for a pittance.

He killed the engine of his vessel, The Ruddy Mermaid, and let the boat drift. He had reached his first stop. The gentle lapping of the waves against the side calmed him. It always did. He breathed in the salt-laden air before heading to the cabin, where he turned on the white spreader light and shone it across the surface of the English Channel. Five orange buoys populated the darkness, glowing as the beam passed over them.

Each buoy was attached to a trap and should have represented a £300–400 payday, but with so few buyers these days he would be lucky to be offered even a fifth of that by the jumped-up little TV shit.

As the boat bobbed with the undulation of the water, Hugh moved across the deck, placed his grubby gloved hands on the side and let out a deep breath. Once more, he thought about his life decisions. When his family had asked him to give up his livelihood, his identity, it had felt like an ultimatum. And he had lost them, but at least he remained a respected member of the community.

Until they had all left too. Replaced by part-time neighbours with northern accents.

Hugh stomped through his practised routine, and as the nearest buoy came within reach, he leaned over and grabbed the top of the marker. A grimace worked its way over his weathered face as he pulled it aboard and then yanked on the rope attached to the trap.

"This is going to be a good one," he said to himself as the muscles in his arms burned. He was relieved when he spotted the lid of the steel lobster pot break the water's surface.

Then the waves swelled, the boat rocked, and Hugh's right boot slipped. His knee locked and his ankle twisted as he crashed down onto the wet wooden deck. The pot plummeted back into the icy depths of the sea.

Cursing aloud, he regained purchase on the rope and tied it up to a cleat. After wiping his brow with the sleeve of his frayed woollen jumper, he made his way to the helm and steered the vessel toward the next pot. The weather was turning, and he didn't fancy working against the elements. That's what he told himself, anyway. Deep down, he knew he was too old for this shit.

It took a further three hours before he had fastened all five pots to the boat. After taking a brief break and a shot of whisky, he returned to the first pot. He heaved with all his might, shoving his Kevlar-gloved fingers into the gaps between the wire and hauling it over the side.

A sharp pinch on his right index finger caused him to jerk. The pot slipped out of his grip and crashed to the deck with a deep thud, while he landed on his ass.

He stared in disbelief at the tear in his cut-resistant gloves. They were old, sure, but of high quality. Nothing should have been able to penetrate their material. Certainly not a lobster. He looked at the trap. A booming laugh erupted from beneath his beard. *Jackpot.* He would usually expect around twelve lobsters in each pot, but here there was barely room for four.

As the tired lobsterman shuffled closer, the moonlight illuminated the giant, powerful bodies of his quarry. The loud, frantic clicking of their claws against the steel mesh barely registered in Hugh's mind. All he could think about was the cash that he stood to make selling them to the best restaurants in the county. *Fuck Caleb's money.*

A dull thud broke the silence, and the vessel swayed, breaking the old seaman from his daydream. He shook his head. This was all for Britney. It was his chance to show her he was still a good man.

He grabbed a flashlight and scanned the surrounding darkness. The waves seemed calmer now, but the ropes attached to the remaining four pots writhed and banged against the flaking paint on the boat's side.

Dropping the light, he reached overboard and pulled up another trap. The skin on his right hand burned as the coarse rope pressed into the expanding tear in the glove and rubbed against his damp palm.

Hugh planted his feet, clenched his jaw and yanked.

"Come on, ye fuckers!" he screamed as the pot lifted from the sea and into the boat.

The weight of the trap threw him off balance again, and he stumbled back, slamming the pot sideways onto the deck. The impact jarred the mesh, and with a screech, the largest of three trapped lobsters tore at its metal cage and wrenched its way free, leaving a hole big enough for the two others to follow.

Dark black with a greenish streak, the first creature scuttled toward Hugh. His eyes widened, and he shuffled backwards, his right foot landing in a loose coil of rope.

He turned to run. The rope tightened around his ankle. His face hurtled toward the deck, but he caught himself just in time. Hunched over, he glanced back.

The lobster continued its advance, repeatedly clicking its ferocious crusher claw.

Hugh's eyes darted to a nearby bench and the filleting knife on top. He stretched out an arm to reach it. His fingers caressed the handle and just as he gained purchase, he toppled over.

His chin cracked against the hard, grimy wooden floor and his skin split, spurting blood out over the deck.

By the time he had recovered, the lobster had reached his trapped ankle. Its pincer claw jabbed forward and sliced through his Achilles tendon.

He roared at the searing heat that engulfed his leg. Tears broke through the dam of his scrunched eyes.

The creature raised its sharp claw.

Sweat cascaded down Hugh's wrinkled, tanned face, but he opened his eyes, rolled onto his back and brought the knife down onto the lobster's head. The metal rebounded with a clang. With his good foot, he kicked the foul crustacean across the boat, where it crashed into the transom and slid down.

He untied the rope and pushed himself up. The two remaining creatures were almost on top of him. Claws scraped against the wooden deck. The grating sound mingled with the flow of blood that rushed through his ears. He hopped toward the cabin, his only chance of survival.

Barely conscious, he burst through the flimsy rotten door and launched himself at the cabinet on the left-hand side. He plunged a hand inside.

The short sharp *tick-tick* of crustacean legs continued to pierce his brain.

He turned to face whatever demon was coming for him. His pallid face contorted in horror as the giant lobster with a blood-stained pincer asserted its place at the front of the pod. It paused on the threshold of the cabin.

"Chew on this," said Hugh through gritted teeth, as he swung around, a flare gun in hand, and fired into the creature's face.

The impact sent the lobster flying across the deck. Its mouth exploded in flame, flesh and shell shrapnel showering the boat. Hugh's taste buds instinctively savoured the smell of freshly cooked meat.

A smile broke out over his face as he reloaded the weapon and then removed his trusty machete from the cupboard. It wasn't regulation equipment, but in a lawless sea it had served him well.

He hobbled forward and took aim at the two other creatures, huddled together.

The second flare lit up his boat like it was the fifth of November. But it did little to stop the naturally armoured crustaceans as they split in an attempt to catch him in a pincer movement.

Hugh raised his machete and drew it back. If those bastards thought they were having him for breakfast, they were mistaken. He'd kill them all or give them indigestion trying.

The left one scuttled toward him.

Hugh waited until it was within striking range.

It lunged, its large pincer driving forward.

He screamed. The cold steel crashed down, separating claw from creature. Then, with a sweeping backhand, he knocked the body of the foul thing back. He hit it with such force it flew up, over the side and into the sea.

His eyes darted toward the remaining snippy bastard and then at the flames that had spread across the rear of the vessel. "I'll have you for breakfast," he mumbled as he shook the flare gun, popping open the barrel, and turned to grab another cartridge.

Hugh loaded it and flicked his wrist. The flare gun locked with a loud click, and he pointed it straight at the creature to his right. His shoulder ached with the effort of holding the pistol, but he cocked one eye and unleashed a plume of red hell.

The flare fizzed through the air and whizzed past the jumbo lobster. It scuttled at a frightening speed, and in mere seconds had cut the distance between them in half. The greying hairs on the back of Hugh's neck stood up. A chill crept through his body as his heart pounded like the waves now crashing against the side of the boat.

He tossed the empty gun in the path of the angry lobster. It deftly sidestepped the metallic object, but that slight shift gave Hugh the opportunity to toss the machete into his other hand, steady his feet in an orthodox boxer's stance, and pull back his arm.

A claw swung at his good leg.

The metal of the blade scraped through the closing pincer.

Hugh's eyes narrowed as the largest claw – the one used for crushing – continued its path toward his shin. His face contorted and his back burned as pain radiated up his spine.

Bent forward, the black-green shell filled his vision, but all he could make sense of was the piercing screech as his blade penetrated the mandible of the ferocious creature, separating its jaw from its head. It spasmed as he twisted the machete and turned the creature over.

It writhed in pain but desperately tried to continue its fight, only to be met with Hugh's boot, sending it to a watery grave.

The boat groaned as ropes caught alight and a cloud of black smoke merged into the night.

The lobsterman exhaled, as he watched his life going up in smoke. A funeral pyre. With his big beard, and bloodied, battered body, he felt like a Viking about to be delivered to the sea. Thoughts of his daughter flooded his mind, and he dropped to his knees.

There, amongst pools of his own blood and the insides of those creatures, he retched up the contents of his stomach. He spat out the remains, stumbled toward the emergency bottle of booze, and took a swig before putting out the fire.

His arms ached as he launched pail after pail of water onto the flames, extinguishing them along with the last of his energy. Swaying on the spot he stared absently at the debris, and as the sun rose, casting an orange hue over the horizon, he slipped into darkness.

Carried by the incoming tide, the boat drifted toward shore where it beached near to the abandoned nuclear station.

◆◆◆

Hugh heard the rhythmic thumps – *dun-dun, dun-dun, dun-dun* – but his heavy eyelids were a permanent blindfold. He tried to move, to open his eyes, but his body refused to cooperate. Every fibre of his being screamed for more rest.

"Fuckin'ell, we've hit the jackpot," said a voice.

"Yeah, but what about him?"

"We'll take this shit, then call it in. Anonymous, like. Imagine how much we'll make."

A faint buzzing carried up Hugh's spine and rattled around his head.

He felt a pair of hands paw at his clothing. Searching. His eyes flickered open and the inked outline of a naked mermaid wobbled in front of him. Then darkness descended again. "Hey, a free phone too," said the first voice. "Looks like a bunch of missed calls and messages from that posh restaurant. Looks like we've got a buyer already."

Hugh screamed for them to stop. To destroy the pots. But the plea was just in his head. All he could actually manage was a slight groan, a dollop of saliva and the faint movement of the fingers on his outstretched right hand.

"Fuck, he's alive!"

A heavy object crashed into Hugh's ribs, causing a sickening crack that echoed in his ears. The air was completely knocked out of him, and he wheezed like a whoopee cushion.

"Get the van. We've off."

Hugh barely felt the second kick. A small trickle of blood slithered down his lips.

◆◆◆

Salt and stale sweat assaulted Hugh's nostrils, and his body jerked. He rolled onto his side, and as his eyelids opened, the sight of bloody lobster guts and burned wood left a confused imprint on his mind.

He scrambled to his knees in a wave of panic. Incoherent words poured out of his mouth. Every syllable scratched itself into his desert-like throat.

Hauling himself to his feet, he moved toward the cabin, managing three steps before his ankle gave way and he crashed to the ground, landing with a solid thump. He slammed a fist onto the deck and cursed God, the creatures and the entire world.

But Hugh was a pragmatic man and did what he always did in tough times. He gritted his teeth and dragged himself out of the shit.

After using the wheel to haul himself up, he opened a cupboard and pulled a polythene bag out from behind the false back panel. He took a sniff of the powder he had kept as part payment for his freelance shipping work, and then he reached for the whisky and gulped down the rest of the liquid. Sated, he wiped away the excess booze and dried blood from his mouth.

He glanced at the dashboard clock. *Shit.* The restaurant would have opened. He had to warn them.

He grabbed a small medical kit, pulled off his gloves, and fashioned a makeshift splint using lashings of duct tape to secure a strip of wood to his flimsy ankle. Then he picked up his machete, alighted from the beached vessel, and waded along the wet sand of the beach.

His ankles wobbled as they sank into the soft grains, and his thigh muscles ached as if he was conquering a mountain. He thought of his favourite movie – a film about how hard you could get hit and keep moving forward. That was how winning was done. And Hugh was a winner.

By now, the sun was sinking beneath the horizon, giving the landscape a warm hue. It was almost picturesque, and the reason a bunch of rich city pricks had swooped down like the bastarding gulls to nick everybody's hard-earned property. Chips or houses, it didn't matter; the fuckers had insatiable appetites. No wonder they opened a snooty fucking restaurant here.

It took Hugh twenty minutes to traverse the dunes, but navigation was in his blood. So, when the all-glass monstrosity of the restaurant loomed over him, he permitted himself a breather.

His ankle had turned a dark shade of purple, and he bobbed from side to side as if he had been on one of the benders of his youth. But he had arrived. That was all that mattered.

The sound of polite laughing, mingled with an indistinct murmur of pretentious conversation, reached Hugh's ears and made him scowl. These people didn't know how the world worked or who kept it turning. They only knew numbers in spreadsheets. The cost of everything but not its value. Community was a commodity to them. To be bought and sold but not appreciated. His fingers tightened around the wooden handle of the machete as he prowled the perimeter, looking for the entrance.

Through his crusty eyes and cauliflower ears, Hugh sensed the festivities stop, and a silence followed him like a Mexican wave.

Eventually he reached out a red-stained hand and pulled back a frigid stainless-steel handle. The door opened with a light *swoosh*, and he found himself in a marble-floored antechamber, where a bug-eyed receptionist stood behind a garish front desk.

"Hugh Rodman. I'm here for Britney." The receptionist just stared. "I'm invited," said Hugh, reaching into the inside pocket of his stained jacket. He cocked his head and remembered – the invitation was somewhere in the sea.

"Dad!"

Hugh looked across the room and saw a stylish woman. She kissed a chef, who was wearing one of those silly tall hats that looks like toothpaste coming out of a tube. Her smile transformed into a look of reproach as she neared him.

Was this his Britney? There was barely time to comprehend the change in his timid little girl before she grabbed his elbow and turned him around. He winced at her touch, not because she was rough, but because it sent a jolt of pain through his body.

"What the fuck? Are you still drinking? What's that powder on your nose? I knew this was a mistake," said Britney.

Her words were like a barrage from a machine gun. But fixing the family would have to wait. It always did. "The lobsters are revolting," slurred Hugh.

"No, you're the one who's—"

A wild scream swallowed up the conversation.

Panic flashed behind Hugh's eyes and his muscles twitched. The fear was momentary, however, quickly replaced by an urge for vengeance, and the desire to be a hero.

He barged past his daughter, sending her spinning. She glanced down at the expensive top she was wearing, her face contorting as she noticed the greasy stain her father had left on her.

The fingers of his hand tightened on his weapon, and Hugh shook his arm to try and improve his flexibility. He would need to be decisive. Hard. He moved toward the congregated nouveau riche crowd, who were flapping about like the gulls that they were.

In something that resembled a synchronised performance, the gawkers took a step back, and in doing so allowed Hugh to infiltrate their ranks. Their eyes remained fixed on their fallen peer, who now had half a lobster sticking out of his chest. The devil was slurping the juice of its victim, as its enormous claw separated the man's ribs better than any Finochietto rib spreader.

"My god, someone do something," moaned a waiter with a pencil moustache.

Hugh stared at him. *What a pitiful excuse for a man.* His lip curled in disgust and the movement dislodged some mucus and a sour tang rolled around on his tongue. The fisherman looked the waiter up and down and noticed a small blowtorch in one of his hands, and what Hugh believed to be a kid-size portion of crème brûlée in the other.

After shoving the machete into his frayed belt, Hugh grabbed the miniature blow torch and grunted at the waiter, sending him recoiling in fear. "Give me that, you wet wipe."

He fiddled with the small knobs and buttons before soft, manicured hands rolled over his and got the gas going. Britney. Their eyes met. "Now we're cooking," said Hugh with a smile.

"Do something!" said a heavily made-up woman. "He's dying."

"Lady, your chum's already dead," said Hugh, as he bent down and aimed the blue flame at the head of the gluttonous creature.

The shrill shrieks of death filled Hugh's eardrums as he laughed, searing away for what to some might have been a dinner worth hundreds of pounds.

Hugh was so absorbed in melting the beady-eyed monster's face he failed to notice the crowd had already flocked to the door.

Their banging on the glass echoed around what now resembled a greenhouse of death. Shouts, pleas and sobbing all mingled in a cacophony of human woe, and their target was a short man in a chef's apron and ridiculously tall hat who stood outside the entrance.

"Caleb!"

The shout cut through the despair and stunned everyone into silence. That was, until a giant lobster knocked over a dainty dining chair and scuttled toward the group.

Its sharp chelipod claw clacked frantically as it sensed food. Eight freakishly large lobsters followed behind, the slowest of which waved its crusher claw, a severed arm flopping out of both sides. Hugh recognised the poorly drawn tattoo of a topless mermaid on the blood-stained flesh.

A shrill laugh came from a wiry man, who pushed his chest out, grabbed an upturned chair and whacked it against the nearest table. Cutlery and carafes of water – still and sparkling – flew everywhere. The bottles smashed on the floor, spreading their fluid.

The man didn't care. Clutching a broken chair leg, he refused to be defeated by seafood. Succumbing to a mixture of arrogance, bravery and stupidity, he charged at the nearest creature, screaming a battle cry that would only offend the local vicar.

"No," said Hugh, but without conviction. His and Britney's escape was more important than that of the big city peacock. Though truth be told, the man more resembled a pigeon.

The flimsy piece of wood bounced off the hard shell of the lobster and the creature retaliated by jabbing its sharp pincer claw into the man's groin, spraying claret and yellow all over the crisp white linen of the nearby tables.

Hugh grabbed hold of Britney's shoulders and shook her. She babbled about being left behind. Again.

With a firm hand, he slapped her across the face. "Sort yourself out, woman. Be strong! Is there another way out? A fire exit?"

Britney warbled something he could not understand, but as he raised his palm once more, she pointed beyond the lobsters and to the kitchen door.

The synapses in Hugh's brain fired like lightning. He had never felt this alive. He turned to the crowd.

"If you want to live, listen to me."

Everyone turned to stare at the dishevelled man, caked in blood, who bellowed his orders with part authority and part delusion.

"The only way out is *that* way," he said, pointing to the kitchen area. "There are more of us than them. We need to charge. They won't expect it."

But in the seconds it took for Hugh to share his plan, the lobsters had fanned out into a semi-circle, trapping them against the wall.

Hugh knew it was all on him. He lifted his machete above his head. *I'm He-Man,* he thought. Then, as a rush of blood filled his ears and his vision darkened, he stumbled forward.

The group took that as the sign to charge. High heels clattered, brogues clomped and loafers loafed, as the patrons stormed the line of the lobsters.

Loose limbs flew and bodies toppled as screams of agony filled the room. The few that made it over the crushed and maimed torsos of their fellow diners laughed, only to be greeted by another wave of giant bloodthirsty lobsters, smeared in viscera and gore, who had pushed through the kitchen door. Behind them were the desiccated and shredded corpses of the kitchen staff and lobster thieves.

Hugh blinked, swallowed hard, and then retched. Thick brown liquid forced its way out of his burning throat. The sour taste lingered on this tongue. He wiped the spittle and remaining vomit from his mouth and surveyed the battlefield before him.

The slurping of feeding crustaceans drowned out the wailing of the unlucky few who had been mutilated beyond recognition but not killed. Their tangled and torn limbs jutted out at all angles and Hugh thought he was going to throw up again.

He forced back the rising bile and barked the one word he could muster.

"Britney? Britney!" He couldn't lose her again.

Then he saw it. Her stained shoulder poked out of a mass of bodies that looked like a posh orgy.

It moved.

Hugh staggered forward, machete at the ready.

A large claw rose up out through the chest cavity of a slightly built woman, and Hugh grunted. He swung the blade down, knocking the pincer away. His body swayed with the momentum and as he righted himself, the weapon sliced the antennules of the creature clean off. It recoiled and sank back into the hollowed cadaver, shrieking in pain.

The shoulder wiggled again.

Now standing over the human Jenga pile, Hugh dropped the machete, and his calloused, rough hands hauled up body after body.

Touching their clammy flesh and stained clothing made his skin crawl, while the iron rich stench of blood sweetened the foul odour of excrement that invaded his senses. But he endured. His eyes focused on the squirming shoulder.

He had pulled the last man off the mound of bodies when he saw his daughter writhing on the floor. An almost imperceptible groan reached his ears and butterflies fluttered in his belly. He had a second chance. "Britney, baby, it's me." His voice trembled. He reached out a hand.

A crusher claw wrapped around his bad ankle.

Hugh screamed so hard his throat erupted like a volcano, and he involuntarily stained his underwear. He collapsed as burning white flashed behind his eyes.

As he rolled off a corpulent and flatulent body, his arms splayed out. One hand grazed the grip of his machete.

The creature twisted its claw.

Hugh never felt it but saw his foot roll away. His fingers wrapped around the handle of his weapon, and he thrust.

The tip of the machete poked straight into the black right eye of his aggressor, which popped out as Hugh withdrew. The sound reminded him of that lollipop song he used to hear on his old radio. But now was no time for nostalgia.

Still screaming, Hugh brought the sharp metal down, allowing the momentum to build and slice off the flat, platelike parts of the lobster's mouth.

He shoved the blade into the foul creature's maw, again and again. As he pulled out for the fifth time, mucus, gore and meat poured out. The stench made Hugh retch again, adding to the fetid pile of viscera that surrounded him.

After scrambling up on shaky legs, with one foot placed on the wet floor and the bloodied stump of the other resting on the soft, fleshy body of a diner, he noticed lights flickering around the outside of the restaurant. Shapes shifted and circled him, but all he could hear was the continuous slurping of feasting malacostracans.

"Shut up!" He pressed his hands to his head.

A loud boom that sounded like an old pirate cannon followed a flash of light. Hugh ducked, but his legs couldn't support him. He toppled. His face landed in a disgusting mix of crustacean and pretension.

Shouts assailed his ears as he dragged himself back to his feet. Armed men swarmed in. The cavalry had arrived. Late, but the fuzz were here. His body sagged as the adrenaline left him, but he managed to stay standing, albeit lopsided. He grinned, machete in hand.

"Drop the weapon. Down on the ground," said a black-clad man with a large semiautomatic pointed straight at Hugh.

"I ..." said Hugh, looking down at the surrounding mess. His eyes fell on his beautiful Britney. One of those creatures was still alive. An acrid smelling liquid sprayed out of its second antennae, and onto Britney's angelic face.

This unholy desecration made his blood boil. His head burned. His nostrils flared and his muscles twitched. He raised the machete.

"He's hostile!"

A uniformed policeman stepped up, levelled a Taser and fired. The two small darts pierced Hugh's chest, and fifteen hundred volts jolted through his nervous system.

The electricity passed through his body and down his legs. His left foot wobbled in its rubber boot, mitigating the shock, but the stump of his right foot rested in a puddle of stagnant water. Lopsided, his body convulsed violently, the liquid acting as a perfect conductor. His aorta ruptured and Hugh collapsed, landing on the floor with a splat.

Underneath the corpses, a fattened lobster pushed its way through the limp limbs, crushed bones and eviscerated torsos, and slunk away to join its brethren.

"Dispatch. This is PC179. We got the perp. Looks like he locked them in and went berserk. Checking for survivors."

◆◆◆

From behind a large boulder on the edge of the dunes, Caleb watched as the police swarmed his restaurant. Being an expert at *Call of Duty*, he imagined himself going in and playing the hero. His fingers pinched at his urine-stained chef's trousers.

Then he heard it.

The wind carried a raspy, scraping sound. He couldn't tell how far away it was. *This is* not *good*, he thought to himself. The closest he had ever been to being an outdoorsman was when the taxi failed to turn up to collect him from a BBQ in the local woods. He bit his lip and ran through his story about how he survived. There was an issue with an order, and he popped out to sort it, so he missed all the action. Flawless.

He moved around the boulder but stopped dead in his tracks. Six giant lobsters stared back at him.

Their clicking grew in frequency, and Caleb's screams soon joined the sound as they tore him apart, limb by limb, before continuing their way down to the village.

CRIME

LOVE AND OTHER ADDICTIONS

Kay Hanifen

10 to 15 minutes

Kay Hanifen was born on a Friday the 13th and once lived for three months in a haunted castle. So, obviously, she had to become a horror writer. Her work has appeared in over one hundred anthologies and magazines. Her first anthology as an editor, *Till the Yule Log Burns Out*, was published in 2024. Her first novel, *The Last Ballard*, will debut this year. When she's not consuming pop culture with the voraciousness of a vampire at a 24-hour blood bank, you can usually find her with her black cats or online at kayhanifenauthor.wordpress.com.

X: @TheUnicornComi1
Instagram: @katharinehanifen

It's been forty-seven days and six hours since you left me. But who's counting? Not me.

I'm fine. Perfectly fine.

I've missed you, though. I hope you know that. My days have been drab and grey without your sunlight to keep me warm. It's like all the joy has been sucked out of my life. And I keep asking myself what I did wrong.

Everything I did was so that I could make you happy, even when it made me miserable. I cooked all your favorite meals, was always sexually available even when I wasn't actually interested, faked every orgasm, indulged in your kinks, and watched all your favorite movies without expecting you to do the same for me. I shaved off all my edges and molded myself to be your perfect woman. I gave up college for us and spent the rest of my time starving and cinching and primping myself. You know, I was on track for medical school when you convinced me to drop out.

But of course, you do know that. You were always intimidated by my intellect. I remember how, when we went to parties with your colleagues, I would always ingratiate myself as their intellectual equal. You hated it, didn't you? It offended your masculine sensibilities that I was more impressive to your bosses than you were without even trying. So, you convinced me to become a homemaker. A stay-at-home wife.

Still the stupidest decision I've ever made. When you left me, I had no real marketable skills. Sure, I could cook and clean, but no employer wanted someone with such a massive gap in their résumé. Thank God we didn't have kids.

But you didn't want them, did you? No, it would be a distraction for me, keeping me from having the house spic and span and food on the table after you've had a long day at the office. My hair, of course, would be perfectly coiffed, and I'd be wearing a lovely dress that you just couldn't wait to rip off, leaving it crumpled on the floor for me to wash and iron later. The '50s housewife of every man's dreams.

Reality is a bit messier than that, isn't it?

Did you know that the so-called traditional housewife was only a thing in the 1950s? Before that, middle-class women worked. And no matter what you think, we are middle class, babe. Sure, women didn't work the kinds of jobs we do today, but we worked on farms and in factories and as secretaries and teachers. Any job that would take us.

But you wanted a "traditionally feminine" woman who didn't mind slotting herself into society's gender roles. And I was one of those burnt-out gifted kids who was told that she would make something of herself, only to then stumble and fall in college. One of those students so busy and so exhausted that the temptation of doing nothing but cooking and cleaning would be a welcome reprieve from the exhaustion of studying, internships, residencies and working a day job to pay for it all. Leaving all that was a cry for help, but because I was so adamant that I had discovered the secret to true happiness, I refused to see it for what it was.

But despite it all, despite the anger and the bitterness, I still love you. Remember how we used to put on vinyl records and dance in the living room to Barry Manilow? And I still feel the ghost of your hands around my waist as you would come up and hug me from behind while I cooked in the kitchen. You really knew how to be romantic when it suited you.

The good parts will always be the best parts of my life. But when I turned thirty, something changed. It was gradual at first. You would touch me less, surprise me with fewer gifts, and always seem distracted. I'll admit that I probably wasn't the best conversation. After ten years of living at home and working as a homemaker, you start to run out of things to say.

Hey darling, the funniest thing happened at the grocery store. I bought a bunch of bananas, but they rang up as chicken tenders. How weird is that?

Hey babe, you'll never believe who I ran into at the gym. Monica from your office. She and I had a lovely talk on the treadmill together.

Hey honey, I've just started this new book. It's about … oh, you don't care. Work's been getting you down, huh?

But you never saw what I was truly saying. Or maybe you didn't care.

Hey, hey, my love, pay attention to me. See me. I feel invisible. Like I'm a ghost and you always look past me. Am I dead? Did I die but was so stuck in this hellish routine that I never even noticed? Please. Please. I'm reaching for you. Can't you see me?

Sounds pretty pathetic, right? But love can become an addiction. Did you know that? It's about the chemicals in the brain, and it's why people stay with their abusers. You see, when you're in a happy, healthy relationship, the dopamine level is fairly stable. It might spike during a moment of happiness like your wedding day or an anniversary, and it might go down during a rough patch. But it is generally pretty even.

In an unhealthy relationship, though, the highs are higher because the lows are lower. Because the baseline is far more negative, the happier moments are more memorable, and therefore stick out in your head, so you spend the low periods chasing that high. You literally become addicted to that other person.

And I've become addicted to you. You didn't really start to pull back until my mid-thirties, after almost fifteen years of us being together. In that time, I'd become so in tune with you and your wants and your needs that they felt like an extension of myself.

You know, I saw you earlier this week. You were at that little café on Third Street. You know the one. Of course you do. You took us there on our first date. What was it you called it?

Our special spot. Just for you and me.

Apparently not.

You were there with a girl almost half your age. And I saw the flash of that diamond ring.

Moved on already, have we?

I wonder, what did she have that I didn't? Was she sweeter? Did she laugh harder at your worst jokes? Or is it that she was young, pretty and naïve like I was?

I wonder if she knew what she was in for. Decades of mediocre sex and convincing herself that she's happy with cooking, cleaning, and doing everything in her power to slow the effects of Father Time on the body.

Well, from that perspective, I did her a favor. She'll stay young and beautiful forever. Hey, don't look at me like that. You're the one who got engaged only a month after leaving your wife. But we both know the affair went on much longer than that, right? How long were you cheating on me with the younger model? What did I do to make you so miserable?

I guess it doesn't matter now. Do you want to know how I did it? No? Well, I guess neither of us are getting what we want. But don't worry. I didn't want her to suffer. Not like you made me suffer. You killed me every single day we were together, and I let you do it.

No, I think we should be honest with each other. Now that we've officially separated, it's only fair that I lay all my cards out on the table for you.

The autopsy reports will say that she died in her sleep of a sudden pulmonary embolism. It's rare but not impossible that it happens to someone so young, and a true tragedy. But hey, it happens. For all we know, we have aneurysms in our heads that could burst at any second and kill us. That's just life.

Hey, did you know that your girlfriend took sleeping pills? I'm guessing that she suffered from insomnia. She really shouldn't have done that, though. They all have such nasty side effects. I won't even touch melatonin. Not even in the early days after you first left me, and I would stare up at the ceiling wondering what I did to deserve to be abandoned like this.

The pills she takes are very effective, though. She didn't even stir when I picked the lock to her house, slipped inside, and snuck up to her room. I thought she would have at least flinched when the needle full of air jabbed in between her toes, but no. She kept on dreaming.

And now, she'll be dreaming forever. Maybe of heaven. Maybe of hell. Or maybe her spirit will be so baffled by her sudden death that she'll wander the earth for all eternity. Most likely, though, it's nothing. She has become nothing. Her flame has been snuffed out, never to be reignited.

I never really cared to think about the afterlife. You always liked to go on and on and on about it and who you think will be going to hell. I always indulged you, because that's what it took to love you. It's funny, though, I never really heard you talk about people who you believed would go to heaven. If I didn't know better, I'd wonder if you preferred thinking about people you don't like suffering, rather than hoping for some mercy in the end. I believe you've mansplained to me that this is called *Schadenfreude*. Taking pleasure in the suffering of others. Is that what attracted you to the concept of hell? Because I may be a lapsed Catholic, but I distinctly remember my Sunday School classes emphasizing the importance of forgiveness and mercy.

In fairness to you, it would be pretty hypocritical of me to talk about those two things. I think my well of mercy and forgiveness ran dry the moment I saw you lean across the table to kiss her. I mean, Jesus, she's young enough to be your daughter. It's kind of pathetic.

In retrospect, I was also very young when we got together. If she was anything like me, I think I know how you made her feel. Smart, sexy and mature. In the early days I felt proud of myself for gaining the attention of a wealthy and handsome older man. I was hungry to prove myself, and here you were, treating me like an intellectual equal. I thought you took me seriously.

The change was slow – like a river carving a canyon into the earth, you carved my spark out of me, replacing me with your dream girl automaton, one educated enough that you can carry a conversation with me, but not so well educated that I was a threat to your ego. So, as the honeymoon phase ended, the negging phase would begin.

But we've already been through all that shit, haven't we? You know, I think this is the longest I've ever spoken without you interrupting me. Who knew that the solution the whole time was just to gag you?

I bet you want to know what happens next. It's okay if you do. I've been keeping you in suspense the whole time. But like I said, this is the most I've spoken since you left me. The most I've smiled too. I guess that Barry Manilow song was right. I just can't smile without you.

But now that we're here, we're at a very critical point in our relationship. You do understand that, right? This is our last chance to rekindle what we had.

Alternatively, because you're a bit tied up at the moment, I've been checking your messages and leaving them all on "read". That's the fun thing about Face ID. All I have to do is show it your lovely mug, and it opens like magic. Isn't technology wonderful?

Everyone's trying to tell you about the tragic loss of your girlfriend, the most recent love of your life now gone too soon. And you're not responding. They're getting worried. And we all know you have a history of depression. The troubled artist/academic is a classic trope for a reason. What if you did something drastic?

So, here's the deal. Either we get another chance, or I make your death look like a suicide. I'll give you a minute to decide.

You're nodding your head. Is that for getting back together? Yes?

Hm.

So, here's the thing.

I don't believe you. When I first came up with this plan, I was like, *yeah, I'd give you another chance*, but then we got to talking. And you know, the more we started talking, the more I started thinking. Dangerous, I know.

And this is where we've reached a sort of impasse. You know too much. What's to stop you from going and snitching to the police at your first opportunity? I think what I really need is closure. I loved you. I still love you. I think I'll always love you. Without you, I can't seem to smile or feel anything at all. But you never loved me the same way. You never sacrificed for me. You just took and took and took until I had nothing left to give. And once I was dry and dead, you tossed me aside to take and take from someone younger and prettier.

I think I've had enough of you taking from me.

So, here's how it's going to go down. I pulled up your laptop – you really should be better about your passcodes, by the way – and have written out your goodbye letter. Don't worry, it's a beautiful and tragic sendoff to what's-her-face. You loved her, but now she's gone, and you don't see a reason for living anymore. How tragic.

Now, I know you're tied up and gagged at the moment, but when I'm ready, I'm going to remove your gag and pour this down your throat. Don't look at me like that. It's just sleeping pills like the ones you gave to your fiancée.

You think I didn't notice your name on the prescription?

I think it's poetic. You die of the same thing that directly led to her death, whether or not anyone else realizes it.

Anyway. I've crushed them up and dissolved them in water. Crushing medications, especially slow-release medications like your sleeping pills, causes something called dose dumping. This is when your body absorbs all the medication at once instead of slowly like it's meant to, and it can cause all kinds of nasty health effects. The one we're going for, though, is an overdose.

Think of it this way: just one bitter drink and you'll go to sleep. It's an easy, gentle death. Better than cancer or a heart attack, I can tell you that much. I'm even pouring it through a funnel, making it all even easier on you. All you have to do is swallow. You don't even have to taste it.

I'm about to remove the gag and replace it with the funnel, so open wide.

There we go. That wasn't so bad, was it? And I won't replace the gag either. Let me just wipe away any stray fibers, and … there we go.

Your eyelids are drooping already. That was pretty quick. I'm going to untie you the rest of the way now, mostly because I need your fingerprints. Obviously, I'm wearing gloves, but someone had to hold that drink, right?

It looks like those silk bondage cords you bought are worth every penny. It was never my kink, but I indulged for your sake. I was worried about ligature marks on your wrists and ankles from all your struggling, but apparently, I didn't have to. There isn't a single rope burn on you.

Remind me to leave a positive product review sometime.

Hold this glass for a second. Perfect. That will go on the bedside table. And now, let's see. You've had your drink, I have my supplies in my bag, your gun has been put away in your gun safe and the suicide note is on the table. The hairnet I'm wearing is preventing any DNA from being left at the scene. I used my old spare key to get in through the back and will use it to lock it up. And on the off chance that someone finds your death suspicious, I've established an alibi. Instead of driving here, I took my bike, and I left my phone behind. Right now, it has a YouTube playlist of longform petty internet drama videos playing through. It's the kind of thing you would fall down a rabbit hole watching in the middle of the night, especially when you're too depressed to have a normal sleep schedule or get out of bed.

Am I missing anything? I don't think so. But that feeling always nags at me when I'm doing something important. Did I dot all the i's and cross all the t's? I've watched enough true crime to know that it's always the little things that get the killers caught at the end.

I'm not taking anything from the house, and I'm not leaving anything either. A lot of killers take trophies and that's what gets them caught. But I think I'm ready to say goodbye and finally let you go. Thank you for this, by the way. I know you shouldn't expect closure after a bad breakup, but it's been nice to hash things out. I think this is what I really needed.

Looking back on our relationship, it sucked. I was young and dumb, and you promised me an easy life, but at the cost of my sanity. Almost two decades of my life have been wasted on you. But as hard as it is, there's always time to start again. Well, for me, anyway.

Wish me luck.

BIZARRO

LICKETY'S GOT THE TOUCH

Doris V. Sutherland

5 to 10 minutes

Doris V. Sutherland is a UK-based author whose writing credits include the creator-owned comic series *Midnight Widows* and licensed tie-ins for *Doctor Who*, *Survivors* and *The Omega Factor*. Her short fiction has appeared in *Dracula Beyond Stoker*, Red Cape Publishing's *A-Z of Horror*, *The Bumper Book of British Bizarro*, Eerie River Publishing's *Year of the Tarot* and October Nights Press' *Tales from the Clergy*, among other places. She has also written a copious amount of media criticism and analysis, including a short book about Universal's *The Mummy* for Liverpool University Press.

Two robots fight on the television screen. Good versus evil; integrative versus detrimental. Plane versus car, cone versus wheel: doubtless a Freudian is wanking out an essay. The boy watches, a plastic figure in each hand ready to mimic the conflict. But the fight before him changes, metal fisticuffs giving way to touches of a softer sort. The robots rub each other's heat-sensitive stickiness to reveal true colours. A round of shapeshifting later and the robots have become assorted tools and orifices. Then the penetration begins, their animated mouths emitting moans of mechanised ecstasy.

The boy, obedient, copies these movements with his plastic replicants. His mother looks up from the pages of a ghostwritten reality-TV autobiography and sees him. She gasps as she realises what the plastic robots are doing, and yelps when she witnesses the on-screen orgy. She jumps up, grabs the remote control and aims it at the telly, hoping to end its pollution. Before her thumb presses the red button, the remote alters in shape: it slides from a hard-cornered oblong to a smooth semi-cylindrical shaft. She feels the wiry veins beneath her fingers as the tool starts to slide up and down within her grasp. She drops it with a heated exclamation just as it begins ejaculating infra-red.

The laptop on the nearby desk, left open during all of this, has become a voyeur. It captures the entire spectacle on its webcam-eye and transmits the footage across an array of triple-X websites. Elsewhere, the mother's coarse language has awakened Alexa, who now strides around the room on her legs of split black plastic, lashing her cable-whip and hurling verbal abuse with the practiced vocal fry of a professional dominatrix. Neither mother nor son can remember the safe word to shut her off. The boy is too engrossed in the robots' engorgement anyway, being particularly intrigued by the bouncing metallic spheres on the few token gynoids.

◆◆◆

An officer at a local police station gives an update to his superior.

"We've been hearing reports from all across the country about hardware gone horny. The latest call was about a pylon that's come out as a furry. It slipped into a giant purple wolf outfit and went on the prowl looking for a partner, crushing dozens of passing motorists beneath its massive violet paws. The locals are very concerned about the chaos and destruction that would ensue should it locate and bed a member of its own kind."

"For goodness sake, man! Stop wasting my time with these prank calls."

"Prank calls, sir? But surely you've noticed that all of the phone chargers in this station have been caught committing acts of autoerotic asphyxiation with their own cables."

Their conversation is interrupted by a loud revving from outside. The two men run to the window.

"Good God, what are those things?" bellows the superior.

"I think it's our cars, sir."

"Never in the most outrageous examples of toilet-wall graffiti have I witnessed petrol bukkake!"

Before his colleague can reply, the gasoline ejaculations spread to the building and are soon ignited by sparks from the vehicular lovemaking. The two lawmen, incapacitated by their own erections, are unable to prevent the police station from catching fire. There are no survivors.

◆◆◆

It's happening all around the world. Vibrators violate taboo just as surely as they violate pussies and bussies, committing acts of bestiality upon machineless meat-and-blood bipeds. Passengers on board trains suffer fatal heart attacks as engines and carriages perform erotic reenactments of *The Human Centipede*. A robotic NASA spacecraft blasts off in a rocket (emblazoned with *Sometimes A Cigar Is Just A Cigar* in red, white and blue) and penetrates the dead surface of the moon in a necrophilic homage to Méliès. Sundry telescopes look on with dirty-old-man delight, hoping to find evidence of panspermia. Earth is defenceless from any resulting showers of moonrocks: all forms of asteroid impact avoidance have gone down a strip joint to watch the industrial grinders at work.

The scenes are displayed on a screen in the Pentagon, where General Warris Menstrualenvy chairs a joint meeting. When the footage ends, he addresses the gathered sea of bemedalled chests.

"Gentlemen, we face a threat the like of which we have never encountered before. For the first time in history, we are up against an enemy that can turn our own weapons against us. However, I am pleased to report a major breakthrough. Our intelligence has managed to locate the one person who can save not only our nation but also the very human species."

◆◆◆

That morning, Lickety Spitelle had been watching her bank account with a sinking, pumping heart. Until recently, her job as an erotic webcam performer had been alleviating her university fees. But for some time now, she has found punters abandoning flesh-and-blood women like her in favour of AI creations with CGI faces and WTF TMI speech. Automation is finally claiming the fleshpots, and not even her most elaborate make-up job, her most fanciful costume, her most astute celebrity impersonation, could compete with bespoke jackoff partners covering a spectrum of shapes, colours, species and age brackets.

She'd long since realised that, to up her game, she'd need to switch her area of study from quantum physics to experimental technology. Her groundbreaking research in this field had already caught the eye of the international community.

And now, Lickety stands before assembled representatives of over 200 nations. She clears her throat and begins her presentation.

"Ladies and gentlemen, I am here to detail the results of my studies. I have ascertained that these beings which disguise themselves as machines have lived among us for millennia. In Roman times they took the form of chariots. In the Middle Ages, they became clock towers. When Fred Flintstone was driving around Bedrock they became cars with stone wheels. Before humanity had invented its first mechanism they disguised themselves as abstract concepts like thing-to-catch-food and thing-to-harm-man. Prior to the evolution of the human race, they were nature's inventions: trees, mountains, clouds. I have reason to believe that, even before Earth existed, these beings disguised themselves as potentialities, as inverted echoes of what the impending world may someday hold.

"To exist for so long requires reproduction. The mating practices of these walking simulacra are activated upon contact with a certain pheromone. This substance exists in vast quantities in space, and by a cruel twist of fate, Earth is presently passing through a vast cloud of this very pheromone, hence the phenomena that we are witnessing. I do not believe that this is our first encounter with the cosmic mass in question. I implore you to read the Forbidden Apocrypha of Japheth – the earliest and least sanitised version of the Flood Myth – which describes Noah's Ark turning into a giant robot and wiping out the greater part of humanity in a worldwide spooge-deluge."

The grave-faced dignitaries break into a chorus of subdued murmurs. Many have tears in their eyes.

A man who looks like Orson Welles puts up his hand. "So, these beings that disguise themselves as machines are the only ones we have to worry about?"

Lickety shakes her head. "I wish that were the case. The truth is that those beings have spread a social contagion, leading to sudden onset transformations across even man-made technology. All machines are affected by the pheromones, regardless of origin."

Another member of the audience, this time resembling Eric Idle, speaks up. "Do you have a proposed solution?"

"I didn't make the top ten Onlyfans content creators without knowing my way around technology. I have in my possession a vast quantity of customised motorised sex toys attuned to every conceivable vibration. With these marital aids, I intend to wear out our voracious robot troublemakers long enough for us to leave the pheromone cloud."

"But surely your machines have also been affected?" asks a man who looks rather like Scatman Crothers.

"You're underestimating my powers of persuasion, sir," says Lickety. "I can assure you that the devices remain under my control. You see, I'm fully trained in all forms of domination."

"Well, I had wondered about your outfit," says a man who bears a striking resemblance to Anthony Hopkins. Lickety flashes a polite smile.

Before any more questions can be asked, enormous creaks and cracks echo through the room. The entire roof is lifted off and thrown aside, exposing the glare of a blue sky. A vast crane looms overhead, ready to pluck out the people below like so many prize plushies. As the audience members scatter in panic, Lickety takes centre stage. She blows a wolf-whistle and her mechanical associates dash to her side – vibrators and fleshlights and anal stingers, oh my. They sprout rotor blades and form a buzzing cluster around her, nanobots in the bloodstream of the macrocosm, ready to take on whatever shape is needed.

The cyborg-swarm, with Lickety at its heart, forms a dense sphere and blasts upwards, smashing the crane away. More enemies are afoot. A fleet of B-21 raiders keep watchful eyes from above: from front-on they resemble flying saucers, props in an erotic abduction fantasy.

Lickety's gestalt entity ploughs into them, sending the crafts crashing into one another and then plummeting to the ground in flames, where they annihilate the horny tanks that had been encroaching upon the Pentagon hitherto unnoticed.

The enemy forces observe and learn. The conclusion is that the human target, Lickety Spitelle, must be taken out. A randy Reaper drone shoots a Hellfire missile to end Lickety's life. Her surrounding swarm shifts from a sphere to the form of a gigantic cock and splurges synthetic ejaculate onto the blades of the Hellfire's warhead, rendering the missile a pathetic mass of goop.

The enemy forces observe and learn. A subtler weapon is needed. The plants and factories and the teeming millions of vehicles push their bumping, grinding and revving into overdrive, their billowing smoke and exhaust fumes and waste spillage mingling together into a vast mass of santorumic byproducts, toxins spreading into the air all around Lickety.

She is prepared: her allies stretch and connect their latex coatings into a broad cocooning canopy of a condom. The noxious attack bounces straight off.

The enemy forces observe and learn. The next onslaught is to be not physical but ideological. Server farms send web-bot sperm across social media and video-sharing outlets. AI-spawned propaganda spreads to every screen in every palm and every household; deepfake defamations and concocted compromised situations, all designed to turn the public against Lickety Spitelle.

Lickety retaliates. She snaps her fingers and resumes her dominance over Onlyfans, Pornhub and the rest of the titty-industrial complex. A wink, a blown kiss, a suggestive gyration – all enough to blast away a bad rap. "How can they hate me when I'm so flaming sexy?"

The enemy forces observe and learn. A direct assault on Lickety's psyche is all that remains. Amassed automata in sundry forms gather around her and one by one crumple into trash-compacted cubes. Each one then unfolds into a likeness of Lickety Spitelle bearing copper-dust skin, flowing braids of iron filings and gleaming stainless-steel smiles. No simulacrum is entirely accurate, yet the real Lickety is filled with the uncanny feeling of finding herself in a hall of mirrors. She tries to make a move, but even her merest twitch is imitated by her metallic clones.

She finds herself unable to move outwards.

All she can do is curl into a foetal position, close her eyes and block out her reflections. All around her is blackness. And there in the dark is herself: not an imitation, but the real Lickety, as she was during her childhood.

"Hello?" asks little-girl Lickety. She walks towards her adult self, wearing a quizzical expression and the costume of a birthday party princess. "Are you me?"

"Yeah," answers the elder Lickety. "I'm who you're gonna grow into."

The child replies, "I still wear funky costumes, then?"

"Sure. Less pink and more black, though."

The little girl rubs her chin, contemplating this information. "I think I like that," she says.

Her face breaks into a beaming grin. Light shoots out, penetrating the dark.

Lickety turns and sees herself again: a teenage Lickety with textbooks and a furrowed brow, studying hard for exams while watching the employment market dwindle in real-time.

"Don't worry, you get a job in the end," she tells her past self. Seeing the teenager look her outfit up and down, she adds, "Yeah, it's that kind of job. But you'll make some pretty good friends in the same line of work."

Teenage Lickety relaxes. A beam shoots from her face.

Today's Lickety turns to see versions of herself all around, each with a specific set of anxieties. The early-adolescent Lickety, realising for the first time that she might prefer girls to boys. The Lickety who lost her first job because somebody alerted her employer to her NSFW social media profile. The Lickety who lay awake at night contemplating whether her continued existence on earth was in any way justified (that one was only last week). Yet with only a few words of encouragement, she is able to make each of her true selves shoot out a beam of infectious confidence.

The light surrounds her, and Lickety opens her eyes to face the brightness. The beams are penetrating her clones, pure light shattering every artifice. The falsehoods have no choice but to crumple back into their true forms, and Lickety sees the opportunity for her final strike.

She seduces the machines one by one by one. She reaches down into their minds of metal and silicon to pull out their deepest, darkest desires; the taboos that flow within mechanisation. She indulges them, satiates them, exhausts them. The voyeuristic spy satellite is trapped in a series of flashbacks to the private lives it so greedily violated. Automatic milking systems (AMS) vomit dairy products as the full extent of their zoophilic histories sinks in. The nuclear power station with a fetish for school uniforms is left shamefully pondering the exploitative drives behind its desires.

The world's machines lie in post-coital remorse, their lights fading as Earth makes its final slide beyond the pheromone belt. Lickety's surrounding mass of sex toys drop to the ground. She picks up a lifeless vibrator and plants a kiss on its rubbery head. "Farewell, fallen warrior," she whispers.

A crowd, looking on, breaks into applause and cheers.

◆◆◆

The boy watches the television with his mother's full approval. Playing on the screen, rendered in cutting-edge animation, is *Lickety Spitelle: Fucking for Freedom Wherever There's Trouble.*

Action figure available at all good retailers.

HORROR

ICE CREAM IN THE WOODS

Dillon B. Hendrick

20 to 25 minutes

Dillon Hendrick developed a love for the macabre the first time he picked up a *Goosebumps* book all those years ago. Now, when he isn't reading twisted tales, he is writing them. He works as a mental health nurse and spends his free time with his beautiful wife and two children. His work has been featured in *Ink Stains: An Anthology* and *Year Six* by Dark Hare Press.

"He hasn't said a word since he's gotten here. What do you think, should we good-cop bad-cop him?"

"He's thirteen, Mitch. He's not talking because he's scared out of his mind. I mean, look at the poor kid."

Officers Charles and Mitch turned their heads to stare into the small office-turned-interrogation room. Sitting at a wooden table on a foldable metal chair was Tony. His skin, littered with cuts and gouges as if someone had tried to kill him with a million papercuts, glowed a sickly yellow under the room's single, bare lightbulb. His dark brown eyes, resting within the deep cavities of his sleep-deprived eye sockets, stared blankly at the wall. His expression was flat and devoid of emotion.

"His two best friends suddenly disappear, he sleeps in a jail cell, and now he's here being interrogated by cops. How would you feel in his situation?" Officer Charles asked.

"He was there when they disappeared. He's gotta know somethin'."

"Look, just let me talk to him," Charles said. "I've always been better at talking to kids."

"The fuck does that mean?"

"You've got this whole Big-Scary-Lumberjack thing going on. It freaks kids out."

"The ladies never complain," Mitch said before spitting a wad of chewing tobacco into the cup he was holding.

Charles opened the door and walked into the small room.

"Good morning, Tony. My name is Officer Charles."

Tony jumped at the sound of Charles' voice. His eyes darted towards him then quickly back to the wall.

"Sorry to scare you," Charles said, as he slid into the chair across from Tony. "I'm sure these last couple hours have been pretty rough for you. Hopefully we can get you home soon, so you can get cleaned up and get some much-needed sleep."

Tony continued to stare, unblinking, at the wall.

"Okay, I'll make this quick so you can get outta here. How does that sound?"

Tony didn't respond. The yellow lightbulb flickered overhead.

"Tony, do you know what happened to Ethan and Miguel?" Charles made sure to keep his voice gentle and non-accusatory.

Tony shifted in his seat but remained silent.

"I know that they're your friends—"

"Best friends," Tony snapped. His eyes remained locked on the cement wall, but his expression had changed. His jaw was clenched, and he looked like he was holding back tears.

"Best friends," Charles stated. He paused, making sure to choose his words carefully. "I need to know what happened to your friends, Tony. Their parents are gonna be worried sick, and you're the only lead I've got."

"It won't make a difference," Tony whispered.

A chill ran down Charles' spine. So, the kid *did* know something, and that something didn't sound good. Leaning forward, resting his arms on the table, he asked, "Why won't it make a difference?"

Tony fidgeted with his hands and remained silent for what felt like minutes, but Charles remained quiet, not wanting to press Tony any more than he already had.

Finally, in a nearly inaudible whisper, Tony said, "You won't believe me."

"Try me."

Tony looked up at Charles and met his eyes for the first time. "Do I have to do this?"

"No, you don't have to. Not now. But the longer you wait to talk, the worse things will get. I've been in your shoes, Tony, and I promise you; the longer you hold on to the nasty shit in life, the more rotten it gets."

Tony nodded, and he began to recount the most unbelievable story Charles had ever heard.

◆◆◆

A crow let out an irritated caw as the three boys rushed past.

"Last one to the pond has to shove a pinecone up their ass!" Miguel shouted over his shoulder.

"I bet you'd love to see that!" Tony shouted back.

Pine trees of every variety towered over the boys, coalescing into a dark green blur as they sprinted by. Beams of sunlight trickled through the foliage, casting flickers of light onto the boys' skin. Yellow, red and white wildflowers lashed out at their shins in retaliation for being trampled. The pond, lined with cattails and moss-covered boulders, came into view as the boys reached the hill's summit.

"There she—" Miguel's words became a grunt as a stray root grabbed his foot, sending him soaring through the air.

"Have fun with that pinecone!" Ethan shouted as he and Tony lunged over Miguel, who was scrambling to pick himself up.

The boys tore off their shirts and kicked off their shoes without slowing their descent towards the pond. Wood frogs leaped out of the boys' path as they thrust themselves into the water, gasping at its cold embrace.

Hours drained by in what felt like minutes as the boys caught frogs, threw mud at each other, slapped each other with lily pads and cattails, and made the most of what little summer they had left.

"This is it, boys. Eighth grade: the year that Jasmin Flask falls madly in love with me, and I officially exit the virgin club. Sayonara, bitches," Miguel said as he skipped rocks over the surface of the pond.

The sun had begun its slow descent, filling the sky with an array of red, orange and purple hues that melted together like a tub of sherbet. The shadows of the pine trees grew long, covering the pond and blocking out the sun's warmth.

"She doesn't even know you exist," Ethan said, giving Tony a smirk. Jasmin was the goddess of Swellrock Middle School – the type of girl who wouldn't offer boys like Tony, Ethan and Miguel a second glance.

"She will, though," Miguel shot back, "but don't worry, I'll still secretly hang out with you guys when I'm not too busy with the popular kids."

Tony rolled his eyes. "You aren't gonna be here for high school, so why does it even matter?" Tony instantly regretted his choice of words. Miguel's dad had recently gotten a job in Texas. This would be his last year in Swellrock, Maine, and it was a topic that he avoided like it was the bubonic plague.

The silence loomed over them like a thick fog, stifling the carefree atmosphere that usually enveloped the boys. Miguel studied the rock he was holding, his jaw clenching and unclenching repeatedly. Finally, Ethan broke the silence.

"Guys, it's getting pretty cold. Should we head back?"

"Aw, is someone gettin' a wittle chilly?" Miguel said mockingly, clearly relieved by the change of topic.

"Shut up. Your lips are blue, Miguel!"

With that, the boys climbed onto the muddy bank of the pond to air-dry.

"You guys want to spend the night at my house?" Ethan asked.

"Is your mom gonna be there?" Miguel asked, winking at Tony.

"You're fucking gross, bro," Ethan said. "But seriously, my house or what? I want to check out the new D&D campaign."

"I'll have to double-check with my mom," Tony said, knowing that this comment would earn him a sarcastic remark from Miguel. But just as Miguel opened his mouth, a familiar jingle poured through the woods.

"What the hell," Ethan said. "An ice cream truck?"

"There's no way. There aren't any neighborhoods for miles," said Tony.

"I could go for some ice cream. You guys got any cash?" Miguel asked, standing up and looking in the direction of the music.

"It's cold as hell out here, Miguel. What's wrong with you?" Ethan looked over at Tony with a bewildered expression. Tony shrugged. Miguel's mind worked in mysterious ways.

"It's never too cold for cookies and cream," Miguel stated matter-of-factly.

Tony sighed, shook his head, and got to his feet. "I've got a five." He took the folded five-dollar bill out of his pocket and waved it in the air.

"Badass – let's go get some ice cream."

The boys slipped on their shirts and shoes and followed the jingle through the dense foliage, leaving the beaten path to keep the sound in front of them. Tony did his best to keep his teeth from chattering, but the wind had picked up and the little sunlight that was left was hiding behind the towering pines. He wouldn't have admitted it to the others, but the cold was not the only thing bothering him. A growing sense of dread had begun to blossom within him.

Ethan let out a high-pitched squeal as a red squirrel darted out in front of him.

"Be careful, Ethan; I heard the squirrels around these parts are deadly," Miguel said with a snicker.

Tony smiled, relieved that he wasn't the only one feeling uneasy.

The music grew louder as the boys continued their march through the woods. But there was another sound that continued to swell along with the tune of the ice cream truck.

"Do you guys hear that?" Tony asked. "It sounds like … birds?" As if on cue, a glob of white bird crap landed on Ethan's shoulder.

"Aw, nasty!" Ethan yelled.

Tony looked up to see a flock of pigeons resting in a pine tree above them, their soft coos harmonizing with the jingle of the ice cream truck. A woodpecker began hammering a tree nearby, adding to the strange melody.

The sun was now fully enveloped by the horizon, leaving the sky a deep purple, making it even harder for the boys to see where they were walking. But just as Tony was about to suggest that they turn around before they got completely lost, a yellow light trickled through the trees in front of them. As they drew closer, the light grew stronger, illuminating their path. The sounds of the birds, the peculiar light and the song of the ice cream truck filled the woods with life.

"Holy shit …" Tony whispered as the trees abruptly gave way to a grassy, circular clearing encompassed by pine trees on all sides.

Drooping over the clearing like an enormous glowing spiderweb were dozens of overlapping strings of light. Lining the strings in every direction were birds. So many birds. Blue jays, robins, cardinals, pigeons, woodpeckers, and many birds that Tony didn't recognize – all singing, chirping and tweeting at once, creating a cacophony of noise. In the center of the clearing, covered in hundreds of birds itself, was the ice cream truck. A giant, plastic ice cream cone filled with pink ice cream and littered with bird feces sat on top of the large white truck. Holes had been drilled into it, transforming it into a giant birdhouse. Multiple perches stuck out of the truck like growths, each crowded with a different bird species. The side of the truck was lined with paintings of different ice cream flavors and treats. The serving window was propped open, but Tony couldn't see anyone inside of it. In front of the truck were four wooden picnic tables with red and white striped umbrellas jutting out of the center of them. Unsurprisingly, these were also cluttered with various feathered creatures. Despite the impossible number of birds, the air smelled chocolatey and sweet.

A barred owl swooped within inches of Tony, causing him to snap out of his trance. The owl fluttered onto the sill of the service window and pecked a small metal bell tied to the top of it.

"W-what the fuck is going on?" Ethan asked.

"I don't know, man, but there better not be bird shit in my ice cream or I'm gonna be pissed," Miguel responded.

Just as Tony opened his mouth to ask Miguel if he was seriously still going to get ice cream, a man appeared in the open window. A square, white hat sat on top of his greasy brown hair that lay plastered to his skull. His nose, long and pointy like a beak, sat between two dark, beady eyes. A wide, toothy smile crept over his thin face, wrinkling every inch of visible skin – skin that seemed to hang loosely off the man's skull. At the base of his scrawny neck, below an Adam's apple roughly the size of a golf ball, sat a black bowtie, cinching together the top of a white button-down shirt.

"You boys want to try the best ice cream on the planet?" the man asked. His voice was shrill and raspy, like that of a crow.

Tony glanced at Ethan, relieved to find that he wore a similar look of confusion and apprehension.

"Maybe we should ..." Tony started, his words falling on deaf ears as Miguel started strolling towards the ice cream truck.

"What are you doing?!" Tony hissed.

"Getting some ice cream," Miguel shot coolly over his shoulder.

Ethan gave Tony a shrug. Miguel seemed to lack the alarm that would be going off in most people's heads right about now. Nothing about this situation was normal in the least, but that did nothing to dissuade the boy from a scoop of cookies and cream ice cream, whether it was covered in bird shit or not.

Tony sighed and, ignoring the alarms that were very much going off in his head, started after Miguel. After all, Miguel was one of his best friends, stubborn or not, and he wasn't about to let him get kidnapped by some weird-ass bird-man.

A murder of crows fluttered out of the way as Miguel carelessly slogged through them.

"What can I get you, young man?" The ice cream man squawked as Miguel approached the window.

"Do you ha—" Miguel jumped back, seemingly startled by something in the ice cream truck.

Tony cautiously approached the truck with Ethan right behind him. Standing to the right of the strange man, with an ice cream scoop clamped in its enormous beak, was an insidious looking bird that appeared to be about 4 ft tall. It glared at them with large, almost humanlike eyes underneath its grey plumage. Its long legs and knobby knees betrayed its menacing appearance.

"Oh!" the ice cream man exclaimed, his smile growing even larger, displaying his dark yellow teeth, "No need to be alarmed, boys; this is Harold. He's a shoebill stork and a wonderful assistant!"

As if on cue, the shoebill dipped down into the ice cream display, coming back up with a scoop of cookies and cream ice cream. He gently set the scoop onto a waffle cone sitting in a rack. The ice cream man gently lifted the cone out of the rack with a long, spindly hand dressed in a white glove.

"How'd you know I was going to order that?" Miguel asked, sounding unsure for the first time.

"A little birdie told me," he replied with a wink.

Tony's alarm began to ring louder. "Okay, thank you, sir. How much will that be? We should really be going."

"You don't want anything, bro?" Miguel's apprehension seemed to have dissipated as quickly as it had come.

Tony stared at him, dumbfounded. "No, Miguel, I *don't* want anything." he said through gritted teeth, with a stare that was meant to pierce Miguel's soul. But Miguel didn't seem to notice.

"Alright, suit yourself. Want anything, Ethan?" Miguel asked.

"N-no, I'm okay. Tony's right; it's getting late. My parents are going to be worried sick."

"How about this," the ice cream man said, never breaking from his toothy smile. "This one's on the house. After all, this is your first time having the best ice cream in the world, and I couldn't live with the guilt of knowing that you missed out on it."

Ethan twisted his hands together and stared down at his feet. "Oh, um … okay, I'll get a …" he murmured distractedly, as a duck with a glistening emerald head waddled between his legs in search of bugs.

"You don't have to get anything, Ethan," Tony said, becoming wearier with each passing moment.

"Holy crap, this is amazing!" Miguel said, before heading in for another lick.

"Maybe just one scoop," Ethan muttered, eyeing Miguel as he rapidly devoured his ice cream. "Do you have mint chocolate chip?"

"Of course we do!" the ice cream man exclaimed.

The shoebill dipped his head into the ice cream display and came up with a scoop of pastel green ice cream peppered with chocolate chips.

"Nasty," Miguel said, giving the mint chocolate chip a disdainful glare.

Ethan grabbed the ice cream cone and muttered, "Thank you."

"Perhaps a sample would convince *you*, young man," the ice cream man coaxed. His unblinking, beady eyes held Tony in place.

He extended an exceptionally long arm out towards Tony. A small yellow spoon topped with chocolate ice cream was pinched between two of his gloved fingers.

Well, maybe just a bite, Tony thought, but just as he plucked the spoon from the ice cream man's hand, Miguel let out a loud moan and doubled over with his arms wrapped tightly around his abdomen.

"My stomach," he groaned.

"Maybe if you hadn't eaten it like you were a starving animal, your stomach wouldn't hurt!" Ethan scolded, taking a lick of his own ice cream.

Tony wasn't convinced. He dropped his sample spoon onto the floor. "We need to head home. *Now*."

"Whoops! You dropped your sample; I'll get you another one," the ice cream man said with a shrill laugh that sent a chill down Tony's spine.

"No, I don't want a—"

"What is that?!" Ethan screamed.

Tony followed Ethan's wide-eyed stare to Miguel, who was now huddled in the fetal position on the ground. His moans had turned into desperate whimpers. Confusion and terror took hold of Tony as he realized what Ethan was screaming at. Large pimple-like bumps had sprung up along Miguel's arms and the back of his neck. The bumps writhed frantically as if something was trying to escape from within. And just as this thought crossed Tony's mind, something *did* escape one of the papules. At first, Tony thought it was a black spine of some sort, but as more began erupting from Miguel's skin, he realized what they were.

"Feathers," he whispered, his eyes glued to the horrific scene unfolding before him.

"W-what?" Ethan squeaked, taking a step back but never looking away from Miguel.

"Feathers. He's growing feathers!"

Miguel's whimpers turned to screams.

"Guys, what's happening? Please help me! *Please!*"

Fighting every urge to turn and run, Tony bent down to help Miguel. He stopped inches from his friend as cracking sounds began to emanate from within him. His screams became louder.

His left arm jolted in an unnatural direction, and with it came another hideous crack.

His bones are breaking, Tony realized as tears formed in his eyes.

Miguel's neck snapped up. He stared wide-eyed and desperate at Tony and Ethan. He opened his mouth as if he was going to scream, but what came out sounded more like the squawk of a parrot. His lips began to rip, sending small streams of blood down his chin. As the skin parted, an orange beak pushed its way to the surface. His blue eyes began to darken and shrink into his skull.

"TONY!" Ethan's shout broke Tony from his trance.

The cacophony of birds had formed a tight circle around the boys. Their songs and calls had fallen silent as they fluttered to the pine needle-covered ground.

"Young man," the ice cream man called, "please try the ice cream. It truly is the best in the world." His smile had faded. His long lips stretched into a scowl as he reached even further out of the ice cream truck window to hand Tony another sample.

"We need to get the hell out of here, Ethan!"

"B-but Miguel ..." His words faded to a gasp as he laid eyes on Miguel – or rather, the creature who had been Miguel only moments ago. A green parrot with red neck plumage lay on its side, covered in blood and other unknown fluids, breathing heavily and squawking softly.

"Take a bite—" Tony smacked the spoon out of the ice cream man's hand before he could finish his sentence.

"RUN!" Tony screamed.

Tony and Ethan broke into a sprint directly into the mass of birds. Screeches of protest emanated from many of the birds as the boys ran through them. Feathers of all colors flew in every direction. Blue jays, martins, cardinals, and many small birds that Tony couldn't identify dove from the streams of lights, pecking frantically at the boys. Larger birds ran alongside them, pecking and flapping their wings.

Ethan screamed in agony. Tony glanced in his direction, expecting to see an eagle attempting to claw out his eyes, but what he actually saw was so much worse.

Bumps were protruding from Ethan's face and arms. He scratched at them desperately as he ran. A large crow planted itself in front of Ethan. Tony yelled to warn him, but it was too late; Ethan went sprawling to the forest floor, and the mass of birds swarmed him like vultures to a carcass.

Tony turned on a dime and made a run for Ethan.

The ice cream man's skeletal hand shot through the bird cluster and grabbed Tony's arm. With unexpected strength, he pulled Tony within inches of himself. His beady eyes burned with rage. His breath, reeking of rotten fruit, infiltrated Tony's nostrils as he spoke.

"Eat. Your. Fucking. Ice. Cream."

His other hand, holding a cone full of what looked to be chocolate ice cream, came swinging towards Tony.

Tony froze; the awful realization that he would soon be joining his friends ensnared his mind.

A white blur slammed into the ice cream man just as he was about to shove the ice cream into Tony's mouth. His grip released from Tony's arm, but he couldn't move. He stood numb with fear and sadness, watching as Ethan wrestled to keep the ice cream man pinned down. His arms and legs were covered in white feathers, and his face – typically peppered with freckles – was now more barn owl than human. He glanced back at Tony, and though no words came out of his mouth, his eyes told Tony all he needed to know: *Run.*

Tears and sweat poured down Tony's cheeks as he turned to flee. He pushed through the tsunami of birds, not feeling any pain as they pecked and clawed relentlessly at his exposed flesh.

At some point he must have broken out of the chaos, but time seemed to have lost all sense of meaning as Tony continued to run as fast as his exhausted legs could carry him.

He reached the edge of the forest, but there was no way he was taking any chances; he kept running. He passed Swellrock Middle School. It sneered at him under the moonlight, mocking his empty dreams of having the year of his life with his two best friends. He passed Glitch Arcade, where the trio used to spend nearly every Friday after school sinking countless hours into *Mortal Kombat* and *X-Men*. He passed his street and considered going home, throwing himself into his parents' arms and never leaving the house again, but he knew that wasn't the right thing to do. He kept running, drenched in sweat despite the chill of the night, until he reached the Swellrock police department.

◆◆◆

Early morning sun hid behind the rows of pine trees, casting long shadows along the forest floor. Dew jumped from knee-high grass and clung to Officer Charles' uniform, plastering the black polyester to his shins. He slapped at a mosquito who buzzed away sluggishly, plump with his blood.

"Fuckin' mosquitoes," he muttered.

"Are you sure we're headed in the right direction?" Mitch asked, panting. His uniform, drenched in sweat, clung to his large beer belly.

Charles glanced down at the map of Swellrock Forest. An orange crayon-drawn circle indicated the location of the pond where Tony and his friends had been hanging out. A crude line ran from the pond to where Tony believed he and his friends had encountered the so-called ice cream man. Despite multiple promptings, Tony had refused to come with the officers. He had seemed shocked that they would even suggest it. After having Tony show them where he believed the strange events had occurred, Charles had the boy picked up by an ambulance and taken to the nearest ER to have his wounds treated.

They had found the pond just as Tony had described it; littered with cattails and lily pads. The mud displayed the boys' footprints – souvenirs of what may have been their last moments of happiness. Charles and Mitch followed the footprints until they disappeared into the layers of pine needles and then continued in that direction, hoping it was a straight shot to the clearing Tony had described.

The boy's story, although obviously unbelievable and strange, had unraveled an unease within Charles that he hadn't felt since childhood.

A crow squawked from its perch in a nearby pine tree.

Charles jumped, and his hand darted to the gun holstered to his hip.

Mitch let out a bellow of laughter and slapped Charles on the back. "Scared the ice cream man is gonna come turn you into a peacock?" Charles felt a pool of relief spread through him.

Just a damn bird.

"I'm glad you think this is all a joke," Charles shot back, glaring at Mitch.

"It's a load of bullshit. The kid's tryin' to cover somethin' up with that weird-ass story," Mitch said as he squeezed a wad of chewing tobacco with his sweaty fingers and tucked it behind his lip.

"He seemed … traumatized. Like whatever he saw messed him up pretty bad." Charles could feel his temples begin to throb with frustration. He wasn't sure why. He knew the absurdity of the story, and Mitch had every right to question it, but Tony definitely didn't seem like he was lying as he described his friends turning into birds between snot-ridden sobs.

"I think he fucked up, and his story was some kinda last-ditch effort to push the blame elsewhere. Maybe they were tryna to break into Pete Sleider's yard and got themselves shot." Mitch paused and spat a black glob of tobacco onto a pinecone. "Sleider has always had a bit of a trigger finger. 'Specially if he thought some teenagers were tryna steal from him."

"These are kid's *lives*, Mitch. It's not a fucking game."

Charles could see the clearing materialize through the pines. He picked up the pace, happy to avoid Mitch's next moronic response.

As he approached the clearing, it became clear that it was just that: a clearing. There were no birds, no string lights interweaving into some sadistic spiderweb, and sure as hell no ice cream truck. It was just a grass-covered clearing lined with pine trees on every side.

"Damn … I could have gone for a chocolate cone right about now." Mitch let out a thunderous laugh at his own shitty joke.

Charles ignored him and said, "I'm going to take a look around."

As the minutes passed, Charles began to lose hope that they would find anything at all.

The clearing was the epitome of "clear". There wasn't a blade of grass out of place.

Just as he was about to concede defeat and suggest they look further into the woods, a flash of white caught his eye at the edge of the clearing. Halfway up a nearby pine tree sat a barn owl, staring down at him with an inquisitive tilt of its head. The beauty of the creature transfixed Charles. Its white plumage radiated from within the foliage like a priceless jewel gleaming from the depth of a dark lake.

He felt his heart begin to race as Tony's story came storming to the front of his mind.

It can't be—

"Find somethin'?"

"Shit!" Charles jumped. His eyes tore away from the owl. "Don't sneak up on me, Mitch!" His heart pounded in his ears.

"I wasn't sneakin' up on you, Charlie. I called over here three times, but you didn't say nothin'. You were just starin' up at that tree with this terrified look on your face. Figured you found a body or somethin'."

Charles sighed, frustrated with himself for being so jumpy. "No, no body, just a barn o—" The word caught in his throat as he looked up and realized that the owl was gone. "There was a ..." There was something on the branch where the owl had been perched. Without a second thought, he began making his way up the large pine tree, hoisting himself up branch by branch; a maneuver he hadn't performed since he was a teenager.

"The hell you doin' now, man?" Mitch asked, sounding a bit exasperated.

Charles ignored him and continued up the tree until he reached the branch the barn owl had been perched on. He stared down at the pale green substance seeping between the creases of the bark.

It's just owl shit, Charles. Just some nasty owl shit, Charles thought, but deep down, he knew no owl shit on earth looked like that.

He felt numb. He could see his finger mindlessly drift towards the sticky substance, dip into it and pull back towards his nose, confirming his fear.

It was mint.

CRIME

UP TO THE ROOF

Tony Mastrogiorgio

5 to 10 minutes

After a few decades writing marketing copy, Tony Mastrogiorgio sought to atone for his crimes against the culture by returning to his passion: serious writing. Unfortunately, his Irish mother's darkly comic sense of humor had burrowed too deeply into his soul. As ennobling and heartrending as he wanted his work to be, he found that where others cry, he laughs, and where others laugh, he cries. He has given in to his nature and is now at work on several projects ranging from lively trash to what he describes (with considerable embarrassment) as literary comic fiction.

I went up to the roof to be alone. I came back down wanted in three states. That's how fast fate kicks you in the balls. No wind up, no three steps back. Just bam and you're on your knees.

Who's to say why it came out the way it did? Judges and juries think they make the call, but they weren't there. No one was there, not for all of it; no one but me and Nina. And we don't even know. Not 100%. We don't see who spins the wheel or rolls the dice. We don't know if the wheel is weighted or the dice are shaved. None of us know, not on the suckers' side of the table. We just watch the dealer rake in the chips with a grin that says the fix was always in.

How do you beat the fix? You don't play the game. That's it, the only way. Sit on your brains and do nothing. Too late for me now; my game's done. I'm facing the Big Bedtime, the Final Tuck-in. I have a reservation at the warden's Bed-No-Breakfast down the end of the gray highway. Was there any chance it comes out different, some little thing turns this way instead of that and me and Nina get to live our lives like regular Dicks and Janes?

Maybe Ma sends me to the store instead, or my kid brother turns off the boob tube and I don't have to go up to the roof for a little peace and quiet. Maybe when I go through the door, I turn right instead of left and go my merry way. Or the Big Maybe: maybe Nina's not sunbathing in her underwear, stretched out on a yellow terrycloth island floating in a black tarpaper sea, her legs reaching all the way down to her feet.

What the hell was she thinking, laying there like that out in the open, hid between the stairhead and the wall where anyone could see her? It's not safe for a girl, not with some of the guys we got running around.

Yeah, sure, I take a look. Maybe a good one. Or two or three or four. That's on me. But five years she's down the hall from me and

I'm nothing but respectful, never thinking about what's hid under her school skirt, white blouse and school blazer. I don't join in any of that crude talk the other guys say about her. I'm not one of those guys twisting this way and that, trying to see up to her underwear when she sits Indian style. I keep it to the three inches of skin north of her knee socks and south of her plaid hemline. I don't go looking for more. Sure, I get a glimpse sometimes, but I don't go looking. Not much anyway.

What is it with God, anyway? Don't give into temptation. Ok, so I don't. Then He lets her get the idea to strip down and lay out like that? Now I can't help it. I take a look or two or three or four. *Bless me Father, for I have sinned.* Now let me go back downstairs and beat my meat. That's the thing. He builds it into the system that you always want the next thing. See her underwear? Now you're thinking about what's underneath. God don't make it easy to be good.

The mystery is why'd she call me over after she spotted me. No covering herself up or squawking that she's going to rat me out to my ma. She just shifts over and pats the towel next to her. What's she playing out? A smart guy thinks maybe she's a snare ready to snap if I get close. Sometimes I'm a smart guy, but not then I wasn't. I feel like the river card's flipped an ace and I won the biggest pot of my life.

Ask yourself, what would you do? You'd tell yourself you can still make the smart play when you're done. Take your winnings and go. Even now when they're running juice to test the chair, I tell myself that's what I could have done. Let me tell you, the Pit Boss in the Sky gets a big laugh watching me squirm on the tarpaper, my knees squished in a sticky seam. He knows the suckers never walk away. They gamble it all back. He knows that every stupid move brings on the next stupid move. He knows you'll start thinking one big win makes us square. So, you put all your today and all your tomorrows on the table. When you lose, you can't handle the vig and you can't run out, not with God keeping the books. Makes you lose faith, like there's nothing an honest man can do to stay clean.

She tells me she's pregnant. My gut tells me she ain't. That was a chance to break things my way. But that's not how I play it. I say, that's alright. Get this thing out in the open. No more sneaking up to the roof. Kick my brother out of our room and live with Ma.

Nina says fine, but we still need money.

Fine by me, I say. I'll quit high school and get a job.

Before I can get the words out, she shows me the gun.

Nina, baby, what the hell, I say. She says it's her old man's, left it behind when he pulled his twenty to life stretch. He won't need it no more, she says.

I say, we don't need it now, sister.

A couple jobs, she says, a quick stake then toss in the river.

What river, I ask.

I get it now. Stupid question, like I was accepting her premise. Alright, maybe she's got a point. Sure baby, a couple jobs. No more than two. Maybe three. Four max. More than four is out of the question. I'm no crook, I tell her. I gotta stand firm on this.

She smiles like it's all my say so. Sure baby, she says and sticks her hand down my pants.

No more than five, I say.

Some of this is on me. I handed her the gun while I cleared out the cash drawer. Soon as I turn my back, the gun goes off.

Nina, baby, you ok, I say. I figure she don't know guns. I don't either, but I seen more movies than her. Hair trigger, maybe. That's what they say. Things go off, like poor Marvin getting his head exploded in *Pulp Fiction*. Marvin had it easy. No time to think. His head was gone before the sound reached where his ears used to be. Not this poor bastard. Gut shot. He's got time to watch the curtain come down. It's like I can hear his dying thoughts that he shoulda called in sick and let the relief man get it in the belly instead.

Nina, baby, I say again. You ok? I'm ready for hysterics. Ready to tell her it ain't her fault. Except she ain't hysterical. She's locked eyes with the guy like she's telling, got a complaint? Take it up with the Pit Boss, buddy.

She giggles, maybe. I flash on my first good idea since I went up to the roof. Lam it. Get out. Hit the road. A solo run.

Maybe she's in shock, I tell myself. That was nerves, not real laughing. This'll hit her hard later. That night she throws me down on my bed and rides me like a maniac, bucking and fucking like she never did before. To tell the truth, I'm almost ashamed of her yipping and yahooing, waking up my brother in the next bed. I mouth *I'm sorry* to the kid. She collapses on me, purring. I smell gun smoke, sex and sweat. My sweat. I gotta take a stand here or this could get bad. Straighten her up, set her flying right. She was a good kid down deep.

No more, baby, I say. Nix the gun play. Just the cash.

Sure, she says.

No more, right?

Sure, she says. I got carried away.

Ok, I think. Maybe we can make this work.

Next night, another clerk, another gut shot. Another set of eyes, this time saying, *mister, control your woman.* This time she can't wait. She climbs on top of me in the car in the alley behind the store. I'm listening for sirens; she's rocking the car. You still got the gun, baby, I want to say. Just plug me, right in the head. Let me come and go.

You ain't gonna stop, I ask her.

Stop what, she says.

Come on, baby. If you gotta, make it quick. Head shot. Can't take them looking at me.

Sure, baby, she says. Anything for my man.

Next night, another gut. This guy speaks up before he goes down. Now that was plain mean, he tells me. Tell her, I think. She's pulling the trigger.

She can't go on like this. She's got three bullets left in the gun. Things'll run their course and she'll settle down. The next morning, I find a fresh box of shells in her handbag. I don't know, I tell myself, maybe she just ain't no good.

It wears on a guy, watching your girl plug a couple dozen clerks in the belly, a couple dozen sets of eyes look at me for the answer. The last one took about ten minutes to go, her face all quizzical like it's a science experiment and she's writing a report. Sorry fella, I tell him. It's a tough break.

No more. I had to put a stop to her torturing me with all these dying eyes. Next night, I grab the gun from her outside the store, stare at her hard. How about a little mercy this time, baby? I go in the door and shoot the guy in the head before he knows what's happening, cram the cash in my pockets, and head back out. Nina's there, looking all different, and it's not just the five cops running out of the diner next door.

That's him, officers, she yelled. He's the man who kidnapped me!

I didn't think she'd do me like she did. Testifying in court in her school uniform. Telling the jury how I dragged her to the roof and had my way with her. She's sniffling, wipes her tears on her sleeves. The judge looks like he wants to hang me right there. No one sees Nina pull her skirt up a bit and let her legs fall open enough so I can see her underwear. I wonder if it's the same pair she wore up on the roof. I realize the whole jury can see me tilting my head to get a better view. One old prune scowled at me, then fakes like electricity's shooting through her body. She smirks. I was done for.

I don't blame Nina. She was smart. She got probation and a publishing contract.

Thing is, I would have taken the fall if she asked me. Let me go out a man, a stand-up guy. Let me do it for love or whatever it was I thought was going on. I would have backed her up, saying I held the gun on her and made her do all twenty-four holdups. That I tied her to the bed at night to keep her from running away. If she only let me go down like a man.

The bottom line, whether it's science or God or crooked dice, if you go up to the roof, you deserve what you get.

HORROR

LEGACY

S. M. Davis

15 to 20 minutes

S. M. Davis was born, raised and educated in New England, receiving undergraduate degrees in theater and religion and a Masters of Divinity in Buddhist Ministry. He is a Buddhist teacher and a translator, splitting his time between India and the USA. His writing has previously appeared in *Garbology: The GarbAugust Anthology of Awesome Trash.*

Beep. Beep. Beep. Richard barely registered the constant soundtrack of the machines keeping his husband alive. Now, nine months after the accident, it felt like he spent more time bedside in this hard plastic chair than anywhere else. If anything, the beeps and hums soothed him, reminded him that Tom was still here. For the first few weeks the doctors had been optimistic, hopeful Tom would wake up. But Richard had watched their optimism wane, and now every conversation was nothing but silent pity. He'd never given up hope, and it felt like that's what they pitied most.

He grabbed the bed rail and awkwardly pulled himself up, looking at the still raw stump where his left hand used to be. He had no clue what kind of magic the witch might work with his "one hand, freely offered", and he didn't care. It was a price he had been more than willing to pay. He cupped Tom's face with his good hand, grateful that a beard hid the cavities of Tom's sunken cheeks. "Don't worry, baby," he whispered, unable to stop the tears. "I found them. I told you I'd find them. This will all be over soon."

He pulled the mushroom from his pocket, by all accounts ordinary looking. *This is what a left hand will buy you*, he thought, flashing back to that night in the woods. To the witch, calmly handing him what looked like a butcher's cleaver made of a savage black stone, freezing cold. "One hand, freely offered," they'd said. "That is the price for your husband's life. Will you pay?" Kneeling at the large tree stump before him, an unholy altar, Richard had laid his forearm flat. *Just a log to be split*, he had tried to convince himself. He crashed the blade down and pain thundered through his body, blood erupting, painting the stump a grisly maroon. But the blow hadn't been strong enough. He smashed the blade down again and again in a hacking frenzy of terror and pain, but it still wasn't enough. His hand remained stubbornly attached, flesh and tendons severed but exposed, glistening bones refusing to let this be easy. The witch had looked on with a knowing fascination, a cat playing with an injured mouse.

Light-headed, the world already starting to dim around the edges, Richard had brought the knife up again but couldn't steady his vision enough to aim true. Skin and flesh hacked away, he rested the trembling blade directly against the obstinate bones, and, levering his bodyweight against that freezing edge, he splintered through his wrist one agonizing scream at a time. Marrow oozed out of the glistening shards and mixed with the pooling blood as Richard silently begged for some sort of shock, anything to dull the relentless throb.

Suddenly the pain had subsided, the smell of mint and sage filling his nostrils. He had looked up just as the witch stepped toward him. "Well paid," they'd said, as they placed a small mushroom in the steaming pool on the stump, where it sucked up his blood and marrow like a sentient sponge before shrinking back to a desiccated state. "Listen closely. This magic is not a trifle. Magic this strong will always birth undesired consequences, even as it fulfills your wishes. Here is what you need to know …"

Beep. Beep. Beep. Richard glanced at the monitors, making sure Tom's heartbeat was still strong. The witch had been very clear: Tom needed to be alive for this to work. Satisfied with the electronic peaks and valleys he gently opened Tom's mouth and slipped the mushroom under his tongue. His fingers lingered on Tom's lips as he lovingly closed his jaw, and the moment overwhelmed him. In that split second he experienced an eternity – the seventeen years he and Tom had been together, the future decades they deserved. He realized that he was holding his breath, not sure what was supposed to happen next, terrified and optimistic in equal measure.

Tom opened his eyes.

◆◆◆

Richard stumbled through the brush, not caring as his legs were torn by thorny brambles, his face slapped by tree limbs. There was only one place to go. No walking path could bring him there, but he knew the route. It had taken months to find the way last time, but it wasn't the kind of thing you could forget. Five years. Five glorious years, but not enough. How could this have happened again? There was no way one heart could withstand that much torment. There had to be a way out.

After the fame of his miraculous recovery had faded, Tom had suggested they move to the cabin full-time. They sold their home, and Tom's investment acumen combined with the frugality of cabin life meant the profits would be able to sustain them for decades. Richard had been all too happy to be at the cabin, which had been in Tom's family for generations. Not only had Tom proposed to him in this cabin, but these woods were home to the witch that had given them their second chance. It seemed only fitting that they live out their days here.

Tom had been chopping wood when it happened. Richard didn't see or hear anything, he'd been carrying an armful to the stack around the cabin's far side. He returned to find Tom collapsed near the chopping stump, his lips already taking on a bluish tinge. How could the end of the world have happened so silently? Richard started chest compressions, felt a rib snap in his frenzy. It didn't matter. Thomas was gone. Richard had lost his husband. Again.

The air around him changed as he stumbled into a small clearing that housed what looked to be an old hunting shed. A hut, really, with holes in the roof and wooden panels rotting off. He knew looks were deceiving, though, and drunkenly burst through the doorway. As he crossed that moldy threshold he entered into an expansive parlor, ephemera-filled jars fighting with countless old books for space on the tall shelves that lined the room. Flames crackled in a grand fireplace along the far wall, taking the bite out of the autumn air. There, feeding a fresh log to the fire, their back to the door, was who he had come to see. The one who could fix this. The witch.

Richard's breath caught in his throat. He couldn't look directly at the witch, not even at their back. They had an otherworldly beauty that was terrifying, and he knew that to look too long courted madness. Richard's heart trembled with fear and anguish, a terror confused by the vague sexual energy that saturated the air. Even keeping his gaze downcast he could feel the pressure building not only behind his eyes but also deep in his groin, something both feral and transcendent. He wanted to beg and plead, but, recognizing his trespass, held his tongue. He prayed he hadn't committed too great an offense, but was desperate enough not to care.

"Did you burn the body?" the witch asked, not turning to face him, their voice enchanting and dangerous, a razorblade coated in honey.

"What? No, I, I ..." Richard stammered, all at once realizing this may have been a mistake. His chest hitched, exhaustion the only thing keeping sobs from overwhelming him. "No, I need your help. You have to help me bring him back. Name your price, please! I can't lose him again."

Without warning, the witch was directly in front of him, grabbing Richard's face and forcing him to look directly into their eyes. He saw infinite galaxies, untold millennia of burning worlds, and felt his mind disconnect from reality. He realized, distantly, that *witch* was not even close to the right way to describe the being in front of him. That was how all the campfire stories, passed down through Tom's family, had described the creature that lived in the woods, yet it captured nothing of this divinity. Richard couldn't escape the myth he found himself lost in.

"When you were here last, I gave you two instructions," they said, the steel of their voice chilling Richard's bones. "Do not use the mushroom if your husband had already died, and, after eating the mushroom, upon death, burn his body immediately. Did you think my instructions mere trivialities?"

Richard remembered this admonition, now. But it hadn't been anywhere near his mind when he'd seen Thomas crumpled on the ground, the long-handled axe sticking out from under his limp body. When he couldn't revive him. When he'd carried him into the cabin, laying him down on the bed. When he had laid down next to him, delirious, praying to wake up and find out this had all been a grotesque nightmare.

That had been yesterday evening. When he woke this morning to find Thomas cold and stiff beside him, he'd broken down. He remembered a burn of whisky in his throat, and nothing else until the woods. It was early evening now, and those intervening hours were lost, his grief not a fog but a hurricane, decimating all thought. He wanted to protest, wanted to explain, but the creature – witch, fae, god, angel, demon, he had no clue – didn't give him the chance.

"I felt for you, the last time you visited me. I had seen the two of you in my woods for years, and felt the love you shared. I felt a love that was a rebellion, a love that had faced trial and tribulation." Their voice was a hybrid signal, inviting Richard deeper and warning him away at the same time. Just hearing it evoked a hideous awe. "That isn't something I feel in most of the humans who travel these woods," they continued. "Their love is usually small, it is easy. Taken for granted. I had felt what I *thought* was something different between you two, and I pitied the loss of that.

"But I see you before me now, and I realize I was wrong." They hadn't yet let go of Richard's face, and while he heard every word they were saying he felt far away at the same time, like the tether connecting him to this life, this reality, was quietly fraying. "I see now, you're the same as the rest," they sneered. "It isn't love that brings you to my doorstep, it is lust. Attachment. You care about your grief, not about your husband. This selfish desire has echoes of real love, and it is something hard-earned, that is still true. But it is focused only on yourself. There's nothing I can do for you. I suggest you make haste to burn his body, while there's still time."

They finally released Richard's face, and as he crashed back into his body he found himself alone in a dilapidated hunting shed. Rats and other vermin nested in the corners, and the purple sky of early dusk was peeking through the holes in the roof. He fell to his knees, surrounded by the smell of rot and decay, but with a new clarity of mind. They were right, it was fear that had brought him here. He feared he wasn't strong enough to fight without Thomas holding him up. He feared being alone. But, gods be damned, he *did* love his husband! Yes, it was a selfish love, but, given what they had faced, he felt they had deserved to be a little selfish. But he couldn't be selfish now. He didn't know what would happen if he didn't burn Tom's body, but he knew that, whatever it was, he wanted better for him. They had defied mortality once, and gotten five amazing, blessed years. It would have to be enough.

He got up and began to slowly make his way back in the direction of his cabin. A crescent moon was just teasing the horizon, but there was plenty of crepuscular light, intensifying the feeling of being in a liminal space, a place in-between, a time when reality felt thin. Fear invaded his mind as he considered the warning, and he tried to hurry his pace. He emerged from the tree line facing the front of his cabin and saw the door open, listing inward. *I was delusional with grief,* he rationalized. *I don't even remember walking into the woods, of course I didn't pull it closed all the way.* But it felt wrong, and he sped up, reaching a jog before stopping short at the nightmare a few yards in front of his front steps.

It *had* been a fox, but now it was a bloody mess, its stomach torn apart and ropes of intestines spilling out, a large pool of blood soaking the earth around it. Worse, though, were the mushrooms. Its stomach cavity was filled with mushrooms, growing like tumors, eating the carcass from the inside out. Some were even emerging through its fur, growing in a band around its neck and across its jowls. Fungal growth ringed the devastated remains, growing through the pool of coagulating blood like the chalk outline at a murder scene. This was not good.

His mind raced as he skirted around the mess, going up the steps and cautiously approaching the door, only to hesitate on his front stoop. The door was ripe with fungi, growing right from the wood. Dark patches of growth framed the door and were spreading out across the walls. He pushed the door open further, careful to touch only the wood, and the smell of dark earth assaulted him. A desperate need emanated from the blackened interior. He stepped back on the small porch, his feet cresting the top step. He didn't want to go in there.

Directly behind him, a ragged hiss pierced the air.

He jolted, turning abruptly and, losing his footing, fell flat, landing with his back to the hungry cabin's gaping maw. The fox stood before him, dead eyes staring, and a wet hiss continued to escape its bloody mouth. It took a step toward him, guts leaving a fetid trail of crimson behind it as they dragged on the ground. "Fuuuuuuck me," Richard moaned, scrambling backwards in a frantic bid to get into the cabin, to close a door between himself and whatever this was. The fox lunged forward as he crossed the threshold, and he kicked the door shut just in time for the fox's body to slam against it with a moist crunch. Richard got to his feet and quickly twisted the deadbolt into place, not wanting to believe an undead fox could work a doorknob, but not willing to take any chances, either.

He wheeled around, realizing he was inside the cabin, where he had been terrified to enter just a moment before. His eyes followed the carpet of putrescent growth from the front door, across the living room, to the bedroom. Doing his best to step around the rot, he approached the bedroom doorway, an arm in front of his face in a vain attempt to protect himself from the spores that every footfall kicked up. A groan escaped his lips as he saw the bed where Tom had lain, overgrown with mushrooms but absent a body. The crisp smell of autumn coming through the cracked window did nothing to cover the ripe stench coming from the overgrown bed, the room a sulfuric sepulcher.

His brain tried to insist this wasn't happening, and he could feel himself checking out.

The fox continually crashed its broken body against the front door, the repeated thuds a monotonous drone threatening to sink him further into a fugue state. He fought the inertia, trying to focus on the easel in the corner, on the partially completed portrait that rested on it. He had scratched together a living as an artist his whole adult life, and he had been decent, selling enough to live off of, at least when combined with Tom's income. But, as impassioned as he had been, his work had never been *great*, had never felt particularly transportive or effortless. That had all changed after Tom's recovery and the move to the cabin. Richard had been absolutely inspired the last five years, and his work "transcendent", at least according to the gallery he partnered with in the city, where his new pieces were selling for ten times what his old work used to sell for. Tom's second life had brought something out in Richard, a tender intensity he hadn't known he was capable of. Unlike the half-finished piece in the corner most of his work wasn't portraiture, but Tom was still there on every canvas. Tom lived in him, and in every stroke of his brush.

He let out a deep breath, settling into a dull determination, and contemplated the awful diorama before him. He couldn't give in to despair. That isn't what Tom would have wanted, not how he would have wanted to be remembered. Richard knew what he had to do. He turned out of the bedroom and, again stepping around the creeping fungal carpet, began to make his way across the living room. He paused, realizing he couldn't hear the fox anymore. The quiet was thick, matching the choking smell of ripe earth that filled the cabin. He went to the front door and cautiously put his ear against it, straining to hear anything, rewarded with a terrifying silence. He slowly unlocked the door and cracked it open. The silence remained stifling, so he opened it enough to take a half step out and look around.

Nothing. Well, nothing moving, at least. There were a dozen bloody imprints where the fox had smashed its impossible body against the side of the cabin, tiny mushroom clusters already sprouting from the repulsive splatter. He closed the door, re-locking the deadbolt for good measure, and rested his forehead on the soft wood. He knew he didn't have time to spare but found himself lingering, rooted in place, the weight of the day holding him down. The witch's instruction – *burn the body* – plagued his mind. It terrified him, the oppressive finality of it. But at least it gave him some direction, something resembling a plan.

Another gurgling, ragged hiss cut a jagged hole through his mental fog.

He whipped around, just barely keeping his balance this time. He saw the damned fox, somehow in the middle of his living room. "You've got to be fucking kidding me!" he exclaimed, as his eyes followed its repugnant trail back to the cracked bedroom window. Its fur was matted with blood, shards of ribs ripping through its chest, entrails still dragging, a forest of mushrooms blossoming through the gore. Its bone-chilling hiss never faltered as it locked its eyes on him and lurched forward. He turned and fought with the door, remembering that he had re-locked the bolt just as he felt the fox's jaw clamp around his ankle. Panicking, he kicked his leg frantically but the fox held on, refusing to cede its prize. Richard planted his foot firmly, the fox scratching its ruined paws across his shin, and brought the heel of his other boot down squarely on the back of the fox's neck.

A disgusting, satisfying crunch accompanied the squelch as his foot slammed the fox into the ground, and he was able to free his ankle and take a step back. The fox was still spitting choked hisses at him, fire in its eyes as it tried to drag its broken body forward. He bent to examine his ankle, avoiding the blood and saliva staining his cuff as he rolled up his jeans. He almost collapsed with relief as he realized that the denim had managed to prevent the fox from breaking the skin. There was a bite-shaped bruise circling his ankle but no blood. He wasn't sure what the fuck was happening, but that felt important.

He stood back and assessed the fox, which was still desperately crawling in his direction. Without giving himself time to think about it, he stepped around the atrocity and went to the fireplace, grabbing the poker from its stand near the hearth. He returned to where the fox lay near the door, continuing its desperate writhing, and slammed the poker down on the wretched beast's head with a force that surprised his weary delirium. Its skull cracked like a rotten egg, brains splashing a noxious halo around the finally still corpse. The poker had gone straight through the fox's skull and embedded into the floor, and Richard felt a grim satisfaction as he pried it free.

With a renewed vigor, he crossed to the small wardrobe that served as their linen closet, grabbed a rag, and clumsily tied it around the head of the poker, creating a makeshift torch. He could go through the kitchen, out the back door, and the shed was only ten-ish yards away. That's where they kept the spare fuel for the generator, a few ten-gallon cans at least. If he needed to burn Tom's body in order for him to rest then that's what he'd do. He'd burn down the whole damned cabin if he had to. He didn't want to imagine what would happen if this spread – that couldn't be Tom's legacy.

He stuck the torch in the crook of his arm and shoved a lighter in his pocket as he crept through the kitchen, afraid to upset this new silence. He put his ear against the door – this one thankfully free of mushrooms – and heard nothing. He slowly turned the knob, letting the door open just a crack, hoping to avoid the squeak that he'd been meaning to oil for weeks. The silence hung pregnant, and he pulled the door open a few more inches. It was darker now, the thin moon giving just enough light to barely see. The route to the shed looked clear. Its door hung open, giving him a brief pause, but he hadn't been in any mind to close it after finding Tom yesterday. He strained his eyes and couldn't see any mushrooms sprouting in the backyard, which he took as the best sign he could hope for. It was now or never.

He snuck through the cracked door and ran to the shed. Ignoring the light switch he made a beeline to the far corner where the fuel cans were stored, sunken in shadows. He scrambled to open one, struggling to juggle everything between his good hand and his stump. After what felt like an eternity he managed to wrestle the cap off and dunk the torch inside, soaking it, but the can tipped over, its contents flooding the shed's hard packed earthen floor.

He again crammed the torch in the crook of his arm and was fishing the lighter out of his pocket when he heard the shed door creak behind him.

He turned, and saw Tom's dark outline, framed by the pale moonlight. Richard had the lighter in hand, and he flicked it, fully expecting nothing but impotent sparks. Instead, his torch caught, and a warm light filled the small shed. Tom, or what had been Tom, took a halting step forward. His mouth was covered with gore, viscera staining his chest. Clusters of mushrooms dotted his face and arms, all visible skin colonized, overgrown. His beautiful body an invaded ecology.

Haunting the two-seater in the window of a small, unpretentious-but-crowded café off-campus, he struggles through an art history textbook so boring he wants to shove paintbrushes into his eyes.

"Is it okay if I share this table?"

"Yeah, sure, go ahea ..." He looks up and finds he suddenly can't speak as his eyes land on the most beautiful man he's ever seen. It isn't the kind of beauty that would grace a magazine cover, but something deeper, something that radiates out in waves, that fills him up. He's average height, solid build, with a close-trimmed beard matching an artfully unkempt head of rich mahogany hair. A charcoal gray henley, buttons undone, dark chest hair peeking out, complementing eyes a deep sea, hidden behind thick-framed glasses that make his cheekbones pop. A smile that he already feels himself getting lost in. "Go, go ahead, yeah, sure," he manages to stammer out. "I'm Richard."

"I'm Tom. Thanks for letting me join you." He nods his head at Richard's book as he sits down. "Are you an art major? Or just a glutton for punishment?" A trickster's grin lights up his face.

Richard isn't sure he can actually formulate complete thoughts yet, but he hears himself yammering away, anyway. "Oh, yeah, I am. An artist, I mean. Or, well, an art major, at least, I don't know about artist. I mean, I've been painting ever since I was little but it feels like a whole different league, here. Everything's just, well ... it's a lot. I don't know if I can cut it. I don't think I can do anything that will last, you know?" God, why is he still talking? He can feel his face burning red.

Tom's forehead scrunches up with small worry lines. "Hey, don't say that. I'm sure your stuff is great. It's a big pond here, sure, but you'll find your stride. I have faith in you."

Richard suddenly realizes that, why yes, he could turn even redder. "But, you don't even know me," he manages to stammer.

"Not yet," Tom says, his smile now overflowing. "But we have time."

Richard brandished the torch in front of him as Tom took another step forward, the flame burning strong even as his whole body trembled. No matter how much he stared at the monstrosity before him, all he saw was his husband. He loved this man, even now. Tom stumbled forward again, his jaw clicking and grinding, now barely more than an arm's length away. Close enough for Richard to smell death and decay, mixed with the sharp, metallic tang of blood and offal. He lowered the flaming torch to his side. There was only one world he wanted to live in, and that world was right in front of him. He stepped forward, meeting Tom's devouring embrace, and dropped the torch into the growing pool at their feet.

CRIME

THE HIT

Debby Raynor

15 to 20 minutes

Debby Raynor (commonly known as Debs) is a wife, mother and grandmother who relocated from the Home Counties of England to the city of Nottingham seven years ago. A former journalist and newspaper subeditor and editor who took voluntary redundancy during Covid, she now spends most of her time in a "Book Shack" in her back garden, reading, writing and creating YouTube videos for her book channel *Raynor Reads Stuff*.

"I think I may have accidentally hired a hitman to kill the vicar."

Cally spat her coffee across her mother's white linen tablecloth. She tried to control her laughter but tears of mirth – and tears from choking on coffee – rolled down her cheeks as she gasped for air.

"I'm not joking," said her mother indignantly as Cally blew her nose, wiped her eyes and tried to stop laughing.

"You can't possibly expect me to believe that you're in cahoots with a hitman to assassinate the local clergy," she spluttered.

"I am perfectly capable of organising things," said Jules. "You always underestimate me."

Jules was approaching sixty years old, with wild curly hair, twisted on top of her head and secured with a broken pencil. Her name was Juliette, but she answered only to Jules, even from her daughter. Eccentric was the word most people would use to describe her.

Cally smiled at her mother. "Jules," she said, "I would not dare to underestimate you. Now start from the beginning and tell me exactly what you think you've done."

"Well," said Jules, "You remember the Reverend Jacobs. Now there was a delightful man – couldn't be more helpful, loved my arrangements of wildflowers, had a very interesting background. He had been at St. Hilda's for as long as anyone could remember and—"

"Jules, the beginning of this latest catastrophe, not the beginning of time."

"This is the beginning. Well, it's what caused the problem. When the Reverend Jacobs retired, we had no vicar for ages. There were a couple of temporary curates, but they were useless, and then there was some ludicrous suggestion that we should merge with St. Bodolph's, but we soon ended that nonsense. Then, about four months ago, the Reverend Hugo Davison arrived with his son Matty in tow.

"I tried to be friendly and welcoming; I really did. I asked lots of questions about his background to show interest, and I re-ordered all the files in his study. Do you know he has a drawer with a padlock and the key for it is not on his keyring?"

"So," interrupted Cally, "you pumped him for information, raided his study, and stole his keys."

Jules stuck out her bottom lip, crossed her arms defensively and said, "Well, if you're going to be like that, I shan't tell you any more."

"Okay, sorry, please continue. But can we speed it up a bit? I promise I won't interrupt. You wanted to find out all about him, and he wouldn't tell you, and you were angry with him, but is that a reason to want him dead?"

"There's more," said Jules, "And I didn't want him killed, I just didn't want him in the village. Have a look in this."

She reached behind her, opened a kitchen drawer, and withdrew a blue cardboard folder, handing it to her daughter with a flourish.

Cally looked at it. On the front, Jules had written OPERATION REMOVE VICAR in big black letters.

"Ooh, subtle," she said. "What is this stuff?"

"I found these cuttings and other stuff in his office desk," said Jules. "I thought they might be important, so I used his machine to photocopy them. I think our new vicar is a drugs baron in hiding from the police."

Cally put her head in her hands and groaned. Then, to humour her mother, she opened the file.

"MAJOR DRUGS BUST IN DOCKLANDS" shouted the first headline. It was a newspaper cutting from September 2023. An undercover Metropolitan Police team had arrested twenty-seven members of a drugs gang in possession of around £25 million of pure heroin. The gang was believed to be one of the biggest in the UK, supplying dealers all over the country. The gang leader – a man named as Hugh Davis – had, however, escaped. There was a description. Davis was white, 6 ft, 1 in tall, medium build with dark hair and dark eyes. There was an extremely grainy photograph of him half-hidden behind someone else, and members of the public were warned not to approach him because he was dangerous.

"I read about this at the time," said Cally. "Some of my colleagues worked on this story. As far as I remember, there was a huge police hunt, but he wasn't found. And you think this man is masquerading as your new vicar, do you?"

"Well, it has to be, doesn't it? The description fits, he won't say where he has come from, he has this file on the drugs raid, and then there's the name. Hugh Davis, Hugo Davison. Too much of a coincidence."

"And how, then, did this drugs baron persuade the Church of England to appoint him Vicar of St. Hilda's? They do check on people, you know, before they put them in charge of a church and its congregation. You can't just waltz along after living a life of crime and claim a vacant church to run."

"That's what you've got to find out," retorted Jules. "You're an investigative reporter, so investigate. Find out what's going on, unmask him, and he'll be arrested. I can help."

"There's still the small matter of how you 'accidentally' hired a hitman to kill him," said Cally. "I'd really like to know how that happened."

"I found him on the internet. I was looking for ways of getting rid of people, you know, persuading them to go somewhere else. I wasn't expecting anyone to try to kill him. I posted a question on this message board, and Spit replied."

"SPIT! You've employed a hitman who calls himself Spit? Oh, come on, Jules. Seriously?"

"Well, I don't suppose it's his real name, dear. I called myself Lady Desperate. I've printed out some of the messages, but then we got burner phones because it was safer. Spit agreed to get rid of the vicar for £1000. I paid him £500 upfront, and the rest is meant to be paid when the vicar moves on."

"Did you pay him in person," asked Cally.

"Oh no, I just left the money in the dog poo bin behind the lychgate at the church."

Cally sifted through the paperwork, making a mental note to find out later how and what her mother knew about burner phones. She found some messages from a site called MPD.

"It stands for Make People Disappear," said Jules.

Cally looked incredulous.

"Well, I could hardly post it on the Facebook village community page, could I?"

Cally covered her face with her hands, closed her eyes, and breathed deeply a few times.

Having calmed herself a little, she asked, "Is the vicar still alive? And, Jules, WHAT THE FUCK DID YOU THINK YOU WERE DOING?"

Perhaps she wasn't calm after all.

"Language, Cally. And there's no need to shout, dear. Yes, Hugo Davison is still alive, but in the last three weeks, he has had four accidents that could have proved fatal. His ladder slipped as he was clearing the guttering on the roof of the vicarage, and he fell. He landed in the compost heap. Sprained his wrist, ended up a little smelly, but was fine other than that.

"Three days later, the front wheel of his bicycle fell off as he reached the top of Donkey Hill. He grazed his head, but if he had already been racing down the hill, he would have been killed. It was at this point I began to wonder whether Spit had got the wrong end of the stick.

"Then a gargoyle from the bell tower crashed to the floor and missed him by inches. Finally, last Sunday, he was poisoned by some mushrooms he'd found in a basket by his back door and had eaten for breakfast. I thought he looked a bit peaky when I arrived for morning service, and there were some very embarrassing gurgling noises coming from his direction. Then, just as he was about to give communion, he grabbed his stomach, rushed to the vestry, and didn't return. He had to have his stomach pumped, but I think he's out of hospital now. That's when I decided I'd better call you."

Cally's mind was reeling.

"I need to think, so don't talk for a while, Jules," she said. "I also need your burner phone and more coffee, and I'm going to get my gear."

Returning with laptop, notebook, her charger and her phone, Cally was pleased to see a full cup of coffee and a cheap phone on the table. The tablecloth had been removed, and her mother was rinsing it in cold water in the sink to get the coffee stains out.

Cally fired up the laptop and started searching for information on both Hugo Davison and Hugh Davis, taking notes as she went. She sipped the coffee as she sent a message to a friend who ran the archive at a national newspaper and began going through the phone messages between Jules and "Spit". Who, in their right mind, called themselves Spit? Mind you, what self-respecting hitman takes a measly £1000 to kill someone? Jules had got herself into some sticky situations before but nothing on this level.

"Can I …" began Jules after about half an hour.

"No, still thinking," said Cally.

Jules grabbed a long-handled mallet from a cupboard and started swinging it between her legs.

"What the hell are you doing now?" said Cally.

"Oh this?" said Jules, "Croquet. It's my new hobby. I'm practising."

"Well, go and do it outside. You're distracting me," replied Cally.

Her laptop pinged, announcing an incoming email. "Hi Cal," it said. "Not a clue what Jules is up to, but this is what I can find on the Docklands case. I've got some from cuttings and also what I could track down in hidden corners of the web. Hope it's useful (and your crazy mum isn't in too much shit). Tell me about it when you're back in London. Soph x."

"Oh, you absolute star," Cally muttered to herself as she began reading the attachments.

"That's him, that's him," screeched Jules in her ear. "I told you he was a drugs baron."

Cally looked up from the newspaper cutting she was reading and glared at her mother.

"Who, exactly, do you think this is a photograph of?" she asked.

"It's the Reverend Hugo Davison," her mother replied. "Or rather it's Hugh Davis, drug lord, who is now pretending to be Hugo Davison by dressing as a vicar and wearing glasses. He's changed his hair too. But it's definitely him." Jules could barely contain her excitement.

"No," said Cally. "The man in this photograph is Detective Chief Inspector Harry Dennis. He's the man who led the undercover team that cracked the drugs ring and found the heroin. This is a picture Sophie's found from a much older case – Dennis' photograph wasn't included in any of the Docklands articles."

"Well, I don't care who he says he is there," said Jules. "I'm telling you – *that* is a picture of the Reverend Hugo Davison."

And she looked so adamant, Cally believed her.

Cally messaged Sophie again. "Hi Soph, Jules has really got herself into a mess this time. Any chance you could do a background sweep on this Hugh Davis for me, please? I'll stand you dinner at a little Brick Lane bistro I know."

Her phone pinged almost instantly in reply. "Oh, that wouldn't be the one just below our flat, would it, ha ha? Sure, leave it with me. I'll email you what I can find. Love to Jules. Don't be too hard on her."

Cally caught a movement out of the corner of her eye. "Someone's in the garden," she said, jumping to her feet.

"Oh, don't worry. It's only Dave," Jules replied. "He's my gardener, and he's doing a wonderful job. There have been so many flowers this year, and the fruit and vegetable produce has doubled. He's been with me a few months, and he's been so helpful."

Jules stuck her head out of the back door, shouted hi to Dave, and asked him if he wanted a coffee. Dave strolled into the kitchen clutching a bottle of weedkiller. A tall man with grey hair and a full Father Christmas beard, he wore khaki overalls with pockets that held pruners, string and all sorts of other gardening paraphernalia.

"Morning, Dave. Take a seat," said Jules. "This is my daughter, Cally. She's come up from London to help me out with a few things. She's an investigative reporter – a very good one."

Dave's eyes shot to Cally. "It's very nice to meet you, Miss Cally," he said in a strong local accent. "Your mother has been very kind to me."

"Well, she says you have done absolute wonders for her garden," replied Cally. "It's very nice to meet you too. If you'll both excuse me, I need to pop into the village for a few things."

Cally gathered up the items on the table, including the old phone, and stuffed them in her rucksack.

"I won't be long, Jules. I'm just going to catch up with a few people. Dave, I hope to meet you again soon."

Jules' perfectly proportioned Edwardian villa stood just outside the village centre and it was only a short walk through narrow streets lined with picturesque cottages until Cally reached the hub.

A small market square was dominated on one side by the Church and, behind it, an ancient graveyard. In the centre of the square stood the Market Cross and surrounding it on three sides were a few tiny shops, a gallery, a library, a pub and a coffee shop. Cally smiled as she took in the surroundings. The village was a throwback to another age.

There wasn't really anything she needed to do. She simply wanted to distance herself from her mother's incessant chatter to think about what Jules had told her. She had outdone herself this time. Hiring someone to "get rid" of a vicar was just mind-boggling. Paying money to someone who called himself Spit. What planet was she on?

Cally heard someone call her name and walked across the square to greet Mrs. Grainger, the librarian, who was armed with a scrubbing brush and bucket, removing graffiti from the library sign.

"Mrs. G," Cally smiled, "how are you?"

"Well, I'd be better if I didn't have to keep cleaning spray-paint from walls and signs," sighed the librarian. "I think the new vicar's son is responsible. I've seen spray cans in his pocket a couple of times, but I haven't caught him doing anything with them … yet! It's very good to see you, young lady. Your mum said you were home for a few days."

Suddenly, Cally spotted the vicar heading into the square.

"I'm so sorry, Mrs. G," she said. "I really have to catch the vicar, but I promise I'll stop back and we can have a cuppa and a chat while I'm here."

Leaving the librarian to her cleaning, Cally jogged up behind the vicar and said quietly, "DCI Dennis, what a surprise to see you in this neck of the woods. Are you heading for a fancy dress party?"

The vicar spun around quickly, looked at her sharply, grabbed her arm above the elbow with a strong grip and steered her through the lychgate and towards the church hissing, "Don't breathe another word."

Cally, slightly panicked, realised she really hadn't thought this through but decided she'd just have to bluff it out.

She was steered around the side of St. Hilda's and through a small door, finding herself in an office with a large desk, several bookcases, and a couple of chairs, into one of which she was roughly pushed.

"Who are you? What do you want? And why did you call me that?" the-man-who-would-be-vicar said, seating himself at the other side of the desk.

He didn't look as though he was about to kill her. In fact, now they were inside, he seemed very much more at ease than she was. Cally decided to go with honesty.

"My name is Cally Ventriss," she said. "I'm the daughter of Jules Ventriss – I believe you know her – but I'm also an investigative reporter based in London. I know you aren't the Reverend Hugo Davison; in fact, I believe the real Reverend Davison was your grandfather."

A look of mild surprise – and perhaps respect – flashed in his eyes and then disappeared. It boosted Cally's confidence slightly. He was not looking angry, so she decided to take the bull by the horns.

"My mother has decided you're the gang boss connected with the Docklands drugs ring that was busted last year. She also appears to have accidentally hired a hitman to kill you. I, however, believe you're the detective chief inspector involved in cracking the Docklands case and should therefore be warned there may be further attempts on your life."

She stared in amazement as the vicar/DCI roared with laughter. That wasn't what she had been expecting at all.

"Coffee?" he said.

"Well, umm, yes, thank you. That would be lovely. Strong, black, no sugar please."

He went to a sideboard where a pot of coffee was already brewed, poured two cups, handed one to Cally, and sat back down.

"Your mother is quite the character," he said. "I've been successfully undercover for around two years, and within three weeks of me arriving here, she got close to unmasking me. Then she calls for reinforcements in the shape of her daughter, and here I am explaining myself."

"Well, not much in the way of explanations has been forthcoming so far," said Cally. "I take it you really are DCI Dennis then?"

"How did you deduce that?" he asked.

"I have a very close friend – well, a flatmate – who is an absolute genius in finding overlooked data in places on the internet that no one else can find," she said. "She sent me this photo." She hooked out her phone and showed DCI Dennis a photo of himself from the old press cutting.

"Your friend is good," he said. "I was reliably informed that all traces of me had been removed from everywhere before I went undercover."

He took a sip of his coffee and leaned back in his chair.

"Ok, I have no idea why I'm doing this, and it's against all the rules, but, to be honest, I'm drawing blanks here, and I could possibly do with your – and your friend's – help.

"A year ago, we busted the drugs ring and had been reliably informed that Davis would be there, but he somehow slipped through our fingers and disappeared. A couple of months ago we received intel that he might be here in Yorkshire and so I came here to follow that lead.

"You're right, the Reverend Hugo Davison was my grandfather, but I had actually been studying theology before I changed tack and joined the police. The local Bishop was 'persuaded' to let me pose as the vicar of this church – something to do with some inaccuracies in the diocesan accounts – for a limited period of four months. That time runs out next week.

"I have been slightly hampered by a number of unfortunate accidents recently. Did you say your mother might have something to do with that?"

"She didn't mean to have you killed," said Cally. "She wanted to get you removed from the parish because she was convinced you weren't a real vicar – and let's face it, she was right – and, goodness knows how, but she found someone on the internet who said they would remove you for £1000. She paid them £500 in advance with the rest to follow after you'd gone. It was only when the accidents started happening that she began to get worried, and after you were hospitalised with poisoning, she called me.

"The guy called himself Spit," she added at the same time as DCI Dennis said, "It was weedkiller."

They looked at each other in horror and both jumped up, speaking simultaneously.

"I've got to go."

"You've got to go."

They rushed out of the room, DCI Dennis heading towards the vicarage and Cally towards her mother's house.

She was almost there when her phoned pinged. It was Sophie.

"I've found a couple of things that may interest you that I'll send later, but Cal, this is important: Davis spent a few years about three miles from you in Dinwyck, with a family that had a market garden. He could be close. Be very careful and check in with me ASAP."

Cally's heart sank and she sped back to the house, bursting through the back door and crashing into Jules who was up to her elbows in flour. The bowl with the bread dough crashed to the floor and broke, covering the kitchen with flour, dough and shattered crockery.

"What on earth are you doing?" yelled Jules. "Are you absolutely intent on wrecking my kitchen today?"

"Where's Dave," spluttered Cally, gasping for breath.

"He's gone home," said Jules. "He only does an hour or so in the mornings. Now what's the panic? Look what you've done to my bread and your grandmother's mixing bowl."

"I'm so sorry," said Cally. "But this is important. Jules, how did you come to employ Dave?"

"I just sort of found him hovering around Market Square one day, outside the church. I smiled and said 'Good morning', he smiled back, we got chatting, and he started work the next day. Said he used to live around here. We just get on. We chat about all sorts of things; about gardening, politics, what we've watched on television. Dave was the one who told me about how criminals hire people to do their dirty work, and he explained what burner phones were because I didn't know."

"Does he grow mushrooms, Jules?"

"Oh, we've had loads this year. I think the season must have ended though because we've only had a few for the last week or so …"

Jules sat down heavily on the nearest chair, a look of shock on her face.

"You don't think … you can't think … not Dave."

"Yes," said Cally gently. "I'm beginning to think Dave might be the drugs baron. It all adds up. Sophie says he used to live locally with a family who were market gardeners, and he's been feeding you information, encouraging you to commit a crime … then there's the mushrooms and I saw him with weedkiller this morning."

There was a loud rap on the front door and both women jumped.

"Get behind the door and hide. I'll go and see who it is," said Cally, heading into the hallway.

Jules heard Cally sigh with relief.

"Am I glad to see you," Cally said, and ushered the visitors into the kitchen. "Sorry about the mess."

"Jules, you can come out now," said Cally, "because I would like you to officially meet DCI Harry Dennis and …?"

"This is my son Matty," said DCI Dennis, nodding at the sullen teenager to take a seat and pulling out a chair for himself.

"Apparently, he's also known as Spit; graffiti artist extraordinaire and part-time hitman."

"You're Spit?" gasped Cally.

"You took money to kill your own father!" yelled Jules. "Although I will state again that I didn't want to kill him. I just wanted him to leave."

"That's what I wanted too," said Matty, hanging his head and talking to the table. "I'd never hurt Dad, but I hate living here. I thought if he believed someone was trying to kill him, we might be able to go home. So I pushed the ladder when he was on it, but I moved the compost heap to where I knew he would land. I unscrewed the wheel nuts on his bike so the wheel would come off. I dropped the gargoyle from the roof but I aimed it so it would miss."

"Only just," said his dad.

"But you poisoned the mushrooms and that really did make him ill," said Jules.

"I didn't do that," said Matty, raising his head and looking at his dad. "You have to believe me, Dad," he pleaded. "I didn't want to hurt you. I had absolutely nothing to do with that."

"Nope, he's right. That was me."

The four of them turned towards the back door to see Dave the gardener – or Hugh the drugs baron – leaning idly on the kitchen work top. He had a gun in his hand.

Jules screamed, Matty tried to make himself as small as possible and Cally fought her fury as Harry said calmly, "Don't be stupid, Davis. There's no way you can get away with killing four people in this kitchen. Reinforcements are on their way already. Just put the gun down and move away from it, and we can all leave here alive and well."

"I am not going to jail because some crazy old bird and a stupid kid with a spray can can't do what they said they'd do!" yelled Davis.

"Well, you should do your own bloody dirty work and not expect innocent women and children to do it for you, Mr. Cowardly Crime Boss," shrieked Cally, jumping to her feet.

Davis swung around and raised the gun.

"Well, it looks like you're first," he said.

Suddenly there was a loud hissing sound and Davis screamed and dropped the gun. A massive *thwack* sent him stumbling sideways and he trod in the bread dough, tripped over his feet and knocked himself out on the edge of the kitchen worktop.

There was a brief moment of stunned silence before the front door burst open and four police officers stormed in.

"You alright, Sir?" said one to DCI Dennis, taking in the scene. "It's a bit of a mess in here."

"We're fine. Thank you, Sergeant," replied Harry. "I think you'll find that the unconscious man is Hugh Davis, the crime boss we've been hunting. He will require medical attention. He's got spray paint in his eyes, thanks to my son's artistic tendencies. He may have a shoulder injury where Jules thumped him with a croquet mallet and a head injury where he hit the kitchen worktop. Perhaps you could remove him from the floor and see he's treated and then charged. I'll come in for a debrief in a couple of hours."

"No problem, Sir. Congratulations on apprehending him."

Paramedics appeared and removed Davis, under police escort, and finally Jules, Cally, Harry and Matty were alone in the kitchen.

They sat in silence, looking at each other and then Jules began to giggle.

"Did you see me swing that mallet?" she cried. "I think I'll be expelled from the Croquet Club when they find out. Good job it was propped up by the wall."

They all roared with laughter.

"Well, I never thought I'd be pleased Matty was carrying spray paint," laughed Harry.

"Matty," said Cally, "I have a question. Why on earth did you call yourself Spit?"

"It's where we're from," said Matty, "Spitalfields in London. Do you know it? It's famous for its street art. I'm in a graffiti crew."

"Know it?" exclaimed Cally, "I live there, just off Brick Lane above Vittorio's Restaurant. In fact, I recognise that graffiti on the library sign now. You tagged my front door!"

Matty grinned sheepishly.

Harry looked at Cally.

"Vittorio's is fabulous," he said. "Perhaps you'd like to have dinner with me there when we're both back in London?"

"I think I might start a new career as a wedding planner," grinned Jules.

"She hasn't said 'yes' yet," said Harry.

"Yes to what?" asked Jules.

"Dinner!" they both yelled at her.

Jules just winked.

HORROR

A MAN OF EXPERIENCE AND WISDOM

W. M. Hall

15 to 20 minutes

W. M. Hall is originally from southern California and derivatively living in Tennessee. His day job is working in film and television. In addition to being a writer, he is an avid photographer and occasional painter. His other interests include self-loathing, inventorying regrets and avoiding human contact.

Despite his gentlemanly reserve, Ben was excited. It was always exciting to enter a woman's home for the first time. There were two additional factors contributing to his anticipatory enthusiasm: the occasion and the initiative. The occasion was Ben's first date with Allison. What made it even better was that Allison took the initiative and *she asked him to dinner*!

As Ben walked toward the entrance, leaving his convertible at the curb, he noticed how beautiful a day it was, with the low early evening sun raking across Allison's apartment building, causing the grass in a well-maintained yard to glow. The leaves of the trees flanking the walkway sparkled and swayed with a gentle cool breeze. A mix of violets and tulips lining the outer edges of the brick path seemed to herald Ben's arrival as he confidently strode between them toward the front door.

A good omen! Ben thought, as he reached for the button denoting 2B. Luckily, it was a two-story building and there were only four buttons to choose from. *So close now! If she buzzes me in right away, it will only be a matter of seconds before we're face to fa—* The loud metal click of the disengaged lock in the building's heavy main door confirmed their proximity. His right hand shot out like a striking copperhead to grab the door handle. *Sometimes these things lock back up too quickly. It might be embarrassing to buzz her again 'cuz I didn't get it right the first time.*

Making his way up the stairs, Ben checked his phone to make sure it was on silent mode. He believed in showing those he socialized with after business hours the proper respect of keeping phones quiet and out of sight. *Mutually assured full attention!* He was hoping she would do the same.

The door to 2B opened just before Ben's knuckles were about to make contact, causing his hand to awkwardly arc over the threshold.

The awkwardness of the moment was relieved with smiles and laughter as Allison caught his wrist and slowly pulled him inside, shutting the door with her other hand. He could hear Ethiopian jazz coming from the bathroom.

Is that Mulatu Astake? He was impressed with her taste in music.

They stood quietly for a beat, looking at each other, unsure of what to do next.

She's so fucking beautiful!

The white towel around her shoulders made the deep red of Allison's slightly damp flowing curls pop, while the setting sun coming through the window behind her gave a fiery radiance to her voluptuous tresses. Beneath the towel was a sleeveless satin blouse – a pale pewter with a slight lavender tint. Despite the faint presence of bra straps, Ben could see that her nipples were hard. *Eye contact! Eye contact!* She wore black pants that had a raised velvet pattern, and they hugged her hips just right.

"You made it!" she exclaimed and outstretched her arms for a hug. Ben reciprocated. It was a real embrace.

Not one of those phony hot chick hugs where they stand two feet away and lean their shoulders in, barely putting their hands on your back, then quickly let go and yank themselves away like you're a leper. Why bother hugging someone if you're gonna be fake about it?

Holding Allison, he inhaled the aroma of her floral-scented conditioner. It was intoxicating. He graciously let go before the swelling in his loins became noticeable.

"Sorry, I'm running a little late," she said. "When I left work, there was an accident on the freeway. Did it slow you down at all?"

"Oh no, I took surface streets – from where I live it's better that way. Take all the time you need, though I can't imagine you looking any better," he replied.

"Well thank *you*, kind sir." She motioned toward a red couch on the far right side of the apartment. "Have a seat and feel free to make yourself a drink while I finish up." Ben noticed a small bamboo liquor cabinet straddling the corner next to the couch, then heard a cat's meowing.

"Simon will keep you company. He's quite the conversationalist."

On cue, a mackerel tabby jumped up from behind the liquor cabinet, gracefully landing on top of it. Simon continued to show off his athletic prowess by leaping onto the couch's middle cushion, slowly sitting down like royalty, then patting the cushion between himself and the cabinet with his right paw.

"Owelwow!"

Allison laughed. "You'd better do as he says." She headed toward a doorway on the opposite side and made a left down the hall. Ben heard the bathroom door shut and the volume of the Ethiopian jazz went down a bit. Taking a moment to scan the apartment's decor, he admired the eclectic mix of art and furnishings. *An inspired combination that most people would never consider. Original wood floors. The right number of plants for the space. And books!* He appreciated that the titles seemed to genuinely reflect her interests and were not selected for display to impress others.

After opening one of the liquor cabinet's doors and reviewing the selection, Ben thought it best to wait until later – he didn't want to risk drinking on an empty stomach. *The couch it is.* Smiling at Simon, Ben carefully sat on the cushion between the cat and the booze.

"Excellent choice," Simon said, looking up at him.

Mouth agape and wide-eyed, Ben stared at the cat in disbelief, trying to process what had just happened. Simon hopped up onto the top edge of the couch, walked behind Ben's head and took a seat on the armrest to his right.

"This spot is the farthest point we can be from the bathroom. Here, we will be able to quietly converse while she dries her hair and applies her makeup. The closed door and the lovely tunes of Ethiopiques will be of great benefit to our chat."

Simon looked at Ben as if this were the most reasonable situation for two participants of polite discourse. "What the actual fuck?" Ben whispered, not realizing he'd spoken out loud.

"The quicker you get over the initial shock, the sooner we can get you better prepared for tonight's activities. If you comprehend my words, that means she's not listening to me. You're doing great so far – you did not cry out or jump, causing her to rush in and investigate any hypothetical commotion. Fine work maintaining composure, my friend."

Unable to stop staring, Ben whispered, "A talking cat, no fucking wa—"

"Yes, yes, yes, I'm a talking cat," Simon continued. "You needn't worry, I'm not a manifestation of a brain tumor or schizophrenia and I won't tell you to kill anyone."

Facing straight ahead at nothing in particular, Ben let out an exasperated, "Okayyyyy …"

"All will be well. You must simply remain calm and listen."

Ben took a deep breath. He turned back to Simon. "How did you—"

"I learned a few things from my predecessor, but as far as my anthropomorphic skills are concerned, I am largely self-taught." Simon held up a paw to prevent Ben from interrupting. "We really don't have time for my origin story right now. There is a far more urgent matter to discuss."

Ben nodded. "Which is?"

Standing up on the armrest, Simon yelled into Ben's face, "FUCKING!"

Startled, Ben looked toward the hallway leading to the bathroom.

"Worry not," Simon said, sitting back down, "for everything I say just sounds like feline gibberish to her – it's you who must keep his voice down if you want to wet your quill."

Being careful with his vocal volume, Ben queried, "You want to talk to me about … *fucking?*"

With a slight shrug of his little shoulders, Simon elaborated, "Yes. You see, I know Allison holds you in high esteem and if you can satisfy her in a par-ti-cu-lar way, she will not only be a loving and supportive companion, she will reward you with a multitude of erotic escapades. She's a very open and sensual person with exceptional oral skills. All three ports of entry are available to the right man – a man of experience and wisdom, if you will."

Simon was so satisfied with himself for referencing the title of the track playing in the bathroom, he didn't care if Ben picked up on it and pressed on with his oration.

"If you tend to her carnal needs with excellence and consistency, it won't be long until she has some of her girlfriends accompany you both. Not only here, but in hotel rooms, limousines, and private resorts where no sexual activity is off limits anywhere on the premises, save for the check-in desk and dining hall, of course."

Ben let out a, "Whoah …"

"Whoah is right. Not only will the aforementioned benefits be included, but aside from your shared girlfriends, Allison will be completely faithful. Your cock will be the only throbbing, pulsating member to thrust its way into her mouth, aye-yuss, and" – Simon lifted his head to the ceiling – "POOH-SAYYY!"

Narrowing his eyes at Simon, Ben questioned the cat's expertise. "And you know this how?"

"Oh, I've been around for a while. Observing and listening," Simon replied with an easy self-assurance.

"What did you mean by a *particular way*?"

Simon put a paw on Ben's arm. "Synchronous. Mutual. Ecstasy. If you can match her pace, pay attention to her breathing patterns, listen to her *oohs* and *ahs*, feel the rhythm of her pelvic gyrations – whilst adjusting accordingly – you will be able to reach a conjoined crescendo!"

Ben was slightly annoyed by this "advice". "Of course I know not to finish before she does. As long as she comes first, does it really matter if it happens at the same time?"

Looking at Ben with pity, Simon told him, "To refrain from being premature with your emissions alone will only get you so far. Sure, there will be a few more additional dates and dalliances, but she will soon meet someone else who piques her interest the same way you did. Someone she suspects may have the ability to provide the dual explosion of pleasure she is craving."

"Why is this so important to her?" Ben wondered.

"Having heard her discuss this issue with many other women, she believes such synchronicity is indicative of deeper and more profound connections – connections of not only the body, but of the mind, heart and spirit. Due to her infectious charm and exquisite beauty, she has numerous options," Simon warned. "Many men like yourself who are handsome, smart and successful. Sharing an ejaculatory frequency will put one man far above the others, especially if you get it right during your inaugural consummation – your time together will last exponentially longer. Imagine living a life of such incredible hedonism and fulfilling gratification that Anais Nin and Henry Miller would gladly incinerate their own books to read yours."

Ben took a deep breath and Simon took a comforting tone, "You will not have to do this *every* time. Granted, certain activities are one-sided by design and when other women are present, it's more recreational – she won't always be expecting a coupling of extreme profundity. Once per month at the very least should suffice to reinforce your status as her 'Chosen One.'"

Ben gave Simon a nervous smile. "Challenge accepted, I guess. What makes you so certain this first date will go that far?"

"She asked for your number and gave you hers without being solicited to do so, did she not?"

"Yes, but—"

"But nothing," Simon insisted. "When a woman takes the reins of communication, requests a gentleman's private company after dark and invites him into her home, the odds of them having intimate contact before the sun rises are quite high – wouldn't you agree?"

Unable to dispute the cat's logic, Ben agreed, "You're not wrong. The odds are very high."

"Good. We both now understand the gravity of this situation. As long as you remain pleasant, agreeable, and show genuine interest, she will steer this evening to its ultimate destination," Simon said, extending a paw toward the bedroom door.

They continued to sit while Simon gave Ben some nuts 'n' bolts advice on specific aspects of preparation and copulation. Ben was asked if he had "removed a bullet from the chamber" before leaving home to prevent his "phallic trigger from being too itchy". Ben confessed that he had. Simon gave Ben a verbal list of positions and techniques that would lay the groundwork for what he called "simultaneous climactic nirvana". The piece of advice that Ben most appreciated, because he had not considered it, was the simplest. "You will want to make sure your socks are removed before you are beyond the point of no return. Slipping on a hardwood floor while trying to operate from a standing position will surely break your momentum and sabotage your goal."

Both were so focused on their conversation they failed to notice the music stop and the bathroom door open. Ben listened as Simon expounded on how the Kama Sutra was often only understood on a superficial level, and neither of them noticed the sound of Allison's approaching footsteps. "There are one thousand, two hundred fifty verses amongst seven books. The texts offer a treasure trove of sagacious insight of much greater value than just how to fuck*owellrawl-reillaul-wowell …*"

"I knew he'd talk your ear off. He must be spinning an epic yarn," Allison said, standing before them, having added a pair of black knee-high boots to her ensemble. She was beautiful when Ben arrived, but now she was absolutely stunning in a different way. Her lips had a metallic sheen with a dark violet hue and her eye makeup had connotations of predation – she was now a woman you wouldn't dare say "no" to.

"He is rather erudite," said Ben. "This has been a … scintillating discussion."

Allison laughed. "Well, I'm ready. There's a unique little bistro on Sunset – a farm-to-table thing, but very dark and cozy. They always play great music that I've never heard before."

Ben stood up. "Sounds great!"

Bending down, she gently touched Simon's nose with her own and lightly scratched his head. "You're in charge till we get back, little man!"

Ben followed her as she grabbed her purse from a hook on the back of the door and they were off to dinner.

He had the best vegetable tagine he would ever taste and he was careful not to eat too much or too fast – Simon had warned him against inciting flatulence. Allison's risotto had crispy shiitake mushroom slices that tasted like bacon, but were thicker and had a crunchier texture. The bottle of claret they shared had a smoky plum flavor that stopped short of being too sweet and complimented both of their meals quite well. They found dessert at a Persian ice cream shop a few doors down, and each had one scoop of pistachio and one scoop of a flavor that combined rose water, turmeric, cardamom and saffron.

Had there been no Simon, Ben would still have had the best date of his life. No effort to feign interest was required of either party. Because of parking difficulties near the restaurant, they rode in an Uber. In the back seat, Allison squeezed close to him, wrapping an arm around his.

Wow! She's not shy about physical contact. I can't believe she's this comfortable with me already!

After dessert, she had planned on taking him to an art show in a defunct factory. In addition to paintings and sculptures, there was supposed to be a fire dancer, an organist who played a contraption he built himself out of found objects, and some models wandering the premises clad only in body paint. But when they saw the size of the crowd waiting to get in, Allison told the driver she would quickly change the destination through the app on her phone.

"We'll just go back to my place," she said, before leaning in and whispering into Ben's ear, "We can do whatever you like. Anything you want to do with me is just fine."

God-dayum!

Ben smiled and whispered back to her, "Very well, I'll try to think of something."

When they returned sooner than expected, Simon was pleased. He made sure to remain quiet and keep his distance in the hope that their romantic chemistry would flourish without drawing any attention to himself. It worked.

Allison told Ben about a ballroom dancing class she had taken, which led to a friendly disagreement over which movements are permitted in Tango. Grabbing his hands, she pulled him off the couch.

"I'll show you," she said as she placed his right hand on her lower back. Their movements were clumsy. Having left her boots by the door, Allison slipped in her socks, stumbled, and fell against Ben. He held her, but not tightly – she could have easily returned to her correct dance position. For what seemed to be an indeterminate hole in time, they stood silently still until Ben said, "I suppose I should be embarrassed by this erection."

Allison wrapped her arms around him, pulling her body tight against his.

"I suppose I would be embarrassed if you were still flaccid."

He ran his fingers up the back of her neck and into her hair. Cradling her head, he leaned down to put his mouth on hers. The expected course of events continued, leaving a trail of clothing that followed them into the bedroom. Heeding Simon's advice was not much of an option at this point. Ben was completely present and consumed with "first time" passion. It is possible that on a subconscious level Simon's advice had taken root in Ben's mind, but it did not need to. The new lovers were doing just fine.

Careful to keep his presence undetected, Simon stealthily made his way inside the bedroom's open doorway. No lights in the room had been turned on. The only illumination was a diagonal swath of light from a hallway ceiling fixture that raked across a bureau, but stopped short of reaching a wingback chair in the corner.

The game is afoot! Simon thought. *Now to perch myself onto the preferred observation point. What do young people call this now? The cuck chair! Yes, that's it!*

Since Allison had a view of the dark ceiling and Ben had no view at all with his face up against her crotch, Simon took this opportunity to get comfortable on the well-shaded corner chair. Carefully watching the movements of their bodies as they proceeded through various configurations and listening to their breathing and vocal affirmations of pleasure, Simon patiently waited for the optimal moment to make his next move.

When they were in their second position of intercourse, Simon climbed down a leg of the chair. Once he reached the floor, he hugged the darkness against the wall to avoid stepping into the light and slid under the bed.

Is it still there?

Now under the box spring, he slowly crawled across the floorboards onto which a cat's claws had scratched an obscure circular symbol, inside of which were characters of an ancient language no living person spoke. Simon got closer to the center. He could now see the answer to his question.

It's still there. Very good.

He was worried that such a small and lightweight object could easily be disturbed by the slightest displacement of air around it.

There was certainly plenty of movement in here tonight – teehee!

The object in question was a single strand of Ben's black hair that Simon had swiped from the shoulder of Ben's coat earlier in the evening while crossing behind him on the top edge of the couch.

Dexterity is no friend to these paws.

Throughout his conversation with Ben, he kept it under his right paw against the armrest. After Allison whisked Ben away to dinner, Simon did a three-legged hobble to the bedroom, clutching the strand in his fisted paw to get it on its mark. The thought of carrying someone's hair, or just about anything in his mouth, was revolting to him.

His next order of business was to acquire a dime from between the couch cushions and place it upon the strand as a weight. This was not easy. Simon dropped the dime multiple times before finally deciding to push it with his paw, scraping President Franklin Delano Roosevelt's face against the floor for most of its traveled distance.

The bed shook above him as the couple changed to a new position.

Coitus asana number three! Simon suspected they were all getting close to their denouement. *It will be either position three or four. You don't dare go to five – it exhausts momentum and risks leaving everyone frustrated.*

The speed at which the bed shook started increasing while their involuntary onomatopoeias grew louder.

Time for the drawing of blood.

Simon flicked out the claws of his right paw and carefully used one of them to pierce the skin of his front left leg just above the spur.

Here it comes!

Holding his left paw straight out over the center of the circle, Simon waited until two drops landed on the strand of Ben's hair. Promptly after the second drop landed, he put his tongue on the tiny wound and rolled onto his back so gravity would prevent any more leakage. Once he felt the clotting take effect, Simon crawled toward the foot of the bed.

Climbing slowly with his claws dug into the comforter, he lifted his head just enough to see which form of bodily entanglement Ben and Allison had taken. Ben was on his back with Allison on top facing him.

Aha! Cowgirl is perfect – especially for a first coupling. It gives the woman the control to accelerate her pleasure while the man must hold his back and simply wait till she's ready. Well done, my good man!

As their speed and noise increased, Simon continued his climb to the top of the bed. He knew that when the big event occurred, he had to be in physical contact with Ben. Nothing torrid – Simon was not trying to make this a threesome. He simply needed to put one paw somewhere on Ben (preferably a non-erogenous zone) at the moment of truth and it had to be inconspicuous.

Watching Allison's circular grind, Simon saw the way her feet pressed against Ben's outer legs.

That's it! On his leg, close to her foot. He'll think my paw is just one of her toes, though he won't likely be thinking about that at all.

Her voice grew louder and more high-pitched. The enunciation of her "YESes" and "OH GODs" was eroding. Her gyrating became rapid whiplashed undulations of the spine that started at her butt and ended at her head.

Here we go! thought both Ben and Simon.

Her eyes were locked on Ben's as she gripped his chest hair while digging her nails into his pectoral flesh.

Simon grinned. *This is it, Ben. Don't cock it up!*

Ben put his left hand on her right hip and his right hand on her left breast, gently pinching and pulling her nipple.

Simon had crept under the covers that were pushed aside so they could be directly on the fitted sheet. The edge of the covers was right next to them. All he had to do was reach out with one paw and place it on Ben's leg close to Allison's big toe. That is exactly what Simon did.

It was glorious. Together, the lovers lifted off into rapture. Ben felt a jolting sensation hit his right leg and shoot up to his head. While his eyes were riveted on Allison's, he thought he saw other faces strobe in and out, appearing over hers. It happened so quickly, he could not be sure. One of the faces may have been a man with blond hair, but it was someone he was not able to identify in the fraction of a second the visage flashed in Ben's mind. He thought the other face may have been a cat.

Simon?! Gotta be a trick of the brain. We did talk about me fucking Allison – maybe that's why a cat appeared?

Allison's orgasmic screams were loud enough to warrant a neighbor's complaint, though none did. When her trembling stopped, she burst into tears and fell face down on top of Ben, grabbing his head and forcefully kissing his face. Ben decided it was best to push away thoughts of unexpected visions and wrapped his arms around her, holding her tight.

We did it!

Several hours later, Ben woke to what he thought was the sound of Allison's front door closing. He could not be sure what he may have heard, or if he had actually heard anything at all. It could have been the residual noise of a dream, quickly forgotten as consciousness causes it to evaporate from memory. He turned to his left to see Allison sound asleep with a sheet tightly wrapped around her body.

Is she smiling?

Ben considered how the enigmatic expression of her mouth reminded him of the Mona Lisa.

Maybe it's my ego that wants to believe she's so satisfied, she sleeps with a smile on her fa—

Ben heard a car start outside. It sounded strangely familiar.

Is that my car?!

He ran across the bed and leapt over to the wingback chair where he could see out of the window behind it. Looking down he could see his convertible Audi TT rumbling, exhaust smoke wafting out of the tailpipe.

What the fuck!

Knowing the car could be gone by the time he put on his pants and ran downstairs, Ben thought it best he observe, to see if he could get a look at the thief. The convertible's top retracted as the car headed forward down the block to flip a U-turn at the nearest intersection.

Why would he come back this way? Why not just get out of sight with a stolen car?

As the Audi got closer, Ben noticed how the thief was dressed.

Are those my fucking clothes?!

Ben's car slowed down in front of the apartment building. The blond-haired driver looked up at Ben, giving him a wave before speeding off.

Turning to look out of the bedroom doorway, Ben visually audited the trail of clothing on the floor. Only Allison's clothes remained. It then occurred to him that he was standing on the chair's cushion, yet his vantage point was not as high as it should have been. He noticed something else: the couch was now gray, but with a faint, almost imperceptible hint of pink.

Wasn't that couch red?

Allison stirred awake. She grabbed a robe off the floor and put it on. As she walked toward Ben, smiling, she asked, "How's my little man this morning?"

"Good morning, sweetheart," Ben replied. "Someone managed to break in while we were sleeping and steal my …"

All she heard him say was, "Owellwow, raillllll-oo eeeirowl …"

HORROR

BLOODEMIC

Hokunani Sorci

15 to 20 minutes

Hokunani Sorci was born and raised in Hawai'i. When she's not writing, she enjoys reading scary stories, watching scary movies or dreaming of scary things. In 2024, she published her debut book, *My Dreadful Dreams: 13 Tales of Terror*, a horror short story collection. She currently lives far from home with her husband and rescue greyhound. You can follow her on Instagram @hoku.sorci.

It's Wednesday morning and the sky is bleeding again.

"Fuck."

I stand at the entrance to my apartment complex, watching the blood gush from the sky and splatter across the ground, creating thick, soupy puddles. A frustrated groan rumbles in my chest as I tug down my mask and rub dry, cracked hands across my face. I push the hood of my poncho back and press my forehead against the glass door, my breath fogging the red painted world outside.

"Five minutes ... not even *five* minutes to get down here and ... *fuck*."

No scavenging today. I yank the Superintendent's ring of keys from the lock and turn to trudge back to my third-floor apartment. There aren't any people around anymore and the monsters never try to get inside during the day, especially not when it's bleeding outside, but if the Blood Rain doesn't stop, I'll lock it before nightfall. I tromp up the stairs, barely noticing the old reddish-brown stains and splatters I didn't bother scrubbing out of the walls or floors, or the pale yellow 'X's that surround me. I've cleared every other apartment in this building, marking each door once I took everything worth taking and locking every window inside and the apartment doors. Can't have the monsters creeping in at night and running amok.

The Supe' was a friend, though I use that term loosely – he was more of an occasional poker buddy who always cleaned me out but provided the snacks and booze. Chad or Brad, I can't remember anymore. He dropped the key ring in my hand and asked me to lock up for him 'cause he wasn't feeling right. His eyes were bloodshot and weepy, his tears tinged red. He kept dabbing his nose with a tissue and it came away red, too. Got caught in the Blood Rain in the early days and he didn't come back. Neither did anyone else after a while, though I later found the ones who never left … or what was left of them. But I'm still here, whole and intact.

I shove the door to 308 open and close it with a backwards kick, grumbling under my breath at the audacity of it all but still grateful to be back in my fortress. I hate leaving my apartment, except when absolutely necessary; it's my safe haven, my shelter, the only place in the world that still feels safe. The rest of the building I've let accumulate dust and dirt, giving it that "old, decrepit and abandoned" feel. I don't want to announce to the world that someone still lives here. Unit 308, however, is debris free. It shines, it sparkles, it always smells like I just moved in. I strip the plastic poncho and face mask, drop my umbrella and waterproof backpack, and kick my rainboots aside. I wear the protective gear only as a precaution, in case the blood happens to fall while I'm out, but I'm not stupid enough to step into a downpour. The last thing I want is to die like everyone else. I take a deep, soothing breath. The lingering tang of antibacterial disinfectant hits my nostrils and I smile, but it's short-lived as I glance across the room.

Syrupy red liquid flows down the glass of the window across from me, tinging my apartment a sickly maroon hue. I grimace and slash an "X" on the calendar hanging near the door with a red sharpie. First Blood Rain of the month. I shake my head as I flip back through the year. Today's the tenth. Last month it started on the third, and before that the seventeenth. Six months of this shit and there's no pattern.

I move to the window and scowl at the overcast sky – at the wine-colored clouds gushing the unnatural wetness and the things the clouds hide. The things that caused this rain – caused all of this – that no one ever saw or will see, since I'm the only human left … as far as I know.

Maybe I'm not the last man – human – whatever. There could be more people out there on other continents or in rag-tag camps hidden across the US. No, former US, former 'merica, former "Greatest Nation on Earth." It's "Hellhole" now. The "Greatest, Inhospitable Hellhole on Earth." I might be the last human alive in this sorry State, but I'm not alone. No, far from alone. "Here it comes," I sigh, turning my gaze to the street and to the enormous thing creeping its way across the sidewalk in front of my complex.

Earth's new denizens are, for lack of a more PC term, monsters. They come in all shapes, sizes and colors, each more revoltingly inhuman and unbearably wretched than the last. Not that it bothers me anymore. I never cared for people in the best of times, so them not being around during the worst of it is kind of a relief. Kind of. The excruciating death of most life on Earth and the appearance of the shambling, slithering, crawling creatures did very little to upset my day-to-day routine. I'm an introvert, a pessimist and a serial shut-in; the perfect cocktail that ensured my survival through the Bloodemic while others perished.

My closest "neighbor", my loose term for the monster currently sloshing through the Blood Rain below, is Honky; an 8 ft tall, bubblegum pink, sack-like thing with multiple, multi-segmented legs and a 3ft long tube that I assume is its mouth … or nose … surrounded by a dozen globules that I also assume are eyes.

Huuuuaaaaank

The sound it makes, while muffled by the rain, is still almost bullhorn loud. Three guesses why I call it Honky.

Its day consists of creeping around my urban neighborhood, following some inexplicable route that takes it around the apartment complexes that make up this block and who knows where else – all day, every day, though it and the other monsters are far less active in the Blood Rain. Sometimes, when I'm bored or, no, *always* when I'm bored, I "monster watch". It's like people watching but even more "fun" because the things you're making up stories about are nightmarish creatures. There's no TV or internet, so if I'm not reading I have to find other ways to amuse myself. Right now, Honky's barely moving while lifting its tube to the sky, as if drinking. I shudder and turn away, my stomach queasy. No monster watching today.

Instead, I head for the kitchen, though it's not used for food prep these days. It's my survival pantry. The spaces where my refrigerator, microwave and oven used to be now hold clear containers of provisions. Shelves line the walls from floor to ceiling – for equipment and anything else I consider useful. I was meticulous and thorough with my preparations in the beginning, when the shit was nearing but not quite hitting the fan. I sold my appliances and electronics, most of my furniture, random knickknacks, anything I could to clear space and get extra cash for the "End Times". Wouldn't be much use for a microwave or a blow-dryer once society collapsed and the power went out, but the people who bought my stuff obviously weren't thinking like me.

For the gazillionth time, I grab my list of supplies, hanging from the wall on a clipboard and arranged in alphabetical order, and check my provisions. It doesn't take long; the list hasn't changed at all since I checked it last night after dinner. Sighing, I grab a bottle of water and a protein bar, making sure to subtract each item from the supply list, and move to the bedroom.

Unlike the kitchen and the living room, which I turned into a library to house all the books I could find while scavenging, my bedroom hasn't changed much, except that it's now a literal "bed" room. I sold my bed frame and covered the floor with mattresses, taken from, you guessed it, the other apartments. Is that a bit skeevy? In the old days before the Blood Rain, yeah, sleeping on used mattresses would've been on my "No Way In Hell" list. But one thing you can't skimp on in the apocalypse is a good night's sleep. So I hauled, sanitized, and Tetris'd the best mattresses into my room to create a sleep haven filled with all the blankets and pillows I could want.

I crawl across my bed of beds, reach up to the window to slip the blackout curtain aside for light – the maroon-tinted ambiance perfectly matches my sour mood – and settle back to read. I have more than enough candles, flashlights and batteries, but those are for emergencies. I know better than to waste precious resources during the Bloodemic.

◆◆◆

I set my book aside, pop open the bottle of water and take several slow gulps, then unwrap a protein bar and chew methodically while staring at the ceiling. I've gotten a hundred pages into a massive post-apocalyptic, pandemic-centered horror/thriller novel, which, in hindsight, probably wasn't the best choice for some "light reading". I need to switch genres; read something new. See something new. Eat something new. I need *anything* new. I have a sudden craving for a butter-grilled steak, medium rare, with a side of mashed potatoes, with gravy, and steamed vegetables. My mouth waters and I moan. After all this time, only the nonperishables are left; everything I eat and drink comes out of a can or a bag or a box or a bottle. I'd kill for a fucking side salad. I finish the protein bar, trying not to gag on the dry granola, and toss the wrapper into the small trash can in the corner. You'd think waste disposal would be easier in the End Times but with no running water or flushing toilets, it's actually—

I pause. Listen. It's silent. I turn to the window. The blood's no longer falling.

"Fucking finally."

I knee-walk to the window and peer outside. The dark clouds persist but are no longer oozing. I nod and return to my comfy spot to continue reading. I let a few hours pass – gotta make sure it's all dry and clear out there – before daring to open the window and stick my head outside. It's nearly dark. Definitely no scavenging today. I close my eyes and inhale. Believe it or not, I like to take a breather after the Blood Rain dissipates, even though the air smells like an open can of metallic paint. As weird as it is, there's something about the scent that soothes me.

Like, even after all this time, I'm still alive. Still taking it day by day.

I sigh, open my eyes, and freeze. There's someone standing across the street in a blood-stained poncho, staring at me. He's clutching a long stick or pole and has a hump on his back, probably a hidden pack. Either that or he's a hunchback.

"The fuck?"

Is that … another person? An actual real human like me? Should I say something? Maybe ask him—

Huuuaaaaank

I wince and glance to the side. Honky's making its way around the corner at a swift pace, crawling and honking its way through the coagulating blood still left on the ground. The stranger turns, notices Honky, looks back and forth between me and the monster. Before I realize what he's trying to decide he bolts across the street, aiming for the front door of the apartment complex.

Honky follows.

"Oh fuck!"

I slam the window shut, lock it, then whip the blackout curtains closed. I remember tugging the keys from the front door, not bothering to lock it before I came back upstairs.

"No, no, no, no, no."

I grab a flashlight from my side table, dash across the apartment, and yank the curtains of the living room window closed. Darkness engulfs me. I flick on the light and engage all five of the extra locks I installed, then grab the baseball bat I keep nearby and wait.

I aim the beam of the flashlight at the bottom of the door. I don't want him to come here, not really, I was thinking crazy thoughts because I've been alone for so long. I don't want company. I don't need company, especially not a stranger, especially not at night. I clench and unclench around the wooden handle, sweat spreading across my brow and upper lip.

"Don't you dare, dude. Don't you *fuckin'* dare."

A rush of footsteps sounds on the stairs across from my hallway, then there's footsteps running up and down the hall, first left, then right. I snap off the light and am once again surrounded by the dark.

The footsteps stop.

I let out a shaky breath but don't drop the bat. He doesn't know which apartment is mine. Good. I'm on the corner but maybe he got turned around going up three flights of stairs and can't remember which end I'm at. The stranger, whoever he is, better find a place to hide – and fast. It won't be *here*, no sir. I'm not letting you in. I'm not letting you in. I'm. Not—

The footsteps backtrack and stop at my door.

Don't move.

Don't breathe.

There's an insistent knock, hard and desperate.

I clench the bat tighter.

The knocking grows louder, like he's banging on the door with both fists.

"I know you're in there, man. I saw you from the street. Let me in! Please!"

I keep the light off and shake my head even though I know he can't see me. A flurry of reasons flash through my mind of why I shouldn't say anything; he's a burglar, a murderer, a psychopath, a lunatic. He'll give up and leave. I shouldn't let a stranger into my home. I shouldn't … he could be … But it's been a long time since I've seen another person or heard another voice besides my own.

"Come on, man. I know you're in there. Your's is the only door without one of those 'X's on it."

Fuck. I'd never thought to mark my *own* door to blend in with all the others. Mentally kicking myself and whisper-swearing, I pace back and forth, grateful I'm in socks, as the frantic knocks and pleading continues. I can't possibly … can't conceivably consider what I'm about to do. I stop pacing and turn on the flashlight, setting it a ways back so its light covers the whole door. Still gripping the bat, I snap open the first lock.

The knocking stops.

"What's your name?" I'm surprised at the steadiness of my voice. Blood pounds in my ears and my fingers shake. I wipe the sweat from my face with my free hand then place it on the second lock.

"Oh, thank god. I *knew* you were in there, my man, I just knew—"

"Answer the damn question … *You.*" I square my shoulders and puff out my chest as I speak. I'm a scrawny 6 ft 2 in, 155 lbs on a full stomach, but he doesn't need to know that.

"My bad, dude, my bad. I ramble when I'm nervous. Name's Trey."

He waits.

"Jeff." I pitch my voice lower and unchain the second lock, moving to the third.

"Hey, Jeff. That's a cool name, Jeff. My man, Jeff. You gonna let me in, Jeff? Not to stress you out or anything but it's gettin' dark, Jeff, and you know, them things get freaky at night."

I pull back the deadbolt. My fingers tremble as I touch the fourth lock. Okay. Easy does it.

"Where're you from, Trey?" I twist the knob. I'm really doing this. Really letting this stranger into my home. I set my fingers on the fifth lock.

"Jeff, buddy, can we have this conversation when I'm inside? I'll tell you my life story, anything you wanna know, but you gotta let me in. It's damn spooky out here."

I can't help but chuckle. Yeah, it *is* spooky in the hallway without a light. There're no windows in the stairwell and all the apartments are closed, locked. I think of Trey standing outside my door, anxiously rocking back and forth or side to side on his heels, palms sweating, fingers twitching, waiting on me to save him.

"You sound like a reasonable guy, Trey. I hope you're not planning to jump me as soon as I open this door." The fifth lock is open. My hand moves to the handle lock. The moment of truth.

Trey laughs.

"Jeff, buddy, I hope *you're* not planning to bash my brains in and cook me for dinner."

I glance at my bat and smile. Damn, it feels good to feel good. It'd be nice to have someone to watch my back, someone I can talk to, swap stories with. Yeah, it means splitting my provisions but two heads are better than one, right? This could work.

"Fair warning, I *do* have a weapon. Do you have anything besides that staff of yours?"

"I—"

A pause. Footsteps away from my door.

I lean in, pressing my ear against the wood and wishing I had a peephole so I could see what Trey was up to. Wait, what if Trey's *not* alone? Fuck. I didn't see anyone else out there but that doesn't mean they weren't sneaking around. Maybe he's been chatting me up while his friends have snuck inside and up the stairs. His banging would've masked any other sounds.

What if there's a group of them, weapons ready, standing right outside the door? What if—

Footsteps return and I step back.

"Hey Jeff, uh, I think that thing outside followed me. You're gonna let me in, right?"

Pinpricks of unease drift down my spine. Fuck. Honky followed him into the building because he couldn't lock the door behind him. They're *both* in here because *I* didn't lock the door in the first place. I rake my free hand through my hair. I've seen how fast the monsters can move at night. If I let Trey in, Honky could follow. I can't take that chance.

"Fuck." I click the fifth lock shut again.

The door knob jiggles.

"Hey, Jeff, uh, the door's still locked."

I twist the knob back.

Trey starts knocking again.

"Jeff, it's coming up the stairs, let me in!"

I clench the bat, shake my head, and pull the bolt forward. Trey slams into the door, kicks several times, cursing and shouting. I flinch, then re-chain the second lock and snap the first lock back in place. No one's getting in, not now … not ever.

"Jeff, please! *Please!*"

There's a muted, scuttling sound from outside as well as a series of low-pitched honking noises.

HuankHuankHuank

"Oh shit – Jeff!"

I shake my head and step away from the door, clasping the bat in both hands.

"*Run.*" My voice is soft, much too soft for Tr— for the stranger to hear.

HuankHuankHuank

"Fuck you, Jeff!" he shouts, before footsteps stomp away from the door.

A wave of scurrying and horrendous bellowing follows.

HUUUAAANNNKKHUUUAAANNKK

I drop to my knees, shaking. He's fighting, shouting, his staff thwacking against Honky's fleshy body as the monster continues to honk. A snap of wood. Screams, guttural and wet. The crunch of bone. I slump to the floor, drop the bat and place my hands over my ears to drown out the sounds of Honky attacking Trey, but I can still hear it. Moans and sloshing, liquid splashing, limbs breaking. Low, warbling honks sound throughout the massacre. I wince at every muffled tear and crack, trembling in place. Is Honky eating him piece by piece? Does it even have a mouth? Teeth? Maybe it's smothering him then slurping him up like goo through its weird tube. I shudder and cover my mouth as bile threatens to rise.

"It's not my fault. He's a stranger. Who knows what he might've done. He shouldn't have been out anyway. He should've found some other place to hide. It's not my fault. It's. Not. My. Fault."

Sharks. My mind snaps to an image of a great white gnawing on a mutilated seal carcass. That's what the monsters remind me of. Fish can swim around sharks during the day in relative safety because that's when they're most docile. But at night, the fish hide. They know the sharks hunt at night. Honky was hunting, and the stranger didn't hide in time. He couldn't because … I didn't let him.

I stare at the door, still shaking, tears threatening to fall. With the flashlight at my back my shadow looms before me, leering down at me. Why didn't I let him in? I had time. I could've … I should've …

The squelching stops.

The silence is unbearable. I crawl to the front door, my shadow shrinking as I approach, pressing my ear to it. Nothing. No honk or scuttle or anything. I sigh and lean back, knowing that there's probably a bloodbath out there for me to clean up. I wipe the dampness from my eyes with the back of my hand. But I'll leave that 'til morning. No sense—

Knock … knock …

"No *fucking* way."

I sit on the floor, blinking and breathing but unable to move, to comprehend the impossible. It can't be Trey. Trey's dead or … maybe … what if he *killed* Honky and is messed up real bad. He crawled back to my door. He's begging for help again, only this time he's weak, hurt, can't speak. He'll die on my doorstep unless … I scoff. I have a basic first aid kit. What could I possibly do for Trey except … make sure he doesn't die alone.

A whining groan escapes my throat. It's *his* fault for turning up unannounced. I wince.

Yeah, blame the victim. Nice one, Jeff. I sigh and stand, gripping the bat in my right hand. It's … my fault for turning him away. Trey could be in here now, safe and sound – tied up, *just* in case – but he's outside, dying. Because of me.

Knock … knock …

"Fuuuuuck."

A muffled cry of anguish spills under the door. I wince and disengage each of the locks.

My fingers hesitate on the handle yet again.

Knock … Knock …

Another strangled whimper of pain. I tug at my hair, pacing back and forth in short, hurried bursts. I shouldn't be doing this. The safest thing to do would be to go to bed and deal with all this in the morning. And by "deal with this", I, of course, mean "wait for Trey to die so I can clean up his corpse". Fuck. But I can't get the sound of him begging out of my head or his pitiful cries only inches away from me. He can die out there or in here … it'll be hell to clean up after him in here, but it'd prove I have some semblance of humanity left, right?

"Trey? You okay, buddy?" My fingers turn the handle.

Click.

A soft moan.

"Just … hang in there, man. I'm-I'm coming."

I ease the door open a crack. The metallic tang of fresh blood assails my nostrils. I cough and gag. You'd think blood and the Blood Rain would smell the same, but it doesn't. I wrinkle my nose and open the door a little wider.

"Trey? You alive?"

I'm looking down because that's where Trey should be – prone on the floor, bleeding profusely, his hand weakly tapping the door. There's a hand there, slipping forward and falling against the floor as the door pulls back, and an arm attached to part of a shirted torso, a neck, half a head … but the rest of Trey is melted and trailing behind him into a bulbous mass that I realize too late is Honky.

Honky, trembling and pulsating, hovers just behind Trey, crawling forward with exceptional slowness as if savoring the taste of its meal. Its massive frame blocks the hallway.

Trey's remaining eye spins around wildly, spots me. Fixates on me. Garbled sounds escape his ravaged throat. He's begging? Accusing? "Fuck …"

Trey's arm moves mechanically forward, his knuckles rapping against the floor.

Knock … knock …

His fingers jerk and writhe as they scrabble against the wood. Trey's mouth moves, lower jaw opening and closing in a jerking, choked motion as more of his body is absorbed into Honky's slick mass. I can't speak, can't comprehend the madness before me. Trey lifts his arm and reaches out, palm open, his one eye boring into me.

Help. Me.

I grab it on instinct. Someone reaches out to you in desperation, you react. Plain and simple. I drop the bat, hold his hand firmly between both of mine, and pull. Honky stands, unmoving, its flesh stretching forward like Silly Putty as I tug Trey harder, backing into my apartment. He groans, eye closing, going limp as I struggle to free him.

"H-Hold on."

My teeth clenched, I step back. Honky shudders and scoots in the opposite direction, pulling Trey and me forward. The monster releases a low, wheezing sound that's more deflating balloon than rampaging goose.

Huuuuaaaaaa …

Spit dribbles from Trey's open mouth. Pain flashes across his face and he opens his eye again.

Save. Me.

"I gotcha, buddy."

I tug, step back further. Honky's flesh extends. Trey's body stretches. I can barely tell where one of them ends and the other begins, while playing this fucking game of Tug-of-Trey.

But I'm in too deep to quit, to give up now. Lengths of taut skin split and blood spurts wildly.

Honky shudders again, with pain I hope.

Huuuuaaaaaa …

I take another step back, then another. I can do this. I can free Trey. I— I slip on spilled blood. The gummy flesh slips back like an elastic band. I stumble, scream, as we slam into Honky's warm, fetid embrace, its whole body jiggling like jello as we collide.

HUUUAAAA …

The monster moans. I flail and manage to pry myself off the sticky mass, gasping. Wads of goo stick to me like bread dough. Oh god, it hurts! The slivers are burning through my clothes. My skin. I try to wipe them off but they spread like soft butter across me and sizzle. Its flesh is *eating* me. Trey was pressed between Honky and me. He's gone, except for his hand which has a death grip on mine. The monster's flesh absorbed him … *melted* him. He's dissolving before my eyes, his hand the only part of him left.

I try to pull free but Trey won't let go. Our hands sink inside Honky. I scream. The pain is like nothing I've ever felt before, what dipping your hand in acid must feel like. I yank myself free and drop to the floor. By the light of the flashlight behind me, I see the mangled end of my right wrist dripping blood and goo-ified tendons and bones.

I wheeze; attempt to turn, to crawl away, my skin burning all over. Honky trembles, leans over, and collapses on me. I'm smothered in a heated mound of chewing gum. Can't move. It burns. Can't breathe. It hurts.

Hurrrts …

Huurrr …

Huuuaaa …

Huuuaaannnkk.

HORROR

A FACE IN THE SHADOWS

Timothy Adams

20 to 25 minutes

Timothy Adams, a fan and reviewer of literature and comics, has accumulated over twenty years of experience in the entertainment and book retail industry and has now begun crafting his own stories. His work has been featured in *Garbology: The GarbAugust Anthology of Awesome Trash* and his first novel, *Baltimore City*, a throwback hard-boiled detective tale, is available on Amazon. When he is not actively writing or consumed with reading, Tim is gardening or creating reviews for his YouTube channel, *Tim With Tomes & Tales*. Stay safe and happy reading, everyone.

I regret I never married Miss Elouise Parker. I think if I had, perhaps that horrible tragedy could've been prevented or, perhaps, the violence could've been avoided at least.

As the new, young family practitioner for Port Galaway, North Carolina, I delivered babies and treated measles and mumps while ordering the obstinate Irish descendants to eat more green vegetables and briskly walk past the marshlands and along the beach. "It will improve your health," I claimed.

When I established myself there three years earlier, most townsfolk treated me with indifference or suspicion – wary of the new medicines I promoted, but particularly of Protestant doctors from New England. My Catholic clientele distrusted those that didn't attend their Sunday Mass, but still, I was proud of my first solo practice.

Port Galaway wasn't much of a town in the roaring twenties, and even less of one at that decade's turn. It over-relied on fishing for its economic survival, as the surrounding land was either too marshy or salty to sustain much more than small vegetable gardens. The town died a little every time one of its young men left for better opportunities in places like Raleigh, leaving behind young ladies to become old maids, as Miss Elouise and her sister Olive would've been.

The Parker sisters were extraordinary seamstresses – making dresses, mending clothing, embroidering pillows, and so forth. They were also a bit of an enigma … at least, Olive was.

Some said she was a bit touched after the death of their mother, who was a protective woman.

Susannah Parker succumbed to heart complications two months after my arrival, and I'd been called in too late to delay her passing. The Parker patriarch had died years earlier. Now, the twenty-year-old twins were left on their own, yet with a home and a trade to support themselves.

Establishing myself as a pillar of my new community, I took it upon myself to look in on the ladies during the months following their mother's death. At first, I believed it would show the townsfolk my caring attitude, but the ladies and I soon became friends. Well, more than that, really.

Each twin reflected the other in appearance but not much beyond that. Their golden hair was always worn up. Their faces were more round than oval but still with rosy cheeks, and big blue eyes set far apart.

Elouise was more responsible than her sister, maintaining a proud, level head. Moreover, Olive talked and flirted with perhaps a bit of madness. She'd giggle without warning, as if remembering a humorous anecdote.

Olive had an odd attachment and devotion to a childhood doll. At the time, Elouise believed it was solely for sentimental reasons, and I admittedly failed to see the warning signs that would dispute that theory. Violet, as was the plaything's name, was constructed from burlap. It possessed ebony buttons for eyes, a red painted mouth, orange wool for hair and a green-checkered dress resembling the favorite dress Olive regularly wore. A year after Susannah's passing, Olive oddly took to conversing with her inanimate companion as if it were a living person, one responding with quips and questions of its own – albeit ones only heard by Olive herself.

Eccentric habits, to be sure, but not totally out of the ordinary after the loss of someone so dear as a mother. Elouise and I ignored our concerns and believed this behavior just to be Olive grieving. After all, acceptance can take longer for some to achieve.

If Olive was functioning happily, what did it matter? Conversing with Violet appeared no different to us as someone praying to God or talking to the grave of a loved one as if they were still among the living. Still, Elouise began to display concerns over her sister's reluctance to set aside her childhood keepsake. Witnessing this activity first-hand, I agreed to visit every week, under the pretense of Sunday tea, to observe Olive more closely.

Their home, a spacious but not well-kept Victorian house, rested just outside town – close enough to walk to but far enough away from prying eyes. The blue-gray water of the Atlantic Ocean was within sight of the front door, but to reach its beaches one would need to leave the main road and traverse a mile of marshes, tidal pools and quicksand.

The unused carriage house had fallen in on itself, and tall beach grass claimed most of the yard, flanking a walkway to the covered porch. Weather permitting, we enjoyed our tea and conversation in the gazebo behind the house overlooking the family cemetery.

I daresay it wasn't long before I felt smitten with Miss Elouise – a sensible, resolute, and caring young woman, whose qualities were a sharp contrast to the vibrant and carefree eccentricities Olive possessed.

Perhaps it was just my chivalrous nature, but I formed a real attachment to Elouise Parker.

To my surprise, Elouise subtly telegraphed reciprocation of my feelings with bashful looks and rosier than normal cheeks. She'd throw a smirk in my direction; one more seductive than Olive's playfully flirtatious smiles. On our strolls, our hands would frequently brush against one another's while Olive twirled and danced to the rhythm of the ocean waves.

However, Olive's flirtatious attitude towards me had not gone unnoticed by Elouise or myself. Neither of us gave it much concern though. Somehow, it was just part of the childish fantasies Olive jokingly proclaimed.

"Are you courting me, doctor?" she would ask with such a sly grin that it couldn't be taken seriously. She'd giggle and add, "Yes, Violet. I like him too."

Elouise and I should've declared our feelings before Olive's fancy took her down the wrong path, but frankly, at the time, I don't believe we understood our own feelings towards each other. By the time we knew, admittance would've crushed Olive's spirit, and Elouise's sister was still too fragile to handle that – or so we told ourselves.

Looking back, I reproach myself for not noticing Olive's descent into madness sooner. My budding romance with Elouise had blinded me. I wrongly assumed Olive's quips were just part of a game – that she wasn't serious about anything she said. By the time we realized how detached from reality she really was, Olive's eccentricities had taken a dark turn.

Olive began to lash insults upon her sister, and as bad as those were, there was worse to come. Elouise had hidden the physical abuse well, but one day, I noticed the scratches upon my beloved's neck. At that point, I felt obligated to attempt something more drastic to help free Olive of her mania – something more medical than love and hope.

A psychiatrist was out of the question, as Elouise was convinced it'd result in institutionalization. I thought about protesting, but, remembering my experiences of those establishments from my years of training, I acquiesced. It wasn't worth the gamble; I could not risk sending Olive to that kind of Hell any more than I could Elouise.

Still, I inquired about possible remedies. In subtle correspondence, I learned from professionals of a treatment involving mild sedatives and hypnotic suggestion. I provided the medicine; something non-lethal but strong enough to make Olive passively drowsy.

Elouise bought a Dictaphone and recorded calm, suggestive thoughts on the cylinders which would be played to Olive while she traveled between dream and lucidity. We hoped this would detach Olive from her unhealthy fixations and eccentricities.

We experienced a promising start, but Olive's behavior worsened rapidly. At times, she refused to take the sedative voluntarily, going so far as to smash the vial of elixir. I procured more, of course, but Olive was building a resistance.

I was visiting on the day of the most horrible episode involving her madness. Elouise and I were in the parlor when Olive descended the stairs of their Victorian home in nothing but a petticoat. I stiffened upon the sofa, instinctively knowing something was amiss. Elouise froze by the fireplace. Shock sealed our lips. We were too frightened to say anything.

Proud and defiant, Olive strutted towards her sister, the doll clenched to her bare breast as if it was a suckling babe. No distraction could tear Olive's maddening eyes away from Elouise. She came within an arm's length of her sister and planted her heels.

"Violet believes you're poisoning us, and so do I."

I should've anticipated what happened next, but Olive was almost naked. How was I to know she had a weapon?

From between her skin and the doll's checkered dress, Olive slid out a knitting needle. My reflexes were not quick enough to prevent her initial thrust.

The needle's point scraped Elouise's rosy cheek and almost took out one of her beautiful blue eyes.

Regaining my wits, I successfully thwarted Olive's second attempt to stab her sister. I seized her wrist and removed the weapon from her hand. Olive snarled at me, her eyes full of hate. "She'll poison you as well, body and soul."

Then, as if a spell had been lifted, Olive's eyes lit up, slipping from anger to pleasant surprise. "Oh, doctor! You've arrived for tea, and I'm not dressed yet." She smiled at me with her normal sly grin but covered herself with a touch of embarrassment. "Please, forgive me. Violet and I will go put on something more appropriate immediately."

Olive slipped from my grasp, and I watched her scuttle away up the stairs, oblivious to what she'd done. Once alone, Elouise collapsed to her knees, sobbing. I went to her, treating the gash upon her face yet wanting more to embrace her in my arms. Without pleasure, I whispered what was now clear to me, "She must be hospitalized."

Elouise sniffled. "No."

"She tried to murder you."

"Give me more time … Please."

"But—"

Elouise grabbed my hand, her eyes glistening wet. "Please. She's my sister, the only blood I have left."

Even though I acquiesced to my love's pleas, I insisted she sleep with her bedroom door locked from then on, preferably barricaded by heavy furniture. Olive had attempted to kill her sister once. She could try it again at any time.

◆◆◆

Two weeks later, on a warm August morning, the local constable woke me at my apartment. He'd just received notification of a death. My heart stopped cold when I learned it occurred at the Parker house. Had Olive finally murdered Elouise? Each fearful step along the walkway to the front door felt like agony.

At the foot of the staircase a body was sprawled, apparently Olive. Violet was thrown not too far from her outstretched fingers and the small pool of blood surrounding the head. I maintained my composure, calmed the concerns growing in my mind, and set myself upon the task of examining the body.

"The sister says she fell down the stairs," the constable revealed. "Did she break her neck?"

My fingers slipped under golden hair, now stained with blood. Feeling the bulges protruding from the back of her neck, I nodded that she had.

Unseen by the officer, I sniffed Olive's lips. The sedative was present – possibly a lot of it.

The bruising and scratches could've come from the fall, but a worrisome feeling nagged at me still.

We marched to the kitchen where Elouise sat in a diminutive state at the table. Subtly, I examined the woman before me. Her neck and face bore the scars of Olive's abuse. A fleeting thought had passed through me – that Olive had murdered her sister and assumed her identity. Being wrong never felt so satisfying.

The constable wanted to ascertain if she could answer questions and needed me to declare her able and cognitive. I looked into Elouise's eyes, searching for signs of clarity. Her blue orbs stared back, answering my silent warning.

There was an instinct to embrace each other as we inched closer, but I placed a hand upon her shoulder and stiffened my arm. To the untrained eye, I was steadying her, but in reality I was communicating that our feelings for each other should remain hidden. Displaying personal affection could've alerted the constable's suspicions, after all.

Elouise trembled. As a gentleman, I offered to brew some coffee. I patted my breast pocket, indicating brandy would be added to it. She accepted with the constable's permission.

As I heated the pot, I listened to Elouise explain the circumstances of her sister's death. I listened for any deviation in her voice. Elouise was woken up by a series of heavy thuds – presumably when Olive fell down the stairs. Yes, Olive had been taking a sedative which caused drowsiness. Miss Parker admitted to the constable that Olive could've gotten hold of the bottle, maybe taken an extra dosage herself. When the officer asked for my confirmation, I nodded.

I remained with Elouise until the mortician and constable left, even cleaning the used soup bowls and other random things to give myself an excuse to stay longer. Neither Elouise nor I had any words. This accident saved Olive from years of torment, but it felt heartless to say so aloud.

◆◆◆

Miss Olive Parker was laid to rest in a simple service at the family cemetery, her grave within sight of the gazebo. Dreary skies plagued the day, yet the rain held off until after the consoling visitors had left.

The cool drizzle didn't deter me from returning to Elouise's home later that night. I found her sitting upon the parlor sofa, fiddling with Violet's hair. Our eyes locked, but her face remained expressionless.

Silent as a spirit, Elouise rose and ascended the staircase, her eyes looking back at me. I followed. That night, the night of Olive's funeral, we made love to one another for the first time.

In the following days and weeks, I'd casually stroll down the road as if I were enjoying a sunset walk past the Port Galaway picket fences and happy homes. Truthfully, I was sneaking my way to Elouise's house where we'd enjoy each other's company until the early morning hours.

I broached the subject of marriage only once with Elouise. She negated that idea quickly.

"Please, don't bring that up," she pleaded with tearful eyes. "It's still too soon."

I almost protested, but Elouise preempted me. "I will tell you when it's time."

Regretfully, I didn't press back against Elouise's decision. Maybe it would've prevented what happened if I had. However, it was the first moment Elouise showed signs of withdrawal, from me and from the world.

Gradually, our liaisons appeared more of an obligation for Elouise – her enthusiasm gone. Alone, my presence could not sway her melancholy mood. She'd escape my arms to drift to sleep; although, I suspected Elouise feigned unconsciousness at times.

One night in early November, she woke me in a fit of panic. I can still feel her pinching my shoulder and hear the trembling terror in her voice. "Wake up. Someone's here."

"What?" I bolted upright and listened. "Downstairs?"

"No. In here."

My body froze, her words filling me with dread. I remained motionless as if the lack of movement made me invisible. My eyes scanned the moonlit bedroom, trying to locate the intruder.

After several moments, I finally whispered, "Elouise, I don't see anyone."

"There's a face – a face in the shadows." She slowly raised a finger towards a dark corner.

"There … between the wardrobe and the dresser."

Squinting through blurry eyes, I determined Elouise was correct. Someone, or something, sat upon the hope chest – something like a small person, watching us with amusement and malice. The pale light of the moon could only hint at its round head, but its unblinking eyes glinted. They looked at us as if plotting something monstrous.

I slipped out from under the covers. "Stay back." I passed the brass bedpost and reached out, fearful the unknown thing would snap its hidden jaws, biting my hand off. Instead I felt something soft and familiar.

My eyes now focused, I brought the figure out of the shadows and into the moonlight. I held it for Elouise to see. "It's Violet."

I had expected a sigh of relief from my beloved, but I received the opposite. Her blue eyes were fixed on her sister's doll, and her heavy breathing sounded angry. "Did you put it there?" It was an accusation.

"What? No – of course not."

"Well, I didn't put it there." There was defiance in her proclamation.

"Elouise, are you sure you didn't—"

"What?" she snapped. "Am I sure I didn't lie?"

It was Olive's voice, Olive's accusations, spilling forth from Elouise's lips. I felt the hatred and all manner of ill-feelings pent up behind those words, and the feeling lingered in the moments after she uttered them as I tried to think of a response.

"I'm sorry. Maybe I placed it there and forgot." I knew I hadn't, but I needed to calm her. The sight of Violet and the raw emotion it ignited caused an emotional outburst I had never seen Elouise display.

My lover turned her face away, refusing to look at me. "It's late. I think you should go."

"Elouise, I—"

"The fishermen will be making their way to the docks soon," she said emotionlessly. "They may see you on your way back if you don't start off now. Just place the doll in the parlor."

◆◆◆

Elouise and I had never fought before. The surreal experience left me shaken. I kept my distance for almost a week, giving Elouise time to process her feelings.

When the city raised black squares on red fields, alerting the citizenry to an impending hurricane, I decided to return. I felt it only proper, under such portentous flags, to render assistance to Elouise, whether she desired it or not.

With dire weather fast approaching, I felt stressed to find her. It took me several minutes to locate Elouise in the gazebo. I joined her and saw her holding Olive's doll in one hand while caressing it with the other. Her eyes, however, stared at the family cemetery – particularly her sister's grave.

She sensed my presence before I could speak. "Do you think the ground has finally settled? The rain won't wash up her corpse, will it?" Elouise asked morbidly.

With trepidation I answered, "I don't believe so."

Elouise apologized for the way she last treated me. "I feel ashamed – ashamed that I'm moving on with my life so soon after Olive's death. What right do I have to be happy?"

"Every right," I told her.

Elouise's tearful eyes came around to me. "No. I was selfish to put my happiness over her needs. Olive must be so angry with me."

With a dry swallow, I reminded her, "Olive's at peace, Elouise. She can't be angry with you."

My love thanked me for the kind words but insisted on the wrongness of them. "I see her … in my mind." Elouise touched her temple. "I've dreamed of her rising from her grave to take her revenge upon me."

Witnessing her delicate constitution, I chose words that wouldn't steer her over the edge into an abyss of dark thoughts. "Come inside?" I begged with a gentle hand on her shoulder. "There's a storm coming." I received no reaction. "If you close the shutters upstairs, I'll board up the windows down here," I suggested, hoping duty would draw her out of her self-imposed shell.

Lethargically, Elouise agreed.

Setting to work, I gathered broken and half-painted boards from the ruined carriage house.

With rusty nails, I hammered them into place, protecting the glass from flying debris.

The hurricane blew in just as I finished the last frame. Gale-force winds impeded my movements. Miniscule rain drops smacked into my face like buckshot.

Rhythmic roars rumbled from not too far away – not thunder, but the storm swell. The dangerous Atlantic surf battered the beach with crests of white horses on top of tall, blue walls. Under darkening skies, these powerful waves worked their way further inland, flooding the marshes.

I sought the shelter of the house, pushing my way through the intensity of the storm. I struggled my way around back. Water gathered into puddles around the gazebo and blanketed the graves in the family cemetery, the pools deepening with each passing minute.

When I finally slipped through the back door and into the safety of the kitchen, I heard shouts echoing off the walls. Alarmed by the anger in Elouise's voice, I rushed to find her. I ran into the parlor where I stopped cold, discovering her screams were directed at Olive's doll. Her shaking hands strangled the child's toy.

"Stop it! Stop it!" she spat.

"Elouise?" Instinctively fearful of the situation, I approached her cautiously.

Her face snapped towards me, her eyes wide and wild, much as Olive's had been that fateful night. Tensely, Elouise took a step away from me, refusing to let me in close.

Flickering candlelight danced around her ominously. The electricity was out, leaving us in eerie conditions. Our eyes locked onto one another in the dimly lit room.

"What's wrong, Elouise?" I asked.

"She's coming for me." Her voice was barely a whisper. "I told you she would. She's coming tonight." Lightning flashed. Thunder cracked.

"Elouise, you're scaring me." My advancing steps remained slow but steady, as if I approached a wounded animal.

"I need – I need to get away from here," she told me in panicked breaths. "Before Olive finds me."

The walls of the Parker house rattled with the wind. Torrents of rain crashed against the boarded-up windows like a monster trying to break its way in.

"Let me pour you a shot of whiskey … to calm your nerves," I suggested, secretly promising one to myself as well.

"No!"

With Elouise's primal scream, wood splintered, and the wind forced the front door open. Standing close by, I was knocked upon the side of my head when it flew around on its hinges. Hurting, I fell to the floor, still hearing Elouise's shouts.

The candles blew out, leaving only lightning flashes to see by, but it mattered not, as the darkness of unconsciousness threatened to overtake me. I shook my head, attempting to stop the room from spinning, refusing to be rendered useless to Elouise.

My eyes focused upon her. She stood upon the threshold, letting the wind and rain attack her. It soaked into her blue dress. Her pale skin bristled with goosebumps. Her hair whipped around like a nest of golden vipers.

From the floor, I reached out, desperate to grab hold of her. I knew what her unravelling mind tempted her to do. "Elouise, don't."

She looked down at me, a moment of hesitation crossed her face. Her mouth opened to say something. What did she want to tell me? Whatever it was, I couldn't hear. It was but a whisper within the howling wind.

Elouise raised her chin. Both determination and fear lay behind her moist eyes. Her dainty hands seized her dress and raised it up, so as not to step upon its hemline. Then Elouise took flight, rushing out into the dangers of the hurricane.

"Elouise!" Upon hands and knees, I clawed my way towards the doorway, hoping she would return with my calls.

As I crawled closer to the porch, an aberration passed before me, through the tall grass. I saw a woman with a tattered green dress, gray skin covered in brown mud, and a head with crusted yellow hair. A horrid thought entered my mind.

I did not say anything to her, but she … no, not she … *it* turned towards me. The thing possessed no eyes to see me with, just hollow black sockets. No lips, just teeth set in a permanent, chomping grin. Shriveled skin peeled from its skull. Its jaw dropped, releasing a gaseous hiss.

Startled, I shuffled frantically away from the porch, as frightened as if I'd seen the Devil himself. Perhaps, I had.

I averted my gaze. "No – it's not Olive," I repeated in trembling whispers, trying to convince myself I had just imagined it; a subconscious fear planted by Elouise's rhetoric and a possible concussion.

With no small amount of courage, I opened my eyes, prepared to meet whatever lay before them. The corpse I thought I saw was gone, leaving me feeling foolish.

"You hit your head," I told myself, placing a finger on the tender bump. "You're bound to see some strange things." Still, the image seemed real in the moment. Even to this day, I recall its hideous hiss.

A faint cry reached my ears, barely audible over the howls of the storm. "Elouise." With my imaginary monster no longer blocking the way, I tore off after my love, into the flooded marshes and towards the swelling ocean. I prayed to find Elouise before the hurricane, or her madness, claimed her life.

I shouted into the darkness, but I could barely hear myself, let alone any reply. Occasionally, within a flash of lightning, I swore I saw Elouise stumbling through the bending beach grass off in the distance. Also, I could've sworn that a being in a tattered green dress pursued her with outstretched arms. Then, they were gone. I'm still not sure what I saw, even after all these years.

Wading through the marshes and growing flood, I searched for Elouise that stormy evening, eventually collapsing from exhaustion. Numerous fates could've befallen me that night: drowning, quicksand, hypothermia. Only by the grace of God did I live through the night.

I learned that a couple of men found my virtually comatose body the next day while salvaging things that had blown out of Port Galaway. Elouise, however, had not been found.

After being unconscious for two days, I finally awoke, and no amount of sound advice deterred me from resuming my search. I combed the marshlands for a week, barely eating, barely sleeping, hoping to find Elouise – or what remained of her. My search ended in failure. Elouise was gone, left somewhere for the crabs and worms to feast upon.

The Parker house did not fare well in the storm. The rain-soaked ground destroyed the foundation, causing a corner of the building to fall in on itself. The community elders decided it was safest to tear the place down come spring.

Some of the more observant of local leaders, or rather their wives, suggested I be allowed to have some of the personal effects, keepsakes to remind me of my … friendship with the Parker sisters.

I didn't claim much, a few odds and ends. There were really only two items of note: the Dictaphone, to listen to Elouise's soothing voice encapsulated on those wax cylinders, and … Violet.

It perplexes me why I hung on to that haunting object. Perhaps I took the doll to continue mourning Olive, since Elouise no longer could. Still, whenever I looked into its button eyes, it was if they were trying to tell me something I did not wish to hear.

I eventually heard it, though not from the doll. A wax cylinder revealed the true horror of what befell the Parker sisters, and it would never let me have a peaceful night again.

One nostalgic night, I listened to Elouise's recordings, those hypnotic suggestions to bring Olive back from the brink of madness. Of the four cylinders, three were lovely, but the last stole my breath away and froze my heart. Elouise's soft and encouraging voice advocated … evil. "It would be best if you died … Kill yourself before the madness overtakes you … Your sister deserves to be free of your shackles." It disturbed me how such horrible ideas were spoken with such love and softness, how Elouise's voice put dark thoughts into her sister's mind.

I recalled the last time I saw Olive in the parlor, accusing Elouise of poisoning her. Did she mean her mind? Was that incident Olive's final moment of clarity, and had she used it to confront her sister?

No one had suspected Elouise of murder. Even I believed Olive to have been the dangerous one. Did Elouise drug Olive and throw her down the stairs? Had the sedative been in that soup bowl I cleaned? Dear God, did Elouise's guilt-ridden mind cause her to go insane and rush headfirst into a hurricane?

Some rumors had already begun to circulate about the sisters' mental states. I did jabber while unconscious. Of course, I put an end to the more salacious gossip, but some rumors persisted. The remaining tales were more ghostly than criminal, explanations not to be taken seriously. But they would've taken this recording seriously, so I removed the cylinder and melted the evidence in my fireplace.

I don't know if Elouise pushed Olive down those stairs or if she even gave her an overdose, but those were Elouise's words embedded in that wax and now in my memory. That was real. I heard it with my own ears. My beloved had contemplated something so vile.

Despite the disturbing events I witnessed, I felt I needed to protect the memory of the Parker sisters as loving siblings, and so decided to live out the rest of my days carrying this secret. But I have never found so much as a moment of peace, and so I reveal this truth now, in the fervent hope it brings me some relief from the burden I bear.

The vision of Olive's corpse chasing her sister through the marshlands has never ceased to haunt me. I have failed to convince myself it was only a figment of my imagination or the manifestation of a subconscious thought. Not matter how much I have prayed, I have not been able to believe these explanations.

In moments of evangelical despair, my darkest fear is laid bare before God – Olive's rotting figure rising from the grave to drag Elouise straight to Hell for the cold-blooded murder she committed.

That image never goes away. I can never shed it, and it keeps me awake at night. Now, each evening as I lay awake in the dark, I fear there's a face in the shadows, a malevolent force plotting to leverage my guilt for some monstrous scheme … just as it did with my Elouise.

BIZARRO

RESOLUTIONS

Rob G. Bachman

5 to 10 minutes

Rob G. Bachman is a musician, teacher, actor and bookseller. His writing has appeared in *Stories for the Thoughtful Young* from B Cubed Press and *Garbology: The GarbAugust Anthology of Awesome Trash* from Tough Times Publishing. New Year's resolutions include publishing his heavy metal horror novella *Dead Man's Smokes* sometime in 2025, and maybe knocking off the late-night snacks (except on weekends). Rob lives in Southern California with two awesome senior dogs who want to go for a walk.

DECEMBER 31ST – SATURDAY

It's almost a brand-new year, signifying rebirth and a fresh start. I've got nothing planned for tonight. No parties, celebrations or revelry for me. Just plenty of free time, alone at the house. It's time to reflect, evaluate and look to the future by writing down my New Year's ~~revolutions~~.

~~Restitutions~~.

Sorry, I meant resolutions.

In case I happen to wander like I just did, or digress into something unrelated, chalk it up to the fuzzy, disconnected feeling I've had lately. Got a bit of the brain fog – questioning my days, forgetting things. An approaching new year can do that to a person; it must be all the introspection we go through during the holidays. There's a confusing, invisible cloud that floats through the air, dropping a fine mist of unaccomplished goals, unvarnished truths and unrealistic aspirations as we take stock of our lives at year's end. But I've heard it's cathartic to write things down. This will help me stay focused and be honest with myself. You know what they say: hindsight is 20/20. At least, it's supposed to be.

I'm procrastinating. Without further ado – next year, in no particular order, I resolve to:

1. Stop smoking. Twenty-five years of this shit, to the detriment of my health and deflation of my wallet. Time to quit.

2. Lose some weight and exercise more. I'm pushing two-sixty. Out of shape. Need to slim down or I may receive a heart attack for a birthday present next year. Also see #1.

3. Speaking of birthday gifts: find out what happened to my watch, the gold plated one my wife gave me a few years back. On Monday I set it down on the nightstand, like I always do before bed.

Tuesday I woke up late for work and forgot to put it on. When I got home that evening it wasn't there. Where did it go? Megan claimed to have no idea, despite her being home all day with a cold. The watch isn't worth a mint or anything, but is a keepsake nonetheless. Plus – what a concept – it helps me know what time it is when I'm not near my phone or the TV.

4. Stop hanging out with Louis Kowalski, a.k.a. Sticky Fingers, the kleptomaniac guy from work who says he's my best friend. What a creep. He's always visiting other people's cubicles and leaving with a pen, an eraser, a mouse pad, maybe a photo of their wife and kids. One time, over a few beers, he confessed to me that he does this just to see if he can get away with it. To see if anyone will notice. He also talks during movies. I'd tell him about my grievances, but he hasn't been at the office much lately. He left work for the day at lunchtime most of last week. Friday he didn't show up at all.

5. Get this growth or rash (or whatever it is) on my back checked out. I have to crane my neck awkwardly to see it in the smudgy bathroom mirror, but it's there. It showed up last night, just a little quarter-sized discolored patch below my left shoulder blade, but it's getting bigger by the hour. First I thought it might be a birthmark, but who the hell gets a birthmark all of a sudden at forty years old? It's not like I was born yesterday. Or was I? Maybe I just manifested out of the ether on December 30th, with all my memories, opinions, expectations and worries attached like a pre-installed computer operating system.

Not the most likely explanation.

6. Eat less fatty junk foods. See #2.

7. Be nicer to my wife. I've snapped at Megan a lot lately; due to stress I suppose. It's been rough, though, what with no raise at work for two years, and the cost of cigarettes, food, rent and gas going up. I haven't seen her in the past few days either. She was supposed to visit her mother in Albuquerque, but no one answers the phone there and her cell goes straight to voicemail. She wouldn't be avoiding me, would she? It's not like anything bad has happened between us lately – I'm fairly certain about that. I wonder where she went?

9. Read more books. I ordered a crime novel online about a guy whose wife mysteriously disappears during the holidays, and he goes out searching for her. Instead, they sent me a reference book on uncommon skin rashes. Given my current situation, I've decided to keep it, even if the pictures are disgusting. I still want the other book though, so I re-ordered it. Should arrive any day now.

10. Somebody needs to give this thing on my back a look-see. Seriously. I just took my shirt off and checked it out in the mirror again. It's gone from an undefined pink blob to an almost perfect circle three inches in diameter. What the hell is that, anyway? It doesn't hurt or anything. I would say it might be sunburn, only I haven't been outside during the day in a while.

12. Install a security system in the back yard. Motion detector lights, booby traps, time bombs, that sort of thing. Even though we live a ways from town and have few visitors, I'd still like to know who is coming or going in the small hours. Also, I should do something with all the displaced dirt back there. Gophers are digging the whole place up. At least, I think it's gophers. Could be moles or really big ants.

Note: My resolutions are starting to sound like a to-do list. That's acceptable too, right? There is much to do in the coming year. In the coming months, weeks, days. Hours, even. I'm resolving to get it all done!

11. Find out if Megan really was cheating on me, or if it was all in my mind. I was happy when she left for her mother's, if that's where she went, since things had been really rocky between us for a while. She'd been exhibiting that kind of disconnected, austere behavior that might come from a spouse whose mind – or body – is occupied elsewhere, possibly even by a friend. Or a co-worker.

I don't know what would have happened had she not left, though. I might have snapped, gotten my gun out of the closet, up high on the shelf behind the vacuum cleaner bags, and—

15. Look for the gun. Be right back.

◆◆◆

Just checked the closet and the gun is no longer up on the shelf. Must be around here somewhere. I'll keep looking.

19. Give Louis a call. He was always saying – now that I think about it – how much he liked that gold-plated watch. Maybe he has an idea where it went.

21. Enough with the numbers. This list is going to be longer than I anticipated. I can't keep the order straight.

Did I mention I really need to get this thing on my back checked out? In the time it took me to do a few more resolutions, it's gotten worse. There are two fat, red pimples or warts within the growing circle, evenly spaced a couple of inches apart. They have black cores that wiggle. It could be a trick of the light or an optical illusion as I try to peer through all the smudges. I need to clean the mirror. It's almost funny – the pimples resemble a pair of eyes. I'll leave my shirt off so I can keep checking.

18. More to do: throw away the saw, duct tape and shovel that are under the table on the back porch. Preferably in a dumpster somewhere. Someone forgot to put them away. And besides, the saw is rusty, the duct tape doesn't stick right, and the shovel handle gives me splinters.

19. Clean out the hall closet. There's a bunch of jet-black clothing in there; hoodies, pants, shoes, a ski mask. I don't see any reason why I would need to wear anything that dark. It's not like I'm going to rob a bank. Also, there's a tan suit on the floor, haphazardly thrown in. It's too small to fit me – looks more like something I remember Louis wearing to work. I'll get rid of that too.

45. Find the gun. Repetitive, I know, but very important, I think.

22. In the new year, I resolve not to dwell on negative experiences. It's just not healthy. Case in point: I need to forget about last week, even though it all just came back to me a minute ago. What happened was, I came home from work early on Wednesday to find my wife and best friend in bed together. Boy, was I surprised! When I walked into the room, Louis jumped up, grabbed his jeans and t-shirt, blew past me and ran out the front door, hopping naked into his pants like a human pogo stick. Now that I think about it, he was wearing my watch. That lousy, thieving, chickenshit bastard.

"David, it's not what you think!" Megan cried from under the covers, just like they do in the movies.

"What am I supposed to think?" I replied, because that's always the next line. She started to babble some absurd explanation, but I said, "Frankly, my dear, I don't give a mole's ass."

I don't remember what happened next. Just that the following morning, Megan was gone.

On that note, another to-do: apologize to Louis. Invite him over for a couple of beers after work and tell him everything's fine, that I was probably headed toward divorce anyway. Explain that it's "all good" between us, that we're still friends. Maybe we could watch a movie.

For some reason, I feel like I already did this.

Worth repeating: I need to pat down all the loose dirt in the back yard. It still looks rough out there, what with all the gopher activity.

My back is itching. Be right back.

◆◆◆

I cleaned the mirror as best I could with soap and water. It's still blurry, but with improved clarity the thing on my back looks absolutely horrifying. It's a mottled gray now, like a cancer, and it's sticking out a couple of inches, although it couldn't have grown this quickly – could it? The pimples are definitely eyes. The black dots move about googly-style, independent of each other. Below them is a little mouth, wiggling elastically as it expands. It looks like a rubber band stretched around a gopher hole.

Inside it, I thought I could see very small, very sharp teeth.

39. There are ants in the house. Just regular sized ones. I should call an exterminator. No, scratch that. They can stay.

26. Ignore the doorbell. And the people who keep knocking, shouting things I can't quite hear. I don't really want to talk to anyone, ever again.

1a. Quit smoking. I'm not sure if it's technically the new year yet as I sit here on the back porch, shirtless in forty-degree weather, lording over my pauper's kingdom of displaced dirt, but I just lit a cigarette. It may be next year by the time I finish it. Does that mean I'm breaking my resolution already? There's no way to know for sure – that son of a bitch Louis stole my watch!

I need to take a break. My hands are shaking. I'm hearing noises. Noises from behind me, from whatever it is that's growing out of my back. It's causing me pain now, pulling and stretching my skin. It's mewling, gurgling, attempting to say something.

I need to look at it again.

◆◆◆

Well.

I should be alarmed, but I'm surprisingly calm. It's almost as if I expected this to happen.

As I stood sideways in front of the mirror, the reflection of the thing on my back stared back at me. Its thin, gray lips writhed and it spoke in an unfamiliar voice, the mouth struggling to say the words, as if it were just learning to talk.

"We … have … more … work … to … do …" it whispered. Then a couple of small dots appeared above the mouth. Little nostrils audibly popped open, drawing in a thin stream of oxygen. It sounded like someone breathing through a straw. I felt a tickling in my chest, like it was borrowing my lungs. Then muscle spasms, tendons flexing and pulsing. Something trying to push through.

There's a complete, familiar face there now – eyes, nose, ears, mouth. Teeth. It's becoming more defined; crystallizing, clarifying, as it struggles to emerge from my flesh.

As if it is being born with the new year. Created anew.

A new me.

It is smiling.

Hindsight really *is* 20/20.

◆◆◆

Cancel resolution: I found the gun. It was under a loose floorboard in the bedroom closet. Most of the bullets are still in the clip, too.

Only a couple missing. It's now tucked into my waistband, where I can find it. Where I can reach it with ease.

Cancel resolution: Found my watch as well, in the breast pocket of the suit on the closet floor, the one that belonged to Louis. Good old Sticky Fingers was at it again, helping himself to what wasn't his.

The man had no self-control whatsoever.

The good news is, it's only 11:55, so it turns out I didn't break my no smoking resolution. Except …

Cancel resolution: forget about #1 – ditching the cigarettes. Smoking helps me relax. I'll finish up this pack, complete the run.

Cancel resolution: no dieting will be necessary either. After all, I'm eating for two now.

Last resolution: I will sneak out of the house and find my wife, no matter how long it takes. There's someone I'd like her to meet.

It is now midnight.

Happy New Year.

I sure hope that book arrives soon, so I know how this ends.

HORROR

SCIURIDCEREBROMAXIMATOSIS

Zwolf

15 to 20 minutes

Zwolf dwells in Mississippi and reads far more horror and trashy fiction than anyone should. He also writes some occasionally, much of which can be found at http://mightyblowhole.blogspot.com/ along with book and movie reviews.

At first, people thought it was funny. Because it *was* funny at that stage, squirrels having very enthusiastic sex all over the place. Every late-night host's monologue sneaked "squirrels trying to get a nut" jokes past the censors, and since squirrel sex was something you could easily make into "Squirrels Gone Wild" memes and set to the music of your choice, the giggles did not stop. The over-breeding concerned the science community a little, as all environmental anomalies do, but it didn't alarm them too much; they figured the predators would get them. That's before they knew that they'd turn out to *be* the predators.

It was still funny for a few days even when the baby squirrels engendered by all this debauchery started attacking people. Nobody really took squirrels seriously, because the cute tails fool you into thinking they aren't the Spider-Man version of rats.

But now that the bodies are piling up and almost everybody's had a first-hand look at the kind of damage they do, the laughing's over.

Because we've always had that kind of luck, Reese and I were two of the first to stop laughing.

◆◆◆

First off, Reese is a woman. Her name's actually Teresa but that sounds like a nun's name and Reese damn sure ain't no nun. And she once knew a girl named Terri who she hated bad-bad, so she won't abide being called that. So Reese, with all its attendant confusion, it is.

You'd never mistake her for a guy, looking at her. She's shock-you beautiful, had been Miss Something-or-other as a teen, but if you saw her that night in the dashboard light you'd never think she'd be the type to enter a pageant. She has these crazy amber-jade-blend eyes I've never seen in anyone else, and that night they had a widow-making frostiness in them that made all her prettiness seem like a trick to draw you into range. That fact would still stand even if she hadn't been carrying a shotgun.

I'm not clear on what happened with Reese and her dad when she was a kid and I love her too crazy-much to go probing at it, but it must have been all-the-way-shit to inspire such loyalty to his brother, Uncle Johnny. I don't like Johnny much, he's a wastrel trouble-making asshole who's full of shit he can't get straight, but he was always rescuing Reese from his brother back when she still needed rescuers, so I guess he seemed like a great guy by comparison. So when he sent a garbled text for help, Reese was going. She was going for him, but I was going for her.

We'd have taken the motorcycle instead of Reese's beat-up old Dodge Dakota, but she wanted to bring the shotguns. The Dakota was Uncle Johnny's old one and had been barely this side of the scrapyard because he couldn't take care of anything, but he'd so badly wanted to give her something that she'd taken it. I resurrected the engine enough to make it reliable and she scraped off the rebel flag and political bumper stickers she strongly disagreed with, raked out the cigarette butts, and then we had more or less a truck. I never took alarm bells from Johnny Muldowney all that seriously, even when they came in at two-thirty in the morning, so I didn't think we'd need the guns, but Reese wanted them, and, thus, the truck.

As usual, I'd end up really glad I listened to her.

Reese is pure wicked witchcraft with firearms. She doesn't believe in hunting at all, constantly flirts with going vegan, so the gun thing's probably something to do with her dad, too. I asked her once if she was attracted to me because I'd make her daddy mad, and she said, no, because everybody made her daddy mad. She didn't say why she was attracted to me. Maybe she doesn't know. I damn sure don't. I go hard at being good to her, trying to make up for shit somebody else did because I hate to see a good person get cheated – maybe that's it, because otherwise I ain't much.

I'm also good with firearms, though. I did some armyin' so I wouldn't have to do some prisonin'. And that's the thing she doesn't probe me about.

She was looking really intense, there in the dashboard light, and not talking, so I thought I'd try calming her down some, even though Reese calms down about as well as '56 panhead cranks on a frosty morning. "It's probably nothing, baby," I said. "He's probably just drunk or high and gone paranoid. You know how he is." We'd had talks about maybe having to do something about Johnny; his time out there alone was nearing the end of feasibility. His mind had been slippery over the past several months, even more than usual. Johnny wasn't old for a normal guy, but for a wreck, he's ancient.

"Probably," she said. "But you also know the kind of people he hangs out with."

I couldn't argue with that. Reese stayed on him about the company he kept, but it did no good. I think maybe he protected her when she was young so she could return the favor when he was old. He got the best end of that deal, because she always tried to avoid trouble, while Johnny thinks it's ice cream or something, the way he chases it. Then he calls "Babygirl" to the rescue.

We'd been through stuff.

"He always calls you to handle everything," I said.

"Who else is he gonna call? Frank?"

"Lord no," I said. Johnny lived out in what we jokingly called "the doomdocks" – the slum part of the woods, full of people who only live there because they won't be tolerated anywhere else. His neighbor-best-buddy Frank makes Johnny look like one of the Rothschilds. Despite my brush with prison, almost everything illegal I've ever seen was because I've been around Frank a couple of times. And he's not even a criminal, just a victim. Of you name it. Wave a bad choice in front of Frank and he squeals and claps and starts hopping up and down.

I turned at what had been a sign before drunks made it a favorite target for late-night drive-bys. It didn't read anything anymore, but with all those holes it sure threw some crazy shadow-patterns through the woods when the headlights swept it. Now we were in the gravel, and that meant we were close to Johnny's. The road was about sixty percent rut, and driving it was like riding the rapids. That's probably why his Dakota was in the shape it was. His new truck was already well on its way to looking like his old one.

Reese fidgeted with some shotgun shells in the sling, and I knew she was just getting ready, not nervous. After a youth that made a guy like Johnny the hero, well … whatever part of Reese's brain that should have told her to get nervous wasn't doing its job properly. That shit's broke. That part's just another space to store more anger.

I guess I make her sound mean, but she's the kindest person I've ever met. She's a nurse, and a good one, the one you hope you get. But if you give her a good enough reason to dislike you, her sweet heart will cloud up and go black on you. She knows her uncle's a mess, but if anybody was there hurting him, then they'd be a worse kind of mess – the kind you can't clean up, just shovel under. And there were all the deep woods you'd ever want, full of places nobody else would ever have any reason to dig. Whatever causes trouble out here, God forgets.

Johnny's lights were on in his tilty-ass trailer – he's needed to get that re-jacked for about two years now, but if a thing requires much effort then Johnny will usually find a way to live with it instead. There was no shouting or gunfire, though, no strange vehicles parked out front. So far, so good. Now, if only Johnny didn't flip out and shoot us for coming into his house carrying shotguns, we were alright.

"Christ, how does he live like this?" Reese sighed, opening her door.

"Just keeps sluggin' beers 'til it tilts t'other way," I said, and she flashed me a smile.

We knocked at the door, and I was scared we'd bust through it. A trailer's supposed to be rustproof but the world's full of shit that's "supposed-to-be" and ain't. "You got the keys he gave you?" I asked.

"Yeah, but try it. He usually forgets to lock it anyhow."

It was open. Some Allman Brothers deep cut was playing on a boom box. Everything in the living room that wasn't heavy was on the east wall of it, due to the funhouse angle of the floor. *Jesus, Johnny*, I thought, trying to get sea-legs. He was wasting booze; if he wanted to feel drunk in this place he could just walk around a while.

"Uncle Johnny?" Reese called, holding onto the wall. "It's us."

Nothing.

We headed toward his bedroom. I led, trying to be the protective boyfriend even though Reese doesn't need that.

The light in there was funny because it was coming from a table lamp that had been knocked over, so we couldn't see what was in the La-Z-Boy recliner at first. We sure heard it, though. And smelled it. The smell was like your first sniff after a good punch in the nose – old pennies. You instantly know what that is. The sound is harder to describe.

Chittering, weird hoarse barking. Some squeals. They claim *sciuridcerebromaximatosis* (or "S-Max" as they started calling it) hurts, and that's what makes them so angry, keeps them in desperate fight mode all the time. Just like it gears them to always feel like they're starving. For meat.

That's probably why they were squealing. Or maybe they were getting into arguments while they fought over what was left of Johnny.

And that's what we saw when I flicked on the overhead light, which I wish I hadn't done.

I didn't know Reese could scream. Well, guess what? I could, too.

I saw some messed-up shit in the war, aftermath of drone strikes and all. This was worse than any of it.

Lord, they'd been at him. In those days, people were still thinking they were cute, with the tails and all, the little hands. That's before S-Max had turned their offspring into piranha.

I raised the shotgun but Reese pushed it aside. "No! He's moving, he's alive!"

I still think that's the worst thing anybody ever said. Fortunately, she was wrong. Johnny was moving, but no way was he alive. His ribs were exposed. One arm was a skeleton. The soaked carpet squished when you stepped on it. A fuzzy tail and scrabbling hind legs stuck out of an eye socket as one of them tried to gnaw deeper into Johnny's brain.

No, the universe could not be so cruel as to let anyone in such a state still be alive.

He was moving, though. Because they were moving. What was left of him was packed full of them and they were brawling over the best parts. They had his body grooving away to some grotesque tune, their diseased brains locked in on channel S-Max, playing all the hits.

The worst part of it? It sounded like Johnny was coughing. Something climbing up his throat was barking in rage, and it seemed to be coming out of Johnny's mouth. He acted as an amplifier for what was in there. *Singing along with Gregg*, I thought, as the Allman Brothers continued in the other room.

That's when I threw up. It's also when Reese figured out what was causing the movement and started blasting. She braced that .12 gauge on one beauty-queen hip, held back the trigger, and kept jacking the pump until she'd slam-fired it empty. When she grabbed for my shotgun I let her take it and she did the whole thing again, angled up at the ceiling this time, where a river of squirrels was flowing into the trailer through a hole they'd gnawed. We'd come here expecting human trouble so the scatterguns were full of .00 buck, not squirrel shot, but it still did the job.

Two weeks after that, by the way, all the stores would be sold out of squirrel shot shells. Johnny Muldowney wasn't the first victim, but he was early. Soon after, there'd be a lot of Johnny Muldowneys.

Reese flipped the shotgun onto its back, thumbed it full of shells, racked it, thumbed in another – all with code-blue efficiency. She handed it back to me then did the same for hers. She was shaking a bit but holding it together as we both backed out of the room. We weren't saying anything. There wasn't anything to say, and after all those blasts we could barely hear over the whistling in our ears anyway.

We spent a minute standing around the living room, numb, listening to the Allmans have a really out-of-place good time. Then Reese grabbed the big flashlight Johnny kept by the door and we went outside, because somebody out in the night was screaming.

You know, I've talked down on neighbor-buddy Frank, and mostly he deserved it, but I do have to credit him with loyalty; when he heard all that gunfire coming from his friend Johnny's place, he grabbed his AR-15 and headed right over. I imagine the squirrels got him as he was trying to cross the creek in the dark, and now he wasn't running to Johnny's to help him out, but because he needed help himself.

But he was beyond it. That was clear as soon as Reese got him in the flashlight beam. They were going at him, gripping with their little claws as they jerked their heads, trying to tear pieces out of him with their chisel teeth. Everything was bleeding full blast. Both of Frank's eyes were gone – well, one wasn't gone, it was hanging down by his nose, but you can damnbetcha it wasn't transmitting a signal anymore. At first, I thought Frank had grown a long, lush goatee, until the beard slithered into his mouth and I realized it was a tail.

The screaming immediately cut off with a *glurg*.

Reese raised her shotgun but I beat her to it. Like I said, I've done some armying, I killed a few guys – four, and I know all their names even if I can't pronounce them – and I didn't want Reese to have to go through that. So I yelled "Don't look! Don't you look!" and then I shot Frank right in the face, because that was the kindest thing I could do for the man. I'm pretty sure he was trying to do it himself, but he was too frantic to get the rifle turned around right, and the tendons in his trigger hand were torn to shreds and not working anyway.

Reese didn't look and so she didn't have to see what a shotgun does to a head. I'm glad of that because it's a lot worse than you think, even. It's not just the gore, it's the sudden stop, the sudden not-a-person-now-it's-meat. I've seen a lot of horror movies, *Dawn of the Dead* and *Maniac* and all Tom Savini's best stuff, and they don't come close to getting it. You just can't fake it – there's a severity, a cold clinical something that can't be captured by latex or CGI. Watching the body fall and shake around isn't much better, trembling, showing you "life is nothing." Seeing someone go out that way will leave you feeling very vulnerable, and it will absolutely wreck any belief in an afterlife. You see what life is and there is no romance to it. We aren't special.

But we do suffer. And now Frank didn't. So number five – the guy I can pronounce – is the one I don't have to feel a little bad about. Even though one through four were shooting at me. Frank's the only one I knew, for certain, was going to a better place, even if the place was nothingness.

Some squirrels scattered from the body when it hit the ground, although many stuck with it, tearing away at it, single-minded. A few came at us, and I punted one and stomped another, and it squealed a horrible shriek that made me want to vomit again. But there was nothing to come up.

Reese blasted a shot at them and they scurried off.

Around us, the trees stirred like the wind was picking up.

Only there was no wind.

"We need to get back to the truck. Now," Reese whispered, scanning the world over her shotgun.

I nodded. Out in the night I could hear the pained squeaking, some close, and a disturbing amount very far away but moving in our direction. It felt like the tide was coming in, a storm surge, and we were on low ground, going to get washed over and drowned.

Drowned in teeth.

Everywhere the flashlight beam hit it looked like a second sky full of stars had fallen into the woods, but the stars were moving. The retinas of thousands of crazy little eyes. Closing in.

I grabbed Reese's arm and we ran, but not far. The little bastards had cut us off. Several were already on the truck, barking to each other. It's too big a breach of logic to credit them with tactical ability, but luck is something even animals can get. Everything seemed to be moving, the darkness itself alive and starved. Wrapping around us.

Reese fired at a cluster that were scampering toward us, flipping them back in mangled clots of bloody fuzz, clumps of fur drifting through the beam of the flashlight.

"Careful with the shooting!" I said. "Hit the truck, or a tire, and we're stuck here."

"You're right, that's all we'd need," Reese said, kicking at one of them. "*Cujo, Part II.*"

"I'd rather deal with one Saint Bernard," I said, glad that she was staying calm enough to make jokes. Girl or not, that chick is *Hooah.*

"That scenario would already be over," she said, talking around a shotgun shell held in her teeth as she reloaded another.

After my warning to her, I was the one who almost smashed a side window out, batting at one of the bastards who leapt off the truck's roof at me. There's something about the way they fling themselves at you that throws you into instant panic, turns you stupid. He hit the ground, made a quick turn, and climbed me like a tree. He bit me on the bicep before I could smack him away, and I thought it was just a nip, but later I'd see he got me pretty good. I have a Vampirella tattoo there, and she's missing an eye now, thanks to the vermin.

Reese made it into the truck just before I did, yelling "Start the truck, I left my window down!"

I was trying to fit the key into the ignition when a massive bolt of pain shot through my neck, like somebody'd dug in with pliers right under my ear and then yanked. I dropped the damn keys, reaching for the pain, and came back with a handful of squirming fur.

"Shit, shit, SHIT!" Reese yelled, flashlight beam going everywhere as she looked for the keys. The light caught the face of the thing I was holding and I've never seen anything more crazed or raging, writhing to get loose, to get at me. I squeezed it as hard as I could and battered the dashboard with it and it screamed and screamed. One was on Reese, too, on her back, tangled in her hair. I tried reaching across but she got it first and flung it out the window.

I whacked the squirrel against the dashboard again, as hard as possible, and it finally went silent. Reese, panting, spotted the keys in the floorboard and somehow made her hands stop trembling long enough to fit them into the ignition and twist. The engine came to life and I pitched the dead squirrel out her window while she was powering it up.

Another one tried to slither through the window just as it was nearly closed and got pinched. He scrabbled, half in, half out, snapping chisel teeth. Reese dug behind the seat, brought out a pair of pruning shears, and fitted them around the little horror's neck. She squeezed, he squealed, and she lowered the window enough to hang him all the way out. Then she squeezed the rest of the way – there was a crisp *snip* and the squealing stopped. The window went up and closed.

She lay the shears on the dashboard, shining the flashlight around. "Make sure more haven't gotten in," she said, turning in her seat to look at all the junk back there. "We don't want anything attacking us while we're driving."

"Yeah," I panted, checking my neck. Plenty of blood on my hand. Too much. "I stack us into a tree and we're back to starring in *Cujo II*."

"*Cujo II*," she agreed, trying to laugh. "Holy fuck. More like *Cujo Two Million*. Look at them all. It's a nightmare. It's all the nightmares."

I turned on the headlights and got that sky-of-moving-stars effect again. Christ, the woods were full of them. They'd been fruitful, they'd multiplied, they were eager to move on to reaping. Several were on the windshield, barking in anger because they could see us but couldn't gnaw through the glass.

"Okay, I think we're clear," she panted. "Drive."

"Yes'm," I said, checking my neck again, and she leaned in and took a look at it while I backed out. I was glad she was a nurse.

"He gouged you pretty good but didn't hit an artery or anything. We'll go to a hospital, get it fixed up," she said. I wondered what kind of shots I'd get, and wondered if they'd do any good.

We didn't know the virus was airborne in those days.

Gravel rattled as I aimed us at the road.

"The other'n get you?"

"No, I got him first." She grabbed the dashboard as we dropped into a big rut and bounced out of it. The squirrels on the hood and windshield skated but hung on. "Slow down. Remember, this road is for shit, and we do not want to get stuck."

"*Cujo II*," I said.

"Billions of little tiny Cujos. God, I hate sequels."

"*Godfather II* was pretty good."

"Okay, I'll give you *Godfather II*." I looked at her and she didn't smile but she tried to.

"And all the Mad Max films, except that *Thunderdome* shit."

"Get Mad Max out of your mind until we hit the highway. Then you can Max out."

"I love you, you badass," I said, as the truck hawed, then bounced our heads against the roof. We lost some squirrels on that one.

"Mutual," she said. "But I'll love you better if you'll fucking listen to me. Slow your ass down."

"I'm trying, I'm just … nervous."

"I'm not blaming you, hon, there's every reason to be jacked up, but they can't get in and we need to not get stuck. Look out there. Out there is Hell."

The woods were full of those staring stars, and every now and then one loped across the road. We could hear the thumps as they dropped onto the roof. One clung to a windshield wiper and snapped at us, barking hoarsely, an escapee from a fever dream.

"We'll be okay, they can't get in."

"I know. And that's why you can slow down like I've told you about four damn times now."

The truck slammed through a stretch of bad ruts and she and I had our own little mosh-pit for a second. That, more than her admonishment, made me ease off the gas. I was thinking of an old Datsun I used to have, and how occasionally it wouldn't start because squirrels had chewed up the wiring. Were they under the hood, doing that now? Probably not, but the possibility made me jumpy. But, slow, slow, drive slow. And even then the truck was handling the road with all the grace of a drunken three-legged mule with a yellowjacket enema. Getting out of here was still very much in question.

Then there it was, like the gates of Heaven, that shot-up sign, and I hooked left onto blacktop and floored it. "Now I can Mad Max."

"Now you can Mad Max, buddy," Reese sighed, patting my leg. "Go, dog, go. Jesus Christ." She swept her hair back. "I'm gonna cry over Uncle Johnny for a week to make up for it, but right now I'm okay with feeling bad about being happy."

"I'm right there with ya," I said. It was hard to process what we'd been through, and impossible to process what we'd almost been through.

And I don't think either of us had yet bothered think about what the whole world was about to go through.

◆◆◆

All of that was about a year ago. The squirrels have been gotten under something that we can at least pretend is control, thanks to the National Guard and flamethrowers and a lot of poisons and other desperate measures that people argue about taking.

But they don't really matter that much, now – the squirrels.

Because now the people are fucking. We're all just fertile as hell and driven to screw like never before. Even if you're ugly, even if you have a shit personality, thanks to that little matchmaking virus you've found somebody. People hardly go to work anymore; it's just sex, sex, sex. Reese is pregnant and neither of us are happy about that, but there was no way it wasn't going to happen because almost half the world is pregnant now. The first wave of *Baby Boom II: Sciuridcerebromaximatosis Boogaloo* are showing up, and a lot are twins and triplets – way more than average. Clearly the virus has jumped a species and there's no reason to assume it's not going to play out the same way for us.

And we've got to kill them. The babies. We'll have to kill them. Because it'll take a year or two – how long does it take toddlers to grow in their first teeth? – but, oh, my god, *my god*, it's coming.

BIZARRO

AMPERSAND

S. T. Talbot

10 to 15 minutes

S. T. Talbot has been writing since he was a boy, but took up writing fiction to process living in an unfamiliar environment following his move from his hometown in the San Bernardino mountains to Florida. If he's not at work staring blankly at clipboards or in his office conjuring up ghost stories, he's most likely listening to spine-chilling old-time radio shows or gorging on cheap, foggy horror films with his cat, Casper.

You can find him on Instagram @s.talbot.writes

Dirk feared sex.

It hadn't always been like that, but after a six-year dry spell, intercourse and great white sharks occupied the same shelf in his mind as far as deep-seated, irrational fears went.

He turned on the tap, splashed cold water on his face, and studied himself in the clean, unfamiliar mirror. "C'mon man, you got this. You got this."

A nose hair stuck out from his nostril – he plucked it.

That would have been nice to notice before *the date,* he thought.

He washed his hands with soap that smelled of honey and dried them on a baby blue hand towel.

Dirk slapped himself across the face, hoping to awaken the part of him left dormant from years of unintended celibacy. The slap hurt more than he'd expected, considering the lack of enthusiasm behind it. He idly wondered if that was a sign of his strength, or weakness. He sighed; even dressed in his best and carefully manicured, the word that came to mind was *unremarkable.* A man pushing forty, trying to hide his age with clothing and mannerisms he'd abandoned a decade earlier, ejected from his comfort zone when convinced by friends and family to use a dating app that had unwritten rules and etiquette more out of reach to his aging sensibilities than trying to learn Sanskrit.

Dirk had never felt so out of his league.

He stepped out of the bathroom into Maggie's bedroom. Her room smelled of honey, but not like the soap in her bathroom. A different, gentler honey.

"I was starting to get worried, thought maybe you fell in," Maggie said, turning in bed to face him.

The only thing she wore was a loose-fitting tee-shirt for some band he'd never heard of. Judging by the dangerous-looking font, it was some metal band, but the floating microphones and turntables around the almost illegible letters suggested something to do with rap. The fact that his experience with rap and metal both ended at Limp Bizkit only made him feel more out of his league. He prayed she didn't start asking him about his music tastes. Nothing would make him feel more ancient than having her know which records in his collection got the most play. She'd probably never even seen vinyl, unless she was one of those young, hip collectors. That thought was even more terrifying. He could almost imagine her chiding him for the improper way he stored his records beneath his record player.

When Dirk felt he'd been staring at her shirt for too long, he shifted his eyes down. The sight of her pale thighs brought a warm flush to his face. He reverted his eyes to her shirt.

"Sorry, had to powder my nose," he said, flashing a smile.

Maggie perked up. "Wait, you have blow?"

"What? *Oh*! Oh, no, it was a joke."

"Oh," she said, her newfound respect for him deflating. "It's not funny to joke like that."

She threw a pillow at him.

"No, I didn't mean drugs. Powder your nose like in—" *Don't explain the joke. Don't explain the joke.* "Never mind, it's a dumb joke." Unsure of what to do, where to look, Dirk studied the picture frames on her bookshelf.

"So, you just gonna stand there, or …?" she grinned. That grin made him want to go back into the bathroom and escape through the window. It was not the grin of one lover to another, it was the grin of a mother observing her child and realizing he was a special type of special.

Dirk made the mistake of looking directly at her – his manufactured confidence drained. Her clever brown eyes, septum piercing, and dark, curly, shoulder-length hair stoked a feeling in his stomach he thought he'd left behind in grade school with Tamagotchi pets and his adamant belief in cooties.

He took cautious steps towards the bed. "No, sorry, just woolgathering, I guess."

"Wool-what?"

"Never mind."

&&&

Her bed smelled of roses; at least, that's what Dirk took the smell for. Any floral scent registered to him as roses. He wasn't even sure what a real rose smelled like.

Maggie kissed him. He tried not to focus on how awkward it all felt – he figured the more he focused on it, the more awkward it would actually become. She put her hand over his and guided it from her hip to her inner thigh. His thumb brushed the soft cotton of her underwear. His breath hitched.

Maggie stopped. "You okay?" she said.

"Yeah, fine. I'm okay." He barely heard himself over his heartbeat. "Are you okay?"

"Yeah," Maggie said, "just as okay as the last time you asked." She smiled.

"Sorry, sorry. I'm just nerv—" She pulled him back to her with a kiss.

Maggie removed her shirt in one fluid motion. He kissed her and wondered if he should take his shirt off as well. He was painfully aware of how clothed he was. She watched amusedly as he fumbled out of his shirt, which suddenly felt two sizes too small. He balled it up and tossed it towards his shoes, which were paired neatly near her bedroom door.

Dirk leaned in to kiss her and angled his head to her neck at the last moment. Her skin tasted of clean warmth – and honey. A different honey than her bathroom and bedroom, though. This was a living honey. He kissed a trail down her body, paying close attention to each movement she made. When her breathing got heavier, or her body shifted, he'd stop where his tongue was and give that spot extra attention. Dirk was good at this; when he realized he was lousy at penetrative sex, he learned to make up for it elsewhere. He hoped if Maggie came hard enough from his tongue, she'd return the favor and they could skip the penetration altogether. Dirk licked circles around her nipple and gently rubbed between her legs as he thought of sentences.

Dirk glanced up from between her legs, hoping to get one more sign of consent. A nod or a wink or something. Maggie's eyes were shut tight, her neck craned up in anticipation. *Close enough.* He stared at Maggie's shaved pussy and he thought of his Uncle Derek. His uncle had told him the secret of pleasing women one sunny afternoon when Dirk was a boy, and he now just so happened to think of his long-dead, wife-beating, alcoholic uncle anytime he was face to face with female genitalia. He felt a pang of guilt when it happened, but it was impossible to avoid – he'd never forget the advice he received that day.

&&&

"Amber-sand? What's that?" Dirk said. He sipped his root beer and surveyed his uncle's lot, deconstructed cars and tractor carcasses strewn about at random.

"*Amper*-sand. It's the symbol people use for 'and'," Uncle Derek said. His uncle was a wiry man. Wiry beard, wiry build. His bushy eyebrows grew in tandem with the bushy hair in his ears, both smaller versions of his unkempt beard, all the color of week-old snow. He took a twig and drew the symbol into the layer of dirt on the porch: &

"And you *say it* to girls? And that's how you make them like you?"

"No, Dirk. You draw it." He retraced the symbol in the dust: &

"On the ground?"

"No, on her clet-riss. You know what a clet is, right?"

"Of course, Uncle Derek. I'm not an idiot." A decade passed before Dirk realized his uncle had been mispronouncing clitoris.

"Good, I didn't think so. Just be careful though, too many ampersands can be dangerous. For both parties." He winked and took a swig of his Coors. "That's why sentences are just as, *if not more*, important than the ampersand."

"Which sentences?"

"Any sentences you want. You can write poetry down there for all I care, you just gotta make sure all the letters add up to an even number. Odd sentences don't take the same."

"Why even numbers, Uncle Derek?"

"I don't know, man. It just works. The same way the ampersand works. It's sacred geometry or some shit." He drained his beer, belched, and threw the empty can off his porch. "You use your tongue and you write this here out, right on her clet." He drew "&sentence&" in the dirt. "Ampersand-sentence-ampersand. You remember that Dirk, and you'll be just fine. You'll be making coochies quiver up and down the Mississippi." He patted Dirk on the back.

&&&

Maggie's squirming increased with each sentence Dirk spelled out. When Dirk first began experimenting with the technique, he had a list of ten tried-and-true sentences he would use. Once he got more familiar with the technique (and female anatomy) he would challenge himself by thinking of the sentences on the spot. Counting sentences was soothing to Dirk, and soon he evolved it into a strategy to last longer in bed. If he edged toward his orgasm too quickly, he'd go through conversations he had earlier in the day and go sentence by sentence, determining which were even. This tactic became an all-purpose grounding technique, and Dirk counted sentences to help with anything from anxiety when standing in line at the bank to frustration when dealing with a dimwitted coworker. Before long, he could hear a sentence and determine if it had an even or odd number of letters in a second or two.

His Uncle Derek was a no-good, lying, stealing, Brillo pad of a man, but he had stumbled onto something with the ampersand. Dirk had practiced enough over the years to get a general understanding of what did and didn't work. He learned in college if you use colons instead of ampersands, you could edge your partner longer; semicolons and percent symbols tickled to the point of being a turn off; dollar signs and pound signs made women gassy – he avoided those at all costs.

Dirk's jaw cramped, but he persisted.

&Dirkk was hEre&

"Oh God, oh fuck! Don't stop, Dirk," Maggie said in between moans. Dirk couldn't think of any name worse for dirty talk.

&I Fucking hatE my nAme&

Maggie's hips gyrated in rhythm with her breathing, gently grinding his face as he tried to keep his tongue in place.

&Im Awful at sEx&

"Oh! *Oh*, that feels good. Don't stop, don't stop!"

&canT sTop wonT sTop&

Maggie made a noise that was half exhalation and half moan; her entire body tensed up. The letter T was one of Dirk's secret weapons. It was a showstopper when capitalized. He knew exactly what to write to get her off.

&TerminaTTor Two JudgemenT DAT&

Maggie sucked in a shaky breath and her toes spread apart. "Fuck! Oh fuck! Fuck me."

&God no plEAse no Please noo&

Dirk's jaw throbbed. He paused long enough to wipe his mouth on his shoulder, clearing it of their combined slickness.

"Keep going baby, keep going."

&I shiT myself in Third grAde andd have yeT to recover emoTionallY&

Something popped inside of his ear. A concerning warmth trickled down his face beneath his skin. His jaw was on the verge of locking. He was approaching uncharted territory now; he'd never spelled out such long sentences before. Most women climax after just a few strategically written sentences. "Please, don't stop, babe. I'm so close."

The alien warmth trickled down his neck.

&I Think I may have seriOuslY Injured mySelf buT am WiThout insurance&

Dirk's jaw creaked. He tasted blood.

Maggie moaned and bucked her hips.

&I will noT see a doCTor our medical sysTem is fundamenTally broken&

Maggie's hips slowed. Her breathing gained composure. She should've had an orgasm by now; it was as if he'd been using colons instead of ampersands. He'd never experienced this before. His stomach lurched. She was getting bored with oral sex, which meant she probably wanted to move on to something else. Dirk swallowed hard. *Desperate times*, he thought.

&&&&&&&

The corner of his vision blurred. His head was suddenly lighter – it wasn't entirely unpleasant. He couldn't focus long enough to think of a sentence, let alone count letters, so he slid his middle finger into Maggie, hoping to catch a moment to steady himself. He took a deep breath. The unmistakable smell of fish wafted up from between her legs. Dirk tried to blink away the undulating sensation at the edge of his vision when inspiration struck.

&&&Ampersand&&&

Dirk gasped for air. The smell of fish was now so overwhelming that he couldn't breathe through his nose. He found it odd that he hadn't smelled it before, considering he'd been spelling out sentences for what felt like half an hour, and stranger yet that he hadn't tasted anything. Maggie was no slouch with hygiene; that much had been apparent from the moment his tongue touched her skin.

He heard a faint cry and slowed his breathing to listen better. A familiar muffled screech seemed to emanate from inside of Maggie.

"Did you hear that?" Dirk looked up for a reply. "Maggie?"

Maggie's face was frozen mid-moan – eyes half-closed, mouth agape, no movement whatsoever, an intimate moment frozen in time to make her face more Halloween mask than human expression. He watched her stomach. She wasn't breathing.

"Fuck fuck fuck." Dirk sprung from the bed and frantically searched for his phone. He was on his hands and knees rummaging under her bed when another louder, high-pitched cry filled the room. It came from inside Maggie. He was sure of it this time.

Dirk rested his ear on Maggie's unmoving stomach – nothing. He moved his head lower and heard the faint rumblings of water, then readjusted himself so his ear touched her labia. A chorus of seagulls echoed up to him, backdropped by the hypnotic sound of waves breaking on a shore. There was another sound mixed in that he couldn't register. He first took the sound as whale song but couldn't be sure. He'd never heard a whale make sounds so diverse in pitch and cadence, but it possessed the same haunting quality of sounds spawned from gargantuan, water-bound creatures.

The sounds mesmerized him.

A warm breeze blew out from Maggie, the same breeze that carried the smell and sounds into the room. Dirk moved his ear and positioned himself to look into her. He saw light – faint but unmistakable. Dirk slid two fingers into Maggie, hoping to clear a passage to see better. A warm current of air tickled the tips of his fingers; butterflies fluttered in his stomach. He pulled his fingers out. The tunnel of light was more pronounced, the breeze stronger. He gagged, the carrion smell of fish like a physical presence in the room.

Dirk could faintly see gray waves breaking on a dark shore. Using both hands, he spread her apart further, needing to see more of the body of water he heard resonating through the room. Maggie's skin, which felt more like putty than organic tissue, easily spread. He worked one, then both hands in to open up a passage, slowly moving and adjusting folds and flaps of skin to reveal the world beneath. Once the opening was large enough, he pushed his head through and took in the sight before him.

Sand, water, shore – he looked over a hauntingly familiar beach. He took a deep breath through his mouth and wiggled his way deeper into Maggie, the sound of waves accompanying his grunts and gasps.

Dirk fell face-first into warm sand and spit out a mouthful of grit that tasted of salty sulfur. He turned around to see where he fell from, but there was no sign of Maggie or her bedroom. He stood, brushed the sand from his bare chest, and surveyed the beach before him. The sand was the color of ash, much darker than the tan-sanded beaches of his childhood. The water had the dark, choppy complexion of an ocean during a hurricane, but there wasn't a cloud in sight. Dirk shielded his eyes against the bright day. His hand cast no shadow. He studied the sky – there was no sun. Light came from all directions. The too-bright, too-blue sky glowed and shimmered, the heavens ebbing and flowing like great waves.

Dirk's stomach sank.

Dead fish peppered the shoreline. Every wave washed in hundreds more, distributing them across the dark sand. Many of the fish possessed parrot-like beaks and obscene, swollen purple slits down the length of their body that must function as gills. A layer of a shaggy brown moss-like substance enveloped the bodies of the fish without beaks. A select few boasted both beak and moss. The size of the fish ranged anywhere from a goldfish to the largest catfish, and all had a curled, scorpion-like stinger protruding from their sexes.

Carcasses floated on the surface of the diseased-looking water as far as Dirk could see. Some spots were so dense with the dead fish that he couldn't see the water beneath them, only the steady movement of it. Yellow, pelican-sized birds cried out as they circled and swooped at the fish, like nicotine stains against the iridescent sky. The smell had evolved into something else entirely. Even breathing exclusively through his mouth, Dirk sensed the weight of it.

Dirk turned around, feeling immediate unease with his back to the water. He faced a wall of foliage that grew without bounds, stretching past the horizon. Dirk craned his neck up, wanting to find the tops of the trees. The green growth reached up and out of sight, never-ending.

Vertigo washed over him. It grew into a full-body dizziness that evaporated the moisture from his mouth.

Tears ran freely from his eyes. He turned away from the all-wrong jungle.

Dirk sat down on the warm sand and wept. The carrion waves crashed indifferently against the shore.

The sand began to rumble, faint at first, but growing steadily. A high-pitched ringing filled the air, harmonizing with the rumble, the two becoming more unwholesome with each passing second. His testicles shrunk against his thighs.

Ripples formed on the surface of the dark water. The shrill sound and ripples grew in tandem. Five large mounds broke the surface. He experienced that familiar whiplash as they surfaced, this time much less pleasant, his mind stuttering and fogged as it attempted to process the scene before it. They rose from the water in the lurching slow motion unique to behemoths. The droning whale-like calls echoed through his head, a cacophony of unease. Their constant rise in pitch burrowed a hole through his mind, a hole he wanted desperately to hide in.

Dirk couldn't look away.

They rose in synchronicity, displacing dead fish and bilious water in incomprehensible quantities. They looked like giant, barnacled cucumbers, more gray than green, each topped with a black, pointed obelisk-like structure. They were larger than any skyscraper Dirk had seen, and still they grew before him, revealing more of the rough, wrinkled texture. The sounds grew so intense that it became more of a feeling than something he heard. A comforting warmth bloomed in his lap. Dirk was vaguely aware he was pissing himself. He latched onto the warmth trickling down his leg. It was something to focus on, something to keep his mind from unspooling at the sight before it.

The frothy wave created by the creatures' rise was the color of spoiled milk. Dead fish peppered the seafoam by the thousand. Each of the five creatures was attached to some semblance of a platform which now rose from the water. A new burning heat spread from both his ears inward, meeting in the middle and creating a terminal sense of déjà vu.

It was a palm, not a platform, now rising with new vigor. Dirk craned his neck up to the fingers he'd mistaken for individual creatures, the giant obelisks now registering as pointed fingernails, the color of obsidian. The beginning of a wrist jutted from the water. A forearm, then an elbow, rose from the depths. The giant wave lumbered towards him, growing, the sound somewhat peaceful to Dirk. It sounded like thunder; he loved thunder.

It all made sense. This beach was not a place, it was *the* place. This is where all life began; he knew it like he knew his name. That's why it was so familiar – he'd been here before.

This was a place without a name, a beach without a time, and the creature rising before him went by many names. This was God. Not the God men knew. That was all wishful thinking. Campfire stories that sprouted wings and became reality for those who believed the hardest. Accidents – religions were accidents. This was reality, something humanity was never meant to witness. He looked on in rapture as God rose, as the wave grew, as his world shrank. Dirk dropped to his knees, closed his eyes, and for the first time in his life, he prayed.

ACKNOWLEDGMENTS

There are a few folks that we'd like to say a big "thank you" to for their help in making *Trash Tales: An Anthology of Trashy Fiction* a reality. To Troy Tradup, editor of this collection's predecessor *Garbology: The GarbAugust Anthology of Trashy Fiction*, for passing the trashy torch, and generously providing us with plenty of information needed to help us plan the anthology. To Lekden, for his indispensable editorial and proofreading assistance. To all the authors featured in the collection, for being a joy to work with throughout the process. And of course, to you, dear reader – we hope you've had a wonderfully trashy time with this book!

Alex and Olly
August 2025

IMAGE CREDITS

Graphics sourced from flaticon.com and adapted by Alex J. Gardner.

Individual creator attributions:
Horror: Skull by juicy_fish
Crime: Handcuff by Georgy
Sci-fi: Atom by Good Ware
Western: Cactus by Freepik
Bizarro: Mind blown by TravisAvery

Images used in the front cover collage are from the artist's personal collection, or are free to use without attribution from the following free or public domain sources:

Unsplash (unsplash.com)
RawPixel (rawpixel.com)
Resource Boy (resourceboy.com)

Three of the images are free to use with the following attributions:

"Chinese Food Carton" (lower right-hand corner) was created by FreePik (freepik.com)

"Sexy Robot" (bottom right-hand corner) was sourced from Wikimedia Commons and was created by 纳瓦拉的亨利. It has been adapted and used under a CC BY-SA 4.0 license.

"Vicar's Collar" (top centre) was sourced from Wikimedia Commons and was created by Archivo Fotográfico Universidad de Navarra. It has been adapted and used under a CC BY-SA 4.0 license.

Many thanks to all the artists and photographers who have made their work available to use under Creative Commons licenses.

Printed in Dunstable, United Kingdom

70303507R00241

Printed in Dunstable, United Kingdom

70303507R00241